THE LADY THIEF OF BELGRAVIA

ALLISON GREY

Storm

Ebook ISBN: 978-1-80508-222-4
Paperback ISBN: 978-1-80508-224-8

Cover design: Sarah Whittaker
Cover images: Sarah Whittaker

Published by Storm Publishing.
For further information, visit:
www.stormpublishing.co

To my husband, Dave – he has never once doubted I could do this, has encouraged me every step of the way and kept the kids busy so I could write in peace. And to Avery and Ronan, who, while occasionally distracting, are nevertheless the loves of my life.

ONE

LONDON, 1879

Hyde Park teemed with crowds; dozens had gathered to catch a glimpse of the latest attraction, for Punch and Judy had come, and not even the oppressive heat and stench of London in the summer could keep the onlookers away. Della had no particular interest in the anarchic puppet and his wife, but it was a useful distraction. For the past fifteen minutes she had stood at the edge of the park, whistling aimlessly to herself, as though waiting for the show to get started. She was careful to keep her expression curious, not bored, so as not to give herself away as an outsider, but always with a sharp eye on the lookout.

She had found her target.

He stood to the edge of the throng, taller than most around him, dressed in a fine grey jacket and fawn trousers. *More for the takin'*, she told herself. She almost smirked as she finally straightened from where she leaned against a tree and made her way towards him, looking for all the world as though she were simply trying to get closer to the colorfully painted booth around which the people had gathered. Her gaze fell on the expensive-looking watch fob at his waist and a small smile curled her lips. She edged closer to him, careful to use the noise of the crowds to cover her approach. A few more paces, and she was within touching distance of him.

A burst of laughter erupted as Punch squawked that he had defeated the Devil, and everyone surged forward as they tried to get closer, jostling the man in front of her. Della made her move. She darted forward, caught the fob and the watch attached in one practiced palm, and turned to retreat.

A hand snaked out of the mass of bodies and ensnared her wrist. She whirled in an instant, saw that her mark had her in his astonishingly tight grip, and tried to yank herself free with an outraged gasp. It was no use. She looked up, but the sun was behind him, and his features were cast in shadow.

"Let me go!" she snarled, grabbing his wrist with her free hand. She glanced around, looking for an escape route while trying not to draw too much attention to herself. Growling at his relentless grip, she finally abandoned caution when she lifted her leg and drove her heel into his instep. He loosened his hold with an angry grunt, and she took the opportunity to turn and run.

Della sprinted towards the edge of the crowd, not daring to look back before she took cover behind a bandstand, pausing only to catch her breath. Staying hidden behind the structure, she made her way down an alley through to the mews behind the shops lining the street before finally turning to see if she had been followed. There was no one around, and she took a seat on a packing crate to examine her new treasure.

Engraved into the polished gold cover of the watch were the initials *C.W.* Well, whoever C.W. was, he must have eyes in the back of his bloody head to have caught her in the act. She *never* got caught, and her skill had earned her the reputation as the best diver in all of St. Giles – and the moniker of Rosie Diver. She frowned at the engraving. Her fence would have to christen the watch for her, removing the engraving which would lower its value.

She pursed her lips as she flipped open the cover to see the time. A minor slip-up, she rationalized. Next time she would be more careful in choosing her marks. She glanced around the alley, saw she was still alone, and pocketed the watch. One more step closer to her goal of escaping the rookery; that much closer to her dream. She smiled in anticipation as she stood and made to go back the way she had come.

She stopped dead in her tracks when she glanced up and saw her mark blocking her exit. Her stomach lurched in a moment of surprise. She hadn't heard a single footfall – how had he snuck up on her like that? His features were clear now at least, and he was undeniably handsome in the sort of square-jawed, broad-shouldered way most ladies would swoon over – but not Della Rose. He offered her a polite nod as she took a small step backwards.

"I believe you have my pocket watch, young lady."

Della drew in a deep breath and shrugged. "Don't know what you mean, sir. I ain't got no watch."

He smiled. "Odd, I saw you examining a watch identical to my own just this moment. Perhaps I was mistaken?"

She narrowed her eyes. He didn't know who he was dealing with. "Maybe." She spoke in a low voice, never taking her gaze from his.

"Then perhaps I am also mistaken in identifying you as the young woman who nearly broke my foot not five minutes ago?"

Della allowed herself to smirk as she faced him, arms crossed, and responded with the smallest tilt of her head. His smile never faded. He even chuckled a little.

"No, I don't think I would forget a thief quite as interesting as you."

She shook her head. What in the hell was wrong with this man? Why hadn't he called for a copper yet to have her arrested?

"Get out of my way," she said with a scowl and tried to step past him, but his large frame blocked her way.

"I have a proposition for you."

She glanced up to find him looking earnestly down at her and responded with a withering glare as she tried to step past him. "Not interested. I'm no whore," she said, moving to the other side of the alley to get around him.

"I have no need of that. How would you like to earn yourself five thousand pounds?"

She halted in her tracks and gaped at him, unsure as to how to reply. Was the man completely off his head? An escaped resident of Bedlam, perhaps? Those people could be dangerous. She looked away from him, trying to draw his attention away from her.

"Don't think so," she muttered as she tried to slip by him once more. Again, he moved to stand in her way, and a small swell of panic tightened her chest.

"May I ask your name?" The lunatic was still smiling! She backed away from him, certain the man had taken leave of his senses.

"My name?" she repeated, attempting to distract him. A narrow lane on the other side of the alley caught her attention. Her muscles tensed as she readied to sprint for the way out. She caught his eye for a moment, and he must have sensed her fear, for his smile faded and he took a step back from her.

"Forgive me. I can see I've confused you. I'm not an escaped Bedlam patient, I assure you." He laughed at the wary look she gave him when he read her thoughts so effortlessly. "Allow me to introduce myself." He paused and bent in a slight bow. "My name is Cole Winthrop, and I am in need of a thief."

She raised a brow at this statement, still not convinced that this man was altogether right in the head. He held up his hands in supplication and gave her what she had to admit was quite a winning smile.

"You think I'm mad." It was a statement, not a question, and she shrugged.

"Couldn't say for sure, sir, but you'll have to find yourself another thief. I work alone and I ain't for hire." Seeing now that he meant no harm, she stepped past him and headed back for the park.

"Wait!"

She turned and he came towards her, hesitant now, his smile replaced by a look of desperation. "Please, I need your help. I need a thief... and you're perfect."

Della scoffed as she settled her weight onto one hip and crossed her arms. "I can take you back to the park and point out at least ten boys willing to do your dirty work for you. As I said, I ain't for hire."

He shook his head. "I don't need a boy. I need a woman... an attractive woman, to be precise."

Della burst out laughing as she looked down at herself. Her skirts and jacket, both nicked from a dressmaker's shop to blend in with middle-class crowds, had been over-mended and repeatedly patched, and she was aware of the tangled mess of her hair, and the effort she had made to stuff pins in it to create a passable chignon.

"Then I'm no use to you at all," she said, laughing as she turned away from him once more.

"You're wrong. You're exactly what I need."

Della pivoted to face him at this abrupt statement. She huffed out an exasperated breath and, tired of his riddles, reached into her pocket for his watch and tossed it to him. He caught it, his brow furrowing as he met her gaze.

"I'm not for bloody hire," she repeated, angry now. Who the hell did he think he was?

"If you think I'm propositioning you as a prostitute, you'd be wrong. I need a thief... only a thief. At least let me explain before you dismiss me."

Rolling her eyes, Della dropped onto a stoop, put her chin in her hands and gazed up at him, expectant. "Go on."

He appeared momentarily perplexed by her actions but shrugged and drew in a sharp breath. "Somebody has stolen something that belonged to my father. Something very valuable."

Della stared at him for a moment. "Couldn't you just go to the coppers?"

At this point, the man shook his head and drew himself up to his full height. "I'm afraid that would be impossible. This is a... delicate matter, one beyond the scope of the police. I am also in a position to help you should you agree."

"Help me?" Della raised an eyebrow at this. It was now that the man's cheerful expression grew a shade more cunning.

"I feel it is safe to say that law enforcement would appreciate the opportunity to have one less pickpocket on the streets, no?"

Her eyes narrowed in suspicion. "And?"

"And I could ensure that any investigations our local police have open into your... doings... as I'm certain they do, would be permanently closed. I have many friends in very high places. A clean record and a large sum of money could be the start of a new life for a young woman from the streets. But in the meantime, I do require someone... unscrupulous."

A small smile lifted Della's lips. "Ten thousand pounds."

The man frowned at her. "I beg your pardon?"

She stood and brushed off her skirts. "You said you'd pay me five thousand pounds. But I ain't without some scruples. It'll cost you twice that for me to lose 'em."

"You don't even know what I want you to steal yet," he said, his brows raised in an incredulous expression as though he hadn't expected her, a thief of all people, to ask for more. She almost laughed.

"Does it matter?"

Suddenly, and to her shock, the man's smile returned, and he stuck out his hand. "Done. We have an agreement."

She hadn't expected him to agree to such an outrageous sum, and she stared at him for a moment. That she was even considering his proposal was absurd, yet the idea of ten thousand pounds to her name made her heart race. That amount would set her up for years to come... for life. No more picking pockets, no more living in a brothel. That one dream she had carried deep in her heart for so many years would be within her grasp. Biting her lip, she looked away from the man named Cole. What would Violet do? She drew in a deep breath and glanced up at him.

"What exactly would I be nicking?"

His smile faded and his gaze slid away from her as though to search for eavesdroppers. Seeming satisfied they were alone, he looked back at her. "Some important documents were taken from me and I need you to steal them back."

Della couldn't help but grimace at this. "Documents? You mean to pay me ten thousand pounds to steal a load of papers?" Somehow, she had expected something more exciting than that – rubies or diamonds or priceless artifacts.

He shook his head. "They're more than just papers. They contain information I would rather not have become public knowledge. My life and the lives of many others are in danger if that information is released."

Della tilted her head. "And it hasn't been yet?"

"The information is written in code, but the person who has it will almost certainly be working to decipher it. I need to get everything back before they do so." He paused. Della said nothing to this, but looked down, frowning. Ten thousand pounds was a huge amount of money, more than she could hope for in a lifetime, vastly more than she could ever make diving at Punch and Judy shows. The man seemed reasonable enough, and she'd spent enough of her life around untrustworthy people to know when someone was just that. Still, she hesitated. It was a dangerous business trusting others where she came from.

Cole's smile returned. It was a damn fine smile, she had to admit. "If it helps, you will be staying with me in my home near Belgrave Square. Your own room and three square meals a day."

Her stomach rumbled at this, reminding her of the hunger that was a constant part of living in Seven Dials. She glanced down at her shabby dress once more. "And new clothes?"

He chuckled and extended his hand. "Only the best."

Della paused, staring at it. The hunger must be making her delirious, but she was ready to say yes. Cora had been generous in letting out her only spare room to Della, but she had been waiting for any excuse to get out of that place.

"I'll have to get my things..." she began, glancing up at him.

"Anything, but we must hurry. It is only a matter of time before the thieves break the code."

Della took his hand and managed a wry smile. "Pickin' a pocket only takes a few seconds. It's the plannin' that takes the most time."

"Then let us be on our way."

TWO

When they arrived at the outer edges of Seven Dials, Della stopped and put her hand out. "Wait 'ere. You can't come with me."

Cole looked at her with a furrow between his brows. "Whyever not?"

Della rolled her eyes as she drew him into a dingy doorway. "'Cause I can't be seen 'ere with the likes of you."

She didn't wait for his reply but pushed him back and walked away. "Stay put," she said over her shoulder as she moved around the corner and into the alleyway. There was no sun in this part of London, though it had blazed across Hyde Park not half an hour earlier. There was never any sunlight to be seen in the back alleys surrounding Seven Dials. She nodded to a hunched figure shuffling towards her – one of the workhouse tenants she knew. He made no acknowledgement of her greeting, but continued past her, his head and back bent. She craned her head about once he had left the alley to see if the toff had stayed put. There was no sign of him, and so she hurried on, sidestepping the pools of filth that invariably filled these streets.

She stopped at a door, once painted a lurid red, though now it had peeled and chipped and faded until it was a dirty brown. She did not knock; it was home for her, as much as she hated the bloody place. It reminded her too much of a home she had once known and fought to forget. She stepped into a dark, unlit hall that reeked of cheap alcohol and other scents to which she had long become accustomed. The sounds of Cora at work came from beyond a closed door to Della's right, so she continued past to the broken stairs at the back of the hall. She climbed up to the second floor, careful to keep quiet, for Cora's customers were an angry lot if disturbed... and too often interested in having Della join the fun. She shuddered at the thought and drew in a deep breath before opening the door at the top of the stairs.

"Violet!" Della's furious shout startled a blonde-haired woman and one of the pub owners who frequented the place out of the bed. The woman gasped as he flung her to the ground and let loose a string of expletives. Della marched forward, took her by the arm and hauled her up.

"Hey, leave off!" she cried as she tried to pull her bodice back over her small breasts. Della shoved her away and turned to pick up a dusty vase on the nightstand.

"Get out!" she shouted and flung it against the wall over the bed. The vase shattered, the fragments showering the man who was busy tugging on his trousers.

"What's this now? I paid for—"

"Get out, *get out!*" Della's voice rose and her body shook as the man stumbled out of the bed. She shoved him towards the door and slammed it behind him. When she turned to face the young woman, she was shaking her head, scraping up the pile of coins on the washstand.

"He wasn't finished," she said, her tone sharp. Della bit back an angry growl.

"Dammit, Violet, I've told you, no men in my room!"

Violet let out a frustrated huff. "I got a new easel and there's no space in mine. I thought you were out."

Della sighed as she crossed to the bed to pick up the mess she had created in her anger. "Suppose it doesn't matter, now."

"Why's that?"

Della faced her friend with a little smile. "I've got a new job."

Violet frowned, her expression laced with suspicion. "What job? You've never had an honest job in your life."

"I can't tell you everythin'. I hardly know anythin' myself. Some toff from Belgrave's hired me to steal somethin' for him. I've just come to collect my things."

Violet's brows arched. "Are you tellin' me that you're going to go with a complete stranger because he wants you to steal somethin'? You can't trust those people, I thought you knew better..."

"Ten thousand pounds, Vi, he's gonna pay me ten thousand pounds."

Violet's emerald eyes widened, and she staggered back a step. "You... you don't really believe him, do you?"

Della shrugged. "I know how to handle myself if he tries anythin'. Besides, this could be our ticket out of here, and I ain't missin' my chance." She turned and pulled an old valise out from under the bed. There was no need to pack. Della never stayed in one place very long – the year she had been living in Cora's brothel was the longest she had ever stayed in one place since leaving the orphanage at sixteen. Her meagre possessions never left the valise. She hefted it up and faced Violet, who frowned again as she tucked a stray wisp of hair back into the loose bun she wore.

"Is this really the best way, though, Della? Countin' on the word of a stranger? I thought we'd been savin' up enough on our own."

"Violet, we couldn't hope to save that amount of money if we picked pockets and lifted our skirts until the day we died. I'll be safe. Tell Cora what's happened when she's finished."

The young woman, still looking suspicious, shrugged and turned to make the bed. "Suit yourself."

Della did not linger to ponder the disappointment in Violet's voice. She scurried downstairs and past the door to the room where Cora did her business. She could hear the familiar squeak of the bed frame, the shouts and moans and gasps that should have sounded pleasurable but somehow never did.

The alley beyond the brothel's doors was empty, and when Della returned to the doorway where she had left Mr. Winthrop, he was gone. A small spurt of anger made her clench her fist around the valise's handle, and she cursed under her breath. She knew his offer was too good to be true. What a fool she was. Damn him!

"Are you ready?"

She spun at the sound of the voice and found him standing behind her. He smiled, but she was too angry at herself to return the expression and scowled at him. "I told you to stay put."

He quirked an eyebrow then gestured to the hansom cab coming towards them.

"I had to pay him a pretty penny to come up this street," he said as he reached out to take her valise. She shot him a withering glare as she pulled it to her chest, pointedly ignoring his offer, and pushed past him. She did not wait for the driver, who looked as though he was uncertain if he should open the door for her or not, and yanked it open herself. Settling against the leather squab, she folded her arms over her chest as she waited for Cole to join her.

When he took his seat beside her, the carriage started forward and he offered her a small grin. "I don't even know your name yet."

Della pursed her lips and glanced out the window. "Della."

"Just Della?" he prompted.

She heaved a sigh. "Della Rose."

His eyebrows rose. "That is an unusual name... it's very pretty."

"It's silly," she said, rolling her eyes and averting her gaze.

"How so?"

"I grew up in an orphanage. The matron gave me a new name when I arrived. She liked givin' us girls silly, fanciful names. She grew roses in the garden... I became Della Rose."

His smile faded. "What did your parents name you?"

That cold feeling in her chest. It always came when she thought of her parents. "Don't remember. All I know is my mother was a whore... don't know who my father was." A lie, but it was none of his damn business. She didn't care to discuss her family, or lack thereof, and certainly not the man who was the cause of it.

He said nothing for a while, and she could feel his gaze upon her. She squirmed beneath his scrutiny, holding her valise tight against her chest as though to shield herself from him. Her stomach rumbled, and, growing miserable and embarrassed in the presence of this man who'd clearly never gone hungry a day in his life, she attempted to burrow into the seat. Her gaze fixed on the city beyond the window as if every building they passed was of crucial importance.

Della then heard Cole shift; there came a rustling noise, and he said her name. When she turned to look at him, he held out a small white box to her.

"Are you hungry?"

She shrugged indifferently. He sighed and reached for her hand. Before she could snatch it away, he pulled it forward and placed the box in it.

"You are my employee now. You needn't be embarrassed to

admit you are hungry. You can have anything you want or need – that is part of the arrangement."

Della frowned at the shiver that raced up her arm from where he touched her so gently before she untied the plain brown string around the box and opened the lid. Though she gave no outward sign of it, her heart soared at the sight of what lay inside the box. Pastries. A dozen tiny, cream-filled, sugar-sprinkled pastries sparkled inside like little golden jewels. Her stomach rumbled in anticipation, and she snatched up one of the confections and shoved it into her mouth. She sighed as the sugar dissolved sweetly on her tongue. Not even bothering to savor the remaining treats, she gobbled them up until her stomach ceased its growling.

"Good?" he ventured.

"Yes..." She almost said thank you, but she'd never had need to say it before, so why start now? After a while, when she licked the last of the crumbs from her fingers, she dared to glance at her new employer.

"So, who am I stealin' from?"

Cole's expression hardened and his body tensed. He glanced out the window before looking back at her. "The Duke of Salisbury. He's a very powerful man, almost royalty. That is why I must resort to subterfuge to get these documents back. I cannot go to the authorities – they will not be able to touch him."

Della chewed on her lower lip as she contemplated this. After a moment, she spoke. "And what makes you think I will?"

At this point, Cole's smile returned, but it was not the easygoing expression she had come to know in her brief time with him. The smile was there, but his eyes were deadly serious.

"Because the duke has a weakness for women. You will be able to get close enough to infiltrate the most private aspects of his life."

Della stared at him for a moment, her face growing hot with rage. She narrowed her eyes at him. "I am *not* a prostitute."

Cole shook his head. "I'm not asking you to bed him. His mother, the Dowager, has finally got her way, and he will be seeking a bride. You" – he inclined his head towards her – "will pose as my cousin, come to visit from the north, looking to unload her dowry. You will be charming—" He paused mid-sentence as he caught her gaze, and when Della gave him a threatening look, his lips turned up in that amiable grin and he waved his hand. "You will enchant him. He holds a ball every year for charity, and we can use the event as a cover to get into his home."

Della raised a skeptical brow as the carriage rumbled over cobbled roads. They had left the filth and misery of Seven Dials for the quiet serenity of St. James' Park, but she paid little attention to the crowds and carriages, for it seemed that Mr. Cole Winthrop must be mad to choose her.

"Wouldn't it be easier to hire a cracksman to break into his home?" she asked.

He shook his head. "The duke is not a trusting man. Lufton Castle is basically a fortress – I daresay anyone caught trying to break in there would be punished most severely."

"And why would he look twice at me? I'm the daughter of a whore, an orphan, a thief... I'm no lady."

Cole leaned forward then and placed a gentle hand upon hers as he held her gaze. Della flinched and her body tensed, but she resisted the urge to pull away.

"Utter nonsense, I am sure, Miss Rose. And I know he will choose you because I know his type – I hope you can act."

Della smirked. "For ten thousand pounds, I'd pretend to be Queen bloody Victoria herself."

A small grin lifted one corner of Cole's mouth. The pace of the carriage slowed as they left behind the open space of The Mall for the bustling, private squares where London's elite resided. Della had always been too intimidated to enter such neighborhoods, though the swag here would be considerably greater than the areas she dived in. A smile suddenly lifted her lips, and she turned her face to the window to hide it from Cole. Oh, she was in now. She would walk these streets disguised as one of these people, and she would clean up. Della's fingers twitched in anticipation, and she flexed them as though to maintain their agility. She would need it in the coming weeks.

Della's voice caught on a breathless gasp when the carriage came to a halt. She could not stop her jaw from dropping a little as she looked past the wrought iron gate to the gleaming white stone mansion beyond. She had never seen a home so large – nor so beautiful – in her entire life.

Cole cleared his throat, drawing her attention back to him. That confident smile of his was gone, and he studied her with narrowed eyes, as if gauging her reaction.

"You live 'ere?" she asked, fighting to keep her tone unimpressed.

He nodded. "Most of the time. There is the occasional trip to the country estate."

Della was quiet as she waited for the door to open. "I've never been to the country."

The driver reached in a hand, but she ignored it and swept by him, valise clutched to her chest. She halted before the gate and realized they were at the back of the house. She turned with a smirk to face Cole, who had come up behind her. "Can't be seen comin' home with the likes of me?"

He shrugged. "People will discover you are here whether I want them to or not. Servants' gossip," he said by way of an explanation. "Remember, you are my cousin. My neighbors are already expecting you. I don't think they'd expect you to look like this, though." The once-over he gave her should have made Della furious, but she realized no cousin of this man would ever come to visit dressed as she was, and so she bit back the scathing reply on her tongue and swept past him.

Cole caught up with her as she slipped through the tall wrought iron gate set between brick walls laden with boughs of creeping ivy.

"That building you went into..." he began, reaching out once more to offer to take her bag. She again ignored him. "Is that where you live?"

She said nothing for a moment as she tried to look unimpressed by his home, but it wasn't easy. The gardens they walked through were by far the loveliest she had ever seen in her whole life. Gravel crunched beneath her feet, and she shivered as the delicate silver leaves of a willow tree brushed against her arm. The scent of roses and lilacs tickled her nostrils, and she could see through a gap in a row of neat boxwood hedges a large marble fountain and stone bench. She almost stopped to take a closer look, but they had reached the door, hidden beneath a trellis swathed in ivy.

She turned to face him. "What of it?"

His eyes narrowed on her, but he made no comment, instead turning the knob to allow her into the house. They moved into a cool, dim hallway, a welcome relief from the oppressive heat outside. Clearly a servants' entrance, the corridor's walls were plain white, and several doors led off the space. He gestured to the narrow stairwell to her left.

"Your rooms are on the second floor... the Rose Suite." His voice faltered and he must have seen the scowl on her face, for he turned on that charming smile again. "A coincidence, I assure you. My mother named the room when she had the home decorated. It's pink." He laughed at the grimace she made and shrugged. "I can have another room prepared if you'd like."

"It'll be fine," she snapped, moving to step past him, but he put a hand on her arm and chuckled.

"You seem to be in an awful hurry. This operation will take

more than a day. I suggest you try to enjoy your time here. I've already sent word ahead, and Mrs. Beatty has prepared luncheon. I can't imagine those pastries were enough."

Della drew in a deep breath and tried to ease the nervous flutter in her stomach. She wasn't used to this; manners and being polite and taking luncheon in a dining room with other people. Cole had been right – she would need any acting skills she possessed to pull this off. She nodded for him to lead her, and he gestured to her bag.

"I thought you might like to freshen up a bit first. I can have someone take your bag up with you if you'd like."

A clutch of panic seized Della and she froze. The valise and its contents were all the possessed in this world and hadn't left her side since she escaped the wretchedness of the orphanage. She wasn't about to let some busybody servant poke through her things.

"I promise you no one will take anything of yours," Cole said, his voice soft. Those striking golden eyes of his bored into her until she had to look away, uncomfortable with the strange emotions they stirred inside her.

"I'd rather bring it myself."

Cole's head inclined in silent agreement, and he gestured for her to follow him. They passed through one of the doors into another corridor and finally into the main hall. Della let out a disbelieving laugh as she gazed up at the soaring paneled ceiling, the delicate chandeliers, and massive portraits in gilded frames. It all exuded wealth and luxury and comfort and, for a moment, Della's anxiety eased. If she played this right, she could have some of this for herself.

"What d'you do for a livin'?" she asked as she snatched up a crystal vase from an elaborate sideboard to examine it. She felt his gaze upon her, and so quickly set it back down again.

"I don't work for a living... I'm a gentleman."

Della frowned at the inflection in his voice. From anyone

else, that statement would have possessed the pride of being wealthy enough not to have to work, but Cole's tone hinged on sarcastic. She gave a sniff of disdain. She would be thrilled not to have to pick pockets or glue labels or sweep streets just to get by. She would give anything to sit out in that garden all day and read her books.

When Cole turned to move up the stairs, Della frowned, swept a small china figurine from the sideboard into her pocket, and followed him.

THREE

Good Lord – Cole had been right. Her rooms were, indeed, pink. A cloying, flowery profusion of coral and blush and cherry and rose and every other shade of pink known to man. Della grimaced, almost wishing she had agreed to be put up in a different room. Pink was not among her favorite colors, but the room was stunning otherwise. Della had never imagined such luxury in her life, and she stood transfixed for a moment, trying to take it all in.

Cole smiled as she ventured farther into the room, and damned if it didn't make her heart flutter like the lovesick heroine of some penny dreadful. *Get a hold of yourself, Della.*

"I will leave you to settle in. One of the maids will be up shortly to help you wash and dress for lunch. Please do let me know if there is anything you require, anything at all. And thank you, Miss Rose. I do hope we have a... fruitful relationship." He nodded and withdrew, the door clicking softly shut behind him.

The valise fell from her clutch to land with a thud on the plush and, of course, pink rug. Della glanced down as she took a careful step forward and saw the smattering of dirt left behind by her muddied boots. Grimacing, she kicked them off before making her way to the enormous, draped bed. She reached forth a tentative hand to touch the pale pink bedspread and found it to be soft and sumptuous. A small shudder of excitement went through her.

Della now looked around the room with the practiced eye only a thief possessed, taking careful inventory of everything here that was ripe for the taking. That crystal vase filled with plump white and pink flowers, the collection of silver objects on the vanity for her toilette, the ormolu candlesticks atop the mantel, the very rug upon which she stood, were all worth a fortune. Pursing her lips, Della withdrew the figurine she had slipped into her pocket in the hall and regarded the small porcelain shepherdess for a moment. She certainly knew the difference between right and wrong, but in Della's world, the line between the two was very blurred. Stealing a bit of food to feed a hungry belly should hardly be a more heinous crime than letting that belly go hungry in the first place. Some people had more money than they knew what to do with and Della was happy to part them from it to survive.

Shrugging, she slipped the figurine back into her pocket.

A large, intricately carved clothes press dominated one wall of the room, but Della had no use for it. Her meagre possessions barely filled the valise she carried them in, and so she looked elsewhere to hide her things from nosy servants. She retrieved her bag from where she had dropped it and slid it under the bed, where the voluminous folds of the bed skirt would conceal it before turning to inspect the rest of the room, her hand moving idly over the items she had marked earlier as valuables, for there was no hurry. Cole himself had said this job wouldn't happen overnight, so there would be plenty of time to clean this room out. Better to have things go missing a little at a time than all at once.

Della lifted the lid of a small inlaid jewelry box to see if it contained any treasures within. Empty. She frowned and resumed her circuit of the room before pausing in front of another door that opened to reveal, much to her shock and delight, a small water closet. A gasp left her lips as she took a few timid steps inside to run her fingers over the cool white porcelain of the washbasin, surmounted by a pair of gleaming brass faucets. Having never used anything more than a wooden tub filled with boiled water to wash up, she sucked in a breath as she tentatively turned one of the spigots. Della's grin widened as clear, cool water poured out of the faucet and splashed into the basin. She trailed her fingers beneath the flow for a moment before turning it off and retreating from the room with a smile.

The sudden sound of knocking on her chamber door made her whirl about as though she had been caught doing something improper. She carefully shut the water closet door and scurried back to where Cole had left her standing before clearing her throat and calling out, "Come in."

The door opened and a servant bustled in, severe in her black and white uniform, hair pinned tightly back from her pale face. She swept by Della as if she were invisible to make her way to the water closet, speaking over her shoulder as she opened the door.

"My name is Mrs. Cooper. I am the head housekeeper here at Bradford House. Lord Bradford has planned for your arrival and has had a wardrobe made for you. I shall draw you a bath and have the staff bring up your clothes. Please see to it that you are presentable before coming down for luncheon."

Lord Bradford? A bloody lord? Well, that was an interesting turn. Della would have mulled over this, but the servant turned swiftly once she had opened the door, her sharp gaze observing Della as one might a snake. She was a middle-aged woman, her hair already a steel-grey, her similarly colored eyes narrowed, her thin-lipped mouth drawn down at the corners. If Della had been at all intimidated by her and her sudden arrival, it now turned to defensiveness and her hands curled into tight fists at her side.

"Listen here, I was hired by Mr. Win—"

Before Della could get another word out, the door to her bedchamber swung open and a flurry of servants burst in, footmen with hatboxes and petticoats and gowns, chambermaids with clean towels and jewelry cases. Della's jaw dropped and she could only stare as they scurried about behind the disapproving servant, putting the garments away in the clothes press and setting out items for her toilette on the vanity. The older woman disappeared into the water closet, and the sound of running water shortly followed.

Before long, the flurry of activity came to an end, and the servants filed out of Della's room, scarcely looking in her direction. Once more, she was alone with the dour housekeeper who inclined her head at Della and spoke stiffly.

"This should be all you need for now. Martha will be up shortly to dress you and I will return to bring you down for luncheon."

With that, she strode past a flabbergasted Della, shutting the door with careful deliberation behind her.

A moment of silence followed as Della stared at the door before she shook her head and turned to face the water closet. A smile curled her lips as she forgot about what she was going to say to that uptight old bitch when she viewed the large copper tub, steam curling above it. She flew across the chamber to the water closet where she paused for a moment to clasp her hands as though in gratitude for this luxury before tugging at laces and hooks to drop her clothes in a pile on the floor.

Wiggling her fingers in anticipation, she gripped the edge of the tub, took a deep breath, and lifted a leg to dip a toe into the water. Delicious. She plunged the rest of her leg in, the heat of the water enveloping her before she stepped over the rim and settled herself down.

A delighted shiver shook her, and she closed her eyes, leaning her head back against the rim. Now this, she could get used to, and with the ten thousand pounds coming her way, what was stopping her? She and Violet could finally escape the rookery, a dream they had carried with them all those long years in the orphanage together. No more stealing. No more whoring. They would live as ladies of leisure, sipping lemonade in the garden in the summer, whiling away their days doing... whatever it was ladies of leisure did. She must look into that. But most importantly, she would have books. Stacks of them. Maybe, though she hardly dared even think it, so fleeting a dream it had been, she could go to school. A real school.

Smiling, Della reached for a small cake of soap placed on a silver tray and leisurely scrubbed herself; scrubbed off the rookery which clung to her skin. She then settled back and, for the first time in as long as she could remember, her body began to relax. Her whole life had been lived on the edge – on the edge of poverty, of starvation, of being caught – and she had never had as much as five minutes in her life to relax, to not always have to be one step ahead of everyone around her. She could just breathe. It was heaven.

After a while, and much to her disappointment, the water began to cool, and Della conceded it was time to get out. Sighing, she raised herself from the water and reached for a linen towel folded nearby to dry herself. She lifted a cream silk dressing gown from a hook on the back of the door and slipped it on, shivering as the luxurious material slid over her skin, to make her way back into the bedroom where she crossed to the clothes press. She flung open the doors and inspected the contents, her bottom lip pulled between her teeth. If this was a difficult decision in the everyday life of a lady of means, she welcomed it with open arms.

Should she pick the pale blue silk? A bit formal, she suspected. Dusty rose taffeta? She thrust her tongue out at the notion, for she had her fill of pink standing in this very room. She shoved it aside. Pale lavender? Deep burgundy? She finally settled on the navy cotton, it seeming the most practical of the attire available to her.

She pulled it from the press and laid it across the bed, admiring the beauty of the gown for, though simple and plain, it was obviously well-made and no doubt expensive. She paused to lift one of the sleeves to inspect the velvet edging the cuff when another brusque knock sounded on the door. Before she could even reply, the lock turned and the door swung open to reveal the sinister-looking housekeeper. She took one look at Della, glanced down at the dress, and shook her head.

"No, no, that is all wrong. That is a traveling gown. Goodness, you're going to be a challenge. I don't think Lord Bradford knows what he's got himself into."

She heaved a sigh that seemed to say her burden was great and strode past Della to the press. She withdrew a skirt and matching bodice of rich mustard, both festooned with brown ribbons and flowers, and laid them over the plainer navy gown Della had selected. She sighed again as she faced the younger woman.

"I will send up Martha to help you dress and fix your... um, hair." She frowned as she said this, and Della unconsciously raised a hand to her still-damp hair and the no doubt tangled mess it was.

Shaking her head, the housekeeper spun around and strode from the room, her large key ring jangling at her side. Della's jaw clenched but no sooner had Mrs. Cooper departed than a rosy-cheeked young woman entered, her face wreathed in a cheerful smile.

"I'm Martha, miss. Mrs. Cooper sent me up to help you... oh, I was worried she would pick that dress for you. Not your color at all. I think you'll find Mrs. Cooper doesn't have an eye for these things!" She let out a breezy laugh at this statement and proceeded to the press to withdraw a selection of white, lacy undergarments.

The young servant then stretched a hand out and smiled merrily, her plump cheeks dimpling. "Your dressing gown if you please! I'll help you into these, and then we can get you down for lunch. I think you'll enjoy it – jellied tongue and cold roast beef."

Della almost gagged at the idea of jellied anything, but obediently handed the gown to the young woman. Standing there, naked and damp, she should have felt awkward, but the servant's carefree manner suggested she was used to this, so Della relaxed. Once dressed in fine silk stockings tied at the knee with pink ribbon and a lacy set of combinations that made her feel like some absurd little cream puff, Martha set about lacing up the beautifully embroidered corset.

"You've not got much meat on your bones – shall I lace it a bit tighter to give you some shape?"

Della turned to face the girl with a scowl. "No," was her sharp reply as the maid tucked in the laces and held out a snowy white petticoat for Della to step into. Finally, Martha moved to the press to inspect the new dresses within.

"I don't suppose Mrs. Cooper would approve, but I don't think that gown suits you at all. Here, this will do you much better." She smiled as she turned with the blue dress Della had dismissed as too formal earlier. Martha expertly buttoned her into the gorgeous silk gown before smiling.

"Mrs. Cooper wanted me to do your hair for you... if you'll have a seat, I'll get my things."

Della did as she was bid and watched, self-conscious in the body-hugging bodice, as the maid set out hair pins and ribbons. "So..." she began awkwardly, plucking at the lace trim on her sleeve, "how do you like working for Mr.... uh, Lord... Winthrop?"

Martha grinned again as she gestured for Della to turn and face the ornate mirror. She started pulling a silver-handled brush through Della's tangled hair before she answered.

"It's Lord Bradford... the Earl of Bradford. His family name is Winthrop. I like it here very much. He's a fair employer. And very handsome." She giggled as she began plaiting Della's thick, dark hair. Della's lips turned up in the barest hint of a smile. The girl was right there, she had to admit, but her heart was hard to the effects of good-looking men. There was no space for romance in her life; too much was taken by the need to survive, and in her experience, it rarely ended well, anyway.

"Lord Bradford says you are to stay here as his cousin... are you really a professional pickpocket?" Martha's wide gaze met Della's in the mirror as she threaded a hairpin into her creation. Della frowned.

"Professional? None of us are professionals, we just get good enough to hope we don't get caught. Better than dying in a gutter, anyway."

The maid nodded sagely. "I suppose that's true. I was lucky to land this post. I started out as a scullery maid in another house before Lord Bradford hired me to be your lady's maid. There, I think you're ready," she proclaimed as she tucked in the last hairpin. Della looked up and almost didn't recognize herself in the gilded vanity mirror. Who'd have thought a fancy dress and a decent hairstyle was all it took to make her look like one of those fancy ladies who promenaded in Hyde Park? She looked... beautiful. Della knew she was pretty but had never thought of herself as beautiful. It was a strange feeling, and she bit her lip as she looked back at her reflection.

Martha smiled at her in the mirror. "You look just lovely."

FOUR

Cole Winthrop, Earl of Bradford, whistled softly as he poured himself a splash of whisky and set the decanter back in the cabinet. A knock made him glance towards his office door.

"Come," he called out absently as he raised the glass to his lips and took a swig. He savored the fire that settled in his belly as Mrs. Cooper stuck her head in and fixed him with her usual humorless gaze.

"The young... um, lady, is getting dressed as we speak. Luncheon is ready to be served. Shall I bring her down to the dining room?"

"Yes, Mrs. Cooper," he said, but after a moment's consideration, he turned before she closed the door behind her. "No," he said quickly. "No... tell Mrs. Beatty to prepare a picnic. I think our new guest might like to eat in the garden."

Mrs. Cooper gave him a blank look, perhaps knowing better than to question his ever-changing decisions, nodded, and left.

Cole swirled the last of the whisky in the glass before downing it in one quick gulp. He was not one to drink alone, but he needed the fortification. He wasn't entirely sure if what he was About to do was genius... or complete folly. His hand tightened around the glass, and he set it down before it shattered.

The duke. Charles Lumley, the bloody Duke of Salisbury, a sly, dangerous bastard if ever there was one. And powerful. So damn powerful. No authority apart from the queen herself could touch him, and even she might hesitate to do so, given his status and influence. His only weakness, as far as Cole had been able to ascertain, was women. A certain type of woman. Miss Rose's type.

Cole's hand shook, ever so slightly, as he glanced in the mirrored doors of the liquor cabinet and straightened his already-immaculate tie. Miss Rose clearly didn't see what he saw in her, but if there was any way to get close to the Duke of Salisbury, it was through her. He sighed. It had to be her – nothing else had worked. A man as powerful as the duke was well-protected. There was nothing left for it but to use a thief to catch a thief. Cole had seen something in Della, though – through the biting words and the mended clothing, the hungry eyes and quick fingers – the quality in her that the duke would find irresistible. Cole had watched Salisbury for years, learning his habits, his strengths, his weaknesses – of which there were few. That was, until he had spotted the duke one night at a costume party held by none other than Queen Victoria herself.

Salisbury had been speaking with a woman who was just Miss Rose's type – slender, dark-haired, icy blue eyes, with that rangy, yet graceful movement. Cole saw, too, that she was sharp: perceptive, and not at all taken in by the duke's overtures, though he was almost certainly the best catch in the room that night.

Salisbury's embarrassing, almost slavering obsession with that woman was what piqued Cole's interest. Here was a potential vulnerability. The duke followed her around the entire evening, requesting every dance, bringing her drinks, all evidence of his ordinarily cold and imperious personality gone.

Cole pulled aside the woman, a German princess distantly related to the consort, and asked if she was acquainted with the peer.

"*Liebe Gott*, no!" she had gasped, shaking her head. "He is detestable... I asked him repeatedly to leave me, but he insisted. He said he would like to court me – the very idea! What a strange, sinister man. You would do well to stay away from him," she had added with a shudder as she made her escape.

Cole paused as he passed through the drawing room and glanced out into the garden to espy a woman in a pale blue dress, her midnight tresses gathered up into neat curls which framed a face of stark, haunting beauty. She looked uncomfortable sitting there, and it took Cole a moment to realize who she was.

His jaw fell. He had known Miss Rose was beautiful beneath the flinty gaze and sharp words, but he had never imagined...

He shook his head and continued through the drawing room to the back of the house and out the garden doors. She sat facing away from him on a stone bench beneath the mottled shade of a willow tree. He opened his mouth to call her name but stopped for a moment to simply watch her. She held a daisy, taken from the profusion of bobbing, cheerful flowers which bordered the garden and idly plucked the petals, watching as they drifted to the ground, then seemed to grow bored and tossed the stem away. She shifted on the bench, as though uncomfortable, and turned before he had a chance to say anything.

Her brows drew together in a frown as she caught him staring and she shot up, as though she had been caught doing something untoward. She crossed her arms in defiance and stared back at him.

"I've been waiting for you," she said, as though she had been terribly put out, sitting out here in the warm quiet of the garden.

"My apologies, Miss Rose. I've had Mrs. Beatty prepare us a picnic, so we may eat out here in the garden. I do hope this is acceptable to you?" he replied, moving towards her. Her arms remained folded, but her scowl softened and she gave a reluctant nod.

"Suppose so. I've never been to a picnic before," she added, finally uncrossing her arms.

"Never?"

She looked away and squinted into the sun. "No, course not."

Cole didn't say anything to that. Instead, he smiled and gestured. "Come, you must be hungry."

Della hesitated for a moment before joining him beneath the swaying branches of the oak tree, the sun warm on the soft grass beneath their feet. His assessing gaze stayed upon her as she took a seat on the blanket, before he handed her a sandwich wrapped in paper. He watched as she tore into it and took a huge, grateful bite, her eyes closing briefly. Something warm stirred in the pit of his belly and, rather than choose to analyze the feeling, he dismissed it as simply being happy to help the lady out of a bad situation and took a decidedly more restrained bite from his own sandwich.

He let her eat in silence for a while, with only the muffled sounds of horseshoes on cobbles and the twitter of birds to interrupt the quiet. After a time, Cole cleared his throat and looked over at Miss Rose, who had finished her sandwich, passed over some jellied tongue with a grimace, and was now dipping fresh strawberries into a bowl of cream. She ate them with evident joy, and he felt that same stirring again as she licked a delicate froth of cream from her lip. He shook his head to dismiss the notion.

"So, Miss Rose, now that we are alone, why don't you tell me a little bit about yourself?"

Her expression became shuttered almost immediately and

her lips thinned into a hard line before she looked away from him. "Nothin' much to tell."

"Now I'm certain that can't be true. Where were you born?"

Her gaze returned to his and it was direct, unblinking, and unashamed. "Right where you found me, in Seven Dials. I told you... my mother was a whore. She was born there, and she died there. And if it weren't for this job, I probably would, too."

Cole didn't know what to say to this. She said it with such nonchalance, as if dying in the putrefied streets of some back alley were of no consequence. He decided, then and there, that no matter what came of this operation, he would ensure that she would never have to go back to Seven Dials.

"And what about you? Where were you born?" she asked, her gaze still locked on him, almost unsettling in its fierceness. He grinned as he set down the remains of his sandwich.

"Right here in this house – all of us Winthrops were born here, all the way back to my great-great-grandfather. It's practically a tradition at this point."

"It must be nice knowin' your family that far back." She gave him a wry smile. "I don't even know my real last name." There was a pause as she shook her head, and Cole thought he detected the briefest hint of sadness in her voice before she snatched up a pastry and met his gaze once more. "How'd you find me? Surely you didn't just pick out the first diver you saw?"

He chuckled and chose a pastry for himself. "No, no, I didn't. I had been asking around, looking for just the right person when I got word of a pickpocket of some repute. Rosie Diver, they called her. I chose you a fortnight ago, sizing you up – which is why you now have a full wardrobe – and then it was simply a matter of waiting for you to find me."

She let out a short laugh. "That's me, alright. Quickest hands in the Dials. I'm impressed – there's not many that can follow me without being seen. We make it a point in St. Giles to always know an outsider when we see one."

Cole gave her a sly look. "I'll consider that a compliment, coming from you."

Della grinned as she dusted the crumbs from her fingers. "Why'd you choose me?"

"Your reputation, mostly. I saw a few other ladies that might fit the bill, but they didn't have the right... look."

"And I do?" She looked incredulous, as though she could not believe that she could ever be someone with the right "look". He took a moment to observe her: the soft curls Martha had coaxed to frame her astonishing face, the wide eyes of icy blue, and the full, pink lips that pursed as she watched him, lips simply made to be kissed. He cleared his throat as he realized where his thoughts had started to wander, for in them she wore considerably less clothing, and her skin was like silk beneath his touch.

"Absolutely. I watched the Duke of Salisbury, as well, and he is a man of particular tastes."

Her pale eyes blazed suddenly at this remark. "And you promise I won't have to... do anything with him?"

Cole shook his head vehemently. "I promise you that. He enjoys the chase. He is a man of great means and power, after all. He can have any woman he chooses, and most would not fight him for the chance to be Duchess of Salisbury. He will appreciate a woman who rebuffs his efforts, who makes him work for what he wants. You are quite free to refuse his advances. I would not have you placed in a compromising position."

She looked suspicious but nodded slowly in agreement. "Very well."

"I must ask," he said as he leaned back on the blanket and propped himself up on one arm. "Where did you get the name Rosie Diver?"

She shrugged. "I've been pickin' pockets since I was four-teen, and I've always worked alone. Most of us divers work in gangs, so's to avoid being caught, but then you have to share the swag."

"And have you ever been caught?"

The grin on her face was sly. "Never. Though they've tried. That's why they started callin' me Rosie Diver – Rose is the name, and divin' is the game. I figured it was as good a way as any to hide my real name from the coppers. You must have friends very high up to get them to stop lookin' for me."

Cole was quiet for a moment as she plucked idly at the grass before he lifted his shoulders. "High enough."

Something approaching a smile touched her lips then and he chuckled before standing to brush the crumbs from his lap and offer her his arm. "Shall we go for a walk?"

From beyond the towering brick walls came the bustle and noise of London that Della was accustomed to, but here, in this expansive, private space, it seemed miles away. Violet would call it enchanting, and Della paused as they passed the fountain she had seen earlier. Stepping away from the earl, she approached it to gaze down into the shallow water. Sunlight glinted off the bright orange goldfish that darted in and out of the water lilies, and she looked back at Cole – Lord Bradford, she corrected herself.

"So, what's so terrible in these documents that someone would try to use them against you? You seem to be a good enough bloke," she joked, turning to face him. The smallest smile quirked his lips as he took a seat on the stone bench beside the fountain.

"Another compliment. Careful or I may acquire a too-high opinion of myself. It's not every day one receives the praises of the best pickpocket in London."

She gave a small laugh and took a seat next to him, but he didn't smile again.

"To be honest, Miss Rose, I have not yet decided if it is worth you knowing that information. I have yet to decide if I can trust you."

His steely gaze on her made her uncomfortable, and she looked away, thinking of the china shepherdess she had pocketed.

"Suppose a pickpocket isn't a trustworthy sort," she said, focusing on the water burbling out of the fountain.

"In time, I think. In time I should trust you. Until then, we have much work to do. You're to begin your lessons with Mr. Avery tomorrow."

"Lessons?" she asked, facing him with a frown. As if he could give her lessons on diving.

"Yes, lessons. To defeat one's enemy, one must know one's enemy." He nodded sagely before adding, "And you will take the next few weeks to learn all you can about the duke. And, I'd wager, you also have much to learn about the etiquette involved in moving about in certain... social circles."

Della knew this was true but couldn't help feeling shamed all the same. She would have retorted with some remark about how he wouldn't last a day in Seven Dials, but when she caught a glimpse of his sympathetic smile, she stopped herself. Once again, he seemed to read her thoughts and added, "I still have trouble with it myself. It's a game out there, a complicated game for which there are many rules. We shall have to teach you those rules if you are to blend in seamlessly."

"And what are the rules?" she said as she plucked another flower from a plant that bordered the path. She didn't know what it was, but it was a lovely bright blue and she twisted the stem in her fingers. He chuckled.

"Too many to tell you now. Mrs. Cooper will be helping with much of your tutoring, and I have taken the liberty of purchasing a book on etiquette for you. It came very highly recommended from the lady at the bookshop..." He paused when he caught her glaring at him and faltered for a moment. "That is... I'm sorry. I didn't think. Can you read?"

Della scoffed and pushed herself up from the bench before striding away. Lord Bradford jogged to catch up with her and she said, without looking at him, "I can bloody well read, I'm not stupid. They didn't teach us orphans much, but they did teach us to read. And why do I need all these lessons to steal from someone? Who's going to care if I know how to act like some bloody toff?"

Lord Bradford's hand came to rest upon her arm, and she whirled to face him. His expression was solemn as she glanced down to where he held her, his touch like fire on the bare skin of her wrist.

"Miss Rose, I don't know if you realize what this world is like. At the very top, there are rules... expectations. If they are not followed, you will surely be marked as an outsider. The Duke of Salisbury must never suspect you are anything but my cousin, a lady of high birth who is expected to marry well and have children. She knows all these rules; she was born to them and has been following them since she was in the nursery. She is not Della Rose of Seven Dials; she is the complete opposite. If he suspects you for but a moment, then the plan will fail. I must trust you to behave exactingly at all times when we are not in my home. Please, Miss Rose – this is an exceedingly important matter for me. I would not have brought you here if I did not think you could perform this task. And I cannot fail. I am happy to pay you whatever you want, but I must know that you can follow the rules." His gaze bored into her and the pressure of his hand on her wrist seemed to grow unbearable. She nodded and pulled her arm away.

"Yes... yes, of course I can follow the rules. I'll help you, Mr... that is, Lord Bradford. I'll help you as best I can."

He breathed a sigh and the relief in his expression was evident. "Good. It will not be easy, Miss Rose. There is a delicate balance to all these rules. Any slip will be widely remarked upon."

Della smirked as they reached the house. "There are rules where I come from, as well, milord. Slips are not remarked upon, they get you killed."

FIVE

A knocking at her door awoke Della the next morning. She groaned and rolled over to bury her face in the down pillows, a soft luxury far removed from the scratchy wool blankets of Cora's. Hers had been a deep and dreamless slumber last night and she wasn't eager to leave the delicious comfort of her bed. But it seemed there was no time to waste this morning, for the door creaked open, and footsteps crossed the floor to the window. The drapes parted with a whisper and the harsh morning light made her squeeze her eyes shut and mutter, "Go away!"

"Sorry, miss, I have orders; lots to do today. Mr. Avery will be arriving shortly to begin your lessons and we have to get you washed and dressed," Martha said as she bustled about the room. Della peeked out from under the blankets and saw the maid setting out brushes and curling rods on the vanity before moving to the clothes press. She stood before the piece of furniture for a few moments, finger on her chin, before she nodded and withdrew a gown of soft grey with thin black stripes.

"Did you sleep well?" the maid chirped as Della relented

and pushed the quilt down before swinging her legs over the side of the bed.

"I did, actually... can't remember the last time I slept so well."

Martha nodded in understanding as she moved into the water closet and turned the taps to start the water flowing. Just the idea of sinking into that tub of warm, scented water made getting up a little more bearable and Della rubbed her tired eyes as she stood.

"I'll leave you to it, miss," Martha said as she turned off the taps and retreated from the water closet. Della eagerly stripped from her nightgown and slipped into the tub with a sigh of satisfaction. She scrubbed herself with the finely milled French soaps on the side table and sat with her eyes closed until the water cooled and she reluctantly stood and stepped out. Martha was waiting for her in the bedchamber, having laid out her gown and underclothes.

Once the beautiful grey cotton gown had been buttoned up, her hair styled expertly by the young maid and her shoes slipped on, Della followed Martha downstairs to the dining room.

Lord Bradford was waiting, and a small shiver went up Della's back when he turned to her with that smile. *That damn smile.* Her body hummed in anticipation of that smile; it lifted her whole being and seemed made for her alone, and how on earth could a simple smile affect her so? She almost giggled when he stepped forward to greet her and then felt foolish for it, and so hardened her expression and gave him a curt nod. Della Rose was no simpering twit.

"Good mornin', milord," she said, keeping her voice carefully neutral and bending in a small curtsey. Was that how it was done? She had never greeted a lord before. Were these the rules he had spoken of? Who to curtsey to, and when to do it?

"Good morning, Miss Rose. I trust you found your rooms

suitable?" He pulled out a chair near the large picture window for her. Through the gleaming panes, the sun shone brightly over the garden and glinted off the water in the fountain. A man in overalls and a straw hat was clipping the neat boxwood hedges, while another knelt to dig in the soft earth with a spade. A wheelbarrow full of seedlings sat beside him.

She shook her head and turned her attention back to Lord Bradford. "Suitable enough."

He nodded as he took the seat opposite her before gesturing outside. "A lovely day. I thought we might eat luncheon in the garden again?"

Della followed his gaze back out the window. The gardeners had moved on.

"I suppose. Martha said I'm to begin lessons today. What are they for?"

He smiled again and something stirred inside her, a pang of desire she had not felt in a long time. It made her press her thighs together as though to hold it there. Damn him and damn his winning smile.

"I have a variety of disciplines I should like you to learn in the next few weeks. Mr. Avery will be your music instructor. I thought a bit of piano in your repertoire would lend to the idea of you being a lady of high birth. Mrs. Cooper will also be instructing you on proper etiquette – we will have to attend several parties and balls and will operate under the pretense that you are debuting next Season. I must ask... how old are you, Miss Rose?"

Della's fingers paused where they played absently with the delicate lace trim on her skirt, and she lifted her head to meet his inquisitive gaze. "I'll be twenty-four in a month's time."

He nodded. "I think you can pass for nineteen. You would be too old to debut at twenty-four. I will also be tutoring you myself when you are not otherwise engaged with your instructors."

Della looked up at this. She opened her mouth to ask what on earth he could be tutoring her in when the door opened and a footman entered with the tea tray. Lord Bradford stood and crossed to the sideboard before turning to Della.

"Tea, Miss Rose?"

Della accepted the cup he handed her with a bob of her head and waited as he took his own cup and resumed his seat opposite her. The footman sketched a quick bow and left the room. "Breakfast should be ready shortly."

"I'm fine. I don't usually eat breakfast."

His expression softened. "You mustn't ever think you cannot ask for anything while you're here. I really do want you to think of this place as your home for the next few months. You are to be my cousin – and I intend to treat you as such."

Della's stomach rumbled, but once again, the words *thank you* did not come easily to her after a lifetime of relying only on herself. She gave a tight nod and took a sip of her tea before she found her gaze wandering to his lips as he drank from his own cup. She let herself imagine, for the briefest of seconds, how those lips would feel upon hers, how her tongue might trace the sharp indent of his cupid's bow, how he might taste, and then she shook her head in annoyance at herself.

"You said you'd be tutorin' me. Is etiquette not enough? I didn't think you people cared what a woman thought."

He chuckled. "In some regards, yes... in most regards, in fact. A shame... you have quite interesting thoughts, as a sex." The look he gave her then, with those finely drawn lips turned up at the corner and his golden eyes seeming to suggest he would most certainly like to know those thoughts, made her draw herself up straighter in her chair to return his steady gaze. He cleared his throat and grinned before adding, "That being said, it is advantageous for a debutante to have a wide-ranging education. We shan't be able to teach you another language in enough time, nor any skills in art, but I shall be teaching you a bit of history and literature, and horseback riding. The duke is an avid rider, and this will surely help you draw his attention."

"Horseback riding?" Her voice came out in a squeak as a small flash of fear skated up her back. Horses made her nervous – their size, their strength. There was no occasion to ride a horse where she came from, and less to think of it as a skill. Her stomach quaked at the thought.

"Yes, it will be the quickest way to gain his attention. Time is of the essence, after all. Fear not, Dionysus is a good, placid mount. He'll do anything you ask of him without a fuss."

"Dionysus?"

Lord Bradford laughed again, a deep, reverberating sound that made her skin tingle. She ground her teeth together against the rising heat in her chest.

"Yes. I had a fancy for Greek gods when I returned from abroad after I finished school. You won't have to do much with him apart from staying on his back."

"Sounds like he'd be a drunken mess judgin' by the name you've given him," she said as she stirred a splash of milk into her tea.

"So, you are familiar with the gods of ancient Greece?" Della looked up to see Lord Bradford watching her with an impressed expression, and she cursed herself. *Your life is none of his business.*

"I read a book once..."

"I see," he said as the footman returned, bearing the breakfast cart. Bradford nodded towards the dishes as the servant retreated. "Are you certain I can't interest you in something to eat? Mrs. Beatty is quite renowned for her marmalade."

Della glanced over at the steaming silver chafing dishes as her stomach rumbled once more in protest. It did smell rather appetizing, so she relented.

"I do like marmalade," she admitted as Bradford crossed to the sideboard where the dishes had been arrayed. He smiled as he piled crisp toast, cold, thick-cut ham, a crock of marmalade, and a generous helping of scrambled eggs onto a plate and brought it to her.

"I used to steal jars of this from the kitchens when I was a lad and got no end of grief when Mrs. Beatty found out. In the end, she ended up doubling the batch just so there was extra for me."

Della allowed a small smile as he resumed the seat opposite her. "So, you're a thief as well? Why, you'll hardly need me for this at all."

Bradford let out a deep laugh as he slathered marmalade on a slice of toast. "Ah, but I fear I am not the duke's type." He glanced at the ornate gilded clock upon the mantel and nodded. "Mr. Avery will be here shortly. When you're done, we'll meet him in the music room."

A music room? The very idea of an entire room dedicated to music was absurd to Della, but she cleared her plate – the marmalade was, indeed, delicious – and rose to follow him out of the dining room through the grand hallway with its breath-taking curved staircase. He then turned down another narrower hallway and pushed open the door to another room. Sunlight streamed through a bay of tall windows festooned with expen-sive-looking blue watered silk drapes onto a gleaming mahogany grand piano. The shelves lining one wall were positively stuffed with books and sculptures and her heart soared as she moved over to one of the shelves and leaned closer to see the title on a red-leather spine. Her excitement grew as she scanned the rows of books. Here was knowledge! Here were the great thinkers she had always longed to study! Homer's *Odyssey*. Beside it, the *Illiad*. She pulled out a volume by Plato from nearby and leafed through it before she became aware of Lord Bradford's gaze upon her.

She looked up and saw that he watched her with a slight smile. "Are you familiar with Plato?"

A sudden, insane urge came over her and she shrugged, nonchalant as she placed the book back on the shelf. "I believe his theory of forms really explains nothing about the similarity of objects and another form is always needed beyond the one proposed."

She risked a glance at him and choked back the laughter that bubbled up inside her chest when she saw the shocked expression on his face. She could sound like a toff, too, when she wanted. Stifling a smile, she turned with a serene expression and a swish of her bustled skirts to stroll past him to the piano. She lifted the fallboard with a single finger and tapped out a few discordant notes as Lord Bradford seemed to gather his wits and move towards her.

"That is an... interesting observation," he said, still sounding stunned. She shrugged again and pushed her skirts behind her knees to take a seat at the piano bench. A book of sheet music sat upon the shelf and she flipped it open, frowning at the jumble of notes within the pages before glancing up at him.

"You play?" she asked, gesturing to the keys. He lifted his shoulders and motioned for her to make room for him on the bench. She shifted over and he sat beside her, flexing his fingers. His thigh brushed against the pleated ruffles on her gown, and she pulled away with a jerk as though his naked skin had touched her. He didn't seem to notice her reaction as he turned the page of the music book.

"Passably. But I was never a very good student." And with that, he leaned forward and began to play, his fingers uncertain at first, but then growing more confident. Della stared as the melody took shape; a sad, haunting piece that made her throat tighten just a little. After a moment, she looked up to watch his face as he played and was mesmerized by his expression. He never looked away from the keys, not for a moment, and the intensity in his eyes as the music reached a crescendo made her shiver. After a few moments, his fingers fumbled, and he shook his head.

"I'm out of practice, it would seem," he said, chuckling as he rose from the bench.

"No... no, it was lovely. What's it called?"

"Beethoven... his *Moonlight Sonata*. It's been ages since I played that. Mr. Avery would not be impressed." He offered his hand to her, and she took it to stand.

"Mr. Avery?"

"Yes. He was my tutor, as well. Let us hope he has better luck with you than he did with me."

As though on cue, there came a knock at the door and a footman entered the room.

"Mr. Avery is here for Miss Rose's lessons."

"Ah, very good. Please do send him in," he said and turned to Della. "Well, I shall leave you to it. Mr. Avery is aware of our arrangement, so please don't feel the need to hide anything from him."

Apprehension slithered up Della's back as he nodded to her and left the room. She stood, uncertain, as there was an exchange of low male voices in the hall. The door opened after a few moments and a distinguished-looking older gentleman entered the room, a sheaf of papers and folders tucked under his arm. A warm smile lit up his mustachioed face as he set the papers down on a side table.

"Miss Rose?"

Della didn't move from where she stood beside the piano but did offer him a small nod.

"A pleasure to meet you," he said, signaling for her to return to the piano bench. She drew in a deep breath and sat as he pulled out a small piece of charcoal wrapped in paper from his breast pocket. She leaned back as he bent over the keys and marked one near the middle.

"Middle C," he explained, pocketing the charcoal. "This is

your home key, and where you shall return every time you play."

While he spoke of notes and octaves and flats and sharps, Della couldn't help her gaze sliding away from him out the window to the lofty willow tree in the garden. Its long tendril-like branches swayed gently in the breeze, and she thought how lovely it would be to sit beneath that tree, Aristotle in hand, and while away the afternoon deep in thought. The gardeners had returned and were hard at work clipping the hedges that lined the wall surrounding the property. She watched them for a moment before someone said her name, breaking her from her reverie.

"Miss Rose?"

Mr. Avery looked down at her with a raised brow and her cheeks grew warm. Chastened, she stared at the keyboard and clenched her fists in her lap.

"Sorry, sir. My mind wandered."

Mr. Avery's expression softened, and he drew up a chair to sit beside her. "I take it this is not what you expected you would be doing when Lord Bradford brought you here?"

A heavy sigh escaped her and she peered over at him. "No... not at all. I'm just a pickpocket. I don't know anythin' about music, or manners, or earls or dukes... I don't know how to be a part of this world. I'm not like 'em. But Mr. – that is, Lord Bradford... he's dependin' on me."

Mr. Avery gave a sympathetic nod. "Bradford is a good judge of character and a smart man. I doubt he would have hired you had he not thought you capable. I cannot help you with manners or dukes or earls, but I can help you learn to play the piano. You are a talented pickpocket, and I am a talented teacher. Those nimble fingers must be good for something other than stealing." He gave her a knowing look and she couldn't help a chuckle as she turned back to the keyboard. "Now, let me show you the notes once more. From C, you can count a full octave..." He proceeded to show her and Della, who had only ever taught herself or had any knowledge beaten into her, began to enjoy herself. As the afternoon wore on and they were called to lunch, she set her fingers down upon the keys and played a full scale. Pride blossomed in a chest that wasn't used to such a feeling, and she fought back a giggle as Mr. Avery closed the fallboard to conclude their first lesson. His smile was genuine as he gathered up his papers and turned to her, hand extended.

"It has been a sincere pleasure, Miss Rose. You have some talent; please don't despair – the knowledge will come in time. I shall see you again tomorrow morning."

Della sat for a long time at the piano bench after he had left, her bottom lip pulled between her teeth as she considered his words. Kind words. Rarely were they spoken to her, and rarely were they given, but damned if she didn't enjoy the feeling and her cheeks warmed once more as she lifted the lid on the piano and laid her fingers on the keys. She held them there for a moment, then slowly, deliberately played the scale he had taught her.

The last note rang out as the door opened and Lord Bradford stepped into the room, his straight, white teeth showing in a grin. "That was very good."

Della looked down, flushed, to hide the smile that lifted her lips. She almost thanked him, but stopped short once more and said instead, "He's a good tutor."

"He is indeed. Now, perhaps you would like to join me outside for lunch? I have some questions about Plato."

Della's gaze snapped over to him at this remark and she found him smiling at her. She would have returned the expression but found she could not bring herself to do it, suspicious, as always, of others' motives. She nodded instead. "That would be nice."

SIX

A peaceful quiet had fallen over Bradford House and Della sat
alone in her room. A small fire burned in the hearth as rain
pattered on the windows. It had started to fall shortly after
dinner, relieving the city of the oppressive heat of the past
week. She had stripped off the taffeta and lace and corset of her
evening attire in favor of a loose nightgown and wrapper of the
lightest linen. She settled herself down on the thick, flower-
bedecked Aubusson rug before the fire and laid her battered
valise out before her.

She opened the bag, almost reverently, and reached inside
to withdraw her most treasured possession, a small photo
framed in tarnished silver. A couple stared back at her from the
tiny image; the man handsome with his neat, dark hair, fashionable sack coat and cravat, with the barest hint of a smile, and the
woman elegant in her fitted bodice and wide skirts. Della drew
in a breath and turned it over to push back the tabs holding the
frame in place. She slipped out the delicate square of silvered
paper to read the names and date scrawled on the back.

William and Clara, 1854

She turned the photo over and touched the faces frozen in time. After a long, quiet moment, she gently placed the photo back in the frame and stood, pausing before crossing to the bed and sliding the frame under her pillow. She then returned to the valise and picked it up to remove another one of her most cherished possessions – a cheap, dog-eared volume of Shakespeare's *Romeo and Juliet*. Cora had gifted it to her after a client left it behind and found no need of it herself. Della had read and re-read it until she had it all but memorized, sitting alone in her tiny room at night by the light of a single, sputtering candle.

She pulled aside the quilt – the finest thing that had graced any bed she had ever slept in – and sat on a mattress that was a far cry from her lumpy old straw pallet at Cora's before settling under the covers with a wiggle of her hips to open the book to the first page.

Two households, both alike in dignity,
In fair Verona, where we lay our scene,

By the time she had reached the stabbing of Mercutio, however, Della could barely keep her eyes open and closed the book with a yawn. She extinguished the candle with a single breath and laid the play aside before burrowing beneath the covers and letting the luxurious softness of the bed envelop her. For a long time, though her eyes ached with exhaustion, sleep would not come as she stared up at the coffered ceiling high above. Shadows slid along the walls as the moon peeked out from behind the clouds. The drumming of the rain on her windowpane was soothing, but it could not stop the nervous flutter in her stomach. It had stopped briefly this morning with Mr. Avery, for under his tutelage she had discovered a confidence in herself she only ever had while picking pockets. But now, here in the quiet darkness of her room, surrounded by luxury and warmth and anything else her heart desired, she grew uncertain once more.

Her fingers curled around the edge of the quilt and her chest lifted in a deep breath as she squeezed her eyes shut, willing for sleep to come and release her from this uncertainty. She felt like a fraud in this room; this was not where she belonged and though she had spent her entire life wishing for surroundings such as these, she suddenly missed that old straw mattress and creaky brass bed at Cora's. It wasn't much, and at times she had hated it there – the dank smells, the leaking roof, the clients with their leering smiles, the frequent hunger – but it had been hers. Earned by her and her alone. If she couldn't earn this... if she couldn't learn the piano and the dances and the speech and the customs and be every bit the toff Lord Bradford expected her to be, then she would be a failure.

Della opened her eyes then and sat up. She would not fail. That ten thousand pounds would be hers and she would not have to go back to Cora's; she would not have to pick pockets or steal food anymore. She would choose her own path.

She stood and reached for the fine linen wrapper draped on the chair in the corner of the room. She slipped it on and tied the belt tight before re-lighting the candle and taking it up to move to the door. It opened on silent hinges, and she stepped out into the darkened hallway, the sound of her bare feet on the polished floorboards muffled by the constant low hiss of the rain. She tiptoed to the grand staircase and paused for a moment at the top to listen for any sounds below before grasping the rail. Shadows loomed about her and the steady tick of the grandfather clock in the hallway marked the time as she followed the path she had taken that morning to the music room.

Light filtered out from underneath the door and she stopped outside. Who else would be awake at this hour? She went to return to her room, then reasoned someone may have left a candle lit, for no sound came from within. Straightening, she turned the knob and pushed the door open. Her gaze fell upon the wingback chair set into an alcove of bookshelves where Bradford sat, book in hand. He looked up with a questioning glance then rose immediately when he recognized her.

"Miss Rose, what on earth are you doing up at this hour?"

Della took a step back, startled by her sudden instinct to flee. She had not expected anyone to be up, and certainly not Lord Bradford. Her heart slammed into her ribs at the very sight of him and his golden eyes, and she drew in a sharp breath before shaking her head.

"Sorry, milord. I didn't think you'd be up... I'll go back to bed."

"No, no, do stay. Is anything the matter?" He looked concerned as he laid down the book he had been reading. He took a few steps towards her and she held out a hand.

"I was going to practice, was all. Couldn't sleep."

He smiled and gestured to the piano. "By all means. It would be nice to have some company."

Della shook her head, feeling awkward in the lace-edged wrapper, almost undressed. And damn if she didn't feel a twinge of heat stir in the pit of her stomach at the thought that only a thin layer of linen and lace lay between her body and his searching gaze. She swallowed hard as she lifted a hand to her throat in an attempt to cover herself. "No... I should get some sleep. Mr. Avery said he'd be back in the mornin'. Besides, I'm not much good company."

"Now I'm certain that's not true. Come, sit. I've been brushing up on my Plato in light of your assessment."

A frown creased her brow as she moved to take the seat he offered. "My assessment?"

"Yes. I must admit I was shocked. I did not think Plato would be familiar to someone... such as yourself." He gave her an awkward smile as though realizing what he said might be seen as an insult before taking the seat across from her. The flicker of the branch of candles he had lit against the darkness highlighted the warmth of his eyes and his fine, strong features and she swallowed back the rising heat in her chest. He picked up the book – *Republic* – and gestured to her with it. "Do you read many of the classics?"

Della looked at her lap, twisting the tie of her wrapper about her fingers. "I only read what I can get a hold of. There's a bookseller in Covent Garden who would sometimes slip me a book or two they couldn't sell. That's how I got Plato. An old copy of *Statesman*. He lent me *Republic* as well."

"Well, this is convenient for us."

Della looked up to find him grinning at her and she frowned again. "What d'you mean?"

"I was going to teach you a bit of literature and history to have for conversations with the duke, but as you are already familiar..." He shrugged. "Then we'll save ourselves the time. Perhaps we'll go riding instead."

"Riding?" Della said in a small voice as her heart rose in her throat.

"Yes. We could go out to my country house for the week to get some practice before we go riding in Hyde Park."

"Ah... the one you have for the occasional visit, no?"

He gave her a self-deprecating smile. "Yes, it's all part of the deal – being an earl, that is. Headingly Hall has been in my family for hundreds of years. I think you'll like it. Lots of space, fresh air. Come," he said as he held out his hand and helped her out of the chair. "Save the practice for the morning. You should get some rest."

"Yes, I suppose," she said as he gestured for her to go ahead of him. He stopped with her at the bottom of the stairs and took an appropriate step back.

"Good night, Miss Rose. I hope you sleep well."

"Are you not going to bed?" she asked as she set her hand

upon the rail and looked back at him. A faint smile lifted his lips – fine lips they were, indeed – and he shook his head.

"Not just yet. I have some... work I need to get finished."

"Work? I thought you said gentlemen don't work," she said with an arch lift of her brow.

His smile was rueful this time. "Call it a hobby."

"Oh... well then, g'night, milord."

"Good night, Miss Rose."

A small thrill raced up Della's back as he inclined his head towards her, the light of the candle he held highlighting the dark amber color of his eyes. She turned away to make her way back up the stairs knowing for certain that she would not sleep that night.

Cole watched Della ascend into the darkness of the hall above, the heavy skirt of her wrapper bunched up in her fists to prevent her tripping. Most unladylike, and yet he could not help smiling. He found he rather enjoyed her company. Such a cagey, prickly creature. But committed, with an intellect he admired. And more than he was willing to admit... her stark beauty fascinated him. He was beginning to think he had not erred in choosing her. When he heard her bedchamber door close, he turned away from the stairs and made his way, not to the music room, but through to the very back of the house, through the now-quiet kitchen and scullery, to the hall where he had first brought her into his home.

He paused at the door, looking through the sheer gauze curtain over the window to the garden beyond. No shadow stirred and so he opened the door and stepped out into the cool drizzle. He took a moment to breathe in the damp night air before glancing down to the flagstone stoop beneath his feet. There, as expected, was a small package wrapped in plain brown paper and tied with twine. He made another careful survey of the gardens, saw nothing untoward, and bent to pick it up.

Returning to the quiet of his rooms, his valet, a quiet young man by the name of John Barrow, helped him undress and drew a bath before nodding and leaving Cole for the night. Cole found the man's quiet presence – and his unquestioning ability to accommodate the strange hours his employer kept – comforting. It was one of the few constants in his life. He washed quickly before pulling on a dressing robe and sitting at the desk in front of the window. Rain streaked down the panes as he took hold of the twine on the package and tugged it off before tearing at the paper to reveal a small, plain wooden box.

He raised the lid to reveal a blank folder filled with paper and withdrew it from the box as he took a seat in one of the armchairs flanking the hearth before taking up a fountain pen from a side table. The first few pages were blank, and he quickly noted the date at the top of the page and below it, *Notes on Miss Della Rose*. He wrote everything he had learned about her today – not much, if he was being honest – then turned to the stack of papers that were of the most interest to him.

Pages and pages devoted to the Duke of Salisbury. His schedule, his appearances at the House of Lords, the layout of Lufton Castle, notes from his staff, who he spoke with at his club, what sporting matches he attended, his financial statements, right down to the name of the horse he was training for the Derby. All of it informative, but none of it useful in getting Cole closer to the duke or finding out where he might have hidden away certain documents which had once belonged to the former Earl of Bradford. The small gold clock on the mantel ticked away as he reached the last page, still no closer to learning what he needed to know. He sighed and rubbed the back of his neck before signing his name at the bottom of the last page and returning the stack of papers to the box.

A yawn rose in his throat and he stifled it as the clock

chimed the third hour. He re-wrapped the box and tied the twine tight around it before making his way back down the stairs and through to the hall at the back of the house. He waited once more to watch for any movement beyond the gauze curtain before opening the door and returning the box to where he had found it. He stood on the stoop for a moment to let the cool night air move over him as a long-buried memory began to resurface. A frown tugged at the corners of his mouth as he recalled a high, sparkling laugh and the secret revealed that had ended that joyous sound for him forever. He turned with a clenched jaw to go back inside.

As he made his way to the main stairs in the front hall, he stopped in front of a small credenza and noticed the china shepherdess that had belonged to his mother was missing. His lips quirked as he stared at the spot where the figure had sat beside a silver bowl filled with fresh peonies from the garden. After a moment, he turned away from the credenza to make his way back to his room. He passed Della's room and noted the flicker of light under her door. Stopping, he contemplated knocking to inquire about the figurine, then thought the better of it and continued down the hall.

Once in the quiet of his own chambers, he stripped out of the dressing robe and threw it over the wingback chair before slipping under the covers naked, as was his preference in the summer heat. Though dawn approached and his mind grew still with exhaustion, he lay for a moment to listen to the pattering of the rain and the tick of the clock. He fancied he could hear Miss Rose moving about in her room but knew that was impossible with two other bedchambers between them.

Perhaps it would be good to get out of the city for a week. Miss Rose mentioned having never been to the country, and Headingly was his favorite place to be. It would be easier to keep an eye on her there – and she might even enjoy herself.

Satisfied, he made a mental note to speak with Mr. Barrow

in the morning to make suitable arrangements for them to travel to Headingly by the end of the week. But if he thought that finalizing a plan would help him find the sleep that eluded him, he was wrong. He lay awake until dawn began to lighten the sky in the east, still straining to hear his houseguest, and wondering why he cared at all.

SEVEN

Mr. Avery arrived the next morning, a stack of papers once again tucked under his arm. A bright smile lit up his round face as he entered the music room to find Della waiting for him, nose buried in a translation of Ovid's *Metamorphoses* she had pulled from the rows of books lining the music room. She barely looked up as he greeted her with a cheerful, "Good morning!"

Loath to tear herself away from the story of the death and deification of Julius Caesar, she reluctantly tucked a scrap of ribbon between the pages and rose to greet Mr. Avery.

"Mornin', Mr. Avery," she said, stifling a yawn as she smoothed down the pale yellow sprigged cotton of her skirts. She had spent the night in a state somewhere between asleep and awake, thinking of Bradford. Thinking of that golden gaze watching her, that damn smile, and all the ways she would have liked that encounter to end, her eyes ached with exhaustion as she took her seat at the piano.

"Are you ready to begin?' he asked as he selected one of the papers from the file he had brought and set it on the shelf. By some miracle, she actually recognized some of the markings on the paper and plunked out a few notes on the keyboard.

"Suppose so," she said, holding a hand over her mouth as another yawn emerged.

"Are you well, Miss Rose?" Mr. Avery asked as he pointed to the scale he wished her to practice, and she shook her head as she dutifully tapped out the notes.

"Couldn't sleep, is all."

"Ah. Well, I should say that a week at Headingly will have you sleeping like a baby in no time."

"A week where?" Della's fingers fell from the keys, and she whipped around on the bench to stare at the tutor. He looked confused for a moment.

"Headingly Hall. Lord Bradford said you would be taking the train there tomorrow to spend the week at his country home."

Della's mouth grew dry and she turned back to the piano. "I didn't think it would be so soon," she said in a low voice as she banged out another scale before Mr. Avery stepped up beside her and gently, deliberately, laid his hand over hers. She stopped and looked up at him with a frown.

"Fear not, Miss Rose. I will be here waiting to resume your lessons when you return. There is a fine piano at Headingly; you can practice while you are away. And, from what I understand, you have never been to the country before."

"No, I haven't," she said reluctantly as he drew his hand away. His smile was gentle as he turned to tap the sheet of music in front of her. She took a deep breath and brought her fingers back to the keyboard to move on to the next scale.

"I think you'll enjoy it," he said. "Wide open spaces, fresh air, quiet – a world removed from London."

Those words struck her as she slowly played another scale, her mind whirring. *Removed from London.* That wouldn't do. She turned her attention back to the words Mr. Avery spoke and a restrained smile lifted her cheeks when she played her first piece later that morning – a few bars of Beethoven's *Ode to Joy*.

Mr. Avery grinned at her as he gathered up his things to leave.

"You're a fine student, Miss Rose. I want you to practice at Headingly – take these with you," he said and handed her a file filled with sheet music and tied with a length of ribbon.

Della hesitated for a moment and reached forth to take the file from him. "I will, Mr. Avery."

His head inclined towards her. "Enjoy your trip. I shall see you upon your return."

With that, he was gone, and the next lesson was to begin. Della's stomach clenched in anticipation as the butler entered the music room. "Good afternoon, Miss Rose. Mrs. Cooper is waiting for you in the parlor."

Della closed her eyes for a moment, took a steadying breath, and rose from the bench. She closed the fallboard, straightened the hem of her bodice, and turned to follow Harris. The echo of her footsteps on the shining parquet made her feel small and her whole chest ached with dread as he opened the door to the parlor and ushered her inside. No sign of Bradford, though there was a small table set up near the intricately carved mantel, laid with a pristine white tablecloth, flawless silverware and expensive-looking, gold-rimmed plates. A tall crystal vase had been set in the center of the table and filled with fragrant purple blooms.

Harris nodded to her and slipped out of the room, closing the door silently behind him. Della stood there, awkward, as she had on her first day here. The idea of spending the afternoon with that judgmental bitch made her blood boil and she took another deep, shaking breath to calm herself. *I will not fail. I will not fail.*

The sound of the door opening made her turn, and the sour-faced Mrs. Cooper entered the room, tray in hand. She moved to a sideboard without a word and set it down before lifting off two plates and setting them on the table. Della watched with narrowed eyes as the older woman turned with a huff and gestured to one of the chairs.

"Please have a seat, Miss Rose."

Della hesitated for the briefest of seconds before stepping forward to pull out the chair closest to her.

"No." Mrs. Cooper's voice was sharp, and Della looked up with pursed lips.

"You just told me—"

"A lady never pulls out her own chair. You wait for a gentleman to do it for you."

It took everything inside Della not to roll her eyes and look around for this "gentleman". "Fine."

"Yes, Mrs. Cooper."

The words came out in a hiss. "Yes, Mrs. Cooper."

Della waited obediently as the housekeeper proceeded to withdraw the chair from the table and gesture for her to sit. This was going to be a long bloody afternoon.

"I should like to begin by addressing your accent. Clearly, you cannot go about speaking like some common costermonger. We shall work on this daily, as it is crucial that you speak like a lady when in the presence of Lord Bradford's peers."

Blood rushed into Della's ears at this remark, and it was with a massive effort that she bit back the stream of costermonger-worthy slurs she wanted to hurl at the housekeeper.

"That said," Mrs. Cooper continued, "going forward, you shall address Lord Bradford as 'my lord', not 'milord'. And there shall be no 'ain'ts' or 'oys' or anything else of the sort. And certainly no cursing. Do pay attention to the way his lord speaks, for that is the correct way a lady ought to sound."

"Yes, Mrs. Cooper," Della answered through gritted teeth in the most aristocratic tone she could manage. The older woman shot her a glare as she gestured to the table.

"Second, let us address table manners. At a dinner party, ladies will be assigned an escort. Lord Bradford shall be your escort for any events you attend, as he is, for the purposes of this... arrangement... your cousin and only relative."

Della glanced up at the older woman's pause, hearing the skepticism in her voice. Mrs. Cooper ignored this look and gestured to the table. "As you will see, I have included at this table setting every piece of silverware you could conceivably see at a formal dinner party. At the center is your dinner plate. To the left are your forks: dinner fork, fish fork, place fork, salad fork and cocktail fork. To the right you will see your dinner knife, fish knife, butter knife, cheese knife, and your spoons: iced tea, cream soup spoon, bouillon spoon, hot tea spoon and demitasse spoon. Above your plate is your dessert spoon and fork. Additionally, bread should be placed on a folded napkin to the left of your plate. Your water goblet is located above your dinner knife, and the wine and champagne glasses are beside it."

Della stared with something akin to horror at the vast quantity of gleaming silverware before her, accustomed to a knife, fork and spoon at most, and champagne glasses being beyond her experience entirely. What had she got herself into? Her stomach sank and the enormity of the task began to dawn on her as Mrs. Cooper handed her a napkin.

"A napkin should be placed upon your lap before the meal begins, and conversation should be kept light, free of controversy or intimate details and never over-long or boring. Take small bites of your food, chew with your mouth closed, and never remark upon what you are being served. Eat what you are given, but do not make an effort to finish every last bite. Gloves should be removed at the table. Please show me how you hold your knife and fork."

Della bit back an exasperated sigh and picked up the dinner fork and dinner knife before peering up at Mrs. Cooper to see if this met her approval. Her nod was begrudging as she gestured for Della to put them back down.

"Good – at least there is something I will not have to teach you."

Hot shame and anger burned inside Della once more and she replaced the utensils with more force than necessary. The housekeeper glared at her for a moment before straightening her back.

"I would like you to know, Miss Rose, that I think this whole experiment is utter nonsense. I have spoken with my lord on the matter, and he assures me that he believes you can help him. I, however, think you untrustworthy, and utterly unsuited to this business. You are not a lady, and I am certain that even the best tutelage will not turn you into one in the time required."

Della's jaw clamped together and her fingernails dug into her palms as Mrs. Cooper let out a sigh and turned away for a moment to gather up a plate covered by a shining silver dome.

"That being said, I trust Lord Bradford and he has not yet given me any reason to doubt him or his methods. You will have to do much to prove yourself to me."

She set down the plate with a deliberate clatter. Della swallowed back, once again, a string of expletives worthy of the London docks, thinking only of the ten thousand pounds coming her way, and the promise she had made to Lord Bradford. Pickpocket and thief she may be, but she was a woman of her word. She drew in a sharp breath.

"Listen 'ere, Mrs. Cooper. I will speak your way and eat your way and act like the highest and mightiest of bloody toffs and this is the last time I'll say anythin' on the matter. Just remember, Lord Bradford chose me, and his is the only opinion that matters to me. You teach me whatever I need to pass as one of these people and keep your opinions of me to yourself."

Mrs. Cooper's eyes narrowed as she regarded Della before she sighed and nodded to the silver dome.

"You may eat now."

Cole looked up as Miss Rose entered the dining room, her head hung low, her gaze on the floor. She didn't look up at him as the footman drew her chair away from the table where she sat and picked up her napkin, focusing all her attention on it as if it were of great importance. Cole met the footman's gaze and he withdrew with a nod.

"Miss Rose?"

"Mmm?" She never looked away from the napkin.

"Are you quite alright?"

Her head bent in the slightest of nods and she unfolded the napkin to lay it over the lap of the pale green dinner gown she wore. Warm summer sunlight streamed in through the grand, mullioned windows, and a gentle evening breeze drifted through an open casement, carrying with it the scent of roses and lavender. None of the beauty of the summer evening seemed to affect her and her ordinarily ramrod-straight back slouched as the footman returned with a service trolley and set down the first course. Della selected the appropriate spoon and, with the practiced manners of someone who had been sitting at formal dinner parties her whole adult life, brought a shallow spoonful to her mouth. A faint smile crossed her lips.

"Is it good?" Cole asked as he took a spoonful of the light vegetable soup. She finally looked up at him, and her eyes had lost their vivacious sparkle. She seemed preoccupied as she gave a distracted nod of her head.

"It's very good," she said, and looked back down to take another sip.

Cole watched her for a long time, drawn to the smooth column of her throat, encircled by a simple black velvet ribbon, before he asked, "How were your lessons today?"

She drew in a sharp breath and straightened her shoulders,

shaking her head as if she had just realized how she was sitting. "Mr. Avery was quite helpful. I played my first piece this morning." The pride was evident in her tone, but she made no mention of Mrs. Cooper and Cole made a mental note to speak with the housekeeper about being gentler with Della. It was not in her nature to trust newcomers, an unfortunate side effect of a lifetime working for someone who was also distrustful.

"That is excellent news. I hope you are comfortable here – and if Mrs. Cooper was in any way disagreeable, I do apologize. She is not quick to trust people she does not know. Be assured, I will speak with her on the matter."

Della's gaze met his, but it no longer held that faraway look. The familiar flintiness had returned and she shook her head. "Oh, she was no bother. Mrs. Cooper and I have an understanding."

Cole tilted his head in bemusement. Surely this was not his Mrs. Cooper she spoke of? "An understanding?"

Della lifted one shoulder and took another delicate spoonful of her soup. "Yes. I told her that yours was the only opinion that mattered to me and if she had a problem with me or the way I conduct myself, she ought to speak with you, and that her job is to teach me enough manners to pass this duke's approval, and not to judge me."

He could hear how she formed her words to sound the way Mrs. Cooper had no doubt instructed her to, but the slip in her accent – the hint of Seven Dials – was evident as she spoke. It was not that which surprised him, however, and he was stunned for a moment by her matter-of-fact dismissal of Mrs. Cooper's barbs. She didn't look to him for his approval or disapproval, but continued to eat her soup, her expression now serene. He almost smiled at her cool indifference and, after a moment, raised his brows in a small gesture of acceptance and turned his attention to his own meal.

When the footman had cleared their soup bowls and

brought in another course of a poached salmon with dill sauce, Della once more took up the appropriate utensils and set about cutting into the fragrant fish.

"What were you doing up last night?" she asked without preamble. He looked up at her, keeping his expression expertly impassive.

"I beg your pardon?"

"You went to your room late. I heard you leave and come back after you went up after me."

Cole could not help his eyes widening and he sat back in his chair, mouth agape as she ate her fish with complete indifference. After a brief pause, he said, "I forgot something in the music room."

"You also forgot to tell me that we'd be leaving London tomorrow."

This time, she raised her hard gaze to him and set her fork down, staring at him with jaw set.

"Yes... I do apologize. I suppose I am not accustomed to making my travel plans known to anyone else. I thought it might do to begin your riding lessons, and we can't conduct them here. You must be seen to be an expert, or at least an enthusiast, if you are to gain Salisbury's attention."

"You might have warned me. I've never left London before. My whole life is here."

A hint of fear flashed in her ice-blue eyes, and she picked up her fork once more to continue eating without looking at him. Cole began to suspect that it was not leaving London which had her so upset. Her fear was of the horse-riding lessons to come, though he doubted she would ever admit this.

"Rest assured, Miss Rose, I shan't make any more decisions regarding our arrangement without your input." He smiled at her and thought he detected a small flush warm her cheeks. He took up his own fork and speared a small morsel of fish. "I really do hope you like Headingly. I don't go there nearly as often as I should, but it is rather lovely."

"We shall see." A pause. "I don't suppose…"

"Suppose?" he prompted her and she gestured to her wine glass.

"I don't suppose you have anything stronger than wine? It's been quite a day."

Cole couldn't help but laugh and called for the footman.

EIGHT

The tiny gold clock on the mantel struck the twelfth hour when Della made her escape. She had been planning it since Mr. Avery had told her that they would be leaving in the morning. The silent feet of a thief took her to the balcony doors, past which the rain had returned as a soft drizzle, and she drew the hood of the black velvet cloak she had found in the clothes press over her head. She had donned her old clothes, scrubbed clean by Martha, and paused to blow out the single candle on the writing desk. The room was plunged into darkness and Della blinked to let her eyes adjust to the lack of light before tucking the china shepherdess into her pocket and lifting the latch on the doors. She pushed them open and slipped out into the night.

Pulling the doors shut, she turned to the landscape of shadows before her. Beyond the walls surrounding Bradford's property glowed the lights of London; thousands of gaslights and torches and candles lighting the streets and windows. She took a deep breath to draw in the night air, scented not of bodies and filth and decay as she was used to, but of the garden below the balcony. The fragrance of roses was strong in the air, and she drew in another breath before crossing to the stone balustrade. She glanced into the darkness below, gripped the rail and swung her leg over the edge.

A few steps along the cornice that divided the first and second floors were an easy bridge to the copper drainpipe that trailed down the side of the house. Using the stone quoins that lined the corner of the façade as footholds, she clutched the drainpipe and shimmied her way down the side of the building until she landed with a soft thud upon the damp grass below. Della re-adjusted the hood upon her head and stepped back to glance up at the imposing structure to ensure no cry of alarm had been raised. The windows remained dark and the house silent, and so she gathered up her skirts and dashed across the lawn to the shrubberies lining the wall.

The gate had been locked by now, but she found a small flowering tree growing close enough to the wall that some of its branches brushed the iron-tipped top. With one more glance back at the manor, she grasped the lowest branches and scrambled up the gnarled trunk. It was a simple matter to reach the top of the wall, lift herself over the decorative metalwork, and, hanging by the tips of her fingers, drop to the pavement below.

It was quiet in this part of London at night, unlike in Seven Dials, which always seemed to come to life once the sun went down. Its inhabitants felt concealed in the darkness; with the day's work over, they now had time to drink and socialize and gamble, the one bright light in their often meagre lives. Violet would be busy at this time; her days were spent sleeping, her nights spent entertaining men either at the pubs or Cora's brothel. Della knew just where to find her.

She walked as far as Piccadilly before she saw a lone hansom cab coming her way and flagged it down. It drew to a stop, and she stepped up to the driver.

"It's late to be out alone, miss," he said, peering down through the gloom. She ignored this remark.

"Can you take me to Seven Dials?"

He regarded her with suspicion. "Dangerous place for a young lady."

"Then take me to Soho Square and I'll walk the rest of the way."

He shrugged. "If you insist." He climbed down from his perch and opened the door for her. She climbed into the cab, lit with a single, swinging lantern, and settled down as the carriage lurched forward. It wasn't long before it came to a stop at the quiet, upscale square. The door opened with a click and Della tossed the man a coin before moving south.

Gradually, the buildings grew shabbier and began to lean in upon one another until she was on Great White Lion Street and making her way to Cora's. She paused outside that familiar red door and could hear raucous laughter inside. Thinking the better of it, she turned away and passed by a group of young men shouting and stumbling their way to the next pub. She drew the hood up farther over her head and turned onto Great St. Andrew's Street.

The light from within the Fox and Friar Inn spilled out onto the cobbles, and upbeat fiddle music filled the street. Gaslight flickered against filthy walls and windows, and Della pushed her hood down as she reached the door to the pub. She entered a room overwhelmed by smell and noise; it buffeted her senses, though it was as familiar to her as home. Shouts and laughter burst out, the stench of packed bodies filled her nostrils and Della grimaced as she pushed her way through the crowd. Suddenly, the quiet serenity of Bradford's music room seemed a world away from the pressing crowd, the yeasty smell of ale and the rising and falling murmur of voices. They called for drinks, they called for friends, they called for women, and this is what Della sought. She made straight for the dark corner at the back of the pub, searching for that familiar blonde head she knew would be here at this time.

And there she was, laughing uproariously at one of the

patrons, a young man with pockmarked skin and dusty clothes. Della waited while Violet took a swig of her ale and turned to meet her gaze.

"Della!" she gasped and pushed the man away to make her way through the crowds. She threw her arms about Della's shoulders with a drunken giggle.

"I knew you'd come back!" she cried, taking her friend's hand to lead her to an empty table. They fell into seats opposite one another, and Violet swallowed back the last of her ale with a gasp. "Where have you been?" she asked, her cheeks flushed, her green eyes bright.

"I told you – I got a job," Della replied, slipping back into the comforting familiarity of the voice of Seven Dials.

"But you've been gone for two days now!"

"I'm stayin' with him. Have my own room and everythin'." Della couldn't help but smile as she said this. Though this tiny, dirty corner of London was her home, it had been glorious living in luxury for the past two days.

"With him? Who's him?" Violet raised suggestive brows as she said this, and Della shook her head.

"It's not like that. It's the biggest house I've ever seen in my life. I have my own room and a water closet and everythin'. And this," she said in a low voice, reaching to withdraw the china figurine from her pocket. She revealed it to Violet under the cover of her cloak and her friend gasped.

"Where'd you get that?"

"From him. 'E's got dozens of the things. I don't think he'll miss one. It's for you," she said, holding it out. Violet's eyes widened and she snatched it from Della's fingers and stuffed it into her bodice before anyone around them could see.

"These people have so much, Vi – it's a bleedin' gold mine in that house. And I'm going to take as much of it as I can. I'll come to you when I'm able. You sell it all so we can save up and get out of 'ere. Once I'm done with this job and paid, we can find a flat together and you can paint, and I can read all day." She smiled at the thought of her fantasy and Violet frowned.

"Oh, Della, I hope you're bein' safe."

"He's quite the gentleman. Very professional."

"Well, come on then, let's get out of 'ere. I don't have to work tonight," she added, gesturing to her bodice and the expensive figurine within. They rose from the table and made their way once more through the press of people to the doors before stumbling out into the damp night air.

"I want to talk to Cora to see if she can find a fence for everythin'. The fella I use won't know how to deal with high-end swag."

"She'll be busy," Violet remarked as they turned away from the boisterous noise of the pub to make their way to the center of the Dials.

"I think she'll want to talk when she hears what I have planned," Della said with a grin. Circles of gaslight pooled on the slick cobbles, and they were careful to stay within their glow. In the darkness, shapes lurked – the broken, the weary and poor, and they watched the two young women in their secondhand dresses, walking and chatting happily as they made their way to the outskirts of the slums where Cora plied her trade.

When they reached that familiar, red-painted door, Violet pushed it open and stepped into the dimly lit hall. Laughter sounded behind a door to their right, and shouts further down the hall from the parlor. Violet took Della's hand and led her up the stairs to her room at the back of the house.

"Tell me everything," she said as she took up a box of matches and struck one to light the lantern on the small table in the corner. The dim glow revealed a dingy room with a brass bedstand, a worn table and chair beside a small fireplace, and the remaining floor space filled with an easel and stacks of canvases leaning against the walls. Pots of paint and cups filled with brushes covered every available surface. Violet dropped onto the bed with a sigh and tugged off her boots to drop them to the floor. She patted the space beside her and Della sat, bending her legs to hug them to her chest.

"So," Violet began as she withdrew the figurine from her bodice and set it on the table. "Who's this toff and what does he want you to steal?"

Della's laugh was nonchalant, but her stomach fluttered as she recalled Bradford's warm, wide smile.

"He's an honest-to-goodness lord – the Earl of Bradford of all things. Wants me to steal a load of old papers or somethin', but we're leavin' in the morning to go to his country house. I'm to learn horseback ridin'. I bloody hate horses." Her face twisted in a grimace, dreading what she knew was to come. Violet shook her head, withdrew a metal flask from her pocket and handed it to Della without a word. She nodded and accepted the vessel with a sigh of relief, gulping down the cheap gin inside. It burned down to her belly, and she welcomed the vague fog that clouded her brain.

"What could a lord possibly want with the likes of you?" Violet laughed and Della elbowed her in the ribs.

"Needs a pickpocket – and a woman. I am Rosie Diver, after all."

Violet accepted the flask back before taking another gulp.

"And you should see these houses, they're bloody castles! I'll be invited to parties and balls as his cousin, and I'll take as much as I can get away with and bring it to you for Cora to sell. When this is all done... a little flat in Marylebone with a garden. I could read all day, you could paint..." Della trailed off with a wistful sigh. "This is as close as we've ever come, and we're not likely to get a second chance." She retrieved the flask to take another swig.

"Oh, Dell, can you even imagine? I'll become a famous artist, and I'll buy you all the books you could ever want."

Della's face broke into a giddy grin as she took another sip of the gin. "Let's not get ahead of ourselves. My manners leave much to be desired," she said, mimicking Mrs. Cooper's disapproving intonation.

"Manners? What on earth do you need manners for? You're a thief!" Violet laughed again as she rubbed her stockinged feet, wincing as she hit a sore spot.

"I told you, I'm meant to be his cousin. A lady of high breeding." She tilted her chin up, then chuckled. "Not some gutter trash pickpocket. I have to sound like I belong."

Violet stretched her arms up over her head and groaned. "Easier said than done."

Della gave her another nudge in the ribs and sighed. "And the dresses – they're incredible. He bought me loads of them. One for every time of the day. It's ludicrous the amount of times I have to change. But the dresses..." She sighed and hugged herself, feeling the mended sleeve of her secondhand gown with a frown and suddenly, ridiculously, missing the fine silk and lawn of her expensive wardrobe. "Come on, let's see if Cora's done. I can't stay too long; I don't want to be missed."

Violet nodded and pushed herself up from the bed before tucking the figurine back into her bodice. Della drowned the last of the gin from the flask and handed it back to her friend, who slipped it into her pocket. She shoved her feet back into her boots and led the way down the creaking staircase. The only sounds now came from the parlor down the hall; Cora's room was quiet, and Violet knocked on the door. The flame on the candle affixed to the wall guttered, and the shadows in the hall lurched and bent, so that when the door opened, the figure inside was plunged into darkness. When the flame righted itself, the light revealed a short, buxom, redheaded woman of forty, her gaze fierce but warm. When she caught sight of Della, her green eyes widened and she stepped forth with opened arms, pulling the younger woman into a tight hug.

"Where have ye been, girl?" she said in her thick Dublin accent, pushing Della back to give her a once-over.

"I got a job, Cora. I'll be gone a few months."

The older woman's sharply featured face screwed up in a frown. "A few months? Ye've not gone to the workhouse, have ye?" Her eyes widened in alarm and her grip tightened on Della's arms.

"No, no, some toff approached me in the park. Wants me to steal somethin' for him. He's given me a room while I pretend to be his cousin."

"He's gonna pay her ten thousand pounds when it's done!" Violet piped up. Cora's eyes narrowed in suspicion, but Della anticipated her protest and held up her hands.

"I wasn't sure either, Cora, but he ain't lying. He's an earl, of all things. I'm livin' near Belgrave Square. Bradford House, if you need to find me."

Cora shook her head, disbelieving. "Oh, Della, this all seems so..."

"Strange? I know, but this could be our ticket out of 'ere. I have a plan, Cora, but I'll need your help."

The older woman finally nodded and stepped back to gesture for them to come into her room. Candlelight flickered against red-papered walls, and gauzy draperies hung over a brass bedstand. A small coal fire guttered and spat in the hearth below a gilt-framed mirror. Della and Violet sat in the two faded wingback chairs pushed into the corner of the room and Violet reached into her bodice to remove the figurine and set it on the small, rickety table between them. They waited while Cora puttered around the room, setting an old brass kettle over the flames and laying out cups before she sat on the bed to face the two younger women. She caught sight of the figurine and inclined her head towards it as she smoothed down the gaudy red silk of her skirts.

"What's this?"

"Just the start. I'm going to be going to parties, balls, country houses... I'll pass among these people unnoticed. I'm going to take anythin' I can get away with. They have so much, Cora, you can hardly believe it. He's got a whole room for music. There's more money on one shelf in that room than you have in this whole bloody house. And I'm going to be admitted to all these homes freely. I'll bring you anythin' I take if you can fence it for me. Twenty-five percent of it is yours if you can get me a good deal. Violet and I want to get a flat outside of St. Giles. She's gonna be an artist." Della looked over at Violet and smiled fondly. They had been raised in the orphanage together and had planned and saved their whole lives to escape this place. This was as close as they had ever been.

Cora nodded slowly and stood to lift the now-steaming kettle from the flames. She poured three cups of strong, dark tea and handed the saucers to the two women. Della accepted hers with a grateful sigh, for her head was beginning to spin as the gin fogged her brain. She swallowed a huge mouthful, scalding her tongue, but grateful for the rush of heat to her senses.

"Aye, I can do that," Cora said as she settled on the edge of the bed to sip from her own cup. "I know a fella – deals in high-end goods. He'll get you a fair price."

Della nodded and drained the last of her tea before standing. "Good. I'll get in touch when I can. I should be gettin' back before someone notices I'm gone."

"You just be careful now," Cora said as Violet stood and crossed to the small cabinet in the corner to withdraw a bottle of gin. She refilled her flask and slipped it into her pocket before nodding to Della.

"I will, Cora, I promise," Della said as she handed the figurine to the older woman with a smile.

"I'll come with you," Violet said as they made their way back into the dimly lit hall and out into the night. The drizzle had by now intensified into a pattering rain, and Della drew the hood of her cloak up over her head once more, Violet followed suit and they moved on hurried feet, stepping over pools of dank water and filth as they made their way out of the Dials. They walked the distance to Charing Cross Road and paused under the shelter of an overhang where Violet handed Della the flask with a knowing look. She took it with a thankful nod and gulped it back, letting it settle warm in the pit of her belly before she chuckled and handed it back.

"I fear it's not very ladylike to drink from flasks in the street."

Violet laughed at this, shaking her head as she raised the flask to her lips to swallow a mouthful. "Nothin' about you is ladylike." She smiled. "You're startin' to sound like one of them."

Della chuckled, her mind becoming hazy and her belly warm. She slumped against the rough brick wall behind them as her laughter faded into a sharp sigh. "Mrs. Cooper will have my head if I don't start talking like a lady. Oh, Vi, I want so badly to get this right. But I'm just not like those people. The bloody rules they have to follow – it's exhausting. And now I have to learn how to ride a bloody horse..." She looked over at Violet who was glaring at her. "What?" Della said, bemused, as she pushed herself away from the wall.

"Oh, piss off, Della – what have you to complain about? Livin' in a fancy mansion, gettin' proper meals, gettin' paid to be a bloody thief – we should be so lucky!" She took a quick gulp of the gin. "You're better than this place, and you know it. You're gettin' us out of 'ere" – she pointed a reproving finger – "and if that means you have to ride a bloody horse, then you go and do it and quit whingin' about it!" With that, she shoved the flask into her pocket, threw one last accusatory glare at Della, and stalked off into the shadows.

Della stared after her friend, the growing heat of shame crawling up her chest and neck.

"Violet!" she called after a moment, but there was no reply, just the rough laughter and shouting that were a constant part of living in Seven Dials. A group of dockers, loud and drunk, were coming towards her, and she turned swiftly without missing a beat and moved north, crossing the street to make her way back to the square where the hansom cab had left her. She flagged down the first cab she saw and told the driver to take her to Piccadilly.

Her head lolled on the seat back as the carriage rumbled over the cobblestone roads and she blinked to keep her eyes open as her mind reeled. When they came to a halt and the door opened, she stumbled on the step and the driver caught her wrist to keep her from spilling onto the pavement. She giggled her thanks and pressed a shilling into his waiting hand before standing and making her way south to Belgrave Square.

Here, the streets were quiet and clean; no drunken louts caroused on the corner, no fights tumbled out from the pubs, and no filth dropped onto the streets from the windows above. Della shook her head and kept one hand on the metal railings surrounding the townhouses lining the street to keep her balance. She made her way to Bradford House, recognizable to her only by the distinctive red brick wall and the gatehouse marked by his coat of arms.

She spotted the branches of the tree she had used to get out and found a foothold on the bricks. Shaking her head once more to clear the fog of gin, she hauled herself up the wall and scrabbled to reach the top. She dropped onto the wet grass and paused to draw in a deep, shaking breath before racing across the lawn to the back door, hoping it would be open and save her the climb up the side of the house. She reached the side of the manor and edged her way around it, past the oak tree she and the earl had picnicked under. The memory of that bittersweet afternoon and telling the earl what her life amounted to made her throat grow inexplicably tight, and she shook her head once more. *Stop being a bloody emotional twit.*

Reaching the rear entrance of the house, hidden behind a swathe of ivy, she turned the corner and... there he was. Standing in the pool of light thrown by the lantern affixed to the wall above the door. He was still dressed in his evening finery and held a small, paper-wrapped package in his hands. His eyes widened when he saw her, and he was speechless for a moment.

She stared at him, not sure if what she was seeing was real or if the gin was causing her to imagine things. Finally, he spoke and broke her trance. "Miss Rose? What are you doing?"

She blinked rapidly, struggling to think of an excuse, but her mind was a blur and she could only gape at him. Bradford's head tilted as he contemplated her and, in that instance, she found the whole situation to be so absurd that she burst into sudden, wild laughter. She bent over with the force of it, gasping with mirth while he looked at her as though she had taken leave of her senses. When she was finally able to gain control of herself, she looked up at him with a breathless chuckle and shook her head.

"I'm so sorry... my lord. Oh, I don't know what came over me. I was... I couldn't sleep. Thought a bit of fresh air might help." The lie came easily now, and she gave him a silly grin. She swayed as she stood there before him, and his brow lifted in bemusement.

"Have you been drinking, Miss Rose?"

"Oh, goodness, yes," she said with a giggle and, in attempting to take a step forward, pitched straight into him. He caught her with a muffled grunt and pulled her up from under her arms until her head tipped back and she found herself staring into eyes of the deepest amber flecked with gold. She let out a low purr and reached out to draw her finger down his chest. An impressive chest it was.

"Violet would like you," she said as her heart began to race. Why on earth was her heart beating so fast?

"And who is Violet?" he asked in a low voice.

"She's my friend... my best friend. Oh, I'd be lost without Violet," she whispered, shivering at the warmth of his large hands upon her back. He cleared his throat and propped her up for a moment to set down the box he carried.

"I see. Come, Miss Rose, I think it's time you got to bed. We have a long journey ahead of us in the morning. Please, allow me to take you to your room."

She bit her lip and let out a suggestive murmur as he took her by the arm to lead her into the house, shutting the door behind them and guiding her up the servants' staircase. She leaned against him as he helped her up, liking the feel of him, the clean, soapy smell emanating from him, and the strength of his arm wrapped about her waist. God, he was so warm, and her stomach fluttered as his arm tightened about her waist when they came to her door.

"You know," he said in his husky voice as he reached down with his free hand to turn the knob, "you don't have to sneak out of the house to visit your friends. You're not a prisoner here. Though I do ask that you exercise some discretion."

She glanced up at him, about to protest that she had not snuck out, but the knowing look on his face made her drop her head in shame.

"I don't think my cousin would be sneaking out of the house in the night," he added as he guided her into the darkened room. He set her down gingerly upon a chair by the door and moved to light the branch of candles by her bed. She watched him through half-closed eyes as her head spun wildly. Violet always did like her drink rather strong. She moaned and slumped back in the chair as Bradford crossed the room to draw the curtains and then returned to her with a frown.

"Is there anything you wish to tell me, Miss Rose?"

Della peered up at him, seized with the sudden dread that he had noticed the missing figurine. She struggled to sit upright as he squatted before her, placing his large hand over hers. A frisson of electricity raced up her arm from where he touched her, and she swallowed hard as his intense gaze met hers. His nearness made her undone, and hot and achy and... good lord, his lips were so close.

"What are you afraid of?"

She stared at him, her mouth agape. Ordinarily she would have a snapped reply ready for such a question. *Nothing,* her mind shouted. *I'm not afraid of anything. Fear is for the weak. Fear makes you vulnerable.* Instead, she found herself whispering, "Everything."

She shook her head. What was she saying? The pressure of his hand upon hers increased and his head tilted as he regarded her with a sympathetic smile.

"I sincerely doubt that. Horses, I suspect." He raised his eyebrows and she nodded slowly.

"Yes... yes, I am afraid of horses." Her voice was low, and she wanted to shake off his touch but couldn't find the will.

"Fear not, Miss Rose," he said in a brighter voice as he stood and offered his hand to her. She hesitated before she took it and wobbled as he helped her to her feet. "I'm an excellent teacher. And I shan't make you do anything you're not comfortable with."

Della closed her eyes against the wave of dizziness as she stood too quickly. His low chuckle reverberated against her chest as she fell against him and at that moment, she wanted desperately for him to put his arms around her, to feel the warmth of his skin and inhale the utterly male scent of him. Instead, he gently pushed her away and glanced down.

"Shall I send up Martha to help you?"

"No... no, don't wake her. I'll be fine," she said, squeezing her eyes shut for a moment to block out the room as it spun around her. He regarded her with concern before nodding and pulling away. It took everything in her not to hold on to him.

"Very well. Good night, Miss Rose. Sleep well." The smile he gave her, filled with such warmth, made her look away. It was unfair that anyone's smile should be so dazzling.

"Good night, my lord."

There was a pause before he turned to leave; a long pause during which it felt, absurdly, like something should happen. She found she held her breath as he gazed down at her, those amber eyes as unreadable as ever. Eventually, he gave a sharp nod and left her standing there, closing the door with a quiet click behind him. Della waited for a moment, her heart racing, her inner thighs slick with her wetness. *Dammit.* After a long time spent staring at the door, wishing for something she knew would never happen, she let out a long sigh and shuffled to the bed. She stared down at that profusion of pink before groaning and falling onto the silk bedspread to bury her face in the multitude of pillows and soft velvet cushions. She lay there, fully dressed, until Martha came with the morning sunrise to light the fire.

NINE

Mr. Barrow awoke Cole with a bright, "Good morning, sir," as the first rays of morning sunlight spilled in through the drapes. For once, he did not greet the day with a burst of energy and a welcome reply to the valet. Instead, he stared up at the ceiling, his eyes heavy with exhaustion.

"Morning, Mr. Barrow," he muttered, hesitating for a moment before he sat up. He rubbed a hand over the rough stubble of his unshaven jaw as the valet handed him his dressing robe without a word and moved into the water closet to fill the tub. Cole stood with a sigh and wrapped the robe around his naked body before walking out to the balcony and staring down into the garden. The rain had stopped overnight, and clear morning light shone bright over the roofs beyond the garden wall, glinting off wet tiles and windows.

"Is Miss Rose awake?" he called over his shoulder.

"Yes, sir. Martha says she was quite out of sorts."

Cole gave a wry snort of laughter and turned to face the valet. "Thank you, Mr. Barrow, that will be all. I'll dress myself this morning."

The valet nodded and laid the freshly pressed trousers he carried over the chair by the door. "Very good, sir."

When he had gone, Cole crossed to the water closet, wondering all the while what he would do about his wayward pickpocket. She was a strange creature, that Della Rose. He knew she had snuck out last night, of course he did. It was his duty to know what went on in this house, in this city, in this country and abroad. It was his life's work to know and see everything without being seen himself.

Mr. Barrow had arranged all his shaving equipment with military precision on the small table beside the washbasin. As Cole frothed up the shaving soap, he found himself remembering, with a strange tightening sensation in his stomach, the feel of her falling against him and her hazy, sleepy smile. Damned if he didn't grow hard just thinking about those soft curves and the wild scent of her as she had drawn a brazen finger down his chest. His lips curled as he lathered his jaw and drew the blade of his razor against the strop. She was making progress, at least. Mr. Avery was complimentary in his reports to Cole, saying she had a natural talent and a few more weeks of instruction should give her enough of a foundation to pass through the drawing rooms of the aristocracy unremarked upon. Even Mrs. Cooper had grudgingly admitted that the young woman was sharp and a quick learner, and she rarely had a kind word for anyone.

As he scraped the blade across his chin, he couldn't help but think she was hiding something from him – and not the figurine. He knew she had taken it, but it was a small price to pay, he supposed, to gain admittance into the Duke of Salisbury's inner circle. It was a circle he, as an earl, would ordinarily belong to, but the duke was particular in the friends he kept, and Cole was not one of them. Secrets were kept more easily if there were fewer ears to hear them, and the duke had a good many secrets.

No, Cole would not remark upon the missing shepherdess for it would not do to lose Miss Rose's trust. That, he supposed, was a delicate thing for her. Hard won and easily lost. He hoped that a week away from the city, away from the life she knew and whatever past haunted her, would do her good. He would have to be very gentle with his lessons.

He rinsed his face and dressed before making his way to the breakfast room. She was waiting for him, her pale blue eyes ringed by dark circles, her chin propped up on her palm. She straightened when he entered the room and gave him a hard look. *Ah*, he thought, *now this is more like her*.

"When are we leaving?" she asked, dispensing with any formalities. The plate of bacon and eggs before her was untouched and he glanced at her as he took his seat. The footman came forward to pour his coffee and Della frowned at him, following his movements with her glower.

"Thank you, Daniel, that will be all. We'll help ourselves this morning."

The young man nodded and withdrew without a word. Cole set about filling his plate and sent her a concerned look. "I do hope you're feeling better after last night?"

Her entire face warmed in a fierce blush as she looked down at her plate, poking at the eggs with her fork. "I'm fine. Just needed a bit of fresh air."

"I don't mind. You are certainly welcome to walk in the gardens."

"And outside the gardens?"

"Yes, of course. I realize you have a life beyond this job. I would not keep you from your friends and family."

Her head moved in a gesture of disagreement as she speared a piece of egg and brought it to her mouth, chewing furiously. "I don't have any family."

He cleared his throat as she glared down at her plate. "I am sorry, Miss Rose. I should have realized. You have no siblings?"

"No." She spoke the word sharply, her attention still on the plate before her.

"No... I suppose not." He drew in a deep breath. It was his job to get information out of people, but her... She was like a locked box for which he had no key, and he never quite knew what would set her off. He decided to try another tack.

"If you don't mind my asking... what are you going to do when you are done here?"

She finally looked up at him and her gaze was suspicious. She finished chewing before she spoke. "Violet and I are leaving Seven Dials. We've been planning it since we were in the orphanage together. She wants to be an artist. You ought to see her paintings sometime. She's quite good."

Cole's heart twisted as he imagined her as a slight, pale girl, dreaming of a golden future that must have seemed impossible. He gave her a sympathetic smile. "I should like that. And what of you? Will Della Rose become a lady of leisure?"

She scoffed and speared another piece of egg. "I have far more planned than lying about all day."

He arched a brow and leaned back in his chair. "Oh?" He left the remark dangling, hoping she would open up and, indeed, after an uncomfortable moment during which her gaze went from being guarded to resigned, she looked away and said, "I want to go to school. A proper school. I want to be a scholar."

Cole couldn't help a small chuckle as his heart warmed towards this fascinating woman. She scowled as though he was teasing her and he shook his head. "It is a noble goal, to be sure, Miss Rose. I do hope you are successful in your endeavor."

The frown faded and she lifted her shoulders. "It's always just been a dream, never a goal... until now. I want to study the classics – history, philosophy – all of them, not just the ones I can steal or buy secondhand."

Cole smiled at her as he observed the proud tilt of her head, and that determined gaze of hers. "Then perhaps you might like to select a book from the library to read on the train."

"The train?" This got her attention, and she looked up at

him with wide eyes and something approaching eagerness. "I've never been on a train."

"Well, then I shall be honored to take you on your first. Come, let us see if I have any classics you have not yet read."

She gave a vigorous nod, shoveled the remainder of the eggs into her mouth and pushed back her chair. Cole laughed at her enthusiasm and commented as he rose sedately from his own chair: "Mrs. Cooper would not approve."

Her face twisted up and she opened her mouth as though to make a scathing retort, but then composed herself and inclined her head in agreement. "No, I guess she wouldn't – though I suppose all these manners she's tryin' to teach me might come in handy. No school's gonna let in someone who sounds like me. I'll have to work harder to improve."

Cole grinned as he gestured for her to go ahead. "Not too much – I do rather like a woman with a bit of spark."

Her eyes widened as she moved past him into the hall. When they reached the library, he took a great amount of pleasure in watching her marvel over the rows and rows of books lining the walls. This was his favorite room in the house and seeing the joy it brought her made him inordinately proud. She pulled out volumes one by one, grinning wildly over some, and slipping others back without comment. "How can one possibly choose?"

"Take as many as you like, but Headingly also has a library, so you needn't worry about running out of things to read."

The pure, unadulterated pleasure in her expression at this information made him suddenly and wildly want to take her in his arms and kiss her, to feel but a fraction of the joy she expressed in that ordinarily fiercely defensive face. He shook his head to dismiss the notion as she came to him with a stack of books and a smile.

"I think this'll do."

.   .   .

Cole wanted to spend the train ride getting to know Della a bit better – perhaps why she felt the need to steal from someone who was going to be paying her an exorbitant amount of money. However, not ten minutes into their journey, as the steam train puffed along towards Oxford, home of Headingly Hall, she slumped against the velvet cushion, her tattered valise clutched in her hands, and promptly fell asleep. Her long, dark eyelashes fluttered as she murmured in her sleep and her expression softened. After what he deemed was an inappropriate amount of time to be watching her, he tore his gaze away and reached for one of the books she had brought along. *Pride and Prejudice* by Jane Austen. *Fitting*, he thought, as he thumbed through the pages. Della possessed a pride in herself that would rival that of any Austen heroine.

After a while, though he fought the desire to sleep himself, the swaying of the train car made his eyelids heavy, and he set the book down. His last memory of her sitting across from him before he drifted off was of soft, pink lips, parted as she sighed, and the delicate curl of dark hair that slipped out of Martha's careful hairstyle to fall down her neck.

Cole awoke when Mr. Barrow tapped him on the shoulder, the memory of a warm, feminine figure in his arms dissipating as he blinked.

"We've arrived, sir. The porter is taking out the bags as we speak."

Cole blinked and nodded, casting his gaze across to where Della still slept soundly, curled up against the paneled wall of their cabin. Mr. Barrow followed his line of sight and cleared his throat.

"Shall I wake her?"

"No... no, Mr. Barrow. Please see to the bags and I shall get Miss Rose ready."

The valet nodded and left.

Cole drew in a fortifying breath and stood. He took a

moment, inappropriate though he knew it was, to look over her sleeping form. Martha had selected a gown of navy plaid with red velvet edging the cuffs and bodice. The color highlighted the soft bloom of her cheeks, and he couldn't help but think how lovely she was when she wasn't taut with anger and defensiveness. He coughed to gain her attention, but she merely shifted in her seat, her head tilting back to expose a smooth, pale throat ringed with the simple strand of pearls Martha had furnished for her. He coughed again, louder, and reached forward to tap her shoulder.

She awoke with a start and stared up at him, bleary-eyed before she seemed to recognize him and gave him a sleepy smile. She twisted in her seat, groaning as she arched her back, pushing her small breasts against the confines of her corset. Cole cleared his throat and looked away as she murmured drowsily.

"Mmmm... have we arrived?"

"Yes, Miss Rose. Mr. Barrow is waiting with our bags. I suggest we get a move on — lots to get done this week."

Immediately, the warm cast to her expression faded and she hardened once more. "Yes, of course."

She stood and stepped past him without another word. She remained quiet during most of the ride to Headingly, but as the carriage rumbled over rutted tracks, she spared a glance in his direction. "It's nice out here... in the country. It's so quiet. I'm not used to such quiet."

Cole's heart warmed as a shaft of cheerful, golden sunlight slid over her where she sat across from him, highlighting the inquisitive spark in her eyes. "I hope you like it here, Miss Rose. I spent all my summers here as a boy with my brothers and sister and I have many happy memories." He almost added he hoped she would make a few of her own here, but stopped himself, thinking it perhaps a bit too presumptuous. Her carefully bland expression never changed as she glanced out the window once more.

"I'd have happy memories, too, if I grew up in a place like this."

Cole's brows drew together as he observed her, from the dark silky ringlets arranged atop her head, to the stiff bearing of her shoulders, to the soft curve of her mouth, and he wanted very much in that moment to reach across the space to touch her.

"What are your happy memories, Miss Rose?" He spoke into the quiet and she turned slowly to face him before she scoffed.

"Happy memories? I don't recall a single one."

"Not one?" If not, he was determined he would make one for her this weekend, small as it may be.

She stared at him with narrowed eyes for a beat before she glanced down as though in thought. "Maybe... though I can't say if it's a memory or only a dream. I recall my mother and I sitting before a fire. She was reading to me. I don't remember the story, but I do remember she had a lovely voice. I never wanted to leave her side..." She frowned suddenly and cleared her throat as she straightened her shoulders and returned her gaze to the scene beyond the window. "Nonsense, really... only a dream."

This time, Cole did stretch forth his arm and lay his hand, very softly, upon hers and she turned a swift, hard glare upon him. "If it was but a dream, it seems well worth remembering."

She said nothing but tugged her hand away and returned to her stern perusal of the countryside, her jaw set in a firm line. Cole leaned back in his seat with a small sigh. How would he ever crack that hardened shell? And if he did, what softness lay beneath?

He glanced out the window as they travelled up the long gravel path, the house a small, beige blur in the distance, remembering summers spent here as a youth, though his duties now kept him away far more often than he liked to admit. Sunlight streamed through the branches of the massive Lebanon cedars lining the drive and danced over the interior of the carriage. Della stared out her window with wide, wondering eyes as they passed the glittering pond where Cole had spent many an hour swimming and splashing with his siblings.

The carriage finally drew up in the wide, sweeping front drive and Della sucked in a breath as she craned her head to gaze up at the sharply square turrets and pointed spires that lined the roof of the manor. A handful of footmen in crisp black uniforms waited beneath the shade of the portico and one stepped forward to open the carriage door. He stood wordlessly to the side and offered his hand to Della, who took it with an embarrassed smile. She stepped down into the bright summer sun, holding a gloved hand over her eyes to shield them. The footman reached into the carriage to retrieve her parasol and she took it with a small nod, still holding her valise to her chest. Cole followed, offering his arm.

"Come, I have much to show you."

"Much indeed," she muttered as they entered the great hall, the oldest part of the building and a marvel of Tudor-era linen-fold paneling, black and white checkerboard flooring, and intricate tapestries.

"This was the first part of Headingly that was built – my great-great-great- or some such grandfather. A courtier to King Henry VII. My great-grandfather, the fourth Earl of Bradford, built the east and west wings during the reign of George III. There are gardens in the back I thought you might like, and there's a small chapel down the hill—" He stopped when he caught sight of her wandering away from him to peer through an open door into the adjacent parlor. He couldn't help but chuckle as he leaned against the balustrade of the massive oak staircase and jerked his head in the opposite direction.

"The library's through there."

A blush suffused her cheeks, and she gave him a lame grin before crossing the hall to the doorway he had indicated. She disappeared into the room and her delighted gasp made him smile as he followed to find her flitting about the room, bathed in the bright afternoon light flooding in through the towering bay window. Shelves of warm yellow oak lined the walls, drawing the eye to a massive hearth of carved limestone surmounted by a portrait of a man in a Georgian-era frock coat and breeches. He looked sternly down upon the room, but Della took little notice of anything but for the myriad books.

"I didn't think so many books even existed," she said as she lingered before one of the stacks.

"To be fair, it is a collection three hundred years in the making," he said, pausing to spin the globe that sat before the fireplace. She let out a small laugh at this and pulled out a heavy, red-leather bound encyclopedia from one of the stacks to flip through its gilt-edged pages. Her slender fingers skimmed over the words, and he wondered, briefly, how it would feel to have those fingers move across his skin. He shook his head. The sting of rejection was still fresh in his heart, and he was quite certain that Miss Rose was wholly unsuited to the business of healing it.

"So, Miss Rose, do tell me what made you such an avid reader?"

She took a moment to place the book back on the shelf and her hand hovered there for a moment before she turned to answer. "My mother, I suppose. Those memories of her readin' to me – whether they were real or not – it was all I had when I was brought to the orphanage. An escape, if you will. In books, people were loved, they had adventures, things I never dreamed I would have. Things I lost when she died." She glanced back at him. "An almost happy memory... more bittersweet, perhaps."

He contemplated her, this fiercely determined young woman whose passion was evident by the way she turned back to the books and whose few good memories came from reading them. "If it is not too impertinent... how came you to be in an orphanage?"

Her expression clouded at this question, but she did not rebuff him. "My mother died when I was six – too old for anyone to want to adopt me, too young to work. I was sent to the St. Giles orphanage. The matron at least allowed me to keep my books, though not much else. I was lucky to have Violet with me. We kept each other company. We kept each other safe."

Cole's insides wrenched at the defiance in her voice and the way she turned away from him once more to peruse her beloved books. "I'm very sorry to hear that. My mother also died when I was young of a fever."

"But you still had all of this, didn't you?" She spoke over her shoulder to him, and her voice was cold. Cole nodded slowly.

"I did. I am very fortunate, I know that. And I will do my very best to ensure that you have the life you want when this is over, Miss Rose. You cannot know how important it is that I get those documents back. You will help save many lives."

"And yet, you still can't tell me what's so important about these papers I'm to steal, or who I'm helpin', or why." She rounded on him with raised brows, and the feather atop her straw bonnet bobbed with the movement. She grimaced and snatched it from her head to crumple it in her fist.

Cole drew in a long breath and took a step towards her. "I cannot. It is a delicate matter, and I trust very little to people I don't know. I don't know you yet, Miss Rose." He softened his expression. "But I hope to."

She looked flustered at this remark and returned her attention back to the books. "I hardly think there's anythin' worth knowin' about me. Who am I?" she said with a wry laugh. Cole raised a hand to touch her shoulder and she spun to face him, her brow furrowed.

"You are Della Rose, and *I* would like to know you."

The crumpling of her façade near broke him then, and he fought every urge to pull her into his arms once more and kiss that lovely, sad face. *Who are you, indeed?* The most fascinating woman he had ever met, and he did want to know her – everything about her. He wanted to know the touch of her hand, the brush of her lips, her very innermost thoughts and desires, everything she liked, everything she hated. And yet... and yet, the doubt he harbored deep inside, the walls he had built to protect himself remained, unyielding, even in the face of such remarkable strength and beauty. He withdrew his hand and cleared his throat.

"Come, I shall escort you to the stables. It is time you met Dionysus."

TEN

The sun was warm upon Della's face as they left the sublime beauty of the library to make their way down a gravel-lined path to the stables. Immaculate rows of red-brick buildings topped by slate roofs stood at the crest of the hill. A small swell of panic began to rise inside her chest as they reached one of the glossy black doors that dotted the façade of the main building. An aged copper weathervane perched upon a cupola on top of the building turned in a listless circle as a small breeze flowed through the courtyard.

"Ready?" Bradford turned to her with a confident smile that, for the very briefest of moments, soothed her fear. *You can do this, Della. You must.* She made a feeble attempt to return the expression as he pushed open the wide door and led her inside.

The clean, earthy smell of fresh hay reached her nostrils and horses, hidden in their stalls, snorted and stamped. Wisps of straw crunched underfoot as they crossed the flagstone floor to the far end of the stable, where a large, sleek black head lifted itself over the door to its stall and nickered softly. The earl walked right up to the beast and reached out to stroke its long nose. It nuzzled against his shoulder, bobbing its head in apparent pleasure.

"Hello Dionysus, old boy. Have you missed me? I've missed you," he said in that low, reverberating voice as he gave the animal's cheek a vigorous rub. He then turned to look at Della, who stood as far away as she could manage, hands clasped tight in the folds of her skirts.

"Would you like to come and meet him?"

Della drew in a deep breath and squared her shoulders before marching forward. No sense putting it off. "If I must," she replied and hesitated as the horse stretched its neck towards her and sniffed her. She fought the urge to recoil from it and glanced up to see Bradford watching her with a sympathetic smile.

"He's very gentle, I assure you."

Della frowned, doubting that any animal so large could be gentle in any way, but she held out a shaking hand and winced as the soft velvet nose pushed into it. She gasped, her heart lurching when the horse bobbed its great head, and she jerked her hand away. The earl chuckled and caught her hand again to hold it out.

"He's just trying to get a good sniff. It's how he gets to know you." The warmth of his fingers through her gloves made her shiver and she swallowed hard against the rising heat in her cheeks. She let him hold her hand there so the beast could get a good smell of her before he released her and gestured towards the other end of the stable.

"The chambermaids have been informed of our arrival and I have asked that they lay out a riding habit for you. Come, we'll have a spot of lunch and then you can change. We'll tackle Dionysus later this afternoon."

Della all but ran out of the stables and finally breathed a sigh of relief as they made their way back to the manor. Her chambers here were blessedly free of pink, and an immaculate black riding habit had been laid out for her. A chambermaid helped her dress and at lunch, Bradford was his usual charming self. She found herself hanging on his every word as he told her about his childhood summers here, his brothers – Percy, George and Henry the twins, all younger – and his elder sister, Adelaide, who had moved to America only last year with her new husband, the owner of a shipyard in New York. His brothers had also since moved on to new lives while Bradford was left to manage the family estates, his duty as the eldest son and earl. He also spoke fondly of his parents, who met while his father was stationed in Ukraine during the Crimean War as a diplomat.

"My father was expected to marry some well-behaved heiress – imagine my grandparents' shock when he came home with the daughter of a merchant. He told me she had them charmed within a week and all was forgiven."

Della allowed a smile at this remark. "So that's where you got it. I thought perhaps they taught oozing charm in them fancy boardin' schools."

Cole laughed heartily at this, and damned if it didn't cause a twinge in the pit of her stomach that she did not care to explore the meaning of.

"Another compliment from Rosie Diver – I do feel flattered."

Della grinned again and swallowed the last dregs of her wine. "Well, I suppose we've delayed the inevitable long enough." She sighed as she set down the glass.

"Yes, I suppose so," he replied as he came around the table to pull out her chair. He walked her back to the stables and dread filled her chest the whole way. Damn giant beast was liable to throw her or crush her to death. Her breath hitched in her throat as they reached the courtyard where Dionysus stood, reins in the hand of the stable boy, a young lad with sandy blond hair and a gap between his two front teeth. He tipped his cap at the earl who nodded and took the reins from him.

"Thank you, Jimmy. I'll take it from here."

The boy scurried off and Bradford turned to Della as she smoothed down the front of her plain black riding habit with nervous fingers.

"We'll start with a gentle walk around the courtyard." He laughed when she looked warily at the big black horse who, for his part, stared back at her with a placid expression. "I won't let go of the reins, I promise. We just want to make sure you have the right position in the saddle."

He led Dionysus over to the mounting block at the side of the cobblestone yard, then patted the horse's lustrous neck and gestured to the block. "Up you get."

Della stepped up and hesitated; the sheer size of the big black gelding was overwhelming and when he shifted his weight she gasped and stumbled back. Her booted foot slipped over the edge of the mounting block, and she fell backwards into Bradford's strong, waiting arms; arms she well remembered from last night. The fashionable little top hat she wore, adorned by a veil of gauze, toppled off her carefully coifed hair. He caught it in his free hand and handed it back to her with a smile once she had righted herself.

"Are you alright?" he asked as she settled the hat back into place and jabbed in the hatpin to secure it once more. She glared at Dionysus, who looked back at her with soft, long-lashed eyes. The shame of her defeat made her shake, and she gritted her teeth with determination.

"Hold him tight," she ordered. The earl complied with raised brows but said not a word as she grabbed the polished sidesaddle in her gloved hands and hauled herself up before scowling down at him.

"Now what?" Her whole body shook; she hadn't realized how far up she would be and every movement from the horse made her feel as though she were standing on a precipice, one slip away from falling. Bradford, still holding tight to the reins, gestured to the pommel at the top of the saddle.

"Right leg there, left leg here." He paused to guide her foot into the stirrup. "Keep your right shoulder back." He took a moment to adjust the stirrup for her while her anger faded away, replaced by a strange breathlessness at his closeness and the familiarity of his touch. He finished tightening the strap and dropped her skirts back into place as heat flooded her belly.

"There, all sorted." He smiled back up at her once more. "I'm going to bring Dionysus forward a bit. This is important – your point of balance will be here" – he pointed – "behind your right knee. Only the ball of your left foot should touch the stirrup. You will place equal weight in the seat, and your upper body ought to be turned ever so slightly to the right, with your waist facing forward." He gathered up the reins and looped them back over the horse's head to hand to her. Dionysus shifted his weight and, though a swell of panic filled her, she pressed her lips even tighter together and nodded at Bradford's instructions. He took her gloved hands for a moment to thread the reins through her fingers.

"You'll need this." He bent and took up the short whip that he had left leaning against the side of the building to hand to her. "This is the schooling whip. Not for whipping – it's an aid, to be used as a man would use his right leg whilst riding astride. It's simply for guiding the horse. Now..." He nodded and made a clucking sound as he took a step backwards. Dionysus followed obediently and Della resisted the urge to cling to the pommel for dear life. Once they had reached the middle of the courtyard, Bradford gestured at her.

"Back straight, head forward, right shoulder back. To make him move forward you simply need to touch him with your calves. Go on, give it a go."

Della looked down at him in a wild panic and he shook his head.

"I won't let go, I promise." His golden gaze met hers, and there was encouragement in it, the sincere assurance that he would let no harm come to her. Her jaw was so tight now it ached, but she gave a sharp nod and pressed her left calf into the animal's side. The horse started forward with a jolt and she gasped and pitched forward to grab a handful of its mane. Bradford tapped her hand.

"Keep your balance. You'll feel more secure if you maintain the correct position."

Della grunted and pushed herself up, mindful of the slouch in her shoulders as she fought the urge to lean forward. She straightened herself with a sharply indrawn breath, adjusted her legs and hips as he had instructed and nodded without looking down at him.

"Give him another tap; we'll just circle the courtyard."

She did as he bade, and with each circuit of the light-filled yard, she grew more and more assured. Dionysus was an easy horse to guide and seemed to understand that she was not yet confident in her skills.

"A gentle tug on the left or right rein to turn in that direction," he said after a period when she had relaxed a bit in the saddle. She nodded again and gave the right rein a twitch. Dionysus moved immediately in that direction, and she couldn't help the small feeling of triumph that swelled in her chest. The earl kept a loose hold of the reins where they looped under the animal's mouth, and after a while, she glanced down at him.

"You can let go."

"Are you certain?" There was no doubt in his voice, just a hint of expectation and she bobbed her head. He sent her a dazzling smile full of pride and stepped away to the side of the yard. Dionysus remained still until she tapped his side once more and brushed the whip against his right side. He started forward and she let him go for a bit before she gave the left rein a tug. She made a mental check of her position as the horse turned and made his way back the way he had come. Bradford stood in the shade of the barn clapping, and Della offered him the slightest inclination of her head as any graceful lady might, though the joyous smile on her face belied her muted gesture. He took the reins when she reached him to lead her back to the mounting block.

"I think that's a good start to the day."

"Oh, no," she said, suddenly and inexplicably disappointed. "Must we stop so soon?"

He laughed. "I told you that you would like Dionysus. Wait here, I shall have the groom saddle up Apollo."

"Cor, you did take your Greek gods seriously," she said with a laugh as the earl retreated into the barn, looking back at her with raised brows and a grin. He returned shortly on the back of an elegant white stallion who appeared to possess far more fire and spirit than the placid Dionysus. The beast snorted and tossed his fine head, but Bradford was a far superior rider to her and held the sprightly animal in check as he nodded towards the rolling hills beyond the courtyard.

"Are you comfortable going out into the fields?"

Della was not entirely sure, but she couldn't bear the thought of going back inside and sitting around in her room until dinner. And she would never admit it to herself, but Bradford's smile gave her such joy that she would ride out, uncertain, into those fields just to have him bestow it upon her one more time. She nodded and he sent her one of those very smiles and dug his heels into Apollo's sides. The animal sprang forth, muscles bunching and legs prancing as the earl held him back.

"Just a walk for now, old boy," he said, patting the horse's neck. Della gave Dionysus a little kick and they moved out of the confines of the courtyard and into the vast, verdant expanse of Bradford's land. Late afternoon sunlight rippled over fields of green and gold and scattered into lacy shadows under the branches of towering cedars and oaks. A flock of starlings rose out of the shadowy forest bordering the land and crossed the brilliant blue sky in a twisting, undulating shape. Della watched them for a moment, marveling at their cohesion, before the path dipped to follow the rolling hills. Her stomach lurched as Dionysus' big body rocked to follow the terrain, but Bradford merely reached across to touch the small of her back.

"Mind your position," he said with a reassuring pat. "I'll be right beside you."

Della drew in a shaking breath as he pulled back, her skin on fire where he had touched her through the habit. They rode in companionable silence for a while until they reached the formal gardens which descended in carefully landscaped levels from the wide, sweeping drive at the front of the manor.

"Mr. Avery said I should keep up with my piano lessons while we're here," she said as they skirted the gardens to continue the path which led around what she presumed to be the chapel. Its spire rose into the clear blue sky, the small iron cross at its peak glinting in the sunlight.

"Yes, of course. I am a poor substitute for Mr. Avery, but I shall endeavor not to undo his teachings." He gave a small laugh as he looked over at her. She couldn't help but return the expression as they moved through the shadow cast by the chapel and back into the warmth of the sun.

"I suppose Mrs. Cooper will have more planned for me when we return?" Dread filled Della as she thought of that sour-faced old woman and her judgmental glares. The corner of Bradford's mouth hitched up as he cast her a sympathetic look.

"If it helps you, she did have much praise for your quick learning and thinks you will conduct yourself adequately when the time comes."

"Adequately?"

He grinned at her, and once more she shivered as she took

in that dazzling display of straight white teeth and slightly dimpled cheeks. She shook her head to rid herself of the memory of those sturdy arms around her waist, the clean smell of him, the fire that burned whenever he touched her. *Don't be a damn fool*, she told herself. *As though he could ever feel that way about you, a nobody.*

They made their way down a small hillock dotted with heather, releasing its mossy scent as they descended, to reach the path which circled the large pond they had passed on the way in. Sunlight glinted off the smooth, flat surface, broken only when the wispy branches of the willows bordering the pond in a small cluster dipped into the water. A pair of swans floated elegantly among the rushes near the bank and Della pulled back on the reins. Dionysus drew to an obedient stop and she turned to Bradford, who followed close behind.

"Can you help me down?"

"But of course."

He swung a long leg over his saddle and dropped with easy grace to the gravel trail. Stepping up to her side, he offered her a hand and held Dionysus steady with the free one as she lifted herself from the saddle, resting her weight on the stirrup. She swung her right leg over the pommel and twisted to face him. He reached up to take her waist in both hands and lift her down. When her feet touched the ground, he paused for a moment, perhaps a trifle too long, his large hands spanning her waist, his amber gaze fixed upon hers. Della's breath grew shallow as she stared back at him, her lips parted as a strange heat unfurled in her belly. Finally, she cleared her throat, and he stepped back with a shake of his head.

"There you are, Miss Rose. You make a fine horsewoman," he said as he gestured for her to move ahead. He did not take her arm this time but followed at an appropriate distance as she moved closer to the water. It was, as always, on the tip of her tongue to thank him for the compliment, but a lifetime of naught but harsh words and few expectations stilled the words in her throat. She instead bent to pick up a small rock nestled in the thick grass and tossed it into the pond. It broke the surface with a small plink as the water rippled out in concentric circles.

"So, what's next? What else must I learn to fit in here?" Della spoke over her shoulder as she snapped the stem of a bulrush in half and flicked it through the tall grass. She heard no movement behind her and so turned to see Bradford watching her with an impenetrable expression. His arms were folded before his broad chest and he leaned his weight on one leg as the two horses cropped at the grass behind him.

"Dancing."

Della grimaced. She supposed that the raucous dances presided over by itinerant fiddlers at the pubs, with the tables pushed out of the way to make up a dance floor, would not suit elegant Society ballrooms. She twisted the stem of the bulrush in nervous fingers as he watched her with a sharp eye.

"And who'll be teachin' me?"

"I shall."

Della's heart leapt inside her chest at this answer, and she was suddenly, keenly aware that he had moved closer to her. Just thinking about him with his hands about her waist, guiding her through a graceful waltz, made her chest grow warm and her legs tremble.

"You?"

"Yes. I am no teacher, but I do consider myself a fine dancer. And I would not bring more people into our arrangement than necessary. The more people who know of our plan, the more likely it is to fail. The Duke of Salisbury has many people in his pay – or in his debt."

"Oh. When do we begin?"

"We can begin right now, if you wish."

That smile. Damn it. Damn him. He stretched his arm out and she took a reluctant step forward and placed her right hand in his left. His right arm came up under her shoulder to rest upon her back, and he took up her left hand to place it on the top of his arm. And there, in the billowing shade of the willow trees, he whispered the steps to her, never once taking his gaze from hers.

"Right foot back, side left foot, close your right foot to your left," he said as he moved her about in a little square, the gravel crunching beneath their feet. "Forward with your left foot, side right foot, close your left foot to your right foot." When they returned to their starting position, he looked down at her with what she could only describe as hunger in his eyes, and something stirred low in the pit of her stomach.

"This time, we'll follow the same steps, and I'll count the beats. I want you to rise on the second beat and fall on the third. Like this," and he took her around in another little square, there beside the still and silent lake, counting the beats. "One two three, one two three, one two three."

With each repetition, her heart beat faster and faster and she was suddenly unbearably hot beneath the dark habit, even though a soft breeze blew across the hills and rumpled the surface of the water. Dionysus and Apollo had wandered farther up the hill to crop at the long grass and though she could hear their quiet snorts and the thud of their hooves on the soft earth, she felt nothing beyond the circle of Bradford's arms, the heat of his body, and his whispered voice. She tried, desperately, to draw upon the disdain she carried for most men, knowing what happened to those who tied themselves to them and always lost in the end. But this man... this man seemed genuinely to want to help her and was unbothered by her profession. And the intensity of his gaze, the heat of his hand on her back, made her dizzy with a desire she had long tried to bury.

She thought, wildly, that he had moved closer as they danced; his lips seemed to hover above hers as he counted out the beats in his low, husky voice. How long had they been dancing here at the water's edge? It seemed an eternity had passed before he finally drew her to a stop and they stood there, motionless. Della knew Mrs. Cooper would tut with disapproval at their closeness and the inappropriate amount of time he held her in his arms. And still, she could not find the will to withdraw, nor to voice a word of protest.

"Miss Rose," he said after a long, tense moment. "Della?"

The use of her given name made her start and slowly, very slowly, he dropped his left arm, still holding her hand in his. Once at his side, he released her fingers to trace the length of her arm until he touched her chin.

"Yes?" she said in a voice barely above a whisper. His other hand moved up her back.

"I fear I have found myself..."

"Yes?"

"You are a remarkable woman, and I should very much like to kiss you right now."

"You would?" she whispered.

His small laugh seared along her nerve endings and her mouth went dry.

"More than anything."

She said nothing, but her lips parted in silent acquiescence, and he bent to capture them with his own, drawing her up tight against the length of his body. Something exploded inside Della, and from her cold, hard heart warmth blossomed like a summer day, expanding inside her until the very blood in her veins seemed electrified. His arms tightened around her, causing a wild shiver to streak up her back and then... she was lost. Lost in his scent, in his ragged breath against her cheek as he lifted her to him, in the exquisite heat of his body as he pulled her closer. Della had been kissed before, but this... this was indescribable. His lips were soft and tasted of the wine he had drunk at lunch, he smelled of horse and earth and leather, and when he cupped her face in his large hands, opening her mouth to his insistent tongue, she dissolved with a blissful sigh.

When he finally did draw away, slowly, with shaking breath, she felt as though she were floating, and her heart lifted inside her chest, humming along with the ragged rhythm of her breathing. They stared at each other for what seemed an eternity. What should she say? What did one say after a kiss that made her whole body seem to sing, that left her shaken and trembling and full of an unbearable longing for more?

"I... I don't know what to say," she finally whispered against his mouth as his thumb gently caressed her chin.

And then he smiled, the smile that had drawn her to him in the first place, and he kissed her again and again as the sun began to dip towards the horizon in the west.

ELEVEN

Night had fallen over the verdant green fields surrounding Headingly Hall and Cole was restless. He stood at the window of his bedchamber and looked out at a night sky that blazed with the glory of a million stars. Though his room was peaceful and quiet, and Mr. Barrow had long since retired for the night, Cole's heart raced and he couldn't seem to draw a breath deep enough to slow it.

He could still taste her. God, the taste of her. It haunted him; it filled his senses like a heady wine. He fancied he could still feel her, lips soft and pliant, small breasts taut against the corset and her grip on him fierce and desperate. With an iron will borne of many years of presenting only the façade he wished others to see, he pushed down the growing heat stirring inside him and turned from the view.

Had he been foolish to kiss her? Certainly – this whole arrangement rested on her being at the top of her game, and on his maintaining a professional relationship with her – for her safety, and for his own. And she was in his care as an employee. He had crossed a line and he knew it. He shook his head and vowed that it would not happen again. Tempting as she may be, fascinating as she might be... it would not do to pursue that impulse. Experience had taught him, rather harshly, that he was better off keeping those feelings to himself.

She had been smiling during their ride back to the stables – quiet, but smiling. When she had come down for dinner dressed in a breathtaking gown of deep purple moiré silk with black lace trim that highlighted the pale translucence of her skin, she had looked warily at him. She said little, though did express some interest in resuming her riding lessons the next day. After dinner, she declined his invitation to take a stroll in the gardens and asked him where the piano was. He took her to the parlor, bathed in the warm golden light of the setting sun, and left her to her scales and arpeggios, played with determined repetition that followed him as he made his way out to the gardens alone. He could still hear her in there, through the open window, doggedly hammering out the notes until the music stopped and only the sound of the starlings and blackbirds filled the still evening air. He'd returned to the manor as the sun disappeared behind the hills and the stars came out to blaze across the sky. There was still a light on in the parlor as he passed by on the way to his chambers, and he peered inside to find her curled up on a chaise, knees tucked up under her chin, engrossed in a novel she had plucked from the shelves bordering the fireplace.

He watched her for a beat, remembering with vivid intensity the feel of her lips upon his and the scent of her – not of perfume, but of woman and the warmth of leather. He withdrew quietly and left her to her reading, certain she would not welcome his intrusion.

And now here he was, uncertain after years of certainty, not recalling a single woman who had ever made him want her so badly. Not even the one he had thought he loved, the one he should have wanted. He shook his head to banish the notion and glanced at the liquor cabinet by the fireplace, then decided if ever there was a time for a drink, it was now. He poured himself a healthy measure of whisky and drained it in a few, short gulps that burned down his throat. A soft knock on the door made him turn. Only Mr. Barrow would come calling at this hour, and only about work, and so he called out, "Come."

The valet poked his head into the room and gave a brief nod. "A package for you, sir."

Cole frowned. This was not their regularly scheduled night. The package was not due to arrive until tomorrow. There must be news. "I'll take it, Mr. Barrow."

The valet pushed open the door and held out the familiar paper-wrapped package tied with twine. Inside the box Cole found a sheet of paper marked with a single paragraph. *Salisbury has hired a codebreaker to review the files. Efforts to retrieve documents must be increased.*

Cole pursed his lips, the only indication of his consternation. He turned to Mr. Barrow after a moment of contemplation. "Make arrangements for us to return to London by the end of the week. Dionysus and Apollo are to be brought to Bradford House. And please send word ahead to Mr. Avery and Mrs. Cooper — Miss Rose's tutelage will have to be expedited. In whatever way they deem necessary. Inform the maids that Miss Rose is to be brought to the ballroom by eight in the morning. We have a lot of practice ahead of us."

"Of course, my lord. Will that be all?"

"Yes... yes, for now."

"Is there a reply you would like me to send?"

"No. Good night, Mr. Barrow."

"Good night, my lord."

The door closed and Cole crumpled up the paper before tossing it into the hearth. The corner caught the flame and soon the sheet twisted up, scorched black, and sank into a pile of ashes in the grate. He stared at the flickering flames, thinking of Della — always Della, and always at the back of his mind. But

the Duke of Salisbury had help now. There were so many
people listed in those documents, all of whose lives were in
danger if their names were deciphered. Cole's only comfort lay
in the fact that his father had written an exceptionally difficult
code – he had been the Home Office's top code writer. He
would have to press Miss Rose – perhaps more than she was
willing. More time spent with her was probably not the best
idea in light of the circumstances, but he had no choice. She
would have to meet Salisbury, and soon.

Della slept poorly that night. Her room was quiet and dark, a
strange feeling for her, accustomed as she was to the constant
hum of noise in London. It wasn't the quiet keeping her awake,
however. Her lips tingled at the memory of Bradford's kiss, and
she rolled with a sigh to bury her face in her pillow, trying to
bring back the feeling of sturdy hands on her back, of the clean,
leathery smell of him, the rasping breath and hard, hot body
pressed into her. Her hands fisted in the sheets and she groaned,
wanting him and hating him at the same time. How the hell had
she allowed that to happen? How could she have opened herself
up to someone so obviously wrong for her, so far away from her
in all measures?

    She had been exhilarated at the time; she couldn't erase the
smile from her face as they rode back to the stables in the warm
radiance of the summer sun. But as she dressed for dinner, and
as they ate in an uncomfortable silence, the more she came to
realize what a mistake their kiss had been. She thought of the
little shepherdess in the care of Cora and a slashing guilt went
through her, an emotion quite unfamiliar to her until now. She
hated the feeling; it sat like a heavy lump in her stomach. When
he asked her to take a walk with him after dinner, she knew she
had to say no. She knew if she went with him, she would kiss
him again – she would pull those magnificent lips to hers and

kiss him until she couldn't breathe. She would drink him in, every smell and sound and taste of him; she would hold him tight to her, attempting to absorb him into her body for want of him. And she would be a fool to do any of this.

And so, she would turn from him, and focus all her energies on mastering the piano, on learning table manners, on memorizing the dance steps and acting every bit the part of a well-bred lady. She would harden her heart once more, as it had always been, and remember why she had never let a man in before.

Lifting her head from the pillow, she sighed and reached underneath to withdraw the photograph she had carried with her for as long as she could remember. In the faint light of the single candle that sat beside her bed, she traced her thumb over the photo of the couple in the silver frame. The photo had belonged to her mother, left to Della when she died, along with the pittance she left behind. The photo was all she had left of her parents, for she had never met her father, a respectable shopkeeper whose death forced her mother into prostitution to feed her young daughter. Della would not meet that same fate. She could not fail this mission. This was her only way out of the rookery. She would not let Lord Bradford, handsome and kind though he was, tempt her again.

With this firm resolution, sleep finally came to her.

The sun had barely broken the horizon when a knock awoke her from deep, dreamless slumber. Della willed whoever it was to go away, pulling the covers up tight over her head as though to shut them out. But the knock persisted, and she finally called out, "Oh, just come in!"

An apologetic chambermaid bustled in with clothing in hand and set about relighting the fire, laying out the combs and pins to do Della's hair and pulling back the curtains. Clouds gathered in the east, blotting out the sun and the patter of rain on the window told Della there would be no riding lessons this morning. Dance it was. Her mind screamed in frustration, knowing this would mean a day spent in the earl's strong arms, twirling about a ballroom. Her body, though, betrayer of her innermost desires, trembled at the thought and she groaned as she kicked away the covers. The chambermaid was efficient in her work and soon Della sat at the breakfast table, groggy and irritable and wanting desperately to hide in her bed all day to avoid that damn smile.

A footman offered coffee and she eagerly accepted a cup, trying to blink away the tiredness in her eyes. Then she heard him – in the hall, speaking in a low voice with his valet. Her heart raced at the very sound and she immediately willed away the feeling and set her mouth in a resolute line.

When Lord Bradford entered the room, dressed impeccably in grey trousers, navy morning coat, crisp white shirt and dark tie in a four-in-hand knot, her breath caught in her throat. He nodded to her as he moved to the sideboard to pour himself a cup of coffee.

"Good morning, Miss Rose," he said as he returned to the table and sat opposite her. Keeping the firm set of her jaw, she gave him the slightest inclination of her head.

"Good morning, my lord. I trust you slept well?"

The barest suggestion of a smile lifted his lips as he speared a piece of ham on his fork. "Quite well. And you?"

"Well enough." God, she hated this stilted small talk. "I suppose we won't be riding today?"

As if to emphasize this point, a jagged streak of lightning lit up the hills and thunder rumbled across the sky. The wind pelted rain against the dining room window and Bradford shook his head. "No, not today. We'll practice dancing instead. I trust that is agreeable with you?"

She thought she detected a knowing tone in his voice, but chose to ignore this and simply said, "Yes, of course."

They ate in silence until Bradford glanced at the footman hovering in the doorway and lifted his chin. The man disappeared and he turned back to Della, whose stomach clenched in anticipation of what she knew was coming. "Ought we to discuss what happened yesterday?"

"No, we ought not to," she replied, never looking up from her plate. A moment of silence passed.

"I must apologize, Miss Rose. It was wrong of me to take advantage of you like that. You are, indeed, a beautiful, intelligent and... fascinating woman, but I think we can both agree that pursuing anything more beyond our professional relationship would be foolhardy."

She finally forced herself to look up at him, wishing she hadn't, for the moment she met that intense golden gaze, something inside her crumbled. It took everything within her to keep the impassive look on her face. "I couldn't agree more."

The very briefest flicker of disappointment crossed his face – so brief it may have never been there – and he bent his head in a nod. "Very good. Come, let us finish here and adjourn to the ballroom. I think today, perhaps the galop might be worth practicing."

His matter-of-fact tone made her heart ache – just for a moment – before she reminded herself of her goal. Her future would not be her mother's. She would not die, broken and sick from hunger in Seven Dials. She was getting out of there. And if that meant going into that room today, learning whatever dance he deemed worthy of the ballrooms of Society, and ignoring that thrill that raced through her body where he touched her, then so be it.

She bobbed her head in agreement, finished her breakfast, and followed him out of the dining room.

Even on this dull, rainy morning, the ballroom glittered. Tall French doors lined one side of the space, looking out over those magnificent, stepped gardens, and gold damask covered the walls. A fire had been lit in the hearth on the opposite wall, and a vaulted, gold-leafed ceiling soared above. The earl crooked his arm and turned to her with a smile that seemed forced. Keeping her expression even, she placed her arm through his as he led her across the gleaming parquet floor to the center of the room, beneath a chandelier dripping with crystals.

"Unfortunately, we have no accompanist until we return to London," he said, nodding towards the piano in the corner of the room. "But I shall count out the beats for us."

As he counted out the steps, leading her across the room with graceful elegance, she forced herself to focus all her thoughts on where her feet were going. She never allowed herself to breathe deep the spicy, warm scent of him, nor to sink her fingers into the taut muscles in his arms, nor get close enough to feel the heat emanating from his body. Never once did she meet his gaze, sure that if she did, she would be lost again. They practiced all morning, gliding across the polished floor, until her feet ached.

"I think that's enough for today," she finally said, giving him the smallest push before stepping away and moving to one of the chairs lining the wall. She took a seat and bent to pull off her slippers, rubbing her tender feet with a wince. Bradford nodded, smoothing down the front of his coat and moving to the door to ring the bell.

"Yes, I think we've made excellent progress. You'll be waltzing with the best of them in no time." His tone was light, but Della made no effort to smile at his attempted humor. He cleared his throat at her quiet indifference and turned when the door opened. The footman from breakfast appeared with an inquisitive expression.

"Ah, James, could you please have tea brought to the parlor for Miss Rose and myself? And some ice in a towel?"

The man nodded and withdrew without a word. Della finally looked up at Bradford with a long, indrawn breath. "Suppose I ought to practice the piano for a bit."

"Yes, if you're up for it. I'm happy to tutor you myself, as we don't have Mr. Avery—"

"No. He gave me some sheets to practice myself. I think I'll be fine on my own."

She saw the hurt in his expression, and chose to ignore it, before he offered her a flat smile and gestured to the door.

"As you wish, Miss Rose. Come, you can ice your feet before you begin."

And so, she followed him to the parlor, heart hardened once more. There was something there; it would be foolish to deny it. She already spent half her days wondering what his skin would feel like against hers, how she might taste him, how he would feel inside her. But it wouldn't get her out of Seven Dials. It wouldn't get her into school. And so, though every part of her longed to know what lay beneath that starched linen and fine wool, she knew there was no way that path ended well. Her path was already decided, and it didn't include him.

TWELVE

They finished out the week with another day of riding lessons. Lord Bradford nodded in approval as Della trotted around him in the practice arena behind the stables. Dionysus shook his dark head as she drew him to a stop, laughter bubbling in her throat. They had managed two more full days of riding practice before they were due to leave in the morning. Della, who had feared learning to ride more than she had ever feared anything in her life – and coming from the rookery, that was saying something – had come to love it. Riding came easily to her, and Bradford, loath as she was to admit it, was an excellent teacher. It didn't hurt that Dionysus was a placid, easy horse, and she had been promised that he would be making the journey with them to London to be her personal mount.

"Well, Miss Rose, I wouldn't say you're an expert, but you will certainly do an admirable job. You'll draw the duke's eye with no problem, I'd wager."

Della smiled as he lifted her down from the saddle. Over the last two days, she'd slowly let go of the anger she carried inside at him. There was no gain to be had from it, and she realized it only made them both uncomfortable. Bradford seemed eager to return to the polite, if somewhat prickly, amiability they had shared before they kissed, and, if she was being honest, she found it hard to stay cold towards him. He was just a good man trying to do right by her and though she was usually eager to keep men away, it was trickier for her to do the same with him. It was too much work to keep him at a distance, and she was tired of fighting it. They would be returning to London in the morning as Bradford had been invited to a ball at the house of the marquess of somewhere – she didn't really care to know – and this was to be her first experience with the glittering world of high Society. She had only a week once they returned to turn herself into a lady before the party and secretly, deep within, she was terrified. Surely, they would see right past the expensive gowns and styled hair to the skinny, poor nobody she really was?

Della led Dionysus back to the stables with Bradford following at an appropriate distance behind her. He had made no more mention of their kiss and for this, she was eternally grateful. She wanted to pretend it had never happened even though, lying in her sumptuous bed late at night, it was all she could think of.

"So," he said as they entered the cool shelter of the stables, "are you happy to be returning to London?"

Della gave Dionysus a gentle pat on the neck before she handed the reins to Jimmy and turned, brushing the dust from her riding gloves. "Yes, I suppose. Though, I won't lie, I like the country more than I expected. It's... peaceful."

Bradford smiled that lovely, warm smile of his and crooked an arm for her. She took it after only a moment's hesitation, and he led her from the stables into the sunny courtyard. "I do wish I had more time to come out here. I like the quiet. I wish we could have stayed longer, but I have received word..." He trailed off and Della sent him a questioning glance. "The Duke of Salisbury is coming close to breaking the code. Time is rather of the essence now. I didn't want to alarm you, nor put any pressure on you." He withdrew his arm from hers and turned to face her head-on. "We must step up your tutoring, I'm afraid. I've already informed Mr. Avery and Mrs. Cooper. Your riding is coming along well enough, but there's still so much more to learn."

A nervous tremor skittered up Della's back, and she pushed it back down, reminding herself of her goals. *There is no going back.* "I see." She swallowed. "I'll do my best, my lord."

The corner of his lips lifted, and he nodded and bent his arm once more to walk with her back to the manor. "I know you will, Miss Rose. I have every faith in your ability. I know I chose well – if one can choose a pickpocket well."

She finally did laugh at the humor in his voice and, briefly, felt at ease with him once more.

During the train ride back to London, valise close at her side, Della diligently studied the book of etiquette Bradford had provided her. At times, she couldn't help a snort of derision at some of the sillier rules and he would lift his gaze to her, brow raised.

"Bloody hell, we're breakin' the rules just bein' in this train car alone."

He chuckled and set down the newspaper he was reading. "We are, I suppose, though, as my cousin, it is all perfectly acceptable. I will be your chaperone, of course, to any events we attend, so you needn't worry about your reputation."

Della sniffed. "As though I care about my reputation. If they knew who I really was, they'd all choke on their champagne."

Bradford tilted his head and contemplated her. "But Salisbury will care about your reputation. He will care very much.

After all, anyone he marries will have to be unimpeachably pure and without scandal. And, since you have no past, we can invent one which is suitably scandal-free. Charity, of course. A love of horses, and a quiet upbringing in the north, away from the tainted influence of London. And a relation of the Earl of Bradford."

Della made a face. "Sounds boring."

"It sounds eminently suitable for a potential bride for the Duke of Salisbury."

She shrugged. "Doesn't matter, I suppose. I just need to act the part until I can get what you need, then back to my old life – full of scandal." She smirked at this, and he laughed.

"Well, I hope you shan't forget boring old me when you leave."

The tone of his voice was light-hearted, but the air seemed to whoosh out of her lungs as she stared at him, suddenly unable to comprehend a future without him. She was horrified when tears prickled at the back of her eyes, and she forced a laugh to stop them falling. "Oh, you're not that boring, my lord."

His expression was warm as he looked back at her and damned if that didn't make her feel like the most important person on the planet at that moment. She blinked away mutinous tears and returned her attention to the book to stop them falling and betraying her feelings, focusing all her thoughts on learning what outfits were appropriate for which time of day. What was wrong with her? She couldn't remember the last time she pined for a man, let alone cried over one.

For the remainder of the train ride back to London, she kept scrupulous attention on the book, sure if she looked up at him and his warm, smiling face, she would burst into tears.

"Oh, Mr. Avery, it's good to see you again," Della said in a relieved voice as she waited in the music room the following morning. He smiled at her as he set down his bundle of papers and gestured for her to sit at the piano. She took the seat, eager to show him what she had practiced while they were away.

"It is good to see you, as well, Miss Rose," he said as he set a sheet of music down upon the shelf. "How was your time at Headingly? I used to go there when Lord Bradford was my student, and I do recall it was quite lovely."

"Yes, it was lovely," Della said as her cheeks warmed in remembrance of the kiss she had shared with Bradford; she could almost feel the eager pliancy of his lips upon hers if she thought hard enough, and she coughed to hide her embarrassment as she plucked out a scale on the keyboard. Mr. Avery nodded in approval as she moved her fingers, slowly but confidently, over the keys. She repeated it, over and over again, until the motion became almost mechanical, and she was able to let her mind wander. In a moment of brief self-indulgence, she allowed herself to relive that kiss again, recalling every glorious detail from the intoxicating taste of his mouth to the roughness of the stubble on his jaw against her cheek, to the desperation of his fingers digging into her back and the heat of his body against hers.

Something stirred low in the pit of her belly as she closed her eyes to commit that kiss to her memory. There couldn't be anything between them, but it couldn't hurt to have that kiss tucked away for the future; the long, lonely one she was sure was waiting for her. She couldn't imagine any other. Mr. Avery placed another sheet of music before her and pointed out something about the chords, but she found she could not focus on the notes, even knowing she must master this skill as quickly as possible. Her fingers fumbled over the keys until finally, Mr. Avery placed a hand over hers and she raised her gaze to his.

"Miss Rose, is something the matter?"

"No, why?"

"You seem awfully distracted today. I thought your mind might be elsewhere."

"No... I'm sorry, Mr. Avery. Nothing's wrong. Please, show me again," she said, turning back to the piano and brushing away those fantasies with a determined shake of her head. With the memory of that searing kiss banished, Della spent the morning replaying the same scales and simple pieces until the notes began to blur on the page.

"I think that will do for today," Mr. Avery said as he gathered up his things and tilted his head towards her. "As always, it has been a pleasure, Miss Rose. Do keep up with your practice. I shall see you again in the morning."

As he turned to leave, she took a step forward. "Wait!"

He paused and looked back at her with a questioning glance. Della swallowed hard and took another step forward with a hand held against her stomach as though to ease the nervous flutter within. "Mr. Avery, are you sure – that is, do you think I'll be ready in time? I'd be so embarrassed if I made a mistake in front of Lord Bradford's friends. I don't want to make a fool of myself. I need them to think I'm one of them." It was something she would never voice to the earl himself. He was so very confident in himself, so sure of all things that she would feel like a failure to not rise to his level. She wanted, more than anything, for him to have the same confidence in her that he had in himself. Mr. Avery was, however, the only person she felt she could confide in.

"Miss Rose," he began in his soft voice, coming forward with a sympathetic smile. "Do let me tell you something I have come to learn in my time as a tutor to the very highest ranks of society." He paused and her eyes widened in expectation. "They will forgive a woman almost any failing if she is beautiful and, above all, charming."

Della's expression fell. She didn't possess a lick of charm –

what use had she for charm as a pickpocket? Mr. Avery chuckled.

"I think you can turn your... unique capabilities, to your advantage. Don't hide what you are. Revel in it, utterly and completely. They will never have met anyone quite like you, and if you wield it in the right way, it will be a powerful weapon. You are a clever woman, Miss Rose. Soften those edges just enough to let who you are shine through. I think people will find you more interesting than all those simpering girls of Society."

Della couldn't help a small laugh, and she smiled as Mr. Avery nodded to her and left the room. She pondered his words as she met Mrs. Cooper for another round of etiquette lessons. Today it was addressing aristocracy, and she tucked away the important bit of knowledge that she was not to address the duke as 'my lord'. That was a mistake she did not wish to make. Mrs. Cooper was especially civil today, almost complimentary, and Della could only assume that Lord Bradford had spoken with her. Not that she cared, she told herself – she didn't give a toss what that dried-up old hag thought of her, nor anyone else. But she did care what Bradford thought of her, and, by extension, the duke. It would not do to address him incorrectly, and so she made scrupulous notes as Mrs. Cooper explained the correct way to greet the hostess at a dinner party, followed by reading passages aloud from the newspaper to practice her accent, eliminating any and all traces of Seven Dials.

That evening, after a pleasant enough dinner during which Bradford told her, much to her delight, that Dionysus had arrived from Headingly, she sat alone in her room, staring at the flames of the small fire burning in the grate. The wispy remnants of the wine she had drunk with dinner clouded her mind, but she had never known with such clarity what she must do. Determined, she stood and moved to the clothes press to withdraw her old skirt and bodice. She discarded the fine silk wrapper she wore and donned the patched clothes in its place. She drew the black velvet cloak over her shoulders once more, crossed to the doors, and stepped out into the night.

She stood in the fine drizzle for a few moments, breathing deep the damp, floral fragrance of the garden before she hoisted herself over the balustrade, clambered down the side of the house, and disappeared into the dark.

THIRTEEN

The next morning dawned with no sun to brighten the horizon, only the rustle of rain on leaves and the dull, muffled echo of the bells of Westminster Abbey ringing out to mark the beginning of service. Della looked out through the rain-streaked windows to the garden below, closing her eyes briefly against the throbbing in her head. Nights spent with Violet always seemed to result in wicked headaches the morning after, this being no exception, and while she didn't remember much of last night, she did recall her impassioned apology to her friend.

"I'm so sorry, Violet," she'd told her once she'd found her hidden away in her room, taking her few days off for her courses. "You were right – I'm bein' a terrible coward. I'll do this for us, I promise."

Violet had looked at her with pursed lips and narrowed eyes, and for a moment Della had been sure her friend would tell her to *fuck off*. Relief filled her when Violet's face broke into a wide smile and she gestured for Della to join her on the bed. She hugged her close and whispered, "I know you will, Dell. You're the cleverest person I know. We're so close, now. Don't give up."

Della could still feel her friend's reassuring embrace as the door to her room opened and Martha bustled in with a breakfast tray.

"Good morning, miss. Sleep well?"

And though Della's head still ached, a slow smile lifted the corners of her lips and she glanced back out the window. "I did, Martha. Very well."

Once dressed and coifed, Della made her way to the grand main staircase, but paused when she glimpsed Bradford standing in the hall below. He stood looking down at the credenza whereupon sat a small china shepherdess.

He turned as the velvet trim of her skirts rustled on the stairs, and graced her with a wide, open smile. Her belly tightened as she reached the bottom stair and he stretched forth his hand to take hers, sending a shiver skittering up her back as he took her arm.

"Another rainy day, I'm afraid. I thought today we might focus on perfecting the waltz – if that is acceptable to you," he added as he led her down the hall. She expected to make their way to the ballroom, but instead, he led her to the parlor where tea had been set upon the side table, but no servant waited to pour it. He gestured for her to take a seat and she did as he bade, never once taking her gaze from him as he crossed to the sideboard and took up, not the teapot, but the brandy decanter beside it. Della watched, wary, as he filled a glass, then turned to her and gestured to the decanter. She was about to decline, but then nodded and stretched forth her hand to accept the glass he handed to her. She took a slow sip as he eased into the wingback chair opposite her.

"There is something I need to discuss with you," Bradford began, taking a quick sip of his drink. Her heart immediately skipped a beat, and she was certain he would accuse her of stealing the figurine. A deep sense of dread began to grow in her chest as he cleared his throat before continuing, "I need to tell you something about myself."

A small sigh escaped her, the dread eased, and she took a sip without responding.

"I hope this will answer some questions for you, and why I have employed you. I realize I have been... reticent."

"Indeed," was all she said. She had been trying to work out her purpose for being here since he found her that day in the alley.

"I had to know I could trust you first," he continued as he set down his glass and leaned forward to rest his forearms on his knees. She was very careful not to look away as he said this, though her grip tightened on the glass.

"I am not simply Cole Winthrop, Earl of Bradford." He drew in a deep breath. "I am an operative for the British Home Office. A spy."

Della's mouth fell open. If he had told her he was a unicorn right then, she could not have been more shocked. She sat back in her seat and said nothing as he carried on.

"I hide in plain sight, you see. I hear things... I learn secrets. I'm a trusted peer of the realm, after all. My father was also a spy. He met my mother during the war in Crimea and I was born after they married and returned to England. My father had been working on an important case when he died, involving the Duke of Salisbury's father. He had long suspected the former duke of selling secrets to the Russians in exchange for paying off some significant gambling debts, even intercepting some letters between the duke's father and his Russian contact that he had been trying to decipher."

Della could only gape as he spoke, grasping to find sense in this information. The clock ticking on the mantel punctuated the quiet in the room.

"When he died, and the duke as well, shortly thereafter, the Home Office placed all his documents – the letters he kept, his notes, his journals, everything related to the investigation, into storage. I suppose there didn't seem to be any reason to continue, and it would have been a bad look politically to accuse one of the most powerful men in the country of treason when he was no longer alive to defend himself." Lord Bradford let out a slow breath and took another sip of his drink before meeting her gaze once more. "About a year or so ago, I began to receive intelligence from some of my agents in Russia that the current Duke of Salisbury might be corresponding with his father's old Russian contacts. Unfortunately, his father's debts did not end with his passing, and he is no doubt eager to pay them off, by whatever means necessary."

Della watched, wide-eyed, as the earl now stood, drink in hand, and began to pace, his voice growing tighter as he spoke. "I went into the archives at Whitehall to retrieve my father's files, hoping I might be able to finish what he had started, to confirm whether my intelligence about the current duke was true. And they were gone."

Della met his gaze when he finally turned, pausing beside the fireplace and raising his glass to swallow the remainder of his brandy.

"Salisbury stole them."

He nodded slowly. "He obviously had knowledge of their location – perhaps from his Russian contacts. I can only assume someone was paid a handsome sum to find them and bring them to him. I have no doubt he only intended to take his father's letters to prevent the scandal from becoming public but ended up with my father's other documents, as well."

He didn't look away from her as she considered this. "And what was in your father's documents?"

His jaw tensed now as he set his empty glass down upon the mantel. "Years' worth of notes about important operations, locations of safe houses, intelligence he had collected and who provided it." A dark shadow passed across his ordinarily kind countenance and Della shivered, unconsciously raising her glass and swallowing the remaining brandy. "He now possesses information which could put people's lives in danger. Their lives, and the lives of their families. And when he deciphers the many codes my father used and finds out it was him who gathered all this information... then my life may also be in danger."

Della swallowed back the growing tension rising in her chest as Lord Bradford turned away from her once more to stare down into the fire crackling in the hearth.

"I see..." She trailed off as the immense importance of her task began to weigh upon her. She shifted uncomfortably in her seat. "But surely there must be other ways to get to him than through me? Was he not investigated after the journals were stolen?"

At this point, Cole returned to his chair, dropping into it with a sigh as a frown furrowed his brow. "We did investigate him – but, as I said, he is an extraordinarily powerful man. We have no evidence to prove he was the one who took the documents and no way of knowing where he's keeping everything. In the end, one of my agents suggested something most... unconventional. A thief to take down a thief. A woman, to take advantage of the duke's weakness for them. And that's where you come in." Cole gave Della a wry smile. "You are a last resort, I'm afraid. We're running out of time – the duke has enlisted the help of a codebreaker, and you may be our last and best hope for getting back those documents before the code is deciphered." He gave her a wry smile. "So, you can see why I am not quick to trust others – a lesson every operative must learn, I'm afraid."

Della shifted in her seat, thinking of the guilt which had made her go back to Seven Dials for the figurine. "Why would Salisbury even want that information? Wouldn't having those letters be enough?" she asked, if only to change the subject.

The earl sighed again and shook his head. "The intelligence in those documents could potentially be worth a fortune to the right people – enough to pay off all the former duke's debts, with a tidy sum leftover. And no doubt it is also worrisome to Salisbury that there could be Home Office agents out there who know all about his father's treason." His gaze slid away from her to the fire once more. "They could stand in the way of his future ambitions."

Della frowned and shook her head. "Then why do this? You have all of this – why would you ever want to be involved with the Home Office?"

Bradford exhaled. "I have wanted to be like my father for as long as I've known he was an agent. He was a hero to me, and he sacrificed his life trying to expose Salisbury's father as a traitor."

Della's lips parted in silent astonishment before he continued, his voice low, his gaze never turning away from the fire as it crackled and spit in the hearth.

"He was working with a partner, trying to infiltrate the offices of someone believed to be a double agent, to find proof that Salisbury's father had passed along information to our enemies. He wasn't meant to be there. His partner had been tasked with retrieving the information, but he was set up, and my father was collateral damage." He closed his eyes. "A bomb had been planted. They were both murdered." Della held her breath, unwilling to break the strained silence before the earl opened his eyes and finally glanced over at her. "We couldn't even reveal what he had been doing when he died. It was covered up, and for all intents and purposes, he died of a heart attack." After a pause, a faint smile turned up his lips. "I think you'll find that is why Mrs. Cooper is rather protective of me. She had been with our family long before our parents died, and she stayed on after my father was killed. She was not keen on me following in his footsteps, but I couldn't imagine doing anything else. He passed before he was able to expose the duke's father, and I vowed I would bring the Dukes of Salisbury to justice in his honor. He risked a great deal to do what he did – he was barely allowed to marry my mother."

"Why not?"

He shrugged. "She was the daughter of a shipping merchant. Hardly an appropriate match for a peer. But he insisted – she had provided information to him during the war. Her name is in those documents, as well, as an informant." He gave her a knowing glance, and Della nodded slowly.

"I see..." It took her a moment to gather her thoughts and then let out a slow breath. "We should practice some more."

He met her gaze with the barest hint of a smile, but there was no humor in his eyes. "Yes, we should."

Clearing his throat, he stood to offer his hand to her. She took it with no small sense of foreboding, and the crushing weight of the burden on her shoulders was suddenly overwhelming. Something hot and uncomfortable tightened in her chest as he helped her and suddenly, she could not breathe as tears scalded the inside of her eyelids. She swayed against him, and he caught her as a sob lifted her chest and she gasped for air. She couldn't stop the rising panic and he grasped her arms in his large hands and turned her to face him.

"Miss Rose? Are you alright?"

She shook her head vigorously, not trusting to her voice. His breath was warm against her cheek, and she squeezed her eyes shut against the threat of tears, horrified by her reaction. What was wrong with her? "Yes, I'm so sorry, I just... I just..."

"Miss Rose. Della."

She opened her eyes, and there he was, his golden gaze boring into her. His grip tightened on her arms."If this is too much, you don't have to do this. I can find another way."

A shaky breath lifted her chest and she stared back at him, trying to find something in his tone, in his gaze, that would suggest something she knew to be deep inside everyone she had known in her life: deceit. She herself had it. Violet had it, so did Cora. She had never received anything in her life without the giver wanting something in return. How else did one survive in the world? But she couldn't hear it in his voice. She couldn't see it in his eyes. It was only truth he spoke to her; every word meant to reassure her. And as she tried to keep her heart hard to him, it softened just a little every time he looked at her with that piercing amber gaze and spoke words, not of harshness and aggression, but of warmth and caring.

And so, she swallowed back the fear and the rising sense that she was utterly unqualified for this task and shook her head. She would do as she had told Violet. She would get on with it and stop whinging. What had she to lose? She could not fall any lower, after all. "No. You said yourself I am your last chance. And I said I can do this. I *will* do this. I have to."

"Are you certain?"

"I am. I feel so silly. I have faced far worse things than a party in my life. And Violet will shame me to death if I fail at this."

Bradford smiled at this and released her arms with the softest brush of his fingers. "She sounds very wise, your friend."

"She is. And she deserves better than what she has."

"As do you, Miss Rose. Come, Mr. Avery can meet us in the ballroom."

He gestured for her to follow him and led her down a hall and through a set of tall double doors. Della couldn't help an appreciative gasp and she lifted her gaze to the soaring coffered ceiling of deep, rich oak. Half a dozen massive crystal chandeliers hovered overhead, some lit against the dreary morning. Two grand fireplaces sat at either end of the space, one with a fire banked up high to warm the cavernous room. Spotless parquet gleamed beneath her slipper-clad feet, and she watched as he crossed the space to the shining grand piano that sat in a bay window, awaiting the skilled fingers of Mr. Avery.

Bradford lifted the fallboard and plucked out a few notes, then turned to her with a smile.

"I'm afraid I haven't hosted many events here lately. I worried it might be out of tune."

"Really? I thought you'd be popular with the ladies at least. I thought they'd be beggin' for you to have parties," she said with a note of humor as he returned to her side and held out a hand. He raised a single brow as she placed her hand in his, and the look he gave her was the very definition of devilish.

"And why do you think I'd be popular with the ladies?"

Della's eyes widened and her face burned as she realized the implication of what she had said. His eyes sparkled with humor, and she tossed her head with a nonchalant sniff. "You're young and eligible. I don't know much about this world, but I'm certain an earl is a fine catch."

His lips quirked as he eyed her with suspicion, then his expression broke into a smile, and he lifted her hand, placed his arm around her waist and drew her into the steps for the waltz. "I suppose I am," he conceded as she tried to keep up with his footing.

"So why haven't you married?" she asked, realizing that it was, indeed, very odd that such a man had not yet secured his future with a wife and heirs. He tilted his head at the question, and then sighed as he swept her around in a wide circle.

"I was engaged, rather briefly, a few years ago. A lady I had known since childhood. We were very close, and she was a good friend. It had always been assumed by our families that we would marry, and we were perfectly happy with that arrangement. I suppose I loved her in my own way, and I trusted her. We told each other everything. Shortly after we were officially engaged..." He paused and gave her a fleeting expression of regret. "I decided I ought to tell her about my work. I wanted no secrets between us, especially if we were to be married. She... she did not take the news well. She did not want to be married to a man who did such work; knowing what happened to my father terrified her, and I can hardly blame her. She wanted a different life, one with the Earl of Bradford – and only the Earl of Bradford. She wanted me to resign from the Home Office and... I was not prepared to do that. I still had a promise to keep. We agreed to break off the engagement and I haven't bothered looking for anyone else since. My work takes me away from London often and the nature of it makes it... difficult to meet someone I can trust. What lady would want to be married to a spy?"

Della heard a sadness in his voice she had not noticed before, and rather thought this lady had broken his heart. She shrugged in kind as they moved across the spacious dance floor. "I don't know, wouldn't it be very glamorous? Travellin' the world, keepin' secrets, the danger, the mystery?"

Laughter bubbled up from his throat and he shook his head. "It is not all glamor, Miss Rose. No, I'm afraid it is dangerous and difficult work. And often lonely. It is not a life for a family."

"So, you do want a family?"

"Someday, perhaps. I am the Earl of Bradford, after all... people have certain expectations of me. If I am to continue the line, it stands to reason that I must marry and beget an heir." He paused and a small furrow appeared between his brows. "Though I never seem quite ready for that." He fixed her with a curious look. "And what of you, Miss Rose? Are there any wee babes in your future?"

She frowned as he drew her around in another wide arc. "I... I hadn't thought of it. I suppose I always assumed that life was out of reach for me. Babies don't belong in the rookery. I know that, and I wouldn't wish it on anyone."

"And what about now?"

"I dunno. Perhaps now, I can."

Della contemplated him for a moment as the pressure of his hand on her back increased and he drew her around in another sweeping circle. Those golden eyes of his, usually filled with such easy warmth, were now full of sorrow. She was shocked when she began to feel something that, up until this point in her life, she had thought was reserved for the weak and vulnerable – sympathy. This man was caught between his duty as an heir – something of which was entirely beyond her ken – and the pursual of his passion. Her hard little heart ached for him in that moment as the voluminous folds of her skirts tangled in his long, lean legs, for she well understood having a passion that no one else shared or supported. What she wouldn't give for someone apart from Violet to tell her that her dreams of scholarly education were more than just the silly notions of a silly female of no account, and that they were well worth pursuing.

Suddenly, she was taken back to that warm, sunny day by the pond. How his hungry gaze had devoured her, and how his lips has fallen upon hers as a starving man might fall upon a loaf of bread. She saw it now, the sadness in those golden eyes being overshadowed by a deep desire and she swallowed hard against the mounting warmth in her belly. Her lips parted as she moved closer to him, and his chest rose as the smile faded from his finely drawn mouth.

Not again, her mind shouted, but no other part of her seemed willing to resist and as they circled beneath the sparkling chandeliers, she found her heart racing in anticipation and her fingers entwining with his. He leaned in close and paused just above her lips, his breath ragged against her cheek. His hand moved, just a little, upon her back, and her head tipped back. His mouth touched hers then, barely, a sensation so gentle she couldn't be sure if he was kissing her or not. A moment passed, an eternity, and he pulled back. His amber gaze searched hers and all she could hear was the wild pounding of her heart; it seemed to be bursting from her chest. Time slowed; she began to regain her senses, and the doubt crept back for a moment, but fled as a shadow from the light when Cole's hands slipped up, over her shoulders and into her carefully coifed hair. He touched her face, and then, on a sharply indrawn breath, pulled her into him and claimed her lips with such force that her whole body seemed to ignite.

His mouth slanted across hers as he gathered her against him, his breath harsh against her lips, his fingers digging into the back of her bodice as if he would drag the gown off her right there in the ballroom. Desire pooled at the juncture of her thighs and rippled outwards until she felt she radiated it and she moaned, wanting more, wanting something she knew they couldn't have.

And then came the sound of the door opening and a male voice calling out, 'My lord?"

It was as though someone had thrown a bucket of ice water in her face. Della thrust him away, panting, and whirled to face the opposite wall to hide the naked desire she was sure was reflected in her gaze. Bradford cleared his throat as someone stepped into the room.

"Mr. Avery is here, my lord," the footman announced.

"Very good, Daniel. Do send him in." His voice was utterly calm and composed. There was no hint of what had been interrupted, and the sound of the door closing indicated the footman had left. Della turned back to face Bradford, her breath coming fast. He stared at her, his square jaw tense, before he cleared his throat once more and looked away.

"I am sorry, Miss Rose... I don't know what came over me."

She said nothing, just looked back at him, her chest rising and falling beneath the perfectly pleated folds of ivory lace on her bodice.

"I do," she finally said, took three quick strides to face him, and put her hands on the sides of his head to draw him back down to her lips, devouring him in a quick, desperate kiss that she broke off the moment the door latch clicked. This time, he did not look so composed when Mr. Avery stepped into the room, observed the scene before him, and nodded awkwardly.

"Good morning, my lord," he said, waiting for the earl's acknowledgement before moving into the room, files in hand.

"Good morning, Mr. Avery," he replied. His voice rattled for a moment, and he swallowed before he collected himself and that familiar, bright smile lit up his face.

"Are we ready to begin?" the tutor asked as he moved to the piano. He took his seat on the bench and twisted to look at them.

Bradford nodded, ever unflappable, and turned to face Della. "Are you ready?" he asked in a voice soft with promise. His gaze bored into her, and she stared right back at him, unfazed.

"I am."

"We are ready, Mr. Avery. A waltz, if you please," Cole called out, never taking his eyes off hers. Della nodded, the music began, and he swept her away.

FOURTEEN

"What is the time, Mr. Barrow?" Cole asked as he glanced into the mirror and straightened his bowtie.

"It is seven o'clock," the valet replied as he held up a set of gold cufflinks. Cole nodded in approval and held out one arm for him to affix the stud to his cuff. Once suitably attired, he turned to leave, but paused in the doorway. "Is Miss Rose ready to depart?"

"She is waiting in the parlor."

Cole's face was impassive as he nodded, but inside, anticipation made his stomach muscles tighten and he had to force himself to walk downstairs instead of dashing down like a child on Christmas morning. He reached the door and made himself stop, brush down the lapel of his tailcoat, and draw in a deep breath. His excitement to see her nearly made him forget how important this night was – nearly, but not quite. It was always at the back of his mind that this evening had to go smoothly. It was imperative that Della make an impression on their hosts so that word might reach the duke. An invitation to his annual charity ball would secure their chances of retrieving the letters.

He had confidence in her abilities. She had taken to her

lessons exceptionally well, though when they danced together, all he wanted to do was gather her up and kiss those lush pink lips and push his fingers into her thick, dark hair. It was wildly inappropriate – he knew that – but that enticing look in her eyes as they circled the ballroom floor held the promise of so much more. Under Mr. Avery's watchful eye, it was all they had – the hungry glances and surreptitious tightening of entwined fingers. They had not spoken of their kiss since it had happened; both, perhaps, afraid that they had imagined it and that to speak of it would be to confirm that it had been but a dream.

In the evenings alone in his room, as he pored through page after page of encrypted correspondence, gathered by informants abroad and throughout London, piecing together clues and information from various sources, his thoughts invariably strayed to her. She was but two doors away from him, and most nights it took all he had not to walk down the hall and knock on her door. She wouldn't be there, anyway. He knew she snuck out at night to visit her friend, even though he had insisted she was no prisoner here. It was in her nature to be clandestine, he supposed, for her own safety.

Composing himself, Cole pushed open the parlor doors and stepped inside. His gaze went straight to Della, who stood looking out the damask-draped window, the late summer sun highlighting the smooth contours of her narrow waist and bustled hips. She turned at the sound of the door opening, and his breath caught in his throat at the sight of her, for she was a sight to behold.

Martha had outdone herself this evening, and Della's rich dark hair had been caught up in a sweep of elegant coils wreathed in flowers to match her gown of rich deep blue trimmed in black velvet and lace flounces. Cole couldn't stop his gaze going to the long, smooth column of her neck, encircled by a strand of sparkling diamonds that had belonged to his mother, down to where the low neckline revealed the delicious curves of her breasts. What he wouldn't give to touch that flawless skin; to bury his face between those ripe peaks and inhale her scent. And then, following upon the heels of that thought, came the rational part of his mind to remind him, as always, of a heart broken long ago and the promise he had made to himself not to let it happen again. And Della Rose was a woman who was sure to leave broken hearts in her wake.

Her pale blue eyes were magnetic against the dark sapphire of her gown, the rich color selected specifically to help her shine in a sea of pink and cream and yellow tulle, which the other unmarried ladies were sure to wear. She wore pristine white gloves, and in them clutched a mother-of-pearl handled fan. She offered him an anxious smile as he came into the room and glanced down at herself.

"Cor, I'm bloody nervous... sorry!" she quickly added with an apologetic grimace. "How do I look?"

He paused for a moment, for words seemed inadequate to describe her exquisite beauty, then smiled at her. "Sublime. A stir shall be created tonight, I don't doubt."

Anxious laughter bubbled out of her, and she clasped the fan to her chest. "I don't know how eager I am to cause a stir," she said, slipping easily back into the practiced affectation of an aristocrat as he crossed to the sideboard and poured her a measure of whisky. She accepted it with a grateful sigh and downed the contents in a single gulp. Her fragrance reached him then, an intoxicating combination of powder and soap and lavender, and he cleared his throat as desire made his breath grow short. Damn, he was growing hard just standing beside her, imagining all the ways he should like to remove that exquisite gown and explore the soft curves of this hardened woman. *Stop it, Cole.*

"All part of the plan. The duke will not be attending tonight, so this party will be good practice. Now, you remember what we discussed?"

She nodded and looked thoughtful. "Yes. My name is Rose Victoria Winthrop, daughter of your uncle, The Honorable Robert Winthrop, and his wife Margaret Winthrop, living in Bamburgh, Northumberland, here to prepare for my first Season. I enjoy reading the classics and riding and have worked with the local parish to feed the poor of the northern counties. I seek an advantageous marriage that will allow me to move south and reside in London where my cousin, the Earl of Bradford, will help with my debut. I have had tutors from London my whole life and will serve my new husband well."

Cole nodded as he took a sip from his own glass. "Excellent. Come, the carriage will be waiting."

He bent his arm for her, and she came towards him in a rustle of silk taffeta and slipped her own through his. She trembled against his side, and he gave her arm an encouraging squeeze. "Have courage, Miss Rose. I know you shall dazzle the marquess and the marchioness, and once the duke hears word of you, he will do everything in his power to meet you. Once he does, it is only a matter of time before you charm your way into an invitation to his ball. And then... we will get back my father's documents and spare a good many lives."

Della managed a nod as they reached the front door and the butler gestured to the fine, glossy black barouche waiting in the sweeping drive. "Then let us be on our way."

Della's heart was fit to bursting as the carriage turned onto The Mall. They had rehearsed for the whole of the short ride to St. James' Park, and Bradford had drilled her one final time on proper conduct and how to address the various members of the peerage she was to meet. She must be bright and witty, but not overconfident, her voice must be soft and sweet, and she must act with every thought towards propriety. She kept in the back of her mind, however, the words Mr. Avery had spoken to her, for they gave her a measure of courage that all of Mrs. Cooper and Bradford's tutoring had not. *Don't hide what you are. Revel in it, utterly and completely.*

And so, she made a note that a duke was to be addressed as 'Your Grace', while the marquess should be called 'my lord' but determined that she would use what wiles and charisma she did possess to enchant Bradford's peers.

The elegant red brick mansion at which they arrived blazed with gaslight from every window, and a steady stream of well-dressed men and elegant ladies in their fashionably tight-fitting bustled gowns streamed through the wide-open front doors. Bradford's carriage rolled to a halt before the wide, curved stairs and he turned to her before the footman came to open the door.

"Are you ready?"

Della took a moment to remember why she was doing this, and the knife-edge she sat upon — a return to a small existence picking pockets to survive and losing any chance of leaving Seven Dials, or a comfortable life with Violet as a scholar, with all the books she could ever hope to read. She gave him a sharp nod and steeled herself when the door opened. The footman reached in to help her down and she hesitated for only a moment before placing her white-gloved hand into his and stepping onto the smooth gravel drive.

The strains of a lively polka wafted through the heavy evening air, and she pivoted to watch Bradford step down from the carriage. He looked damned fine, she had to admit, with his dark hair slicked back under a glossy black top hat, those golden eyes that missed nothing, his sharp nose and those sensual lips. He adjusted the lapel of his black tailcoat and was about to move forward when she shook her head and reached up to carefully straighten his white bowtie. He studied her as she did so, and his breath was warm upon her cheek as she appraised her handiwork for a moment before stepping back.

"Perfect," she declared, and he smiled that radiant smile of his and offered her his arm.

They walked up the steps to the main door where a footman waited to receive invitations. Almost immediately, Della could feel all eyes turn to them; words were whispered behind opened fans and brows raised in curiosity. Beside her, Bradford was utterly imperturbable as usual, and he nodded and tipped his hat to the occasional acquaintance. Della's throat was dry, and she'd have killed for another glass of whisky to soothe her jangling nerves. Though she gave no outward hint of it, always careful to keep her expression impassive, inside she quaked with fear and apprehension. Surely they could see it; surely they could see through the fine black velvet cloak and no doubt exorbitantly expensive dress that she was a fraud? But no one called out; no one walked up to her and yelled 'Thief!', and they reached the landing with nary a word of protest.

Bradford leaned close to whisper in her ear, "There, the couple by the door – they are the Marquess and Marchioness of Colchester, our hosts for the evening. She is the one you must impress tonight – it will be her approval that will gain us admittance to Salisbury's ball in a month's time."

Della swallowed back the momentary rise of panic and nodded without looking over at Bradford. They strolled, arm in arm, following the line of guests ahead of them, until they were face to face with their hosts. The marchioness was a tall, slender woman of about forty with a crown of deep blonde hair arrayed with red roses to match the deep ruby silk moiré gown she wore. Her eyes, a friendly green, lit up upon seeing Bradford and she exclaimed to her husband, standing a small distance away, "My darling, it's Lord Bradford. We have not seen you in an age!" Her tone was accusing as the earl inclined his head and gestured to Della standing beside him.

"A fact I mean to remedy tonight. Lord and Lady Colchester, may I present to you my cousin, Miss Rose Winthrop of

Haversham Estate in Northumberland. She is staying with me in preparation for her first Season."

Della dipped into the curtsey Mrs. Cooper had made her practice until her legs and back screamed in agony, rising as the marchioness regarded her with a warm expression.

"Bradford, you did not tell me you had a cousin quite so fetching," the marquess remarked with a raised brow. Della gave him a carefully rehearsed shy smile.

"Thank you, my lord and my lady. It is a pleasure to make your acquaintances. You have a beautiful home." Della's voice was smooth and practiced, not a hint of Seven Dials to be heard.

"Thank you, dear. Lord Bradford, how have you been? I have not seen you since the Earl of Leicester's party in the spring."

"Very well, my lady. Out of the country, mostly. I visited my sister in New York for a spell."

"Ah, how is Adelaide?"

"She is well – they are expecting again. She's due near Christmas."

The marchioness smiled. "How exciting. Will you be leaving us again once the Season is over?"

"I had planned to visit some acquaintances I made in Paris on my Grand Tour."

The marquess laughed and nudged his wife with an elbow. "You see, darling – hasn't a wife and a brood to keep him home so he's off galivanting about the world. Lucky devil." He winked at the earl who returned the expression with a grin and a nod towards the marchioness.

"Ah, but not quite as lucky as you, my lord."

The lady rolled her eyes and grinned before glancing towards Della. "Miss Winthrop, how are you finding London?"

All eyes turned to her, and Della's face grew warm as she called upon the serene smile she had been rehearsing. "It is very different from Bamburgh, I must say. It's very loud and crowded. But my cousin is a gracious host, and I am having a lovely time."

"That is wonderful news," Lady Colchester said before turning a sly smile towards Bradford. "Lady Sarah was asking after you again. I do believe she's expecting a dance tonight."

"Is she?" he replied with mild amusement and Della raised an eyebrow.

"I believe she is determined to become Lady Bradford."

His arm stiffened beneath her touch but the laugh he let out was carefree. "She is a persuasive young woman. She may yet win me over."

The couple shared a laugh as Della swallowed back the rising tension in her chest.

"Have you met Lady Sarah yet, Miss Winthrop?" The marquess now spoke up and Della's cheeks stretched in a smile.

"I have not, though I should be glad to meet anyone who can finally get my cousin to the altar." She leaned closer at this point as if imparting a great secret. "The family is most concerned he shall never marry, and who will look after him then? He's hopeless on his own, as I have come to see!"

The couple tittered with laughter before the marchioness nodded towards Bradford, who looked down at his companion with a raised brow. She grinned back at him.

"Do take care to watch her, Lord Bradford – she's a sharp one!" Lady Colchester's gaze suddenly went past Bradford's shoulder and lit up in recognition. "Ah, my lord, you do remember the Duke of Salisbury? Your Grace, I did not expect to see you tonight!"

Della froze. She turned her wild gaze to Bradford who merely gave his head an imperceptible shake and tightened his grip on her arm. Nothing in his expression changed; if he was shocked it did not register as he turned with her to face the new arrival.

Somehow, she didn't know why, Della had expected a short,

squat man, older, unattractive. Wasn't that how all men in power ended up looking? The corruption marking their physical selves – it always seemed so in the cartoons she read in the occasional copy of *Punch* magazine she was able to pick out of the trash. However, this man was tall, almost rakish in his appearance as he sauntered up the steps, his shoes polished to a mirror-shine, his shirt crisp snowy white against the rich black of his tailcoat and trousers. But where Bradford was dark and magnetic in his appearance, the duke was fair and grey-eyed, lean where the earl was heavy with muscle, and there was something in his eyes – something dark. No one here would see it, but Della did. He lifted a white-gloved hand to his top hat and tipped it towards the earl before lowering his hand to touch his chest.

"Ah, Bradford, it has been some time, hasn't it? How do you do?"

"Very well, Your Grace." Bradford's arm squeezed hers again, and she drew in a deep breath and straightened her shoulders. "Please allow me to introduce my cousin, Miss Rose Winthrop. She will be staying with me in preparation for the Season."

Della held her breath as the duke turned his attention to her. His gaze raked over her, assessing, and his lip curled up in just the barest hint of a smile. He said nothing for a moment, just stared back at her, and she had a sudden, mad inclination.

"It is an honor to meet you, Your Grace," she said, dipping into a graceful curtsey. "Cousin, would you be so kind as to take my cloak? I am quite warm."

She looked sidelong at Bradford, who gave her the smallest indication of a conspiratorial smile and nodded. "Of course."

Della turned back to the duke, looked up at him with batting eyelashes, and never took her gaze from his as the earl reached up to slip the cloak away. She was careful to delicately lift each shoulder as the velvet pulled away from her body before she offered Salisbury the most suggestive smile she could manage as the shock wore away. They now had to rethink their plans, and in a hurry.

The duke seemed to collect himself and bent in a graceful bow, his hand still upon his chest. "The honor is all mine, Miss Winthrop. I do hope you will save me a dance?"

Della bit her lip and allowed one of the other guests passing by to bump into her so that she was forced to step closer to him; close enough that he would be able to smell her perfume. She raised a hand to her décolletage, bared to his gaze now, as though in shock. His eyes followed the gesture and he swallowed.

"How could I refuse?" She kept her voice low, so that he had to lean closer to hear her, and she grinned as Bradford spoke up beside her.

"Cousin, will you allow me to take you to the ladies' room? Lord and Lady Colchester, I do hope we see you again tonight. Your Grace." Bradford nodded to the duke, who still held Della's gaze, and he looked to the earl with an irritated expression. "I will be sure Miss Winthrop saves you a spot on her card."

The duke looked satisfied with this, and she could feel him watching her as they walked away. And then, to be sure that the duke would, indeed, come to find her, she swayed her hips provocatively beneath her bustled gown, letting the train rustle elegantly behind her, a tactic that would make Violet proud. The earl let out a small laugh beside her, but she did not dare look at him as he murmured in a low voice only she could hear in the press of people surrounding them, "Never in all my days."

She finally angled her head to observe him as they left the main hall and moved down a quieter corridor to the ladies' room. "So?" she asked as they paused outside the door. She withdrew her arm from his and looked at him with an expectant expression. He appeared impressed.

"Never have I seen such masterful manipulation. Most of the young women here have been raised to know how to flirt, but I have never seen anything quite as skillful as that display. I think we have secured our invitation to the ball next month."

Della let out a short laugh. "You can thank Violet for that — I learned it all from her. I don't suppose this means we can leave now?"

He gave a rueful shake of his head. "I'm afraid he will be expecting a dance now. Go ahead, freshen up and I will check your cloak for you. I'll meet you here when you're done."

Della bobbed her head in agreement and watched him move back down the hall.

The room she entered was bright with gaslight, and she coughed as a cloud of face powder filled her lungs. A maid in attendance offered her a glass of water and she accepted it with a small smile. She took only a moment to check her reflection in the gilt-framed mirror in the next room, apply the smallest amount of powder to her nose and forehead and adjust the low neckline of her stylish blue gown. She looked around for a moment to make sure no one else was in attendance, then slipped a hand down inside her corset and lifted her breasts up as high as they would sit beneath the stiffened whalebone. She smirked at her reflection and gave her cheeks a pinch for good measure. She would bet the entire ten thousand pounds she was due that no other ladies here would utilize Violet's trick for enhancing her décolletage.

She was about to turn to leave when she espied a group of ivory-handled brushes and combs set upon a delicate gilt table in the corner and glanced around once more before plucking up one of the combs and slipping it down her bodice. She patted her chest to make sure it was secure before smoothing down her hair and leaving the room.

Bradford was not in the hall waiting for her, but someone else was.

"Your Grace?" she said in a careful voice as the duke pushed himself away from the damask-papered wall where he casually leaned. He took a moment to study her, his grey eyes raking down her form and pausing where she had lifted her breasts up so invitingly. Ordinarily, she would have recoiled from such a nakedly lewd look, but instead she tilted her head and turned up one corner of her lips in a sensual smile. "May I help you?"

"Miss Winthrop, I hoped I would find you here. I wanted to make certain we had an opportunity to dance this evening, so I took the liberty of filling out a dance card for you."

He handed over the small, folded card attached to a scrap of ribbon and a small pencil, and she took it with a trill of laughter, noting when he touched his chest once more, seemingly out of habit. He had taken it upon himself to fill out several dances with his name, an amount that was sure to cause a stir.

"Your Grace, though I am exceedingly flattered, do you not think it unseemly to fill out so many spots? I rather think there might be unflattering gossip should I keep you for the whole of the evening."

The duke's face was inscrutable as he stepped closer to her – closer and closer again until she found her back against the wall in an effort to maintain an appropriate distance.

"Perhaps," he said in a low voice. "Perhaps you are right." His arm came up and he braced a hand against the wall behind her, as though to trap her there. Rose would not object; that persona would smile nervously and titter like a schoolgirl at the very idea of a duke paying her such attention. But Della, buried far beneath the weeks of strict tutoring, flinched at his closeness and the vague threat in his voice. The instinct to drive her knee into his groin and shout at him to fuck off rose inside her and he leaned in close as though he would kiss her. Her face ached with the effort it took to keep smiling as the faint scent of his expensive cologne enveloped her.

"I should say that the other ladies would be positively green with envy were you to dance with me. The Duke of Salisbury is a sought-after man."

Della swallowed back the dangerous growl mounting inside her throat and looked down, as though terribly flattered. "Your Grace, I am new to London and would hate to offend the other ladies here. I am certain there are many present who would also like to dance with you tonight. Please do spare them some of your worthy time."

He said nothing. She dared a glance up and saw he watched her with a predatory gleam in his eyes, his face uncomfortably close to hers. "How very gracious of you. I shall abide by your wishes, Miss Winthrop. Let the others have their turn. But I will come find you when I am ready." His arm dropped down, and he was careful to let it brush across her bodice. A spark of rage ignited inside her and her hands clenched at her sides as he stepped away with a smirk. All the while, she kept that stupid smile on her face, and she hated herself for it.

"Cousin?"

A welcome voice sounded from down the hall, and she whipped around to see Bradford advancing down the corridor.

"Ah. Bradford, there you are. I had come to bring Miss Winthrop a dance card and ask if she would favor me with a waltz tonight."

The earl's gaze shifted down to Della's clenched fists and then lifted to the duke and he offered a beatific smile. "I am certain she would be honored. I wanted to let you know that the marquess was looking for you just now."

The duke gave a distracted nod, looked at Della once more with a suggestive glance and stepped away. "Very good. Thank you, Bradford."

He walked away with a confident swagger, Della glaring at

his receding form. "She bloody well would not be," she muttered, the smile wiped from her face.

"What did he do?" Bradford's voice was low and dangerous as his gaze followed Salisbury until he disappeared into the crowd in the lobby.

"He did nothin' that any other man who thinks himself better than others wouldn't do – he thought I would fall over myself for him and made a fool of himself."

Bradford's expression showed his concern as he faced her. "I do hope he wasn't overly familiar?"

Her lips tightened and her face ached from the false smile. "Not more than any drunk on a Saturday night. Don't worry about me; I know how to handle men like him. They've never heard no, and it's best to keep it that way if you want to keep them soft." She turned to him then with the same false smile on her face and offered her arm. "Shall we join the party?"

The earl frowned at her before taking her arm and walking with her back towards the hall. He said nothing, but Della smiled inwardly and touched her bodice with her free hand. The ivory comb lay nestled inside. So, too, did the duke's pocket watch and fob, and she considered that worth a leering glance or two.

FIFTEEN

Cole watched with a practiced eye as the duke swept Della across the dance floor in a lively polka. She looked up at him with an adoring smile, though Cole knew her well enough by now to see the spark in her eyes that indicated her displeasure. She burst out in a pretty laugh as they brushed by where he stood on the edge of the dance floor, champagne in hand. His fingers tightened on the delicate crystal stem as Salisbury's hand slipped down her back – lower than what would be deemed appropriate, but Cole knew that if anyone could manage the duke's indiscretions, it was her.

"It would be quite a match, Lord Bradford," said a voice behind him and he turned to see the Marchioness of Colchester nodding towards the couple.

"It would be, my lady." He took a sip of his drink. "It's everything her family could have hoped for."

"His mother will not approve." The marchioness shook her head. "The daughter of an earl's youngest son who has hidden himself up north? She may have her sights set higher for marriage for her son."

"I don't think marriage is what the duke has in mind for my cousin." Cole's lips pursed, and she chuckled.

"She looks as though she can manage him," she said, echoing Cole's thoughts.

"I assure you, she can."

"I found it odd that you had not mentioned her before today."

Cole finally turned to look at the marchioness, who watched him with narrowed eyes. He shrugged. "I haven't seen my uncle's family since I was a lad."

She frowned. "I thought you were there last summer?"

Cole gave her a knowing look and she nodded slowly. "A ruse?"

"I was in France – one of our ambassadors was causing trouble. As it stands, I have not seen my cousin since she was a wee girl. My uncle does seem keen on maintaining his distance from our family, though he did ask me to do her the favor of finding someone to sponsor her, as she has no other family in London."

"Ahh," was all she said in reply. She watched them dance for a moment, then inclined her head towards the other guests who also seemed enraptured by the couple. "You'll have to watch her. A beautiful young lady like that – she'll break some hearts."

Cole's gaze returned to Della, and he watched her step lightly across the floor, her skirts rustling, her movements economical yet graceful, as befitting a professional thief. As he had predicted, in a sea of pink and cream tulle, she stood out like a rare sapphire, mysterious in her strangeness, magnetic in her undeniable beauty.

"She will indeed," Cole replied, distracted, as the marchioness took a sip of her drink. Something rose inside his chest as he observed Della's fingers tighten upon Salisbury's arm and her eyes flash with rage. Not jealousy – no, how could he be jealous of a man she clearly despised? – but something else. A longing. An unbidden need. And though he knew this evening was pivotal in gaining them access to Salisbury's party, he wanted nothing more than to be out there on that floor with her, fingers laced with hers, hearing the rasp of her breath as she twirled and dipped with the music. It galled him that it should be Salisbury of all people guiding her beneath sparkling chandeliers to the romantic strains of Chopin.

"And what of you, Cole?"

Cole turned when the marchioness spoke up once more, her use of his given name unsurprising considering how long they had known one another. "What of me, Jane?" he replied with a smile.

"What of your broken heart?"

Cole's smile faded and he raised his glass to his lips but tasted nothing as the champagne went down his throat. Jane's look was sympathetic as she observed him.

"It was a long time ago. I have rather moved on since then."

She tilted her head and gave him a suspicious look. "I bounced you on my knee when I was but a girl, and I think I know you well enough by now to know that is utter rubbish."

The weight of that statement sat heavy upon Cole's heart, and he swallowed back the last of his drink. "What can I say, Jane? I thought I had someone I could trust, someone who would accept all parts of me. I will be very careful not to make that mistake again."

Jane shook her head and laid her hand over his. "Just because you cannot trust anyone in your profession does not mean you cannot trust anyone in love."

Cole sighed and glanced out towards the dance floor where Della moved through the couples like a rare jewel in a sea of pastels before he turned his attention back to the marchioness. "Ah, but you see, Jane – it is because of my profession that I find it so very hard to trust anyone I love."

Jane gave a rueful shake of her head and withdrew her

hand. "Does she know?" she asked, nodding towards Della. Cole followed her line of sight and was once again startled by his reaction to her. It always seemed to come from nowhere: a skip of his heart, a tug at his cock, a sudden longing for that fierce, dark-haired beauty.

"No," he said after a pause. "No – my uncle never approved of my father's work, especially after his death. I doubt he would approve of me continuing it."

Jane offered him a quick smile as the marquess waved to her from the other side of the dance floor. "I will keep my eye out for any trustworthy ladies. Enjoy the evening, Cole," she said as she disappeared back into the crowds. Inexorably, his gaze returned to the dance floor and he longed to hold Della in his arms, longed to kiss her again. And he knew he was falling for her.

"You're a fool, Cole," he muttered to himself.

The clinking of glasses and the swelling of the music as the band struck up a waltz surrounded Cole and his head began to ache as he caught snatches of conversations.

"Word has it she was caught alone with Sir..."

"He wants to marry Miss Chamberlain, perish the thought..."

"I wanted five yards of silk brocade, but they only had damask and I simply cannot..."

"Good evening, Lord Bradford," said a soft voice behind him then, and he turned with a distracted frown to see none other than Lady Sarah Eastwood, daughter of the Marquess of Sedgwick. She offered him a shy smile before he remembered himself and sketched a quick bow.

"Good evening, Lady Sarah. You look radiant as ever – how does the evening find you?"

The young woman, fair-haired and petite, blushed furiously and dipped into a quick curtsey. "Very well, my lord," came her breathy reply. "And yourself?"

Cole glanced towards the dance floor and caught Della's gaze before Salisbury twirled her away. If he were not mistaken, her eyes had narrowed at Lady Sarah before she had been pulled across the dance floor, but he quickly dismissed the notion before he turned back to the young woman. "I am well, thank you, my lady. May I fetch you a drink?"

"No, thank you," she replied, holding up the glass that had been hidden at her side. He nodded, certain he could feel pale blue eyes fixed upon him and doing everything in his power not to turn back to the dance floor.

"I understand your sister is engaged?"

She bobbed her head. "Yes, to the Earl of Devon. They are to be wed next spring. The earl has a lovely estate in Cambridge – Wolton Manor. Have you been there?"

Cole caught a glimpse of dark blue silk out of the corner of his eye and forced his attention back to the young woman before him, swathed in pale cream tulle. "I believe so, years ago for a hunting party. He has an impressive stable."

"He does, indeed – my sister is forever telling me I ought to join them at the races, but I find all that fuss and noise so very tiresome. I rather prefer the country." She gave an awkward smile and took a quick sip of her drink. "The marchioness tells me your cousin is visiting."

"She is." Cole willed himself not to look out at the dance floor for Della. "She will be staying in preparation for her first Season."

"How lovely that you will be here. I did not see you much last Season." Her dark eyes widened with delight at the prospect.

"I was traveling abroad. I would be away this year, as well, but my uncle asked that I help my cousin with her coming out. Do you travel much, Lady Sarah?"

Her hopeful expression fell just a little and she shook her

head. "No... I'm afraid I get homesick rather easily. I suppose that makes me rather dull, but I know what I like." She trailed off as she realized the implication of her words, but Cole leaned close and offered her a secretive smile.

"Only the most interesting people are so certain of themselves and aren't afraid to say it. It's very brave, and certainly not dull. I hope you can find someone just as brave to share the quiet of the country with you." He straightened then and offered his hand. "May I have this dance, Lady Sarah?"

An understanding look came into her eyes and she smiled. "I would be honored," she replied in a soft voice as she set down her glass and took his hand to follow him out onto the dance floor. He caught Della's frown across the flurry of dancing couples and offered a slight shrug in reply as he swept Lady Sarah around in an elegant circle.

"Your cousin must be in search of a husband from the city," Lady Sarah said, and Cole looked down at her with a questioning glance.

"Yes, her father hopes she will find an advantageous match and be able to live here. He thinks she's too lonely all the way up north."

There was a pause. "And what of you, Lord Bradford?"

"Me?"

"Yes... I have not yet seen you find yourself a bride. I thought perhaps having your cousin here would inspire you to your own search for a match. When you broke off your last engagement, many had been certain you had done so for another woman."

Cole allowed a small smile for her as they twirled between the other dancers. "Alas not, my lady. No, I had simply not been a good match for her, nor she for me. I cannot seem to stay in one place for very long and I fear it rather puts off many ladies."

"So you require an adventurer?" Lady Sarah asked with an

arch of her brow as a smile played about her lips. Cole chuckled.

"I don't suppose you know of any adventurers living in the greater London area?"

She giggled as the music came to an end with a flourish. "I'm afraid not. But if I can find someone to share the quiet with, I have no doubt you will find someone to share the noise."

Those words stuck with Cole as he took her arm to lead her from the dance floor.

"Thank you for the dance, Lord Bradford," she said in a quiet voice as he guided her back to her chair. "I do hope you enjoy the rest of your evening."

"Lady Sarah," he replied, bending in a bow. "It has been a sincere pleasure. I wish you all the very best."

She glanced up at him with understanding, and then nodded with the faintest of smiles. He paused to think on her words before he turned back to the dance floor, his gaze immediately seeking out the one who set his heart on fire with but a look. He caught sight of her at the opposite end of the floor as she pushed herself away from the duke a little too forcefully. She said something to which he nodded before he escorted her to where Cole waited with an impassive expression.

"Thank you again, my lady. It was a pleasure."

She said nothing, just bent in a stilted curtsey and smiled back at him as he dropped into a low bow and disappeared into the crowd.

When she turned to Cole, the smile had left her face, but her cheeks were flushed pink. She said not a word but grabbed his hand and pulled him away from the dance floor, forcing him to follow. It wasn't until they reached the relative quiet of the refreshment room that she finally turned to him and spoke. "Who was that?"

Cole frowned as he drew her into a small alcove since her voice now fairly seethed with anger. "That was Lady Sarah."

Della sniffed. "Ah, the one tryin' to get you to marry her. She looked rather dull."

"There is no need to be unkind. I have known her for a long time, and she is a good person."

"A little too good, I should say." Della said this in an offhand manner as she gazed out over the room, but the words struck him to his core as she seized upon the very thoughts he had kept to himself – that Lady Sarah would be just as uncomfortable with his being a spy as his fiancée had been. Della glanced back at him with a frown.

"May we go now?"

Cole held up a hand for a moment and turned to fetch a glass of water from one of the servants bearing trays of drinks. He handed it to her and she raised it to take a sip.

"The duke looked rather pleased after your dance."

"I should say so," she said, her breath still coming fast. "He invited me to go ridin' in Hyde Park next week. I told him I'd be delighted."

Cole's eyes widened. "Surely you jest? He's already invited you riding?"

Della tilted her head and gazed up at him with fluttering eyelashes, an exaggerated imitation of the look she had no doubt used on Salisbury. "But of course. I'm not some innocent schoolgirl like the simpering twits here. I know what men really want, and it ain't pretty giggles and hiding behind a fan." She rolled her eyes and set down the glass. "Have they anything stronger? I don't want to remember the feel of his hands on me in the morning. He makes my skin crawl."

Cole frowned as a footman passed with a tray of champagne. She plucked up one of the glasses and drained it in a single mouthful. One of the matrons behind her gasped in outrage and he cleared his throat and took Della by the arm to lead her from the room. When they reached an empty corridor, he turned her to face him. Her otherworldly eyes snapped with anger. "You don't have to go through with this, Della. Say the word and I will pay you for your time and send you on your way."

"Don't be a fool," she spat at him. "I'm not going to let him get away with what he's done. Let him go on being a smug bastard while he threatens others' lives just to save his own damn skin? Not on your life." She jerked her head in the direction of the cloakroom. "But I'm done for tonight. We got what we wanted. You can tell them I have a headache or whatever's suitable, but I want to go."

Cole put a hand on her arm to draw her attention back to him. He caught her wild gaze with his. "I'm so very proud of you, Miss Rose. You did an exemplary job tonight. Of course, we may go. Though I do think the marchioness may be disappointed when she realizes we've gone. I think she's quite taken with you."

"Taken with me?" Della asked in an incredulous tone as they crossed the lobby to the cloakroom. "Why would she have any interest in me?"

Cole handed their ticket to the footman who withdrew to fetch their cloaks. "Lady Colchester does have a fondness for debutants who show a bit of... gumption. She is something of a social director in her circles. She can make you the talk of the Season – or ensure that you die a spinster. You would do well to stay in her good books."

Della snorted in derision. "Why? So I can marry an earl? A baron? The duke?" She accepted the cloak the footman handed to her a moment later with a smirk. "Tell me, my lord, what will you tell these people once I get you what you need and I pack up and leave?"

Cole drew his own cloak over his shoulders before taking hers from her hands. The planes of her face had hardened once more; Rose Victoria Winthrop was gone, and Della Rose of Seven Dials had returned. He laid the cloak over her shoulders and his gloved fingers brushed against her bare skin for a fleeting instant. A shiver raced down his spine as the wild thought of what lay beneath all that silk and lace crossed his mind, and he cleared his throat. "I simply intend to tell them that you did not find London agreeable and that your father has arranged a marriage to one of the Scottish lords for you, and so you returned to Northumberland."

She nodded slowly as they made their way through the throngs to the front door. A footman swung it open for them and they stepped out into the cool night air.

"I'll have them bring the carriage round," he said, turning to the footman, but Della laid a hand over his arm.

"Could we walk? I need some fresh air. It isn't far and it's a fine night."

Cole glanced up at the clear night sky dotted with stars. He looked back down at her, at the flushed cheeks and the wide blue eyes, and how could he possibly say no? "I would like that very much."

Della drew in a deep, ragged breath to calm herself as Bradford asked the footman to tell his driver to go home ahead of them, then turned to her with a bent arm. She took it with a faint smile and drew her cloak tight about her shoulders as they made their way down the steps and out onto the street. Carriages trundled past, but as they strolled farther away from the Colchesters' glittering mansion, the street grew quieter until they reached Constitution Hill. They walked in silence but for the far-off clop of hooves and the faint rustle of the wind through the trees. A few other passersby tipped their hats towards them, and finally Della spoke.

"I suppose I'll have to practice my riding this week."

"There are practice rings at the stables – we'll go tomorrow afternoon."

She glanced up at the dark night sky and the shaky sensation of her rage began to subside. The earl's body was warm and solid beside her, and he slowed his long stride to allow for the heavy, bow-bedecked train trailing behind her. Yes, she knew now what kind of man the duke was, and she was more than happy to do whatever lay in her power to bring him to justice. Just the memory of his words as they had danced made her shudder.

"You are a rare beauty, Miss Winthrop," he'd told her on the dance floor, with an arm around her waist. "Why has your cousin not mentioned you before today?"

Della had released a breathless giggle as Salisbury pulled her along the dance floor. He was a fine dancer, she allowed. But his hand wandered low, down over the curve of her hip, and she worried the other dancers would see and remark upon it. That was not the sort of stir she wished to create tonight.

"I have not seen my cousin in many years. I was certain he had forgotten about me until my father contacted him." She'd needed to think quickly. The sooner she could garner that invitation, the better. "He has been very kind to find a sponsor for me. He has even allowed me to bring my own horse from home."

This piqued the duke's interest, as Bradford had promised it would. "Your own horse? Do you go riding often?"

"Not as often as I should like. Lord Bradford has promised to take me riding in Hyde Park during my stay. I am told a great many marriages are made there." She had made the comment in an offhand manner, but the look she gave him was knowing.

"I can hardly imagine any man would not be interested in your hand." He gave hers a meaningful squeeze and she bit her lip. His gaze dropped to the gesture and his grasp tightened around her waist. Everything in her being wanted to slap him across the face, but she forced a sweet smile. He touched his chest again, she noted with suspicion.

"You must allow me to accompany you. I will be at Rotten Row next week – Wednesday. Be there." It was not a request; it was a command. Undoubtedly, he was not accustomed to asking for what he wanted. She gave him a sly smile and reached up to brush her hand down the front of his immaculate white shirt, fanning to feel for whatever seemed to so occupy his thoughts. He stiffened and she immediately withdrew. "Perhaps. I shall have to check my schedule, of course. I have been so very busy, and there is so very much to see in London." That dark look she had noticed came into his eyes once more, but Della was prepared for this. She smiled again. "But I could hardly refuse the invitation of the Duke of Salisbury. I shall be there."

The darkness evaporated and he offered her a smug grin as the music ended. Relief flooded through her as she pushed him away before the last note had even played, always careful to keep that suggestive smile on her lips and her lashes fluttering prettily. He escorted her to the edge of the dance floor where Bradford waited for her, his expression guarded. She had nodded to the duke and sighed in relief when he disappeared back into the crowd.

Della shook her head to rid herself of the memory of his cloying touch as she and Bradford reached the top of Constitution Hill and, without a word to one another, continued through the small park as though reluctant to turn and go home.

"May I confess something to you?" Della asked as they paused beside Wellington's great monument. Bradford glanced down at her, his gaze searching hers in the light of the gas lamps overhead.

"Of course."

It was on the tip of her tongue; she was going to pull out the watch from inside her bodice and tell him she had taken it from the duke when he had cornered her outside the ladies' room. Her hand inched upwards, then paused. She bit her lip. "I... I took that little china shepherdess. The one on the table by the stairs. I took it the first day I met you. I was going to sell it. But I… but I brought it back. I didn't want you thinking one of the servants had taken it."

A faint smile lifted his lips. "I know."

"You do? Why didn't you say anything?"

He lifted his shoulders and turned to face her. "I didn't want you to distrust me. I wanted the decision to return it or not to be your own. Why do you think I told you—"

Della saw the glint of the knife behind Bradford – the man had materialized unseen from the shadows – and she shoved the earl to the side as she let out an inarticulate shout of warning. The knife sliced down at the empty space and when it reached the bottom of its arc, she snarled and threw her body weight at the attacker. A solid wall of muscle met her, but the man had not accounted for the lady in the expensive ballgown to be a child of the streets. She swore at him as she raked her fingernails down his shadowed face and drove her knee into his groin, cursing when her heavy ruffled skirts impeded her movements. A meaty fist struck her shoulder as a raspy voice snarled 'Bitch!' and she fell to the ground as pain exploded through her side.

She gritted her teeth against the rush of rage and started to push herself up off the damp grass when she heard a shout of warning and looked up to see Bradford collect himself and turn to face the man with the knife. He said not a word, but he shook out his shoulders, lined himself up, and connected with the attacker's nose in a clean, efficient jab. The man stumbled back, stunned, clearly not expecting the retaliation of a well-dressed couple strolling in the park late at night. He swiped at his bloodied nose, lashed out with the knife, and was immediately knocked back with another swift uppercut to the jaw.

"Drop the knife." Bradford's voice was deadly as he stood with fists at the ready, hunched in anticipation, his golden gaze lethal. A muscle in his jaw twitched as Della sat, panting, waiting for him to make a move. The footpad's eyes narrowed as he seemed to contemplate whether the obvious wealth of the couple was worth the fight.

"Drop it," Bradford repeated, his steely gaze never leaving his opponent. Della, heart hammering, pushed herself up from the ground and limped up, unseen, behind the man. With an angry grunt, she grabbed a fistful of his hair and wrenched his head to the side. The man swore as he swung for her with his free hand, but the earl leapt forward, tackling the man to the ground. He landed with a grunt before pressing down on the footpad's free arm with his knee and grabbing the other arm to wrench away the knife. The other man finally shoved Bradford away and jumped up before spitting at them and turning to retreat into the shadows.

Bradford pushed himself off the grass and started forward as though he would go after the man, but Della reached out and put a hand on his arm. "Let him go – he's just hungry and desperate. He'll lose himself in Seven Dials, you'll never find him."

He turned slowly to Della, knife in hand, gasping. She stared back at him, feeling as though her chest was about to burst as she sucked the crisp night air into her lungs.

"Are you hurt?" he asked.

She shook her head, even though a sharp pain shot up her arm when she moved it.

"You saved my life." His amber eyes were wide, his mouth agape as he looked at her.

"I..."

She gasped as he dropped the knife and tugged her against him to crush his lips to hers. In an instant, the walls she had built up inside her to hold her desire for him in check crumbled, and she answered his searing kiss with a groan that emerged from some deep, dark place inside her, a place she had long fought to ignore. She arched her back and reached up to rake her fingers through his hair and pull him down to her, meeting the thrust of his tongue with her own, almost sobbing from the heat which roared through her and burned in her chest.

His fingers slid into her hair, his touch sizzling along her nerve endings, dislodging flowers and hairpins as his mouth slanted across hers, bruising her lips as though he could not bring her close enough. She didn't care anymore; she didn't care that she would be gone from his life in another month. She just wanted him, all over her, inside her, everywhere.

"Please," she gasped against his mouth, and he pulled back, his breath rasping against her cheek.

"Della..."

"Please," she whispered, more urgently, and he hesitated for only a moment before his lips were upon hers again, and they were stumbling backwards until he pushed her up against one of the columns nearby. He took a moment to rip off his fine gloves before his hand was on her leg, lifting her skirts. Her hands found purchase on the base of the column, and she leaned her head back against the cool stone. When his lips touched her stockinged knee, she shivered and sighed into the night. "Della," he murmured against her flesh, lips moving higher, hands pushing her skirts away. She stifled a gasp as his hand slipped beneath the fine cotton lawn and pushed her legs farther apart. He rose to face her, and his gaze held hers for a moment, his fingers hovering so very close to where she wanted him to touch her.

"Della," he said again, and she rose to meet his lips once more, gasping against his mouth as his finger slid through the silky curls, parted the waiting flesh, and slipped inside her. Her chest seemed to burst into flame then; her inner muscles clenched around him as he teased her, kissing her all the while and tasting sweetly of champagne.

"Please." Her whisper caught on the breeze and floated away into the night and her nails dug into his back as she silently begged him for more. His free hand tightened its grip in her hair and he groaned.

"Della, we can't..."

She almost screamed at him as her passion burned, unspent, and she ground her hips against his hand. "Don't make me beg – don't make me beg you to fuck me."

She opened her eyes as he shook his head and raised it to meet her gaze. His look was steady, unperturbed, and she wanted to cry out. How was he so calm?

"I don't want to fuck you, Miss Rose... Della. I want to make love to you. And I don't want to do it here in the park." He bent down so his lips were against her ear, and she squirmed in his embrace. He pulled his fingers out from inside her and she let out a moan and closed her eyes. "This is not where I will have you. It will be in my bed, with candles lit and champagne on ice, and I will make love to you all night, if that is what pleases you." His warm breath fanned across her cheek, and she swallowed hard as his mouth touched the curve of her jaw before he pulled away to regard her. "We should go home."

A heavy sigh lifted her chest and she reluctantly nodded. He retrieved his discarded gloves and his top hat which had tumbled into the grass when she pushed him. He drew the gloves back on and settled the hat upon his head before offering her his hand. They made their way out of the park and towards Bradford House, saying not a word to each other until they reached the front door. He turned the key in the lock, and they entered the hall, quiet and dark but for a few lanterns that had been lit so they could find their way.

He faced her at the bottom of the stairs and leaned down to brush the lightest of kisses against her lips. "It is late. Do you still wish to come to my room?"

She hesitated. Would it be unwise to go with him? Perhaps. But what had she to lose? Her heart? It had not been broken before, and she would be damned if it would be now. That did not mean she could not enjoy the pleasure of his body for one night – and pleasure she was certain of, for that look in his eyes promised pleasure beyond words, and she would be foolish to miss out.

She drew in a shaking breath. "I do."

A sensual smile lifted his lips, and he took her by the hand to lead her up the stairs.

SIXTEEN

Della paused when they reached his door, feeling the weight of the pocket watch against her chest. His hand was warm and possessive as he pulled her against his body and lowered his mouth to hers, his free fingers fumbling with the doorknob.

"Wait," she gasped against his lips. He drew away, his amber eyes dark with lust and his breath coming quick. "I..." She swallowed. "I need to go to my room for a moment. To... to freshen up. I fell in the mud," she said by way of explanation.

He blinked rapidly, then nodded. "Of course. I shall be waiting for you." His voice was rich with promise, and she bit her lip as she backed away from him and fairly ran down the hall to her own room. The door closed with a quiet click, and she leaned against it for a moment, closing her eyes. She drew in a deep breath to slow the frantic race of her heart, her hands quivering in anticipation before she pushed herself away from the door and raced to the bed. She dragged the valise out from beneath the skirt and flung it open before digging under her corset to retrieve the duke's watch and the comb. After stuffing them into the deepest corner of the bag, she pushed it back under the bed and crossed to the water closet.

She turned up the gas lamp beside the mirror and stared at her reflection for a moment before slipping the cloak from her shoulders. Her cheeks bloomed with color and her eyes sparkled. Bradford's fingers had removed most of the flowers from her tangled hair and Martha's careful curls had fallen out, so she reached into the mass and began plucking out the remaining flowers and hairpins until the midnight tresses fell about her bare shoulders in loose curls.

Her pulse fluttered at the base of her throat and the desire began to unfurl in her once again as she thought of Bradford – Cole – waiting in his room for her. She dampened a towel and rubbed away a streak of dried mud from her forehead, then washed her hands. Her shoulder still hurt where the footpad had hit her, but it didn't matter. Nothing mattered as she smoothed down the front of her bodice and raced from the room on eager feet.

Dark shadows loomed in the hall, but her heart was light as she stopped at his door and raised her hand to knock, then shook her head and pushed it open. Her gaze immediately went to where he stood in the small, golden circle of light cast by the branch of candles he had lit. He straightened from where he had been pouring himself a drink from a sideboard and turned to face her.

They said nothing for a moment as she drank him in. He had removed his tailcoat and bowtie and stood there in only his trousers, waistcoat, and shirt sleeves, devastatingly handsome as the light from the flames flickered against his square jaw. She couldn't wait to touch every inch of him; she ached for it, could almost feel his skin beneath her fingers. He inclined his head towards the table.

"I know I promised you champagne, but perhaps you'd like something stronger?"

Della swallowed hard as desire licked through her before crossing the room to where he stood, the heavy train of her gown rustling as she stepped across the fine Turkish rug. She clenched her hands to stop them shaking before she reached up and took the glass from him, letting the tips of her fingers brush against his. She smiled as she met his fierce golden gaze and lifted the glass to her lips to down the whisky in a single swallow. A muscle in his jaw twitched as she handed the glass back to him and took a step away. She then turned slowly, deliberately, from him and lifted the heavy curtain of her hair over her shoulder, presenting him with the row of tiny jet beads that ran up the back of her gown. His low growl echoed in the room and the glass clinked as he set it down before she felt not his hands, but his breath, warm as it fanned across her bare shoulders.

"I have been trying to convince myself all night we shouldn't do this," came his throaty whisper and she shivered as she angled her head to glance at him over her shoulder. Her skin seemed electrified as he hovered, not quite touching her, but the heat of his body unmistakable. She reached back and caught hold of his fingers, desperate to feel him.

"I want you to undress me."

A sharp intake of breath. "Della..."

"Undress me," she said again, more forcefully, wanting him to know that she wanted this. She was not afraid of what came next. *Just tonight,* she told herself. *Just tonight. Why shouldn't you enjoy yourself for one night?*

There was a pause, a moment during which she feared he would step away and leave her on the edge with no relief from the desire pooling low in her belly, her thighs growing slick with her wetness as she remembered his fingers curling inside her. A shaky sigh of relief left her when he pulled his hand from her grasp and lifted it to touch her arm, sliding up its length to reach her shoulder where his breath grew warmer and then he was kissing her there, softly, moving his mouth up her neck and touching his lips to her earlobe. Her toes curled inside her silk slippers as she waited, her breath caught in her throat, until he began to work at the buttons on the back of her gown.

Della pulled her bottom lip in between her teeth as sweet anticipation filled her. Her bodice began loosening around her chest and she squirmed as he drew it away with a sigh before his hands settled on her hips. His lips were still there at her neck, dropping soft, hot kisses upon her skin as he tugged at the ties of her skirt and petticoats before they, too, dropped to the ground in a puddle of silk taffeta and fine linen. She stepped out of the pile of fabric and kicked off her shoes as she turned to face him.

Those golden eyes of his were feral now as he watched her step back and reach up to loosen the hooks at the front of her corset. She was sure he could see her heart pounding beneath her skin, so wild was its rhythm, but his gaze never left hers as she dropped the finely embroidered corset to the ground. His hands clenched at his side as she revealed herself to him in only her fine cotton lawn underwear and stockings before she managed a small, beguiling smile and lifted her chin. "Take your clothes off."

His eyes widened at the command, shocked, and then he opened his mouth as though to protest before she smiled again. "Take them off."

There was another pause and then the corner of his lips curled up and he began working at the fine mother of pearl buttons on his shirt with agonizing slowness. Firelight danced against the sharp lines of his jaw, highlighting the dark sheen of his hair and it took everything in Della not to run towards him and just rip the damn shirt off him. If this was to be their only night together, then she intended to make it last.

Della's mouth grew dry as he tugged the tails of his shirt from his trousers and discarded it along with his undershirt, revealing an impressive expanse of muscle dusted with the lightest furring of hair across his chest. Her stomach clenched in expectation as he reached for the buttons of his trousers, before she held out a hand. "Let me," she said, her voice emerging as a hoarse whisper. His gaze burned into her as he nodded and dropped his hands to his sides. She approached him slowly, itching to run her fingers over those taut muscles. She held back, though, with a will that astonished her, as she stopped mere inches from him, close enough to feel the heat of his body. She stopped to unbutton the few fastenings at the front of her combinations before smoothing her hands over her shoulders to push it down. Cole's whole body grew taut and his breath quickened as the lacy garment fell to her feet, leaving her in only her stockings.

Just tonight, she reminded herself as she finally stretched her fingers forth and touched the ripple of muscles on his stomach. They contracted under her touch and Cole's breath hissed out between clenched teeth, but still, he did not reach out for her. Della let her fingernails scrape down his skin, over his navel, lower, until she caught the button of his trousers in her grasp and pushed them down over his hips. His cock sprang forward, fully erect, and she smiled up at him as she slid her fingers around the rigid shaft, stroking him with the lightest of touches. His throat moved as he swallowed, but still his hands stayed at his sides, balled into tight fists. His eyes were like fire, vivid gold and burning right through her. His scent surrounded her, a heady combination of whisky and smoke and cologne and she closed her eyes for one brief second to breathe deep the wild masculinity of him, to feel the radiating heat of his body. Finally, she raised her gaze to his.

"I want you to make love to me now."

Cole's jaw tensed and he drew in a deep breath but needed no further encouragement as he finally pulled her into his embrace and lowered his lips to hers. Della gasped as his tongue plundered her mouth, tasting, teasing, and his hands were in her hair, drawing her closer. Her nipples hardened into tiny peaks as the hard ridge of his cock pressing against her stomach made her moan. She needed him. Inside her. *Now.*

Instinctively she wrapped her legs about his narrow hips as he lifted her to him, gripping his wide shoulders as he moved with her to the bed and she thought she would burst as his kisses deepened, his tongue thrusting against hers. They fell onto the bed in a tangle of limbs and Della pulled him close, opening her thighs around him, frantic, needing to feel the weight of him pressing down on her.

"Please," she whispered into the fire-lit room, echoing her plea from earlier, and a deep chuckle reverberated in his chest as he lowered his mouth to her breasts, drawing a hardened nipple between his lips.

"Not yet, Della," he murmured against her skin and her fingers immediately tightened their grasp in his hair, drawing a gasp from him. How dare he deny her? She was about to voice a fierce protest when his hands suddenly seized her wrists and pinned them over her head to the mattress. The fire behind him emphasized the sharply defined muscles in his arms and chest as he leaned over her, his amber gaze dark with lust. The smile was gone from his face as she looked up at him, arching her back in a silent plea for more.

"Not yet," he repeated in a deep voice before lowering his head to her breasts once more, this time gently laving her nipples until she squeezed her eyes shut and moaned as the sensation rolled over her like a wave, spiking through her until she could hardly bear it. He tugged her hands down to her sides and, still holding them tight despite her writhing against him, began trailing kisses down her stomach, slowly, deliberately, until she moaned in frustration. His mouth reached the juncture of her thighs and lingered there, his breath warm against the wetness on her skin.

Her hands balled into fists as he pressed a kiss to the soft curls, then another, then another, growing more hurried as he nudged her thighs wider apart. Then his tongue was there at her aching core, parting the moist folds to taste her and her soft gasp of pleasure rang out into the still night air. He was kissing her, oh god, he was kissing her and sucking at her flesh, and she didn't know how much more she could take. She wanted desperately to touch him, but his large hands held her fast and all she could do was moan and shake and push her hips at him as the pleasure mounted. And then, when she thought wildly that she couldn't bear one more minute and her whole body tensed in anticipation, he thrust his tongue inside her. Della bit back a cry as her entire core burst in a shivery wave of pleasure, rippling through her in swell after swell as she shuddered and moaned, still held fast to the bed with Cole's strong hands.

When the waves had subsided into pulses that spread out from her center to her trembling limbs, she opened her eyes to find Cole staring down at her, his gaze turbulent, his muscular thighs now on either side of her legs, holding them together as though he would hold the sensation of release there for her. She licked her lips as she gasped for air and he immediately leaned over to cover her mouth with his, drawing her into a kiss that tasted faintly of her wetness, and she moaned against him as he finally released her wrists from his grasp.

With a guttural grunt, Della lifted her freed hands and pushed against a chest thick with muscle, hooking her leg around his to roll over on top of him and straddle his hips. His fingers began to trail up her calves, but she snatched his wrists and, with a sultry smile, pinned them to the bed at his side.

"My turn," she said in a throaty whisper as she leaned down over him, letting the peaks of her breasts graze his chest. It heaved under her touch and a deep groan echoed in his throat as she pressed her lips to his jaw, inhaling his intoxicating scent, then lower, lower, until she was flicking her tongue against his nipple, reveling in the soft hiss of pleasure she elicited from him.

Just tonight, she told herself one last time before she released one of his arms to reach down between them to find his cock, hard and hot and ready for her. She bit her lip as she stared down at him, never letting her gaze leave his as she lifted her hips and guided him inside her before settling down on top of him and slowly, purposefully, rocking her body against his.

Della sighed as he filled her, then bent to slide her fingers up his arms, pushing them up over his head, holding them there as she rolled her hips over him, letting the sensations wash through her, loving the way he threw back his head in apparent pleasure, loving the straining muscles and sinews in his arms as he pushed against her weight, loving his deep moans. The fire kept building and building where he joined her until she squeezed her eyes closed, tightened her grip on his hands, and let the sensation burst in a swelling flood of satisfaction that made her cry out as she held him down.

And before the last shudder had even racked her body, Cole's eyes darkened, he broke free of her grasp, folded his arms around her, and rolled over to pin her beneath his big body. Della let out a shaky laugh as his mouth descended on hers in a kiss that took away what little breath she had left.

"My turn now," he whispered before he slanted his mouth over hers again and took her waist in his large hands. He tilted her up and began to thrust into her; short, hard strokes that made her gasp, barely giving her pause before another orgasm racked her. She held tight to him as the world seemed to drop away, leaving only the sensation of his lips bruising hers with their ferocity, of his wild scent, sex and man, of the soft grunts he made with each push, of his cock filling her as he buried himself to the hilt. He never paused, not for a moment, even as she arched beneath him, only thrusting harder, faster, until, with a frustrated growl, he pulled away from her to spend himself on her belly.

Cole held himself above her for a moment, gasping, before

he fell to her side and rolled onto his back, flinging one muscular arm over his face. Della sighed; a lazy smile spread across her face, and she wiggled down into the soft mattress, luxuriating in the feel of the cool silk upon her sweat-dampened skin and the hazy bliss of release. Satisfied, she closed her eyes and reached out blindly to feel for him. His hand caught hers and his touch was gentle, easy, as he pressed a kiss to her palm. When their breathing had subsided, he pushed himself off the bed in a ripple of muscle and returned with a damp cloth to gently wipe his seed from her belly. She watched him through lowered lashes as he tended to her, and then, unable to think of anything to say which wouldn't be terribly awkward, remarked inanely, "Where did you learn to fight like that?"

He shot her a swift glance, bemused, before he let out a soft laugh. "It does do to have some knowledge of self-defense in my line of work. My father was a boxer. He taught me."

A disbelieving laugh bubbled up from her throat. "What sort of boxin' was that? That's how the bludgers and mug-hunters fight – and it ain't boxing when they do it."

A small smile lifted his cheeks and he shook his head. "I didn't say he was a professional."

Della pursed her lips and flung her arms over her head, stretching her body out on the bed with a contented sigh. She heard Cole's low moan, and his large hand cupped her breast before his mouth descended and he was lapping at her peaked nipple, making her squirm with anticipation. Her hands found purchase on the bedspread, and she lifted herself closer to his mouth as raw, pulsing need expanded inside her once more. Her thighs parted as if to welcome him, and he took up the invitation with nary a moment's hesitation, pulling her back under him and guiding himself into her with a low hiss of pleasure. The finely worked clock on the mantel ticked away as they made love, heedless of the hour, heedless of anything beyond their bodies, their desire, and their unspoken knowledge that, outside this room, they did not belong together.

Cole awoke, slowly and with uncertainty, sometime in the wee hours of the morning. He stared up at the intricately coffered ceiling high above, hearing nothing but the tick of the clock and the soft breathing of the woman who lay beside him. He turned his head to look at her, and the faint light from the dying embers in the hearth caught the fine, smooth line of her cheek and the sheen of her dark hair where it lay like a ripple of black satin over her small, shapely breasts. He well remembered the feel of them in his palm and of the sweet taste of her as he had buried his face between her thighs. His cock stirred at the memory, and he rose from the bed with a grunt, pulled on a dressing robe, and crossed the room to the window. Outside, the garden was still and quiet and he glanced at the clock to mark the time – nearly three in the morning. He sighed. He would be late now, but his associates in the Home Office would have to wait. He had no new information for them anyway. He had nothing until he found out where Salisbury was keeping those documents. Looking over at the form in the bed, his chest grew tight with some unspoken emotion. That look in her eyes as she had pushed him out of the way of the footpad – that fierce, fearless fire made him want her all the more. Never in his life had he met a woman so unabashedly bold and strong and unafraid to say what she meant. And never in his life had he wanted anyone more than her.

And what of it? he thought to himself as he moved to the door and slipped into the hallway with hardly a whisper. *Will she be your lover? Will you court her as you would some well-bred heiress? Will you marry her?* Cole shook his head. Somehow, he did not think she would respond positively to any attempt at wooing; indeed, he would almost expect her to laugh in his face. And what was it about her that made him want to do any wooing at all, when he knew his current circumstances did not truly allow him to have anyone else in his life. His career left him too busy, his heart too guarded.

Cole moved through the still and silent house, making his way to the back door as he did every night. It was a system of his own devising. He could not be seen to be visiting Whitehall regularly and so the boys he used to pass along his correspondence and intelligence would leave briefing packages outside his back door each night. He opened the door and there it was, sitting unassumingly on the flagstone. Cole bent to pick it up, and, quite liking the fresh night air upon his face, didn't bother going inside to unwrap it. He pulled the twine away and slipped off the wrapping. Inside was a single sheet of paper, written in his carefully devised code.

She is being watched.

Cole instinctively glanced up at the windows above as his mind raced. Who would be spying on Della? Salisbury? He had only just met her, though Cole wouldn't put it past him. He knew she was living here; she had clearly had an impact on him if he felt it necessary to keep watch on where she was staying. He crumpled the missive in his fist and shoved it into his pocket. There would be no reply tonight. He stared out into the shadows for a few moments as though the person watching Della would materialize, but the garden kept its secrets. He turned and went back into the house, stopping in the silent kitchens to put together a small tray of food before making his way back up to his room.

Della still lay slumbering, and he carefully lifted the bedspread over her naked body before moving to the hearth. He banked up the flickering coal fire before sitting at the small desk nearby and rummaging in one of the drawers for a fresh sheet of paper. By the light of the fire, he began scribbling instructions to a spy in his network who would dig around to try and find out who might be seeking information about her.

Though his eyelids were heavy with exhaustion and his body spent from making love to the woman who now slept not ten feet away from him, he forced the words onto the page before folding it up and slipping it into an envelope. Mr. Barrow would deliver it come the dawn. Finished, he leaned back in the chair and plucked a grape from the bunch he had brought up with him. Chewing thoughtfully, he turned once more to look at Della and found she was awake and staring back at him, her pale eyes luminous in the light of the fire.

"Where'd you go?" Her voice was raspy with sleep, and she rubbed her eyes with a balled-up fist as she sat up. Cole's whole body grew taut with desire as he stood and moved towards the bed. As he took in her tousled hair and creamy skin, her lazy perusal of him, he wanted nothing more than to push her down into the soft mattress and make love to her again. Instead, he sat on the edge of the bed and heaved a deep breath. "Work. It's why no one waits up for me anymore. I have had some... information relayed to me, regarding you."

"Me? What about me?"

He noted her expression; nothing changed. She looked mildly confused and twisted her body to face him.

"You are being watched."

Her eyes grew wide, and she frowned. "Watched? By who? When? Nobody knew about me until tonight."

Cole's lips quirked as he nodded in agreement. "I know. I have my suspicions..."

"Salisbury?"

"Perhaps. But my men will investigate it. I'm afraid... I'm afraid I cannot allow you to leave here at night anymore. And we will use the carriage to travel from now on."

Almost immediately, her eyes flared in anger and her shoulders stiffened. "You said I was not a prisoner here. I've been discreet. I go late at night, I take the side streets – what sort of person would follow me into Seven Dials, anyway? Not one of your people, surely. They'd never make it out alive." She spoke in a low voice that simmered with anger, all traces of her carefully practiced accent gone.

Cole held up a hand to halt her rush of fury and shook his head. "I do not blame you, Della. I don't think you've been followed into Seven Dials, but I cannot allow someone to see you go there. It would compromise our entire operation. Until I can find out who is spying on you... I must ask that you not leave this house without me or another chaperone."

Her lips tightened as she glared at him, her eyes snapping with anger, but after what seemed an eternity to him, she released a long, slow breath and shrugged. "Fine."

Cole knew a lie when he heard one, but he said nothing as she crossed her arms over her chest and looked away from him. "Should I go back to my room?"

He contemplated her for a moment, hating that he had to do this, hating that he knew she would probably not listen to him. Mostly, he hated that she still could not trust him, and that she felt he was betraying her in some manner. He wanted desperately to reach out and touch the smooth skin of her arm, but stopped himself and instead said, "You don't have to. I would like for you to stay."

She lifted her obstinate gaze to him. "What of the servants? Will it not look bad if they find me in 'ere?"

"Would it bother you if they did?"

She bit her lip and glanced away. "I dunno... I've never cared for propriety before. I'm sure you've had many women in this bed before me." She didn't say it in an accusing manner, just a statement of fact. He reached out then and did touch her arm. She didn't pull away but did look down to where his fingers brushed against her skin.

"I've told you, Della – my line of work does not allow for

much romance. I have had women here before you. A select few whom I could trust, who wanted to be in my bed and nothing more. But none," he emphasized the word, "has enraptured me quite the way you have."

His confession did not seem to move her; she merely gazed back at him, her expression indecipherable. "I'm tired," she finally said. "I think I'll go to my own room."

Cole opened his mouth to say something – anything – that would get her to stay, for the cold look in her eyes, unchanged from the day he had first met her in that alley, struck him to his core, but thought the better of it. He watched, unspeaking, as she lifted herself off the bed, hands held in front of her as though she were now embarrassed of her nakedness. She glanced towards the discarded mess of her clothes, and he rose without comment to gather them up for her before draping his dressing gown over her shoulders. She nodded, almost indiscernibly, and crossed to the door. Before turning the knob, she spoke without looking at him. "I'll be ready to practice riding in the morning... if you care to go with me." Her voice softened as she said this, and hope budded inside him. Perhaps he had not yet lost her. He inclined his head.

"I would like that very much."

She was gone without another word.

SEVENTEEN

Della didn't leave that night. Nor the next. She spent her days with Cole dutifully riding Dionysus at the nearby stables with him at her side on Apollo. She practiced the piano every morning with Mr. Avery, throwing herself into her lessons with cold determination. Less enthusiastically, but still committed, she met with Mrs. Cooper after luncheon to work out the finer points of etiquette and perfect her aristocratic accent. In the evenings, following dinners marked by stilted conversation and too much wine, she met with Cole in the ballroom and moved through the steps for the waltz and the polka and the galop, knowing she would have to dance with the duke when they attended his ball in another month's time.

The night before she was due to meet Salisbury in Hyde Park, dressed in her fine riding habit, showing off with the rest of the high-born ladies on their expensive mounts, she sat alone in her room. There was nothing left to practice, no book she cared to read, and she longed for Cole as she had never longed for anyone before. Not that boy at the foundling home she had snuck away with at night just to find some manner of pleasure in her drab existence, not that friend of Violet who had tried to pay her for their time together before she slapped him for presuming she would sell herself. Not the bookseller's son who would make eyes at her whenever she stopped by to see if they had anything she could buy with the penny she had plucked out of the gutter. They had given her momentary respite, a spot of color in the life of greys and browns to which she was accustomed.

None of them had brought her such earth-shattering pleasure, none had shown her such kindness or generosity, nor accepted her just as she was, hard edges and all, as Cole had. But him telling her that she could not leave this place only served to remind her that here, she was no longer her own person. She was not Della Rose, born to a loving family, but brought down by a cruel twist of fate and lifted to a marginally better existence than dying in a gutter by the matron of the orphanage. She was Rose Victoria Winthrop, a mystery, an enigma, shaped by the hands of someone else and an actor in every regard.

She kneeled beside her bed to pull out her precious valise and, hugging it to her chest, sat with it near the fire to inspect its contents. There was the small comb, certainly worth a few shillings, and the watch, worth a good deal more. She hated that thing now; she fancied she could hear it ticking at night under her bed, not unlike the beating of the heart in Poe's story, read aloud to her by the matron as a lesson in morality. She wanted it gone, and tonight was the night.

She stuffed it down the bodice of her tatty old dress along with the comb, drew the dark velvet cloak around her shoulders and lifted the hood up over her head. As she had before, she shimmied down the side of the house and lifted herself over the wall on the branches of the small flowering tree. This time, however, she did not take her usual route to Piccadilly to flag down a hansom cab. She headed south to Eaton Square and the rows of gleaming white townhouses which bordered it. She would find a cab to take her to the Houses of Parliament and then approach the Dials from the south. She hoped that having not been outside the walls of Bradford House for nearly a week and taking an indirect route would throw off anyone who might be trying to follow her.

Della paused when she reached Victoria Street and huddled beneath the shelter of an elegant portico to listen for any noises. This neighborhood was quiet tonight; no parties livened the windows of the fine townhomes, no passersby strolled past at this hour, and she saw only one hansom cab moving slowly in her direction. She raised her hand to it and asked the driver to take her to Charing Cross.

When they reached her destination, she pressed a handful of shillings into the driver's hand and asked him to wait for her. It was nearing one in the morning, and she couldn't risk not being able to find another cab to take her home and have Cole discover she had left.

She paused again on St Andrew's Street and searched the dark once again for any indication that someone lurked in the shadows watching her. No shapes shifted in the alleys or shady corners, and so she pulled the hood low over her forehead and moved between two buildings to make her way to Cora's brothel. The streets were quiet now and Della withdrew the key she had kept when she left to turn the lock of the red door. The hall was dark; no lights flickered in the sconces, and so Della felt her way along the wall until she reached the dilapidated stairs at the back of the house and mounted them to reach the second floor. There, to the right of the landing, was her old room, and a faint light glowed beneath the door. She knocked quietly and it opened a moment later on squealing hinges.

"Della!" Violet exclaimed and grabbed her friend's hand to pull her into the room. A small coal fire smoked in the hearth and Della pulled the hood off her head as she shut the door behind her. Violet wore a loose nightgown and her blonde hair hung in a wavy curtain down her back. She held a paintbrush in her hands. "I haven't seen you in nearly a week. Thought you'd forgot us!"

"No, no," she replied, slipping easily back into the voice of the rookery as she reached into her bodice and withdrew the watch and the comb. Violet gasped as she set down the brush on her easel before accepting the items.

"Della! Where'd you get such a bang-up jerry?" she asked, referring to the watch as she took it into her palm and inspected the polished gold cover and intricate engraving.

"From a fella who deserves its loss. That's for you – I want nothin' to do with it. Give it to Cora to sell, I don't need my share."

"Really?" Violet gave her a suspicious look. "You're not gonna want it back like that little china thing, are you?"

Della gave her head a vehement shake. "Not at all. It's yours, I promise. And this, too." She handed over the comb. "I'm tryin' to get more, but I haven't been let out of the bloody house for a week. I'm in Hyde Park tomorrow – can you meet me at Rotten Row at ten o'clock?"

"Suppose so. What are you doin' there?"

"Meetin' the gent who owned that watch for a ride." She held Violet's gaze for a moment. "He's got a key on 'im. Kept touchin' his chest all night – I felt it, he wears it on a chain round his neck."

"And?"

Della scoffed. "He's a duke who's stolen a load of important papers that could ruin him if they're ever found. What do you think he's carryin' that key around for?"

Violet smiled slowly. "For wherever he's keepin' those papers, I reckon."

Della gave her a sly look as she shrugged off her cloak. "A safe? Close by – he won't let those papers out of his sight." She paused. "You still have that mold? The one Richard left behind?"

"The cracksman from Covent Garden? Maybe." She turned to the narrow dresser behind her and rifled around in the drawers for a moment before raising a triumphant fist, key casting mold in hand. "Here it is!" She passed it to Della who shoved it into her pocket.

"Perfect. And tomorrow?"

Violet nodded as she flipped open the cover of the watch and cooed at the inlay of diamonds beside each finely worked numeral. "I can be there."

"Good. I'll be on a black horse. The earl's got a white one – I'll look out for you."

Violet sighed and dropped onto the bed, and it was only now, as she fell into the small halo of light cast by the little fire, that Della noticed the black bruise marring her friend's pretty green eye. She gasped and kneeled beside the bed to take up her hands. "Who did that?"

Violet shrugged and arranged the lumpy pillows behind her back. "Just one of them workhouse lads. Got a little too scammered and smacked me when I told him I'd have to charge him to put a hand up me skirts even though he'd done it for nothin' last week." She gingerly touched the skin around her eye. "Can't make a livin' if I keep lettin' him do it for free, can I?"

Della looked down and shook her head. Tears pricked at the back of her eyes, and she angrily blinked them away before squeezing Violet's slender hands. "I'll get you out of this place, I promise! No matter what it takes, I'm gettin' that money and we're gettin' out of here."

Violet shook her head and pulled the threadbare blankets up around her shoulders.

"I'm fine, Della, you know I'm fine. I've been doing his long enough now, it's all part of the job." She gasped suddenly and glanced up with a smile. "Ooh, does this mean I finally get to see your fancy earl? What's he like? Old and fat, I'd say."

A rush of heat rose in Della's cheeks, and she glanced away to fiddle with the ribbons on her bodice. Her body still felt marked by Cole's touch; his scent seemed to linger on her skin, and her heart raced at the still-fresh memory of his head between her legs and his kisses upon her breast. She swallowed back the swell of desire in her chest and forced out a small laugh. "Hardly. Quite handsome, actually. He's... he's very kind."

Della felt the penetrating stare of her friend and looked up to see that Violet watched her with suspicion. "When have those people ever been kind to us? You're just another servant to 'im, Della. He'll get his money's worth, and then he'll cast you off, back to the gutter you came from. It's a fair bit of money, to be sure, but that's all it is."

"Maybe... but I haven't seen it. You know me, I don't trust anyone outside of you and Cora. And I... I just can't make myself not like him. I mean, it won't matter in the end. I'm sure I'll never see him again after this. But it's been nice, gettin' to know him."

Violet's stare grew harder, and Della became convinced that she could read her very thoughts and would know that not one week ago, they had been entwined on his big bed, naked and writhing and breathless with desire. Her cheeks grew hot, and Violet gasped and shot up. "Oh, Dell, what did you do? Did I not warn you? You can't trust them!"

Della huffed out an angry breath and glared at her friend. "Yes, I was with him – I was with him the night of the ball, and I liked it! He made me feel good; he made me feel somethin' that wasn't misery or hunger or fear! And I don't care if it meant nothin' to him, I felt alive that night. And I don't care if I never see him again when we're done, I'll take that memory with me and remember that someone like him actually wanted me!"

Violet looked taken aback as Della's hands shook and she gasped at what she had said, surprising not only her friend, but herself. She looked up into Violet's wide, green eyes, and smiled. "You see – he can't hurt me. I'm usin' him just as much as he's usin' me. Don't you worry for me. I'll be fine." She stood from where she kneeled at the side of the bed and offered a serene smile. "I'm going to get everythin' out of this I possibly can. I'll nick whatever I can get my hands on, I'll eat whatever they put in front of me, I'll wear better clothes than the queen herself, I'll ride a horse that's worth more than this house, I'll dance at the balls – and I'm gonna let that man do whatever he wants to me, because he is very, very good at it."

It was now that Violet's frown broke into a wide, knowing smile and she rose from the bed to give Della a hug. "Then go now, enjoy yourself. I'll be at Rotten Row at ten. Be safe."

Della grinned and pulled the cloak back over her head before she turned to leave. "I will. See you tomorrow."

"Good night, Della."

"Bye, Violet."

Della closed the door with a creak and made her way back down the dark hall, out the front door, and into the night. The streets were quiet as she reached Charing Cross and looked around for the hansom cab. Nothing. The street was empty, and she swore and stamped her foot as panic set in. If she did not get back to Bradford House – and soon – there was no telling the consequences, and she cursed herself for having come out here.

"Bloody hell," she muttered and turned to head north, hoping she would have better luck on Shaftesbury when she heard the familiar clop of hooves on packed dirt and turned to see a cab coming her way. A sigh of relief lifted her chest, and she raised her hand to flag it down. The driver pulled to a stop and looked down at her with a tip of his cap.

"Dangerous for a young lady to be out here at this hour," he commented, and she made no answer to this as she pulled open the door.

"Just take me to Belgrave Square."

The driver shrugged and once Della had settled on the seat, he called out and the carriage lurched forward. When they finally came to a stop, she waited for the driver to climb down and help her out.

"A young lady like you ought not to be out alone at this hour," he said as she fished in her pockets for a few coins. Something odd in his tone made her glance up at him and he was smiling at her, a smile that made her blood run cold, and she took an instinctive step back before she fairly threw the money at him.

"You head on home, now," he called after her as she crossed the street with a thudding heart, looking back to find him still standing there, watching her from the pool of light cast by the gas streetlamp overhead. When she turned the corner, her instincts began shouting at her, and she lifted her skirts and ran. She heard nothing behind her, no pounding footsteps, no ragged breathing, no rustle of someone in the bushes, but she ran nevertheless, not stopping until she reached the comforting familiarity of the brick wall surrounding Bradford House. She hauled herself over the top of it and dropped silently to the grass below. The manor was quiet and dark, and she raced across the lawn to pull herself up the copper drainpipe, shimmy across the façade and pull herself onto her balcony.

It was only when she reached the quiet sanctity of her room that she stopped and slumped to the ground, chest burning and gasping for air.

"Della, you bloody fool!" she cursed herself, slamming her fist onto the plush rug beneath her. She scrambled up off the floor and crept back to the window to peer out into the garden. She searched every inch below; every shadow, every shrub, but nothing moved. Reluctantly, she withdrew from the window and stripped from her dress before tugging on a nightgown and burying herself deep into the mattress, praying she had been mistaken. She had been so careful. Surely, she had not been followed – surely not.

And though the clock now approached the third hour and her eyes ached with fatigue, she still could not sleep as she replayed the night in her head and the eerie smile that cab driver had given her. Della was still awake when Martha bustled into her room to help dress her, and she groaned and lifted the covers over her head. "Oh, Martha," she said in a voice that rasped from lack of sleep, "I feel awful. I haven't slept a wink."

Martha spoke over her shoulder as she busied herself setting out combs and curling rods. "Will I have Mary bring up a cup of coffee?"

Della sighed and pushed herself up off the bed. "Would you? That would be lovely."

As the maid called for coffee and pastries to be brought up, Della stumbled into the water closet to splash her face with cold water, hoping it might revive her. She groaned at her appearance; dark circles ringed her eyes and her hair was a snarled mess. Martha would have her work cut out for her this morning.

Once suitably attired in a plain tea gown and her hair wrestled into submission, Martha took Della down to the breakfast room where Cole waited for her. He glanced up as she entered the room and his face lit up with that damnably winning smile. She couldn't help returning the expression, albeit a little more reluctantly.

"Good morning, Miss Rose. Did you sleep well?"

Della grimaced as she moved to the sideboard in front of the wide bay of windows. The warm morning sunlight offended her exhausted eyes, and she squeezed them shut before she poured herself another cup of coffee and, holding it in both palms, took a deep, grateful sip. When she turned to face Cole, he was frowning at her.

"I gather not?" he asked, receiving only a groan in reply as she took her seat. "Shall I send word to the duke that you will be indisposed today?"

"No!" she said, straightening in her chair and shaking her head. "No, I don't want to delay our plans anymore. I'll be fine, I promise."

Cole looked skeptical as he reached for a slice of toast and Della sipped her coffee with determination. This was not the time for postponements or mistakes. She shook her head once more to clear the fog and forced herself to feel that cold anger towards the duke that had carried her through the ball and would get her through today, as well. It had to – what other options did she have?

EIGHTEEN

Dionysus was in fine form today, and Della suppressed a yawn as she settled herself into the saddle and brushed his flank with the whip. He started forward in an elegant trot and Cole smiled over at her in approval from atop Apollo.

"I must congratulate you, Miss Rose," he said in a low voice as he tipped his fine top hat to a passing gentleman. "You have made exceptional progress these last few weeks. I did not think we would gain Salisbury's attention so quickly. I was wrong to harbor any doubt."

Hot guilt slashed through Della as she recalled the chilling smile of the cab driver from the previous night, and she shifted uncomfortably in her saddle. Dionysus snorted and tossed his head, and she raised an absent hand to touch his neck. "It's nothing, really," she said, pausing to bestow a most ladylike smile upon a passing couple. "Like I said, I learned most of this from Violet. You just have to know what men really want."

"And what do men really want?" he asked, his voice husky as he looked over at her with hunger burning in his eyes. She should have looked away, should have made some benign comment about the fine weather and got down to the business at hand – ensuring their place at the duke's ball in a few weeks' time. Instead, she looked slowly down his body, from his sensually parted lips to his broad chest, to his strong thighs gripping the saddle, thighs she well remembered pushing her own aside in a moment of passion. Desire spiked through her at the memory, and she glanced back up to meet his gaze.

"I can tell you what other men want. What do *you* want?"

He moved Apollo a step closer with a subtle tug of the reins and his whisper was urgent. "I want *you*, Della – I haven't been able to stop thinking of you since that night. Please tell me you feel the same."

Her breath came faster, and it took everything in her not to reach across the space between their horses and touch him. "I do… but I'm worried. I've been trying so hard to make sure I don't fail. For you. For myself."

Cole reached across and touched her gloved hand. From a distance, it had all the appearance of being a friendly, reassuring pat from a chaperone to his young charge, but to Della, the look in his eyes held the promise of so much more and his fingers lingered slightly longer than proper. *Maybe just one more night.* The thought passed briefly through her mind as a warm, budding ache pooled low in her belly and she took a deep breath and tore her gaze from his as a pair of riders approached them.

"Bradford!" one of the men called out as he kicked his horse into a trot to reach them. "A very good morning to you. We haven't seen you riding in ages!"

Cole tipped his hat to the gentleman as he drew to a stop in front of them, followed by another, younger man on a spirited bay stallion.

"Perrin, good morning," Cole replied with a smile. "Grisham, how do you do?" he said to the younger man who grinned as he tucked his crop under his arm.

"Very well, indeed." He turned his cheerful gaze to Della. "And who is your lovely companion?"

Cole glanced towards Della who drew in a deep breath and mentally checked her position in the saddle as she nodded towards the two young men.

"Gentlemen, this is my cousin, Miss Rose Winthrop. Rose, this is Lord Perrin" – he gestured to the man who had first approached them – "the Marquess of Perrin, and his brother, Lord Alfred Grisham."

Della smiled as the two brothers inclined their heads towards her. Lord Perrin sent Cole a cheeky grin as his horse tossed its head. "Well now, Bradford, had I known you had such a lovely visitor, I'm sure I would have called sooner. You're making me look ill-mannered."

Della's face warmed at this remark, and she offered the marquess another smile. "You do flatter me, my lord. And please do not feel remiss in your manners – I have only been in London a short while."

"Well, that's a relief. And what brings you here, Miss Winthrop?"

"My cousin has been kind enough to let me stay with him for my coming out. We have not seen each other in years and have much catching up to do."

Perrin nudged his horse into a walk and the others followed suit as he pulled up beside her. "So where is it you call home?"

Cole and Perrin's younger brother had fallen into step behind them as Della shifted her hips in the saddle, ever mindful of looking like someone who had been doing this their entire life. "My family estate is in Northumberland, in Bamburgh."

"And how are you finding London?" he asked as they passed beneath the mottled shade of a plane tree.

The response, practiced diligently with Mrs. Cooper, came automatically. "It's crowded, and noisy. I'm rather used to the quiet. But I'm having a lovely time. Cole – Lord Bradford is a gracious host." Della looked back as she said this to meet Cole's gaze and found him staring intently at her as Lord Grisham chattered on about the horse he was training for next year's derby. The sight of those golden eyes, boring into her with their raw intensity, brought back a flash of memory: his head between her thighs; the slick wetness of his tongue on her flesh; of his muscles, taut beneath her fingers as he had thrust into her. She swallowed hard and looked away with a pounding heart. Bloody hell, she was already wet just thinking about it. *Just one more night. One more night couldn't hurt.*

To take her mind off the growing, grinding heat between her thighs, she turned a practiced smile upon Lord Perrin. "How long have you known my cousin, Lord Perrin?"

He looked thoughtful for a moment. "Goodness... since we were lads. Six or seven, perhaps?"

"Oh, then you know him a good deal better than I do."

"I suppose. Still, it is strange..." He paused and glanced over at her.

"Strange?"

"Strange that I have never heard mention of you before you arrived. I know almost everything about Bradford. I've met all of his family – including your father." His gaze was piercing, and Della fought to keep her expression neutral even as panic scorched along her nerves and her mouth grew dry. She risked a glance back at Cole and saw him grinning at her, then turned back to Perrin, who was also smiling. She frowned in bemusement.

"Don't worry, Miss Rose," he whispered, leaning towards her. "I do know Bradford very well – well enough to know what he really is. Your secret is safe with me."

Della's hands trembled in relief as she loosened her white-knuckled grip on the reins and shook her head. "I wish he'd told me."

The marquess chuckled. "All a bit of fun, I assure you. He was the worst of us for playing pranks when we were young. I had to laugh when we spoke earlier in the week."

Della sent him a questioning look and he elaborated.

"When he first told me about this little scheme of his, I thought he had brought on some old flame to work with him, from the way he spoke of you. You're all he could talk about." The marquess laughed. "Just the thrill of a new partner, I suppose. He's always worked alone, you see."

Della managed a weak smile before she looked away, hardly seeing the other riders around them as she absorbed this information, remembering Cole's penetrating stare only moments ago and not daring to turn to see it again.

"Bradford tells me you're a pickpocket," Perrin continued as they moved into the warm summer sunlight. Relaxing a little at the mention of a subject for which she was finally qualified to speak on, she nodded and reached out to pat Dionysus' head as he gave it a shake.

"I am," she said, straightening her shoulders and giving him a coy smile.

"I hear you've never been caught."

Della's smile grew wider. "Never."

"And they call you Rosie Diver."

Della chuckled. "That's me. The quickest hands in the Dials." She raised a hand to her forehead. "My, it is warm today. Might I borrow your handkerchief?"

"But of course." Lord Perrin reached into the pocket of his morning coat and withdrew a fine silk handkerchief which he then handed to her with a flourish. She dipped her head in a grateful nod as she took it and pressed the silk to her forehead.

"I don't suppose you've ever stolen a pocketknife that had a crest with two lions engraved upon it? I lost it in Mayfair years ago and I always suspected a pickpocket got it."

Della touched a gloved finger to her chin and looked

thoughtful for a moment. "No, I can't say that I have. But I did once steal a rather lovely gold cufflink with the initials A.G. engraved upon it." She turned to Lord Perrin with a wicked grin. "What does the A.G. stand for?"

His blue eyes widened in astonishment, and he glanced quickly at his wrist before letting out a disbelieving laugh. "Andrew Grisham."

"Well, Andrew, it is a lovely cufflink." She stretched out her hand and opened her fist to reveal the purloined item. The marquess burst out laughing then as she dropped the cufflink into his hand and he slipped it back onto his cuff. "I, too, enjoy the odd prank," she added with a wink.

"I can see now that Bradford is in good hands – so to speak," he said with a chuckle as he took up the reins once more and tugged to slow his horse so Cole and his brother drew alongside them. "Bradford, you're got yourself a keeper there. Do see that you watch your cufflinks, though," he added with a smile as he nodded to his brother. "We should be off. Enjoy the day. Miss Winthrop, it was an absolute pleasure to meet you." He spoke loudly now for the benefit of those around them and she offered him a secretive smile before he and his brother kicked their horses into a trot and pulled ahead. Cole drew up beside Della and gave her a suspicious look.

"Well, he seemed rather charmed with you."

Della gave a nonchalant shrug. "Well, I have worked very hard on my charm these last few weeks. It's about time it was good for something other than getting into the duke's good graces."

Cole's face broke into a wide grin but as he looked up over her shoulder, his expression fell as he drew in a deep breath and, for the first time since she had known him, he looked... uncertain.

"Cole? Is something the matter?" Della asked as he continued to gaze past her shoulder with something like hurt in his eyes. "Cole?" she asked again, and then turned at the sound of hoof beats drawing to a stop behind her. She followed Cole's line of sight, tugging at the reins to turn Dionysus so she could see who he was looking at.

"Lady Evangeline," he said in a soft voice, dipping his head in acknowledgement to the young woman atop a dappled grey mare, finely turned out beside a person who appeared to be her mother.

"Lord Bradford," she said with an uncertain smile. "This is an unexpected pleasure. I have not seen you riding in months." Her words seemed forced as she tightened her grip on the reins and Cole cleared his throat. Della couldn't help but notice the older woman watching him with narrowed eyes, but smiled at the pair, nonetheless.

"I have been out of the country," he said before turning and gesturing towards Della. "May I present my cousin, Miss Rose Winthrop? Cousin, this is the Lady Evangeline Drake, daughter of the Duke of Cavendish, and her mother, the Duchess of Cavendish."

Della's sharp gaze did not miss the look that Lady Evangeline directed at Cole – a questioning look, perhaps? Content to wait until she could interrogate him later, she plastered a wide smile on her face as she faced the ladies. "It is a pleasure to meet you both."

Lady Evangeline inclined her head in acknowledgement before turning to Cole. "Lord Bradford, you did not tell me you had a cousin – and such a lovely one. Where have you been hiding her?"

Cole's gaze slid across to Della for an instant, full of unspoken words, before he turned a smile, somewhat bereft of its usual dazzle, upon Lady Evangeline.

"Unfortunately, it has been too long since I saw Miss Winthrop last. We have had a great deal of catching up to do.

We did not see you at the Colchesters' ball last week – I was certain you would have been there."

The young woman waved her hand. "I was a bit under the weather, I'm afraid. I heard the Duke of Salisbury made a surprise appearance."

The duchess now spoke up from beside her daughter. "I'm sure the marchioness was quite put out at not having received his response."

Della grew cold at the memory of the duke, remembering his uncomfortable closeness and his off-putting confidence and she frowned.

"Don't be silly, Mother," the young woman said in a soft voice. "It wouldn't have been a party worth talking about had he not attended. I was most disappointed I couldn't be present."

Della had to fight not to sneer in disgust as Lady Evangeline seemed to express genuine regret at not having been able to see Salisbury and she caught Cole's warning glance before she nodded at the pair. "Then you are in luck's way today," she spoke up. "We are to meet His Grace here this morning to ride together."

The duchess looked with wide eyes at her daughter who perked up at this information.

"He invited you here today?" she asked Cole, and he shook his head and motioned towards Della.

"Not I. He invited Miss Winthrop after they shared a dance."

Evangeline's face froze and she looked over to Della, whose cheeks grew hot under the scrutiny.

"Really?" The disappointment in her eyes was very real, and she swallowed hard and looked at her mother, whose lips had tightened as she regarded Della with suspicion. "That is most unusual for him. He must have taken quite a liking to you."

A nervous laugh emerged from Della, and she waved her

hand in what she hoped was a gesture of nonchalance. "Hardly. I told him that I had never been riding in London before and he insisted on meeting me to show me Rotten Row."

Lady Evangeline narrowed her eyes at Della for an uncomfortable moment before her face broke into a smile and she nodded at her mother.

"Well, I do hope you enjoy yourself. It is a lovely day for riding. It has been a pleasure to meet you, Miss Winthrop. Lord Bradford, I do hope to see you again soon. Good day to you both!"

And with that, she tapped her horse with her crop and took off at a sedate trot with her mother close behind. Della watched them go, frowning, before turning to see Cole regarding her with an enigmatic expression.

"A friend?" she asked as Cole flicked his crop against Apollo's side. Della followed suit as they began walking along the iron railings that lined the trail. He was quiet for a moment before answering without looking at her.

"She was my fiancée."

Now it was Della's turn for speechlessness. She bit her lip and cast a concerned glance towards him. "Do you see her often?"

"Often enough. It can be... uncomfortable, but we hold no ill-will towards one another. We are still friends, in a manner of speaking."

"Even after what happened?"

"Yes." Cole glanced over at her now, and his expression had softened. "As I said, we were once very close. I trust her still to keep my secrets. We were simply not right for one another. We've moved on, and now she has her sights set on the duke."

Della snorted and flicked the veil affixed to her fashionable top hat out of her face. "If she wants the duke, she can bloody well have him."

"I don't think she's really what he's looking for. I'm afraid she'll end up learning that the hard way."

Della stared at Lady Evangeline who rode ahead of them, gesticulating wildly at her mother before her shoulders slumped and she kicked her horse into a canter. They were soon out of sight as they rounded a bend in the path.

"She's a pretty thing – daughter of a duke? That would be quite a match," Della remarked as they passed beneath the mottled shade of a towering oak tree.

"Salisbury doesn't just want a pretty thing. He wants someone with fight in them. I told you – he likes the chase." Cole looked at her. "That is why you are the perfect person for this operation. You will lead him on a merry chase, and he'll believe the whole time that at the end, he will bag you as he would a boar."

Della grimaced at this comparison and shuddered. "Won't he be disappointed," she said as they emerged back into the blinding sun. It warmed her skin, and when she glanced over at Cole, he watched her once more with longing in his eyes.

"I would also be disappointed if someone such as yourself denied me her charms," he said in a voice low enough that only she could hear. His gaze slid down her body, and that familiar fire ignited deep in her belly. She fought back a smile and cleared her throat as they came upon another group of riders.

"Well, we can't have that," she remarked as she spurred Dionysus into a trot. She heard Cole cluck his tongue for Apollo to follow suit and allowed a giddy laugh to burst from her as she rode on ahead of him. The very idea that they would, this night, meet once more to share that passion which could not be contained, made her heart feel as though it would burst, and she sucked in a deep lungful of air to calm herself. She was about to turn to Cole when she saw *him* up ahead.

The Duke of Salisbury.

Her heart, glowing with anticipation, dimmed suddenly

within her chest, and the smile faded as though it had never existed. Cole drew to a stop beside her and spoke without looking over at her. "Are you ready?"

Della straightened her back, drew in a sharp breath, and gave a curt nod in response before summoning up Miss Rose Winthrop and her charming smile. "Your Grace, it is an absolute pleasure to see you again," she called out as he drew near on a tall, spirited chestnut stallion. He tipped his top hat to her, offered her a leering smile, and pulled his horse to a stop.

"Miss Winthrop, I am so glad you could come out today. Bradford, good morning to you," the duke added with a brief, uninterested glance towards Cole who returned the greeting with a neutral smile.

"Good morning to you, Your Grace. Fine weather we're having, isn't it?"

"Yes, fine indeed," the duke replied, never looking away from Della, whose skin grew cold under his regard, despite the heat of the day. Her gaze flicked down to the fine gold stick pin he wore, and she swore it would be hers by lunch time.

"Come, tell me about this fine beast of yours," the duke said as he wheeled his horse about to continue in the direction Della and Cole had been going. She flicked her whip and Dionysus started forward, bobbing his head as if he could sense her unease.

"This is Dionysus," she said, reaching out to pat his glossy black neck. "Come all the way from Northumberland to keep me company."

"A fine piece of horseflesh, if I may say so," the duke pronounced, nodding towards the gelding. "And where in Northumberland does your family call home?"

Della cast a brief glance at Cole before answering, "I grew up at Haversham Estate, in Bamburgh, on the coast."

"And how are you finding London?"

She allowed a small, embarrassed smile. "It's very loud here.

And crowded. I rather miss the peace of the country." Della peeked over at Cole, and the look she gave him was full of meaning as the memory of their kiss on the shore of that pond at his country home came back to her. One corner of his lips curled up as he seemed to read her thoughts.

"Ah, you shall become accustomed to it in time. A woman like you should have attention from more than a handful of backwoods Scottish lords. You should have only the finest suitors." The duke's tone was slick as his gaze raked over her, and Della forced out a trilling laugh.

"You do flatter me overmuch, Your Grace."

He went on to speak of his father at length, and his ancient lineage going back to Richard III, and it was all Della could do not to shout that his stories were lies and his father a traitor, but she smiled until her cheeks ached as they followed Rotten Row towards Serpentine Road. When they, blessedly, reached the end of the path, Della turned to Salisbury. "I don't suppose Your Grace would join me in getting some refreshments?"

The duke nodded towards Cole. "What do you say, Bradford? A refreshment for the lady?"

"A fine idea, Your Grace."

They guided their horses to the hitching posts at the side of the path and Cole dismounted in one smooth, graceful motion to move to Dionysus' side. "How are you faring?" he asked once out of earshot of Salisbury.

The serene expression never left her face as she lifted her leg over the pommel and slipped her foot out of the stirrup to drop into his waiting arms. His hands lingered upon her waist, and she swallowed back a small moan of pleasure.

"I have never been better," she replied in a bright, false tone as she brushed her hand over his before stepping away to take the arm the duke offered. A small cart nearby sold lemonade and as they waited in the short line, Della squeezed Salisbury's arm and subtly leaned her hips into his. He looked down at her with something approaching a smirk and jerked his head in the direction of Cole, who stood nearby, as any good chaperone would do.

"I suppose your cousin has told you of the ball I am hosting in just over a week's time? This year we are raising funds for the St. Giles orphanage, a charity rather dear to my mother's heart."

Della's body grew cold at the mention of the orphanage where she had spent ten long, lonely years, but she let her eyes grow wide and her mouth form a perfect little 'o' of surprise. "He has not, naughty thing. Do tell me about it."

A flood of memories returned: the backs of her hands tingled as though she could still feel the sting of the matron's switch upon them, and her stomach rumbled as if it could remember the gnawing hunger. She gulped back a rising wave of sadness and rage and looked away as they reached the front of the line, hoping to hide the tears pricking at her eyes. He handed her a cup of lemonade after a moment and she swallowed it back, letting the sweet tang clear her thoughts before she found her easy smile once more and gazed up at the duke when he spoke.

"Every year I select a different charity to support. It is at the very height of the social calendar. The queen herself used to attend before her husband's passing."

"How lovely," Della remarked, taking another sip of her lemonade.

"I had not known that the cousin of the Earl of Bradford would be in London, else I assure you, my dear, you would already have an invitation."

And this was when Della struck, curling her shoulders forward in an intimate gesture and fluttering her lashes as she placed her gloved hand upon his arm. "A grievous error I have no doubt the Duke of Salisbury can easily remedy," she said with a raised brow and a suggestive smile. She reached up to touch the lapel of his coat as though to adjust it for him and pressed as close to him as she dared, never letting his gaze leave hers. He swallowed.

"Of course. Consider it done, my lady. I will ensure an invitation is sent to Bradford House for you posthaste."

"Good. Else I might have been offended," she said with a raised brow and turned with a saucy look over her shoulder. "A moment, if you please, Your Grace. I think I should like to get my cousin a cup."

"But of course. Please, allow me," he added, handing her a few coins for the drink. She nodded gratefully and fetched another cup. As she returned to where the duke stood in the shade of a tree, she found a conveniently raised root and stumbled upon it, tripping headlong into the duke and spilling the contents of her two cups over the front of his riding jacket. He gasped in shock as she drew back, her hands covering her mouth.

"Oh, Your Grace, I'm ever so sorry! Oh, please, let me help you with that!" she cried, tugging a handkerchief from her pocket and beginning to dab at the wet spot which covered his chest. He held up his hands and shook his head.

"It was but an accident, Miss Rose, please think nothing of it." The words he spoke were certainly what a gentleman ought to say to a lady in such circumstances, but she heard the peevish edge to his voice, and smiled winningly up at him, careful to let her hands wander low as she attempted to dry him. He seemed somewhat mollified by her fingers brushing against his waist, and she held his gaze with a fluttering of her lashes as she dabbed the handkerchief over his collar.

The key was off his neck and in her pocket in a matter of seconds, along with the mold, and Salisbury was none the wiser. But Della had not become the best pickpocket in St. Giles without learning a few things, and she knew that she had only moments before he made that habitual motion of touching his chest where the key should lie. She was careful to take his hand as though beseeching him.

"Oh, Your Grace, can you ever forgive me?"

He shook his head, his expression composed but his eyes flashing with irritation. "There is nothing to forgive, Miss Rose."

"Oh, just look – you must allow me to compensate you for a new jacket if this one cannot be saved. Do hold this and let me see if I have another." She spoke quickly, pressing the used handkerchief into his hands and fishing about in her pocket for another. It was a clever little trick, and it took but a moment to fit the key between the two halves of the mold to make an impression in the clay that had been pressed inside it. The key came out with the new handkerchief, and she presented it to him with a flourish before beginning to press it to his chest once more.

She stood back after a moment to appraise her work and the duke's hand, without him seeming aware of it, went up to where the key hung about his neck once more.

"I suppose that will do. Oh, I'm ever so embarrassed. You must let me know if the jacket requires replacing."

The duke gave her a quick smile. "Thank you, Miss Rose, but I'm certain my staff shall be able to attend to it."

"Of course. And thank you, Your Grace, for the invitation to your ball. I do look forward to a dance," she added, her voice dropping as she glanced up at him, her smile coy. The irritation left his expression at that moment, and his eyes lit up.

"As do I."

She grinned as she turned away to return to where Cole stood facing the trail, watching the other riders go past. He turned when she spoke.

"Cousin, we must stop at the dressmaker on our way home. I will require a gown for His Grace's ball in a week's time." She looked over her shoulder at the duke as she said this, and his satisfied smile suggested she had done her duty for today. She gave Cole a barely perceptible nod as she approached him.

He returned the gesture and said loud enough for Salisbury to hear, "Then we'd best be off. I have some errands to run this morning and you may accompany me." He looked over at the duke now. "Thank you, Your Grace, we look forward to your invitation. Good day to you."

Della never looked away from Salisbury as Cole spoke, her gaze full of promise for him, her lips curled in an intimate smile, and he only nodded in response as they returned to Apollo and Dionysus.

Cole said nothing as they unhitched their horses, waiting for the duke to return to his and ride off. When he was gone, Della released a long, shaky sigh and leaned her forehead against the warm bulk of Dionysus' neck.

"Well done, Miss Rose," Cole said as he gathered up Apollo's reins. Della tilted her head to look at him.

"It's what I came here to do. I'm not wasting any more time on that man than I need to. Best to just get us in on the first try rather than faff about hoping he'll come around on his own."

Cole was nodding in agreement when Della noticed a woman waiting near the lemonade stand. She cleared her throat and said, "I'm afraid I spilled my drink. I think I'll get another cup before we go."

"Certainly."

Della smiled and backed away before turning and crossing the expanse of lawn to the stand. She took her place behind the other woman who ordered herself a cup and moved to the side as Della stepped forward to speak with the vendor.

"Got it?" Violet asked without looking at Della.

Della glanced over at Cole to make sure he wasn't watching before handing her friend the mold. "Take it to Richard. Ask him to make me a copy. Bring it to the gatehouse at Bradford House tonight, at nine o'clock. Oh, and this, as well – this is for us," she added as she withdrew a gold cufflink from her pocket. If she was going to all that trouble for the key, she might as well treat herself to a little swag.

Violet didn't look at the items, just stuffed them in her pocket before she snuck a glance over at Cole. "So that's the earl." A slow grin spread across her mouth, and she made a face expressing her approval. "I can see what you mean, Dell. That's as fine lookin' a man as I've ever seen. It hardly seems fair, does it?"

"What?" Della asked, looking once more to make sure Cole's attention was elsewhere. He was busy unlooping Dionysus' reins from the hitching post.

"I mean it's hardly fair that a man should be so handsome, and be an earl, and not be a complete bastard as well."

Della laughed and gulped back the lemonade before discarding the cup. "And I fully intend to take advantage of it. Must be off. See you tonight."

Violet bent in an exaggerated curtsey. "Good day to you, milady." And she winked and spun around to make her way back through the park, sipping her lemonade. Della smiled after her before returning to Cole, whose whole face brightened as she approached.

"All set?" he asked as he bent and laced his fingers together to give her a foothold to lift herself into the saddle. His touch lingered as he adjusted her skirts and looked up at her with a wicked glint in his eye. It took everything in her at that moment not to drop into his arms and push him down on the grass to kiss him and bite him and taste every part of him.

"I take it that was your dear friend Violet?"

Della gaped at him, and he laughed and swung himself up into Apollo's saddle.

"Don't look so surprised, Della – I am a spy, after all." And he winked at her, dug in his heels, and took off down the path.

She couldn't help chuckling as she clucked to Dionysus and followed them.

NINETEEN

Evening crept over the city, bringing with it another smattering of rain that scented the air with its earthiness. Della sat alone in the parlor with the gaslights burning low, stumbling over a particularly difficult few bars in Beethoven's *Für Elise*. She went back to the beginning of the piece, but her fingers failed her once more and she closed the fallboard with a growl of frustration. Staring at the sheet music Mr. Avery had left for her, her eyelids grew heavy as the long day weighed upon her. She should be in bed after last night's trip to Seven Dials, but she wanted to wait for him. She longed for him now; just a word, a glimpse – it would feed her soul, it would be enough to sate the craving. But Cole was nowhere to be found, and Mr. Barrow was not forthcoming in giving away his master's whereabouts. She had stumbled upon them earlier in the day as she passed by the ballroom, drawn to the slightly ajar door when she heard muffled thumps and heavy grunts.

She bit her lip as she recalled peering through the crack in the door to espy Cole and his valet in the middle of boxing practice, both stripped down to their trousers. Sweat had trickled down Cole's well-muscled back and matted his hair to his forehead as he threw jab after jab, his movements sharp and efficient. Mr. Barrow punched like the bareknuckle boxers she knew, brutally and with little finesse, and yet somehow, the two men remained evenly matched as they sparred. So that was how he had built his impressive physique – and what she wouldn't give for more of it. More of that sweat-slicked skin, more of those slabs of muscle moving under her touch, more of that raw power focused only on bringing her absolute pleasure.

Della rose with an exasperated sigh and crossed the room to the bookshelves that flanked the intricately carved mahogany fireplace, where a small coal fire burned to chase away the evening's chill. She skimmed a finger along the spines and pulled one book out to give a half-hearted perusal before slipping it back between the others. Ordinarily, a quiet evening and a room full of books would have been her dream come true, but her mind wouldn't focus, and she couldn't muster the energy to find anything interesting enough to want to read. She didn't want to read. She wanted *him*.

The sound of someone clearing their throat made her look up to see Mrs. Cooper standing in the doorway. Della frowned, her defenses immediately rising, but the older woman merely nodded towards her and said, "I'm off for the night. Will there be anything else, Miss Rose?"

Surprised at the woman's soft tone, she slowly shook her head. "No, Mrs. Cooper. I was just going to go to bed myself."

Something approaching a smile crossed Mrs. Cooper's face and she glanced towards the piano in the corner. "I heard you playing earlier. You've come a long way in such a short time. You are to be commended."

Della's cheeks grew warm, and she shook her head. "Not me, really – it's all Mr. Avery. He's a good tutor."

"You are too modest, Miss Rose." She paused. "I also wanted to thank you."

"Thank me?"

"Yes... it has been a long time since Lord Bradford went riding in the park. Or attended a party, for that matter. Always working, he is. He has told me of your success so far, and I was wrong to doubt you. You have acquitted yourself admirably."

Della was speechless for a moment in the face of praise from a woman who had once looked upon her as one might a pest. "I have had a lot of good help," she finally replied.

The faintest of smiles crossed Mrs. Cooper's lips before she nodded. "Well then... good night."

"Good night, Mrs. Cooper."

The housekeeper gave her a tight smile again and retreated into the darkened hallway. Della stood by the fireplace for a moment, staring at the doorway, feeling as though she had just passed some sort of test, and faintly relieved because of it.

In the hall, the grandfather clock struck the tenth hour and she conceded that there was no sense in waiting up. Wherever Cole was, he was clearly not going to be back any time soon, and so she turned down the gaslights and retreated to her bedroom.

Martha had lit a cozy fire for her and laid out her nightgown and wrapper on the bed, and Della smiled as she stripped from her heavy silk evening gown with its lace and bows and ruffles of pale mauve. Buried beneath the confines of her corset were a handful of expensive silk handkerchiefs taken from the dress-makers they had visited that day and a signet ring slipped from the finger of a pushy milliner. Della pulled the valise out from under her bed and tossed in the stolen goods before plucking a grape from the bowl on the sideboard. She chewed it thought-fully as she made her way into the water closet and drew herself a bath, tossing in a handful of scented salts before slipping into the delicious warmth.

She closed her aching eyes as she leaned her head back against the rim and released a long sigh of relief. They were so close now, but the weight of her upcoming task was beginning to grow heavy, and a trembling sigh escaped from her. *I will not fail. I will not fail.*

When the water began to cool, Della quickly washed herself and was about to lift herself out of the tub when she heard a quiet knock at her door. Martha must have returned to help her take out her hairstyle and change for bed. She rubbed herself dry and slipped on the light linen wrapper that had been left on the bed before opening the door.

"Hello, Marth—"

She stopped abruptly when she saw who stood there.

Cole, in trousers and, more fetchingly, shirtsleeves, stood in the hallway lit only by a few gaslights. He did not smile when he saw her, but his golden eyes blazed with desire and before she could utter a word of greeting, he came towards her in a single stride and took her into his arms. Della managed a gasp as his mouth descended onto hers and he was kissing her, tugging on her lips with his teeth, fingers digging into her back and buttocks. A moan reverberated in her throat as they stumbled into the room and he kicked the door shut behind them, his mouth never leaving hers. She found herself clutching the front of his shirt, afraid she would fall if she let go, for the world spun around her and her heart drummed against her chest as she reveled in the musky smell of him, the faint taste of whisky on his lips, and the sound of his breath rasping against her cheek. *Just one more night.*

"I have been waiting all day for this," he whispered as the backs of her legs caught the edge of the bed and they fell in a flurry of entangled limbs. "I have thought of nothing else but putting my mouth between your legs" – he pressed his lips to her throat – "and tasting you, nothing but your skin, and your breasts, and how you breathe when I'm inside you, and how I don't ever want to be anywhere else."

Della closed her eyes as desire unfurled inside her belly, thinking of his muscles moving lithely under his skin as he delivered a crushing left hook to his valet, but his lips were upon hers again, devouring her. The weight of him on her made her sigh as he pushed off her wrapper, allowing his kisses to trail down from her mouth, along her neck and down to her breasts where his tongue circled her pebbled nipples until she growled in frustration. She pushed her hips at him, desperate for more, desperate for release. His large hands held her steady, though, and she could only arch her back and sob into the night as his tongue teased and traced along the curve of her breast before descending lower, lower, until she trembled in expectation.

When his mouth found the wet, waiting core of her, she thrust out her hands in search of some purchase and found the intricate scrollwork of the headboard. Her fingers took hold, and she held tight as his tongue lapped at her, teasing apart the folds of her flesh to find the hard nub that radiated with desire. She twisted her body as he sucked it between his lips, tasting and licking and nipping at her until she couldn't bear it anymore. That fire he so expertly tended razed her; it rippled through her as he brought her to climax, holding her steady as she cried out into the night.

"Cole," she gasped as he pulled away and ripped off his shirt. "Cole," she said again, giving voice to the only thing she needed at that moment. He paused only to push off his trousers, but she put her hands on his chest as he leaned over her. *If it's just one more night, I want everything.*

She pushed him onto the bed and bent over him in the flickering candlelight, her pulse surging as she moved down, tentative at first, to take his cock in her hand before leaning down to brush her lips against the glistening head. She gloried in his gasp of shock, followed by his long moan of pleasure as she took him into her mouth and he succumbed to her touch. She brought him in slowly at first, laughing deep in her throat as his cock jumped when she flicked the throbbing head with her tongue. She now held him steady as he had held her, taking him in deeper, deeper, until he inhaled through clenched teeth and his hands curled into fists in the bedsheets.

She licked and sucked and tugged at him, loving his taste, his scent, the silken solidity of him in her mouth, the power she held over him in that moment. It made her wild and breathless as she drew him in deeper and deeper, pulling away only as his body grew tense before she crawled up the length of him, straddled him and settled herself down, impaling herself on him with a shiver as his fingers tightened on her hips. His amber gaze met hers in the quivering firelight, filled with some emotion she was suddenly terrified to examine. She squeezed her eyes shut, blocking him out to focus on the building, budding center of their passion, an emotion she could at least comprehend between them, one which scared her less than the one in his eyes. She gasped and held his hands to her breasts, arching her back as the sensation peaked. Her broken cry filled the room as she found her release, but before the last shudder had even ebbed, he suddenly gripped her waist and rolled her onto her back to settle his delicious weight upon her.

She let out a gasping laugh of delight as he braced those muscular arms on either side of her, pressed his mouth against her neck, and thrust deep, pumping into her with wild abandon as she laughed and cried and sobbed from the devastating pleasure of it all beneath him. Then he paused, hovering above her before he clenched his jaw and pulled out to once more spill his seed upon her belly with a groan.

He fell upon the bed, his broad chest heaving as he gasped for air. Della, smiling with satisfaction, stretched out beside him as the fire faded into embers before snatching up a handkerchief from the bedside table to wipe herself clean. When their breathing had slowed and the night grew quiet once more, Della, purring like a contented cat, eased herself against the length of his body, still damp with sweat. *Just one more night,* she told herself for the hundredth time, trying to convince herself of something she knew would never happen. Her finger traced an invisible line upon his chest as her head rested upon his shoulder. He caught her fingers in his after a moment and stroked the palm of her hand with his thumb while she exhaled against his neck. Only the sound of the clock ticking on the mantel and the soft crackle of the fire filled the room, neither one of them wanting to break the spell of the silence. Words were not needed as they touched and traced each other's bodies, learning all the curves and planes of one another until fingers grew bolder, hands slipped between legs, breathing grew heavy once more and before she knew it, he was inside her again, his mouth slanted over hers, and he was holding her tight to him, rocking with her until her cry of pleasure echoed in the quiet.

Cole blinked as he awoke sometime later, the body beside him warm and soft and as the memory of that night filtered into his thoughts, he smiled and tilted his head to inhale the heady, floral scent of Della's hair. Her head lolled upon his shoulder, and though he was loath to leave her side, with her skin fragranced with sex, her long, shapely limbs and the soft, contented smile upon her lips as she slept, he had work to do. He gently extricated himself from her embrace and slid off the bed to tug on his trousers and shirt.

Bleary-eyed and exhausted, he made his way downstairs to the back of the manor and opened the door to the servant's entrance. There, with clockwork-like reliability, was the package and he bent to pick it up. Not wishing to disturb Della, he untied the string and opened the box to reveal a sheaf of papers marked in his carefully constructed code. The first several pages were simply updates on the actions of the agents who worked under him, and their current whereabouts. All was in order there and he flipped ahead to the pages of the most interest to him.

No information on who is following her. Trail has gone cold; no further sightings.

Agent Tyndall reports suspicious activity in St. Giles. Questions are being asked regarding a gentlewoman of her description – she may be compromised. Location of documents yet to be determined.

Cole sighed and rubbed a hand over his face. *Damn it.* Anger budded inside him. *Damn it!* He crumpled the paper in his fist and stalked back inside. His chest grew tight with fury as he reached her bedroom door and he paused with his hand on the knob to draw in a deep breath. The feeling constricted into a tight ball in the pit of his stomach, and he shook his head before he slipped into the room and closed the door silently behind him.

He walked over to the bed and stared down at her as she slumbered, her expression soft as it rarely was when she was awake, her hair spread in a dark fan over the pillow, a single, lovely breast bared by the drape of the sheets. His jaw tightened and his fists clenched at his side as he whispered, "Della."

She stirred, moaning softly, but she did not wake.

"Della!" he said louder, and this time, she groaned and stretched, her eyes opening to focus on him before a sleepy smile spread across her lips and she reached up for him. He didn't move, and she frowned.

"Is something wrong?"

"Did you go out?"

She blinked and dropped her arms. "Out?"

"Did you go out after I expressly asked you not to?" His tone was calm, collected, but deadly, and her jaw dropped as she pushed herself up onto her elbows.

"I…"

"I told you this operation could be compromised if you went out again – I asked you not to. Did you go out?"

Her mouth closed and her expression hardened, but she did

swallow after a moment and raise her head to meet his glare. "I did. I had to see Violet. I'm sorry—"

"Della, do you realize what you've done? Someone has seen you – someone is asking questions about you in St. Giles."

Della sat up now, holding the sheets against her chest as her expression grew defiant. "Then they're wastin' their time. No one there will speak to any outsider askin' around."

"They don't need to know anything about you, someone saw you go there. They can infer enough by that alone." He waved his hand and began to pace. "Did someone follow you when you went there?" His voice was tight, and his temples began to throb.

She looked down now and when she lifted her gaze to him, tears shone in her eyes. "I was so careful, Cole. There was a driver who brought me back here. I don't know if he was watchin' me, but he gave me a strange feelin'..."

"Christ," he muttered, pressing the bridge of his nose with his fingers. His mind spun as he tried to work out what this might mean. Perhaps something – perhaps nothing. He bit back a frustrated growl. "This could be my last chance, Della. *Years* of trying and failing and we are so close." His fists clenched as though to hold onto hope that seemed to be slipping from his grasp. Della dropped her gaze to the bed and a frown furrowed her brow as Cole stopped in front of the hearth.

"We need those letters." He spoke to himself as he stared down into the dying embers. She rose from the bed suddenly, and he turned as she gathered up the bedspread to her naked body and, pulling it tight around herself, kneeled to drag her old valise out from under the bed. He watched, frowning, as she dug around inside the bag and pulled something out. She crossed the room to where he now stood by the hearth, trailing the bedspread behind her, and held out her fist to him. He looked down as she uncurled her fingers to reveal a small, engraved key.

"What is that...?"

"Did you not notice the way he touches his chest? I suspected he kept somethin' valuable there – and wouldn't you know it, I was right." She smirked. "Now, if I were a rich and powerful duke and I had a load of documents that could prove my father was a traitor and maybe pay off all the debts he left me, I would surely keep those things in a secure location. In a safe, perhaps? And who knows safes better than a Covent Garden cracksman? Got myself a key casting mold and had Violet bring me the copy."

Cole stared down at the key lying in the palm of her hand. "Did... did you take that key from him today?"

"Among other things," she said, smirking and grabbing his hand to give him the key. Cole closed his fist around it and looked back up at her as the smile faded from her lips and she stepped away from him, her gaze on the ground.

"I'm sorry, Cole... you're right. I should have listened to you. It was a stupid thing for me to do and I was wrong to risk your operation – I know how much it means to you to finish this. I... I'm just not accustomed to being told where I can and cannot go. My world is very different from yours. It won't happen again."

That little ball of fury in Cole's stomach began to recede, but his mind, ever analytical, had already started working out how this could be turned to their advantage. He looked down at Della, standing quiet with eyes full of regret in front of him, the flicker of the fire warm against her skin.

"What is your plan?"

She said nothing for a moment as she slowly perched herself upon the edge of the bed. "If he's got a safe, we need to know where it is, no? Got a little something else of his he may want back." She opened her other fist now to reveal the gold stickpin she had slid from his tie when she had been wiping him down. "We simply call upon him to tell him we found his stickpin at the park – got his crest on it and everythin' – and I can have a look for the safe while we're there. Then it's a simple matter of us using our copy of the key to get into the safe the night of the party, take whatever's in there, and get it out without bein' seen." A tentative smile lifted her cheeks, and she raised her shoulders. "And then we're done."

Cole's stomach dropped. *Done.* But he didn't want to be done with her. Her gaze turned sad as she watched him from the rumpled bedclothes. "I will make this right, Cole. I will not let my mistake cost you this operation. I will not fail."

Silence filled the room as he observed her sitting there at the edge of the bed with the blanket wrapped about her body, and a sudden pang of sadness filled him, knowing that in only a week's time, she would be gone from his life. He had never allowed himself to think about where this all ended, but now that it stared him in the face, he could not deny it. He did not want to lose her. He wanted her here, always, in his life. But in what world could they possibly be together? And how could he possibly give up that which he had spent years building?

"I know you won't," he whispered, taking a step towards her. "I knew you would be the right person for this operation from the day we met." He took another step, never taking his gaze off her. "For I have never met anyone so capable, so strong, so determined—" He stopped in front of her and put a finger on her chin to tilt her head up, so she was looking at him with wide eyes. "—so lovely. Della, what will I do when you're gone?"

Her brow furrowed and those haunting pale eyes shone up at him. "I'm here now," she whispered.

"Yes." His finger traced the line of her jaw. "Yes, you are."

She stood then, dropping the sheet she had clutched to her chest to reveal herself in all her naked glory. Silently, she reached for the buttons on his shirt and, with agonizing slowness, undid them as he held his breath in rapt attention. Time slowed as she pulled him down onto the bed beside her and wrapped her legs about his waist, drawing him close with eager arms and breathless whispers that quickly turned into harsh gasps of pleasure as he slid himself between her thighs. When the shudders had finished racking her body, she fell away from him, panting, her skin glistening and her hair in disarray.

Cole was wild now; the thought of losing her made him want her all the more, and when her rapid breathing had subsided, he pulled her back under his body and watched her eyes grow wide in surprise as he drew her legs around his hips and entered her again to the sound of her eager gasp. And, knowing that they both longed for this night to last forever, he held her tight as he made love to her, his throat aching with the effort it took not to tell her what he desperately wanted to say. *I love you.*

TWENTY

"Are you ready?" Cole's words reached Della as she breathed out a deep sigh to soothe her nerves. Her plan to quietly return the stickpin to Salisbury without any fuss had turned into an invitation to dinner and now she stood with Cole at the threshold of Lufton Castle's massive oak doors, dressed in ludicrously expensive ice-blue silk taffeta, trying to summon the persona of Miss Rose Winthrop.

"I suppose so," she whispered back as a footman guided them into a hall so massive their footsteps echoed upon the marble floors. As they followed behind the servant, Cole reached out suddenly to lay a hand upon her arm as he slowed to allow the footman to move ahead and out of earshot. "I would like you to do me a favor tonight, if you would be so kind," Cole whispered to her as they moved down a long, wood-paneled corridor.

"And what would that be?"

"I am concerned that Lady Evangeline has set her sights on the duke. She will be in attendance this evening, and I thought it might do for you to give her some advice – in your own subtle way, of course."

Della frowned. "I'm not helping her to get married to that monster."

"I didn't suggest you give her advice to get him to marry her." He looked down at her. "I want you to – subtly – tell her that perhaps the duke is not the best match for her. I still consider her a friend and knowing who Salisbury really is, I can't let that happen. I think it would be better to hear it from another woman."

Della nodded in understanding as the footman stopped ahead of them to announce them.

"Miss Winthrop, what an absolute pleasure to see you again," the Duke of Salisbury said as they entered the parlor. The rest of the guests had already arrived and turned to face them. Though Della's instinct was to shrink away from such scrutiny, she forced a polite smile onto her face and straightened her shoulders, comforted by Cole's hand on the small of her back as he moved with her into the room.

"I was surprised to receive your calling card this afternoon. I had thought I wouldn't see you again until the ball. I do hope my invitation to dinner wasn't inconvenient?"

Della offered her most charming smile and shook her head. "Not at all, Your Grace. It was most welcome and very kind of you. What an honor to be invited to dine at the home of the Duke of Salisbury."

"The honor is all mine, Miss Winthrop. I must confess I was eager to see you again – a week is far too long to go without beholding such beauty." He bestowed a simpering smile upon Della who swallowed back the bile rising in her throat. Cole watched the duke with an impassive expression, but Della saw the tensing of his jaw before she gave a trill of laughter that sounded false even to her own ears. "You are too kind, Your Grace."

"Come, let me introduce you to my other guests," Salisbury said in a smooth voice as he held out an arm to her. Della sent a brief, chagrined look towards Cole before placing her hand upon the duke's and allowing him to lead her to the guests who stood in small groups chattering, glasses of champagne in hand. A sigh of relief left her lips when she saw Lord Perrin and his brother, friendly faces in a sea of curious stares.

"Ladies and gentlemen, may I introduce Miss Rose Winthrop, cousin of our good friend Lord Bradford."

Della fought back a derisive scoff at that remark as she dipped into a small curtsey and nodded towards the guests.

"We had the honor of meeting yesterday at Rotten Row," Lord Perrin said to the duke, stepping forward to take up Della's hand and press a kiss upon her gloved fingers. He winked at her as he rose. "Good evening, Miss Winthrop. A pleasure to see you again."

Della gave him a conspiratorial smile as the other guests were introduced: the Earl and Countess of Somewhere – she didn't care to remember – a baron and baroness, the Marquess and Marchioness of Colchester, more faces Della was relieved to see and, as Cole had forewarned her, Lady Evangeline, who for her part, greeted Della with a warm smile.

"Lovely to see you again, Miss Winthrop."

"And you, Lady Evangeline."

The footman returned at that moment to announce that dinner was served, and Salisbury appeared suddenly at her side with a solicitous expression. "As you are new to our city, would you allow me to escort you to the dining room, Miss Winthrop?"

Skin crawling at his nearness, she cast about looking for Cole, but he had been designated as the baroness's escort and had already left the room with her. Resigned to her fate, Della gave a reluctant nod. "Thank you, Your Grace."

He took her arm once more and led her down a hall blazing with gaslight and lined with dozens of gilt-framed portraits to the dining room, a space bursting with gold and silver, fine crystal and flowers. She had to stifle the sudden urge to laugh out loud as she looked down at the layers of lace and silk of her dress, to the man standing beside her, one of the most powerful men in the country, and realized that this entire room would be absolutely appalled if they knew who she really was. Why, she was sure the duke would faint away from shock if discovered he had set his sights on the daughter of a Seven Dials whore. Cole caught her gaze as they took their seats across from one another at the massive oak dining table, groaning under the weight of all the silver and crystal and fine china, and raised an eyebrow at the secretive smile on her face. She merely shrugged as a footman came forward to pull out her chair and the duke, much to her relief, took his place at the head of the table.

Lady Colchester took the seat beside her and Della smiled at the older woman as a flurry of footmen came forward with the first course of oysters. "Miss Winthrop, what a delight to see you again. You have been well?"

"Yes, quite well. My cousin and I had a lovely time at your party."

"I'm so glad." Lady Colchester took up her oyster fork and nodded towards the duke. "It seems as though you have caught the eye of His Grace."

Della's heart slammed into her ribs, but all she offered the other woman was a shy smile. "Oh, I don't know that anyone as lowly as myself would be worthy of a man like the duke," she said with a wave of her hand.

"Nonsense. He just wants some quiet, well-bred girl who will give him a handful of sons and silence his mother's nagging. I do hope once he has you suitably betrothed that your dear cousin finds himself a bride – a man like that ought not to sleep alone." The marchioness raised a suggestive brow at Della, who couldn't help a small laugh as they both glanced over at Cole, now deep in conversation with Lord Colchester.

"Lady Colchester, how scandalous of you!"

The older woman waved her hand and chuckled. "I am not

dead yet, my dear. I can still appreciate a man as... virile as Bradford."

Della nearly choked as she took a sip of her champagne, for she had never thought she would hear such words pass the lips of anyone as refined as the marchioness. And, at the same time, despite all that had passed between her and Cole, she couldn't help but agree with her.

"He is handsome, I will grant you that." Della paused. "Why hasn't he married yet? I have not heard of any serious contenders since..." She paused, aware of Lady Evangeline's presence farther down the table and dropped her voice. "Since his engagement was broken off."

"Oh, he has had interest, of course. That's why he rarely attends social events – all those pushy mamas and their daughters are desperate to get their hands on him," Lady Colchester began, leaning closer so they wouldn't be overheard. "But none have ever seemed to capture him – poor Lady Sarah never had a chance, I'm afraid. I think they have all been too... demure. Your cousin is a kind man, with a good heart, but something does tell me he prefers his women a little... wilder."

Della's eyes widened as the other woman sipped her champagne, seeming unaware of the effect her words had had. She made an effort to keep her voice casual when she spoke. "And what makes you think that?"

The marchioness shrugged. "His father was quite the rake in his day, before he met the countess, and she was not quite the decorous lady his parents had hoped for him. I see so much of the late earl in your cousin... including his fondness for bold women. I've known him since he was a wee lad, and he always went after the loudest girls – the ones who wouldn't be considered appropriate by anyone else. It is a shame he has not yet found the right girl. He does have the earldom to consider, after all. Lifelong bachelorhood is not a reality for men like him. And he often seems... lonely. Rattling about in that big house all by himself." The marchioness smiled and speared an oyster.

"Indeed..." Della trailed off as she picked at her own oysters, swallowing them back with a mouthful of champagne before she dared to look up and meet Cole's gaze across the table. She started as she found him staring at her with those magnetic golden eyes and couldn't look away; he held her with an enigmatic expression, and she shivered as that little flame flickered to life. Memories of his lips on hers, of his fingers digging into her flesh and his guttural grunt as he thrust into her flashed through her mind. She bit her lip and looked down, shifting in her chair as a heavy heat settled between her thighs.

Lady Evangeline spoke up as the oysters were cleared from the table and a course of asparagus soup brought in by another flurry of servants. "Your Grace, I understand you will be supporting the St. Giles orphanage this year at your charity ball."

"Yes indeed, my lady. A cause my mother has championed for many years. I do hope you will be attending."

A warm blush suffused the young woman's face and she nodded. "Indeed, I shall. Miss Winthrop," she added, turning her attention to Della. "I do hope you and Lord Bradford will be coming."

"We shall. His Grace was very kind to extend an invitation to me shortly after I arrived in London" – she graced Salisbury with a courteous smile as she spoke – "and I do like to support charities when I can. Especially those which help the less fortunate."

The other woman nodded sagely. "Can you imagine living in one of those places? All those poor orphaned children – it must be terribly sad," she said, shaking her head.

It took everything inside Della to keep her expression neutral as she took another long sip of her wine.

"Yes, terribly," she murmured, fighting back a scowl. What

did these people know of hardship? What did they know of the people like her, living only streets away, who went to bed hungry, who grew sick living among the filth? This sheltered girl would faint if she saw what went on behind the doors of Cora's brothel. Cole sent her a sympathetic look as her throat constricted against a rising wave of anger. She took a deep breath to compose herself and stretched her lips into as convincing a smile as she could manage as Lady Evangeline chattered on about the duke and his various charities. Della wanted nothing more than to slap the pretty young woman and scream that the man was a monster and that no money or titles could be worth tying herself to such a person, but she continued to smile and nod and make silly, inane replies until the last course finally arrived.

It couldn't come soon enough. Talk of the orphanage, of the poor souls who called it home as she had for over ten years, brought back a deluge of memories she did not care to revisit, and she was scrupulously quiet as conversations flowed around her. She caught snatches of them as she ate her sherbet with intense concentration; something about railyards here, about the opening of a new milliner there, and she wished she had been seated beside Cole, though even from across the immense table she was keenly aware of his presence and carefully avoided his gaze.

"Miss Winthrop?"

Della almost didn't react to the name right away as she concentrated her efforts on the dish set before her, then looked up suddenly as someone repeated her name.

"Miss Winthrop?" Salisbury spoke from the head of the table and Della's face burned in a fierce blush as she turned her attention to the duke.

"Yes, Your Grace?"

"We had been discussing an upcoming recital and I wondered if you played any instrument?"

Della stared in bewilderment at him for a moment before she remembered herself and gave a quick nod. "I do, Your Grace. That is, I play passably. The piano."

Salisbury's face broke into a wide grin. "Ah, then perhaps you would grace us with a few pieces after dinner? I do so love the piano."

Della's expression froze into an expectant smile and her stomach clenched in terror. No matter how much she had practiced with Mr. Avery, she still did not feel prepared for this. Cole cleared his throat across the table from her, breaking her from her daze.

"Why, I should be delighted. Though, I am a little out of practice," she added quickly.

"Not to worry, Miss Winthrop. We would appreciate it all the same," Salisbury replied, ensnaring her gaze with his own. She shuddered and quickly looked away.

"If I may suggest it, Your Grace," Lord Perrin spoke up from further down the table, "Lady Evangeline is a quite accomplished singer. Perhaps she could accompany Miss Winthrop for a duet?"

Lady Evangeline turned towards Lord Perrin at this suggestion and her face lit up with a warm flush and a shy smile. "Thank you, Lord Perrin, I would be honored."

As the last course was cleared away and the guests rose from the table to make their way back to the parlor before the men would part ways for their cigars and brandies, Lord Perrin escorted Della, whose heart now raced in anxious anticipation.

"Have you played for an audience yet?" he asked in a low murmur.

Della couldn't find her voice and so merely shook her head in reply. He reached over with his free hand and patted her arm.

"You needn't worry. We'll fill everyone with enough drink

they shall hardly notice. Lady Evangeline is quite a good singer – she will help guide you."

Della looked up at him and saw him gazing ahead of her at the aforementioned lady, his eyes filled with longing. It dawned on her now that Lord Perrin may perhaps bear some affection for the young woman, and she looked away to hide her frown. Only one person had ever looked at her like that, and he walked but a few feet in front of her. But she could not let him in. Oh, she was happy to share his bed and his body, happy to let his mouth search between her legs, to seek out the most intimate parts of her, to bury his cock inside her, but her heart was another matter. There was no future for them beyond this arrangement that she could see, no matter that he made her feel as if she were the only woman on earth, that she was more than just a pickpocket, that she was worthy of a life beyond Seven Dials.

Lord Perrin led her towards the gleaming mahogany piano set into a massive bay window lined with rich red velvet drapes and gave her a smile of encouragement. "Good luck, Miss Winthrop."

Della drew in a deep breath and pushed in the back of her skirts to take a seat at the bench before flipping through the various sheets on the shelf, praying to find a piece she was capable of playing. The words Lord Perrin had spoken to her at Rotten Row came back to her. *You're all he could talk about.* She wanted to scream. It was her own damn fault for letting Cole as close as she had. She was not capable of love. Too many years guarding her heart had hardened her to the emotion, and who was she, anyway? An orphan, a criminal. And him? Far too grand for her. Her hands shook as she set aside a sheet of music before someone laid a hand on her shoulder and she glanced up.

Lady Evangeline smiled at her and pointed to the music book propped up on the shelf. "I will sing that if you can accompany me."

Della glanced at the sheet. Schubert's *Serenade*. Easy enough, and she had practiced it frequently with Mr. Avery. She nodded and took her seat at the bench while Evangeline stood next to her and cleared her throat. She laid her fingers over the keys, took a deep breath, and began playing. A few bars in, Evangeline's sweet, clear soprano joined in and the guests clapped in appreciation. And all the while, Della felt Cole's gaze upon her, watching, waiting, and she longed to turn and look at him. But she couldn't; she wouldn't.

When finally, they finished the piece and she closed the fallboard with a sigh of relief to a smattering of applause, Cole was there with a glass of champagne and Della snatched it a bit too eagerly from his fingers and swallowed it back in a single gulp.

"Well played, Miss Winthrop."

She managed a nod and risked a glance up at him only to be ensnared by that fierce golden gaze. "Thank you, my lord. Mr. Avery deserves most of the credit. And Lady Evangeline. I do believe she distracted everyone enough from my playing that no one noticed how terribly amateurish it was."

Cole's half-smile sent a thrill up her spine, and she silently cursed him for it and its effortless ability to make her weak for him. "Do not underestimate yourself, Della," he said in a low voice as he leaned in close to her. "You have some talent. It might be worth continuing afterwards... if that was something that interested you." A small frown marred his brow for a moment, only for it to disappear as soon as it had appeared. He inclined his head towards Lady Evangeline, who stood alone near the massive stone hearth in which a hearty fire blazed. "Now might be a good time to speak with her."

Della drew in a sharp breath and bobbed her head before smoothing down the front of her bodice and crossing the room to where Lady Evangeline stood, glass of champagne in hand, staring up at the massive portrait which hung over the fireplace.

"Lady Evangeline?"

The woman turned at the sound of Della's voice.

"I wanted to thank you for accompanying me this evening. You have a beautiful voice."

Her cheeks flushed. "Thank you, Miss Winthrop. You are a talented pianist." She paused. "I suppose... I had wondered if your cousin told you about us."

Della cleared her throat and shrugged. "Only that you had been engaged but remain friendly. I am glad you could both remain close – I know he values your relationship."

Lady Evangeline gave a half-smile. "And I his. But I am ready to move on now, lest some come to believe I will die a spinster." She gave a pretty laugh as her gaze wandered out over the other guests and came to rest upon Salisbury, standing across the room with the baron. A dreamy expression moved over her delicate features before she glanced back at Della and said with practiced nonchalance, "The duke seems to be quite smitten with you. I suppose you will save a dance for him – I hear you shared a waltz at the Colchesters' party a few weeks back."

Della tilted her head and observed the young woman. "Actually, I shall do everything in my power to avoid him for the evening," she replied, taking a slow sip of her champagne.

Lady Evangeline looked confused. "I... wouldn't it be rude to ignore the host at his own party?"

"Most certainly. But no ruder than him accosting me outside the ladies' room and demanding I save every dance for him." Evangeline stared at her, aghast, but Della kept her expression neutral as she leaned towards her, speaking low enough that the other guests would not hear. "You would do well to look elsewhere for a husband, Lady Evangeline. He is not an honorable man."

Della saw the confusion and heartbreak on the other woman's face but did not elaborate. This was not the time for subtlety, whatever Cole said. She was not about to spare the feelings of some naive schoolgirl for the sake of propriety. She had a right to know the duke's true nature. Lady Evangeline stared at Della with her mouth agape when a voice sounded behind them.

"Lady Evangeline?"

They both turned to see Lord Perrin with a hopeful expression. "I wanted to tell you what a lovely voice you have. That was a pleasure."

And as Lady Evangeline blushed and smiled prettily, Della winked at Lord Perrin and slipped away to approach the footman hovering near the door. "Might you direct me to the ladies' room?"

He nodded and Della met Cole's gaze for a moment before she left the room, assuring the footman she could find the way back herself when he left her in a gaslit corridor. She made quick use of the facility, pinching her cheeks to bring color into them and smoothing down her hair in a gilt-framed mirror before slipping silently out into the hall and making her way to a door they had passed on the way in. She had glimpsed shelves filled with books and supposed a library was a likely place to keep a safe.

With the stealth and silence only a thief possessed, she slipped into the room, lit only by a handful of gas sconces on the walls. Della lifted her heavy skirts as she made her way across the floor to stop them rustling and approached the oak desk at the far side of the room. She bent to inspect the piece of furniture but it was far too delicate to contain a safe of any substance and so she moved away to the shelves lining the walls, interspersed by elaborately carved panels of rich oak upon which brass wall sconces had been mounted to light the space. Della had spent enough of her time with the burglars and area divers who frequented the more flash parts of London to know where someone like the duke would hide a safe – and where else would a duke keep the very documents that could potentially ruin him?

She held her breath, not daring to make a sound as her fingers felt along the edges of the panels, seeking out the spring that would release a hidden door. She moved from one to the next, her search silent and methodical until she detected the telltale wear on the wood where fingers had grasped for the concealed latch. Brow furrowed in concentration, she slid a finger between the paneling and, on an indrawn breath, pushed the latch and slowly, slowly, pulled the panel away from the wall.

Della smirked in satisfaction as the massive iron safe was revealed to her. Glancing towards the doors once more, she reached down her bodice to retrieve the copy of the key she had hidden away. Holding her breath, she slipped it into the keyhole and carefully turned it, then heard the soft click as the locking mechanism gave way and the heavy iron door opened a crack. Jubilant, she smiled to herself as she gently pulled the door open to find a cavernous space filled with neat stacks of leather-bound ledgers, dozens of them side by side with cardboard boxes stuffed with paperwork and envelopes in bundles tied with twine. And here it was, all the evidence Cole needed to finally end the years of dedication to one man, to keep the promise he had made to his father. And Della knew, if she did nothing else with her life, she would be proud of her part in helping Cole keep that promise.

Nodding in satisfaction that all was where it should be, Della was about to close the door when she spotted, tucked away on the top shelf of the safe, slim stacks of gold bars and polished jewelry cases. She paused for a moment, stared up at that shining gold and flexed her fingers. It would be so easy... the ingrained sense of a thief to grab and run whispered at her. For a moment, she didn't move, though her hands did tremble at her sides. Finally, she shook her head, pushed the door shut, and turned the lock once more.

She carefully noted which panel concealed the safe and, not daring to be away from the parlor for longer than would cause suspicion, she carefully pushed the panel back, eyed the wall and floor around it to ensure that nothing was out of place, and hurried on silent feet to the door. She made her way, unseen, back to the parlor and slipped into the room without remark. Cole caught her gaze from across the space and she gave him a small nod to which he did not react, simply returned to the conversation he had been having with Lady Colchester.

"Miss Winthrop?" came a most unwelcome voice and Della turned to Salisbury approaching her with a smile but no warmth in his cold, grey eyes.

"Yes, Your Grace?"

"Your cousin mentioned that you had an interest in the classics. I thought perhaps I might show you an edition I purchased recently – the complete writings of Socrates. Would you care to see?"

"I would be delighted. Though, it might interest you to know that Socrates never actually wrote anything. Any works of his are simply the words of his contemporaries and members of his circle preserving his memory through his conversations. Quite a nice gesture, wouldn't you say?"

Something dark passed over Salisbury's face for a moment, and it compelled Della to let out a bright laugh and touch his arm, pressing with gentle familiarity. "Forgive me, Your Grace – my philosophy tutor was a strict taskmaster. I'm afraid I made that very same mistake myself and was rather harshly rebuked. How soon we forget!"

Salisbury looked down to where her hand touched his arm, then back at her with an ingratiating smile. "Why, thank you, Miss Winthrop. I would have hated to be misinformed about my own book. Come, I have left it out for the other guests to see."

Salisbury gestured for her to take a seat on the settee near the fireplace, placing himself in the wingback chair beside her, and Della glanced up briefly to find Cole watching them from where he stood nearby. He dipped his head in a small gesture to let her know he was nearby should Salisbury become a little too forceful, but all Della could see was the naked desire in those golden eyes, and so quickly returned her attention to the duke.

In any other time and place, the exquisite leather-bound volume Salisbury presented to her would have thrilled her no end, but all Della could think of was how badly she wanted out of this place and how desperately she wanted Cole's hands upon her again. The wanting him and hating him at the same time was a pain unlike any she had ever known. To take her mind from the emotions churning in her stomach, Della turned her attention back to the duke.

"I realize now, Miss Winthrop, I never did ask the purpose of your calling on me this morning. What, pray tell, did you wish to discuss?" Salisbury inquired as he closed the cover on the book.

"Oh yes, of course. Just a small thing, I'm sure – I believe this is your stickpin." She withdrew the item from her chatelaine bag and handed it over with a smile. The duke nodded.

"That is mine, indeed. My thanks to you." He frowned briefly. "I don't suppose you also found a gold cufflink?"

Della gave a sympathetic shake of her head. "I'm afraid not, Your Grace. I do hear that pickpockets frequent the park – at least I was able to rescue your stickpin before one of them got it."

Cole's gaze shifted to her, but Della ignored him as the duke frowned again and shook his head.

"Damned thieves – should be locked away to rot, the whole bloody lot of them." He caught Della's incredulous expression and composed himself. "Do pardon my language, Miss Winthrop. And thank you again for returning this."

Della merely smiled again and inclined her head. "I'm so glad to have been of service to you, Your Grace. I don't suppose..."

Salisbury raised a brow at her. "Yes?" he prompted her.

"I don't suppose... we might arrange to go riding together again after your party? I had such a lovely time." She gazed up at him with lowered lashes, her small smile full of promise, and his grey eyes narrowed as a rakish grin lifted his lips. His hand was suddenly upon hers where it rested on the arm of the settee, a heavy weight that trapped her there beside him. It took everything in her not to shake him off and she let her gaze wander down to where he touched her so intimately. The smile she gave him made her cheeks ache and, on a wild impulse, she brushed his hand with her thumb. His smile faded and the desire in his eyes intensified, but behind it was something else... a hint of a threat. Della's heart began to pound against her chest and his hand suddenly closed around hers, crushing it in his grasp. She drew in a sharp breath and Cole turned with a questioning look from where he stood nearby, but Della quickly laughed and gave a shaky smile, ever mindful of the other guests who glanced with interest towards the couple.

Salisbury held her for a moment longer, and though her bones creaked and a muscle in his jaw twitched, she never looked away from him, and the smile never left her face. After what seemed an eternity, he dropped her hand and grinned widely as though it had never happened.

"Of course, we should go riding once more, Miss Winthrop." He spoke now in a voice loud enough for Cole to hear. "It would be a pleasure."

At that moment, Cole stepped forward and coughed. "It is getting late, cousin. Thank you, Your Grace, for a lovely evening, but we must be going."

"Yes…" Della murmured, accepting the duke's hand to help her stand. "Yes, we should be going." She glanced up at Salisbury who watched her with narrowed eyes. "Thank you for your hospitality, Your Grace. We shall see you again at the ball."

"Of course. And thank you again for returning my stick pin."

Della looked over to Cole, whose expression never changed; he barely blinked as he bowed to Salisbury.

"Good evening, Your Grace," Cole said before saying his goodbyes to the other guests and taking her arm to lead her out into the hall. They stopped near a small table which held a silver dish for calling cards and a lovely, chased gold letter opener, and Della turned to the footman who waited with her cloak.

"Excuse me, but before we go, might I know the name of the publisher of your master's new book? I think I should rather like to see what else they publish."

The footman nodded. "I will be but a moment, miss," he said, retreating into the parlor. Clenching her jaw, Della turned then, snatched up the letter opener and was about to drop it into her chatelaine bag when Cole put a hand on her shoulder and shook his head. She rolled her eyes and reluctantly replaced the letter opener on the table. The footman returned with the name and Della thanked him before he held open the door for them.

Once they had entered the quiet peace of the waiting carriage, Della finally burst out in a string of expletives as she rubbed her aching hand. Cole said nothing as she gritted her teeth against the flood of tears, growing angrier as they pricked at her eyes, hating that anything about that man would make her cry.

"If I never see that man again, it'll be too soon!" she hissed as she massaged Della the base of her thumb. She raised her head when Cole reached across the space to touch her knee, looking upon her with concern.

"Did he hurt you?"

She gave a reluctant shake of her head. "I'll be fine."

"We're so close now, Della. One more night, and you shall never have to see him again. Did you find anything?"

She drew in a shuddering breath. "I found everything. Safe in the library. Fourth panel from the right – there's a latch beneath the trim on the right side. And don't worry about me, I know what I'm doing. But he nearly crushed my bloody hand. The man's a fucking lunatic," she muttered, wincing as she rubbed her bruised fingers. Cole breathed a deep sigh, the relief in his expression palpable.

"I cannot thank you enough, Della – this is very good news, indeed."

Della merely shrugged. "Just doing what you paid me to do."

Cole's mouth quirked up before he caught her hand in his, gently turning it over to inspect it.

"So," he began, brushing his index finger over her palm, "what else have you stolen from him?"

Della frowned and pulled her hand back. "You wouldn't let me take it. I've stolen nothin'."

"Come now, Della, you know he would accuse some poor servant of taking it and have them sacked for it."

"Well, then there's no harm done, is there?" she said, folding her arms across her chest.

"But what else have you stolen, Della?" His words were slow and deliberate, and she looked up to find him watching her with a stern expression. She gave a nonchalant shrug.

"Nothin' he can't afford to lose."

Cole raised a brow in expectation.

She relented. "His cufflink."

"And?"

She pursed her lips and looked away. "His pocket watch."

Cole sighed and reached over to take her hand into his once

more. She flinched as her bruised fingers bent in his grasp, and he loosened his grip as he raised her hand to his mouth and touched his lips to her palm. "Promise me no more?"

"You know," she said, withdrawing her hand from his, "you did hire me to steal for you. I can hardly be blamed for taking advantage of my situation."

"Della, I hired you to steal something that belongs to me, not to steal from other people."

She huffed out a breath as the carriage lumbered along the banks of the Thames. She stared out into the darkness beyond the windows, punctuated only by the gaslights lining the street. A hot, uncomfortable sensation gnawed at her stomach, but she willed it away, refusing to feel guilty for having taken that man's things. As though he could not replace them a thousand times over. As though it could make up for how he had treated her.

"Della," Cole finally said after the silence had stretched on to the point of discomfort. The very sound of his voice made her shiver and she turned to him – only to look into those mysterious, golden eyes that watched her, seeing through her, seeming to know her very soul. She trembled as though stripped bare by his gaze, and wondered, briefly, if he could read her thoughts.

"I wanted to speak with you... about afterwards. When all this is done, whether we are successful or not."

"What of it?" she asked, her defenses rising, prickling under her skin as she straightened in her seat.

"I... I want to tell you that it has been a great pleasure working with you – and becoming better acquainted." His voice grew husky as he spoke, and his eyes grew warm with meaning. Della frowned as he continued, rubbing the back of his neck as though uncertain what to say next. She had never known him to be unsure of himself. "And... how I should hate to lose you."

She stared at him now, mouth open, and he stared right back, almost defiantly. She blinked as her world tilted around her. Hadn't she just been using him? Getting everything she could out of him – his body, his home, his money – before their time was up? *No,* said a little voice inside her. *You will miss him desperately when you are gone. The very thought of never seeing him again makes you ache.*

Della swallowed; the old habits and walls were so very hard to break. "We knew this would end. You'll get what you need – let's not pretend our relationship was anything more than professional. We were fucking each other. I'm sorry if you thought it was more than that."

The words were like a dagger to her flesh, but nothing in life was easy, and one had to be prepared to say goodbye without emotion. Her heart hardened despite his declaration that he cared for her, for what use was it to return such an emotion? What use would it be to tell him she felt the same way? How could they ever be together? She had to look away as his lips twitched and he nodded slowly.

"I am sorry, as well. Perhaps I misread the situation." A muscle in his jaw twitched. "We shall continue our lessons and plan for the night of the ball." He paused and smiled – a smile of genuine feeling. "And still, it will have been a great honor knowing you, Miss Rose. Whatever you think of me."

Della didn't know what it felt like to have one's heart break. She had never loved anyone deeply enough to feel that way. Perhaps her mother, but she had been too young to remember much about the woman or her final days before she had been bundled into the orphanage. But the look Cole gave her as the carriage drew to a halt before the gatehouse of Bradford House – not angry, not frustrated, just sad – certainly got her as close as she ever would to having her heart rent in two. She stayed in her seat long after Cole had stepped out into the quiet night, wondering what held her back from simply saying, *Thank you.*

TWENTY-ONE

Mr. Barrow was waiting for Cole when he came down for breakfast the next morning, exhausted after a night spent replaying Della's words in his head. *We knew this would end.* And, truth be told, he knew that their relationship was never meant to last beyond the current operation. Why then had he lain in his bed all night, hoping she would knock on his door, hoping she would ignore her declaration that they were not meant to be, and let him make love to her again? He wanted so badly for her to be wrong because he could not imagine a future without her.

"Good morning, my lord," Mr. Barrow said as Cole gestured for him to follow, taking the valet past the breakfast room and down the hall to his study.

"Are Agent Tyndall and Agent Thorne ready for Saturday?" he asked as the valet followed him into the room, shutting the door behind them.

"Yes, my lord, they have been surveilling Lufton Castle since last week."

"Please inform them that Miss Rose has located the missing

documents. They are in a safe in the library, on the north-easternmost corner of the property. I will be at the Home Office this afternoon; we can meet there to look over the plans once more. Anything else I should know?"

"There is a guard who makes a round of the property at the top of every hour."

"Is this consistent? Even if there are guests?" Cole asked as he crossed the study to the portrait of his father which hung behind the massive mahogany desk that sat in the middle of the room.

"It is, my lord."

"Dogs?"

"No."

"Good. I'll go over the specifics with Miss Rose this evening."

Cole swung the frame out on a hinge to reveal the safe concealed behind it. He turned to the desk behind him and opened the bottom drawer. Rummaging around, he pushed aside the papers inside to lift the false bottom and retrieve a small key. He opened the safe as Mr. Barrow watched and pulled out two bags of coins before handing them to the valet, who accepted them without a word.

"Take this to the drop at Whitehall Gardens. I want Agent Tyndall to use it to get whatever information he can. I don't want a word of Miss Rose breathed without me knowing about it. A few sovereigns should help loosen any reluctant lips. I need only keep her true identity quiet for one more week."

Mr. Barrow nodded and turned to leave the room before he paused. "Would you like me to keep an eye on her?"

Cole swallowed hard as he slowly closed the safe, turned the key, and pushed the frame back against the wall. "No," he said, his voice as steady as though his valet were simply asking after the weather. "She will not be leaving again."

There was a meaningful pause before Mr. Barrow finally said, "Very good, sir."

Cole stood there, staring at the painting of his father – a man who so very closely resembled him physically, with the same dark hair, straight nose, and amber eyes. He remembered a man who had poured every bit of himself into his children when he could, for his work did not allow him much time with Cole and his siblings. And then, that work had taken him from them. It had been five years since his passing, and not one day of it had gone by without Cole fearing that same fate. And yet, even his father's death had not compelled him to give up the work himself. Cole did not intend to let his father's death have been in vain.

He mused, as he turned away from the portrait, that his father would have thought Della to be an exceptional candidate to be an operative. Clever, quick-witted, knew the rookery like the back of her hand – and not a bad fighter. He smiled as he remembered her throwing herself at the footpad in the park, with neither fear nor hesitation. And afterwards... he rubbed a hand over his jaw as he slowly sat at the desk. His stomach muscles clenched against the rising heat as he remembered pushing up her skirts there against the column; how overcome he was, how she had held onto him as though she were drowning, how wet she had been for him.

Cole slammed his fist down on the desk in an uncharacteristic fit of frustration. What had it all meant, anyway? Nothing, he thought as his jaw clenched. Nothing to her, at least. *We were just fucking each other*. He swiveled in his chair to the cabinet behind his desk and pulled out a bottle of gin and a single glass. He set the glass on the desk and filled it before pausing and staring at the clear liquid. It would be so easy to let her keep using him, as was so clearly her intention. It would be so easy to let her come to his room, wearing that flimsy linen wrapper, let her undress him, let her spread her legs for him – and each time, lose a small part of himself to her. She would only be here one more week. How much could he lose by then?

The hour grew late that night following the party and Della's cruel words to Cole in the carriage. Martha had arrived in Della's rooms to strip her from her fine silk gown and brush out her dark hair. Della waited after the maid had left for as long as she could bear before she grew angry and then began to feel ashamed for the words she had spoken the night before. She finally rose from where she sat in her bed, the copy of *Metamorphoses* left forgotten on the pillow beside her and donned her wrapper. The hallway beyond her door was dark, illuminated only by the small circles of light cast by the gas lamps on the walls. She paused outside Cole's bedchamber, but no light shone from underneath his door, and she continued down the stairs when the faint sound of the piano drifting up from the parlor reached her ears. She made her way through the shadows of the grand hall and stopped at the door. Pride forced her to draw in a deep breath, clench her fists, and set her jaw before she entered the room, determined she would not show how much she wanted him, nor how ashamed she was to have hurt him. It was better this way.

Cole sat at the piano, plucking out a few dissonant notes and he looked up when she stepped into the room. His expression, as always, was unreadable, and he inclined his head towards her before turning back to the keyboard and beginning to play a sad, slow song she did not recognize. She stood, listening, swallowing back any emotion that dared creep up inside her before he spoke over his shoulder.

"I have good news, Miss Rose. You have received your invitation to Salisbury's ball. I wish to thank you; you have far exceeded my expectations. I had begun to despair of ever catching him – I would not have been able to do this without your help."

Della pressed her lips together and twisted her fingers in the silk cord tied about her waist. "I told you I wouldn't fail. I would not see innocent lives lost to the vanity of one man."

Cole stopped playing and turned then to look at her. Everything in her, every fiber of her being longed to run across the room and throw herself into his arms and kiss those finely shaped lips, feel the heat of his body, hear the rasp of his breath. But she stood there as he observed her, in clothes worth more than everything she owned put together, in a house well beyond her reach, and did nothing.

"I know it has been difficult. The duke is not an easy man to spend time with, particularly for a woman like you..." He trailed off, pressed his lips together and gave a tight smile. "For a woman who attracts him. I wanted to give you something before you go, as a small token of my appreciation."

Della frowned as he stood and crossed to a small table near the fireplace. A paper-wrapped package tied with a length of blue ribbon sat upon it, and he picked it up and brought it to where she still stood by the door.

"The ten thousand pounds is more than enough," she said as he handed it to her. For a moment, she wouldn't take it, but he reached out and gripped her hand in his.

"This is not part of your payment. Simply a gesture of thanks."

He put the package in her hand, and she reluctantly accepted it. He watched, expectant, as she pulled at the end of the ribbon, then tore away the plain brown paper. There, in her hands, was an exquisite red leather-bound book, the gold lettering reading *The Complete Works of Plato.* Della stared down at it for a long time, frowning, her thumb moving over the embossed letters. She pulled her lips in between her teeth as her jaw worked at holding back something rising from deep inside her. It rose and rose until she thought it would choke her, and she swallowed hard and looked up at him, her vision blurred. *Say it*, she thought, *say thank you*. The words were right there at the tip of her tongue, but they died away as she nodded instead. "It's beautiful."

His expression softened, then, and he gave her the smallest of smiles. "I hope it is the first in a large collection, Miss Rose."

After a failed attempt to return the expression, she looked down.

"Despite what happened with Salisbury... I hope you had a good time last night," he added.

She still could not look at him and pursed her lips. "It was... nice. Lord Perrin was very kind."

Cole moved away from her to the sideboard and lifted a heavy decanter to pour himself a glass of port. He filled another glass and handed it to her without comment. "He's a good chap."

"We talked when we were at Rotten Row. He knows about you. About what you do."

Cole nodded and gestured for her to take a seat. She held a hand to her stomach as she sat, feeling rather exposed wearing only her nightdress and wrapper, even though he had seen and tasted the most intimate parts of her body. Nervous, she drained her glass in a single gulp and took a deep breath as Cole sat in the chair opposite her and draped a casual arm over the side.

"He's one of the few. We've known each other for a very long time."

Della wanted to ask what he had told his friend about her but refrained. Just being near him, alone in this room, made her head swim and desire ripple up from between her thighs. *Damn him.* She looked down at the beautiful leather book in her lap and felt the sting of tears, her body betraying her. "He rather likes Lady Evangeline."

"He has for a very long time. I knew you could be counted upon to steer her away from Salisbury."

"She seems too kind to be taken with the duke. I can't see how she could ever love someone like him."

There was a pause. "Sometimes we can't help who we love."

Della finally looked up, trying to steel herself against that penetrating, golden gaze, but it ensnared her, and her heart leapt inside her chest. She drew in a shaky breath and tried to smile but failed. "I... I was waiting for you."

"Waiting for me?"

"I feel like such a fool. After what I said last night, you would have no reason to want to see me. I was certainly mistaken."

"Not mistaken," he said, taking a casual sip of his drink. "I wanted you to come to me."

She frowned and set aside the book. "I don't see what difference it makes."

He took another sip and tilted the glass towards her. "It needs to be your decision, Della. Perhaps I have not made my feelings clear, but I suspect you know them. I will not pursue anything that you have no wish to be a part of. But if you want to come to me – to use me..." He trailed off and drained the last of his port. "I simply don't have the resolve to deny you."

Della stared at him. He had guessed her intentions – to wring every last ounce of pleasure from their time together. That she would take from him whatever she could before they parted ways. She narrowed her eyes at him and stood suddenly, but he did not react beyond tracking her movements with that sharp, assessing gaze.

"And what if I do?" she asked in a whisper, hands clenched at her sides as she fought back that painful need to touch him.

"I told you, I won't deny you. Just know that my feelings do not change."

She eyed him with suspicion. "Do you expect mine to change?"

His shoulders lifted in a shrug, and he set down his empty glass. "What if they did?"

Her throat ached with sorrow now, and she shook her head, fighting back the threat of tears. She let out a short laugh. "What would it matter? Are you gonna marry me? Della Rose of Seven Dials, infamous pickpocket, orphan..." The words choked her, and she dropped her gaze to the floor, covered in thick, expensive carpeting. "Don't be stupid. Whatever I feel doesn't matter. I know there's nothin' for us after this. And you're a fool to think any differently."

Cole stood then and moved towards her, never taking his gaze from hers. "I don't know what our future is, Della. But I know it doesn't end in a week."

He was close now, so close she could smell the delicious fragrance of him – port and smoke – and feel the heat of his body. Suddenly, his fingers were at the tie of her wrapper, and he gave her a questioning look to which she said nothing but took a step closer to him and gently set his hands aside before tugging at the tie herself. His fingers slipped over her waist, slowly pushing the garment off her body and then she was standing there in only her lace-trimmed nightgown. Never looking away from her, and never speaking a word, he worked with unhurried fingers to remove his tailcoat, waistcoat, bowtie, shirt, trousers, drawers... until he stood before her in his magnificent nakedness, fully erect, daring her to look away with his wolf-like stare.

Della's breathing grew heavy with each piece of clothing he stripped from that big, well-muscled body until she was sure she would scream from the sheer agony of waiting. Her throat convulsed and, with trembling hands, she undid the ties of her nightgown and let it fall with a whisper to the floor before stepping out of it. His hungry gaze moved over her, and she was consumed by it, shuddering when he finally reached out to lay a large hand over her hip and draw her towards him. His lips, when they touched hers, were gentle, and moved leisurely down her jaw and the length of her throat until she wanted to sob out loud and beg him to take her.

His other hand moved around her back, pulling her towards him, and a long sigh rasped from her mouth as her naked breasts brushed against his broad chest and his fingers pressed into her waist, pulling her backwards with him. He dropped onto the settee behind them, pulling her down with him as she straddled his hips. Her fingers clenched onto his shoulders as he entered her in one smooth motion, and she sighed against his neck as his arms closed around her, holding her tight to him as she rocked against him.

The sensation of him filling her, stoking against her tender flesh, overwhelmed Della's senses and she gasped as Cole took his mouth from her breasts and buried his face in the curve of her neck, inhaling deeply as though to commit her scent to memory. And as he held her tight and kissed her neck and matched the steady rhythm of her hips, she suddenly, inexplicably, began to cry. A single tear rolled down her cheek and she pressed her face into his hair to hide it from him as raw, aching sadness welled up inside her, burning in her throat. She clenched her teeth against the threat of more tears and clung to him as though she would fall into a dark place from which there was no return if she let go. His breath was harsh in her ear as he thrust up into her and suddenly, the dam burst, and she was clinging to him with tears rolling silently down her cheeks.

She couldn't stop it, and when a shuddering sob burst from her, he pulled away. His eyes widened as he beheld her, cheeks wet with tears, and he reached up to brush them away.

"Della," he whispered, his thumbs stroking her cheeks with soft tenderness, "what's wrong?"

Furious at herself, Della pressed her lips together and tore herself away from him, leaving him sitting, bewildered, as she stumbled back. She snatched up her wrapper and pulled it on, shaking, as he rose from the settee and put a hand out to her.

"Della?"

She shook her head as more tears welled up and she blinked furiously to keep them at bay. "Bloody hell," she whispered as she pulled the cord to close the wrapper before wiping her face with a voluminous sleeve. When he took another step towards her, she snatched her arms back. "No!" she cried out, balling her hands into fists at her sides. "You weren't supposed to do this to me! I'm not this person – I don't bloody cry."

Cole tilted his head as he observed her. "Then why are you?"

"I don't know!" She swiped at her cheeks again. "I feel so stupid. I'm not some schoolgirl heartbroken over her first love. I told myself I'd take every advantage of this opportunity, because I know I'll never get another one in this lifetime." She paused as Cole began to draw on his shirt, then spoke in a quiet voice. "I didn't want to feel anything for you. You were a means to an end – Violet and I are finally going to get out of the rookery. She's going to paint, and I'm going to read. And that's all I need. But then you had to be so kind, and so bloody good..."

Cole raised a brow as he buttoned his shirt. "Is it a crime to be a good person?"

"'Course not." She shook her head. "But I don't know what... I don't know how to respond to it. I'm not like you. I'm not like your friends."

A slow breath lifted Cole's chest. "Why are you trying to be someone you're not? I'm the only one here."

"What are you talkin' about? The whole bloody time I've been here has been spent tryin' to be someone else!" she spat, her rising anger letting the Seven Dials seep back into her voice. How did he stay so damn calm? He reached out then and took her hand in his, and she squeezed her eyes shut as he drew her close.

"I'm the only one here, Della," he repeated. "I have never asked, nor ever wanted you to be anyone but yourself with me."

Her jaw tensed and she met his earnest gaze with defiance. "And what if I were to stay? Do I stay as Della Rose, unworthy of a peer of the realm? Or do I stay as Miss Rose Winthrop, your cousin by day, your lover by night?"

For the first time in as long as she had known him, his expression faltered, and she sneered as she shook off his hand. "You've not thought this through. I 'ave. I think on these matters every minute of every day because this is not my world, and to everyone here, I don't belong."

"Della, you've as much right to be here as I do."

She shook her head in disdain and stepped back. "'Course I do. I know that. You know that. But what of your friends? Your family? Lady Evangeline? The Marquess of Colchester? The Duke of fucking Salisbury? I doubt they would think the same. Would you be willin' to give them up to be with me? Would you be willin' to give up your career for me? I can't be Della Rose unless people know who you are."

He said nothing for a moment and the weight of that silence settled upon the room as she watched him, his brow furrowed as he considered her. He opened his mouth as though to speak but the words seemed to fail him, and she sighed. "I won't ask you to give up everything you've worked for, for me. And I won't give up what I've worked for... I'm so close to having what I've always wanted, Cole."

It was then that Cole closed his eyes and shook his head. "I know you are, Della. And I won't take it away from you." He let out a slow breath and raised his gaze to her once more and the longing in his eyes made her chest ache with sadness. "I am a man trained to anticipate all outcomes, to be one step ahead... I wish I could have better predicted this."

"Predicted what?"

The corner of his mouth turned up, the dimple flashed and was gone, and Della's throat grew tight. "Oh..." The single utterance caught at the end and he swallowed, trying another smile. "You are also a means to an end, my last resort... I am going to get what *I* always wanted. But I cannot deny" – Della held her breath as he paused and lifted an arm to run a hand through his hair – "that I have fallen for you, utterly."

Della was taken aback and her mouth fell open. Her fist tightened where she still held the tie of her wrapper as she drew in a sharp breath. "You... you love me?"

And then he smiled that wide, warm smile that made her heart flutter, and her breath grew shaky.

"You are a fool, Della Rose." He laughed. "I do love you – you are a necessity to my very existence. The thought of never seeing you after this week is unbearable."

Della stared at him. She wanted desperately in that moment to hate him, to keep her life uncomplicated and on the path she had decided for herself. She wanted a quiet, comfortable existence with her books – returning Cole's love and facing an almost certain future of ostracization and ridicule was not part of that plan. And as she stood there staring at him, wanting him as she had never wanted anyone before, she found she did not hate him. How could she? He had made her feel important and valued in a way she had never experienced in her life, had made her little dreams seem so much bigger. But she understood better than he what his people thought of her, and what that meant for any relationship they might have, and so, though it hurt to say the words, she shook her head.

"I'm sorry, Lord Bradford. I'm sorry if I've misled you. But I'm afraid I don't feel the same way. There's no future for us that I can see."

She didn't wait to see what his reaction was. She couldn't possibly face it, and she turned on her heel and left the room.

And though tears burned in her eyes and her chest ached for want of him, she did not turn back. She did not turn back when he called her name as the door shut behind her, nor when she almost convinced herself, upon reaching her bedroom door, that it was not too late to go back and deny everything she had said. She forced herself to shut the door and stood there for a moment, trembling, before moving away to sit upon the edge of the bed. And Della Rose, who so rarely had cause to cry, and decried those who did, wept bitterly, half hoping he would knock at her door, and half hoping he wouldn't.

TWENTY-TWO

"Mr. Barrow?" Della asked as she poked her head into Cole's study to find the valet sitting at the desk making notes in a ledger. He looked up as she spoke and gave her a nod of acknowledgement.

"Yes, Miss Rose? How may I help you?" He set down the fountain pen he held and tilted his head as she stepped into the room, hands clasped in front of her.

"I was wondering... if you might tell me where Co— where Lord Bradford is? I had expected us to practice our dancing this afternoon."

Mr. Barrow cleared his throat and stood, closing the ledger as he did so. He kept his fingertips resting upon the leather cover as he spoke. "Lord Bradford is at Whitehall finalizing the plans for the operation. He asks that you meet him for dinner this evening so he can discuss the strategy for the party tomorrow."

Della hesitated in the doorway and the valet raised an eyebrow.

"Is there anything else I can help you with?"

"No... I mean, yes. It's just that... we were meant to spend this week practicing. I have not seen him since the night after the duke's dinner party."

Mr. Barrow was quiet for a moment as he gathered up the ledger and tucked it under his arm, not meeting her worried gaze until he finally spoke. "He's been rather busy with matters of some urgency. There's a great deal of planning involved for tomorrow. He will be home tonight for dinner and shall see you then."

Della knew when she was being dismissed and frowned at the cool edge to the valet's voice. Had Cole told him what happened? Did Mr. Barrow now hate her, as well? She swallowed back the lump in her throat and tried to smile. "Thank you, Mr. Barrow. There was just one more thing..."

"Yes?"

She drew in a small, fortifying breath. "Would it be possible to have the carriage brought round? I need to see my friend, to plan for our new home."

The valet stared at her for what seemed an eternity and Della had never felt more scrutinized in her entire life. She fought the urge to shrink back as she straightened her shoulders and met his steely gaze without looking away. After a moment, he gave a quick nod. "Very well. But I shall have to accompany you."

Della hesitated. She wanted desperately to speak with Violet, who had always guided her when the path before her was unclear, but the idea of sitting in a carriage with a man who clearly sided with the person whose heart she had broken was painful. She huffed out a breath. "If you insist. As long as you don't mind a trip to Seven Dials."

Mr. Barrow's smile bordered on a smirk as he came around the desk and walked towards her. "That doesn't worry me in the least, Miss Rose," he said, stopping before her. "I also grew up there."

Della's jaw dropped as he moved past her into the hall without another word.

Della didn't speak until the carriage jerked into motion and Mr. Barrow had settled himself on the seat opposite her. "I... I had no idea you grew up in the rookery."

His smile was slightly warmer as he regarded her. "Yes, above the flash-house on Queen Street. My mother ran the lodging rooms and fenced for the owner."

A burst of laughter erupted from Della. "Never say your mother was a fence!"

The valet's smile was conspiratorial now as he leaned closer to her. "Aye. And a good one. She had a whole network of divers and toshers bringing her goods from all over the city."

"Any chance I brought her anythin'?"

Mr. Barrow's smile faded, and he leaned back in his seat. "No... she died when I was a wee lad. Lived on top of that flash-house till I went to work with Lord Bradford."

Della let out a disbelieving chuckle. "How on earth did you meet him? Was he spyin' on you as well?'

He laughed as the carriage approached Piccadilly. "I was spying for him. Lots of Peelers would come into the house for meals and drinks, keeping an eye on things, listening for information. They started using me as a go-between; I'd get them information they needed, and they'd toss a few coins my way for it. Lord Bradford needed someone on the inside to work for him and they recommended me. After a while, he asked me to come work for him as a footman. Wanted to get me out of the rookery. I worked my way up, earned his trust – and I've been his valet for three years now."

Della gave her head an incredulous shake. "Why didn't you tell me?"

Mr. Barrow lifted his shoulders in a shrug and reached up to pluck the fine derby hat from his head and set it on the seat beside him. "I thought it best to keep you focused on the task at hand, and my lord agreed. A great many lives are in danger, Miss Rose. Any distractions could be disastrous."

Her mind raced at this information. One of her very own kind, here in this carriage. This steady, well-groomed young man had come from one of the worst slums in London, and she hadn't known. "So that explains the way you fight."

"The way I fight?"

"I saw you and Lord Bradford sparrin' a while back. You didn't look like a professional."

He laughed. "I'm certainly no professional. Just started out as a lad who had to learn how to defend himself, same as you. The earl asked me to train him, said he doesn't want to fight with rules. They don't exactly suit his line of work." He winked and Della nodded in understanding.

"Does anyone else know? About you?"

He shot her a bemused look. "Of course, they do – why wouldn't they?"

Della frowned. "Well – where you're from. Don't his friends find it... objectionable? Don't they worry about having a criminal in their midst?"

The corner of his lips turned up. "A former criminal. I have left those days behind. All they see now is a valet of the highest order, trusted by a man of unimpeachable reputation."

She said nothing for a moment as she contemplated the valet and saw now the sharpness in his gaze that she so often saw in her own – the look of a man who sees everything and has known hardship.

"What if these names get out? What if everyone finds out what he really is?"

Mr. Barrow angled a long look at her as the carriage jolted over a rut in the road before rolling to a stop.

"He would be devastated. All the other business – the earldom, House of Lords, country houses, all that – he's grateful for it all, certainly, but it's all just a stepping stone to what he really loves. I imagine he'll be doing this work till he drops dead – or he would if all those other things weren't in the way. But he's careful. Only the very closest to him know about it – it's a hard thing, in this business, trusting others."

Della winced as the stirrings of some emotion she did not care to ponder on started up in her belly and she immediately pushed it down as the valet stepped out of the carriage and reached in a hand for her. She took it with a small nod of thanks and saw they had stopped at Soho Square where he moved to the edge of the road and flagged down a passing hansom cab.

"He trusts you," she said as he handed her into the cab and slid into the seat beside her.

"And that took years. I was a lot like you when I started out with him. Bit prickly, bit untrusting, myself. We can't be putting faith in others where we come from, can we?"

Della again said nothing, but she did shake her head. Mr. Barrow gave a small smile and leaned back against the leather squab. "I grew to see, though, that he was someone I *could* trust. I don't want to let him down, you see. I've been working for him since he first set his sights on the duke, and I'll be there when he finally gets him – thanks to you. And when all that other stuff gets enough in the way that he might have to give this up... I'll still be here."

The valet smiled at her, but she couldn't find the will to return the expression. The guilt of almost costing Cole something he had spent years chasing made her stomach clench, and she vowed she would not fail again. She wanted so very badly to ask Mr. Barrow what Cole had said about her after the duke's dinner party, but her pride made her swallow back the words as they turned onto Shaftesbury and the cab stopped to let them out.

They walked to the outer edges of the Dials, where the

houses began to lean in upon one another and the air grew thick. The sun faded from view as they passed into the streets surrounding the infamous sundial at the center of the cross-roads. The valet's whole demeanor changed as he walked beside her. No longer cool and collected, his face took on a hardened, suspicious look – almost everyone here wore it, and his shoulders stiffened as though in anticipation of an attack. Della mirrored his demeanor as she walked close beside him, glad of his size, even though these streets were home. They were dangerous, even for someone like her. She stopped outside the door to Cora's brothel and turned to Mr. Barrow, whose chis-eled face lay in shadow beneath the brim of his hat.

"I won't be long, Mr. Barrow."

A small smile lifted his cheeks. "Please, call me John," he replied, letting the full effect of his Seven Dials accent color his words. She couldn't help a laugh.

"John."

He nodded and glanced behind him. "Not a problem. I've a few people I have to see. Shall I meet you back here in an hour?"

Della nodded and watched as he picked his way through the stinking puddles back the way they had come before turning and pushing open the red door.

It was quiet now in the house. No sound came from Cora's room nor any of the others, so she continued through to the back of the hall and up the dilapidated stairs to her old room. As she reached the landing, a strange sensation skittered up her back and she almost felt... sad. After tomorrow night, she would never have to come back to this place. The part of her life she so longed to leave behind would be gone. Why, then, did she look with nostalgic familiarity upon the faded floral wallpaper and the sunken floorboards? Perhaps it was the only place that had ever felt like a home for her, the only place where she had been welcomed. But as she raised her fist to rap upon the portal, she had the sudden and wild wish that it was another door she was knocking upon, and another person she was going to meet – a person who had also welcomed her. She hesitated, only for a moment, before tapping her fist upon the wood.

It opened a moment later and Violet, paintbrush in hand, looked put out before she recognized her guest. "Della! I didn't know when I'd see you again!" She ushered her friend into the room and cleared away a messy tangle of dresses for them to sit on the bed. Della perched at the end as Violet set the brush down upon the ledge of her easel and dropped onto the lumpy mattress. Her friend nodded at the painting in progress; two bodies picked out in swathes of peach and alabaster, entwined together on the canvas.

"It's good," Della said of the painting in progress. "Is the new flat ready?"

Violet nodded as she leaned back against the wall. "All ready."

"Here, you can add these to our collection," Della said, withdrawing the silk handkerchiefs and signet ring from her bodice. She hesitated for a moment before placing them down upon a table, thinking of the disapproving look Cole had given her and, once again, hating the guilt that nibbled at the edge of her conscience. Perhaps it was time to put her pickpocketing days behind her. Violet rubbed her hands together as though in anticipation and smiled.

"Perfect. I can't wait. I'll finally have a studio, with big windows, and there are bookshelves everywhere for you. And a garden. I've always wanted a garden. We can plant strawberries."

Della's smile was dreamy as she leaned against the faded wallpaper. "The earl has the loveliest garden – there's a big fountain with a bench, and the willows look like silver when the wind blows... and it always smells good. Like roses and lilacs. I want our garden to be just like it."

Violet's eyebrow rose a fraction. "Does he, now? And how is the earl?"

Della's throat tightened and she looked down at her lap, worried her friend would see the despair she felt at having Cole's last words to her be him telling her he loved her, and that she had turned away from them. "He's eager for tomorrow, to get back his father's documents. He's worried for the safety of his agents if they're found out and exposed."

"That duke sounds like a right bastard."

Della had to chuckle as she looked up at her friend. "That he is. I'll be very happy never to set eyes on him ever again."

Violet nodded sagely, but there was a wicked glint in her eyes. "And the good earl? Would you care to set eyes on him ever again?"

Oh, Violet – always straight to the point, straight to the heart of the matter. Della tossed her head, attempting some of the coolness she had used to brush off Cole himself. "His future is not my future. I told him as much."

"Told him? Told him what?"

A lump formed in her throat, and she had to look away from Violet's narrowed eyes. "I told him I did not return his feelings. What good would it do? The very idea—"

"What feelings?" Violet cut her off with a hard look and Della let out a shaky sigh.

"He told me... he said he loves me."

Her friend drew in a sharp breath; her emerald eyes widened, and her jaw dropped. She said nothing for a moment, and Della wished with her whole being that Violet would know what to do, what to say, because she hadn't the foggiest idea. She couldn't be with Cole. She would help him get those documents back, and that would be the end of their relationship... but her heart vehemently protested this path. Finally, Violet shook her head and frowned. "Do you love *him*?"

Della looked up into her friend's assessing gaze. "I... I

dunno. I don't *want* to. He's an earl and what am I? What could I even be to him? A mistress? He'd have to give up everythin' to be with me – his friends, his family. His career. And I'd have to give up everythin' I've worked for."

Violet shrugged and plucked up the hairbrush on the table beside the bed to begin slowly running it through her loose tresses. "Would it be so bad to be his mistress? You'd have a nice place to live, nice things to wear, and him." Her smile was suggestive as she said that, and Della let out a small huff of laughter as she fiddled with the lace edge of her bodice.

"I've worked too hard to get this far just to become a mistress. I have bigger plans for myself. And so do you."

Violet rolled her eyes and gave her friend a knowing look. "You've never worried about me before, Della Rose, and you shouldn't now. I'm perfectly capable of takin' care of myself. If you do have feelings for him, don't deny it on account of me. I want you to have everythin' you want."

Della reached out then and took Violet's hand into hers with a sad smile. "Oh, Violet... you deserve so much more than this. But I can't be with him. I can't be with anyone. I don't want to end up like... her."

Silence filled the small room, punctuated only by the hiss and crackle of the small coal fire which burned in the sooty hearth. Violet continued to brush her hair as she contemplated this, nodding slowly. "I think," she said at last, setting down the brush, "I think you ought to tell him this."

Another lump formed in Della's throat, and she swallowed it back as her head dipped in agreement and she sighed. "As always, you are the level head I need in these matters. I don't know what I *want* to say to him, though I know what I *ought* to... that if he wants me to be Della Rose with him, for I refuse to be anyone else, then he will have to reveal who he really is – how else can he explain my going from being his cousin, to just me, Della?"

Violet's lips quirked in a small frown. "You'll have to let him decide that."

A pause. "Yes, I suppose I will." Della smiled then and nodded towards the painting in progress. "Will you sell it?"

Violet followed her friend's gaze and sighed. "I'll try. I've been tryin' to get into galleries, but no one wants anythin' like that. Too provocative, they say. Lot of uptight old biddies, they are." She shrugged. "Once we're out of here, maybe then I'll have better luck."

"We will have better luck, Vi, I promise." She grinned and glanced at the small collection of bottles on the small table in the corner. "A drink before I go?"

Violet's eyes brightened and she pushed herself up off the bed before crossing the small space and filling two glasses with gin. She handed one to Della who took a sip and then laughed. "You'll never guess what I learned on my way over here."

A raised brow met Della's remark and she continued as her friend returned to her seat on the bed. "Lord Bradford's valet Mr. Barrow grew up right here in Seven Dials. His mother was a fence."

A burst of disbelieving laughter came from Violet as she choked back the gin in her mouth before she wiped a hand across her lips and gasped. "His valet? Really?"

Della nodded. "Yes. Grew up right over that flash-house on Queen Street."

Her friend looked contemplative now. "Barrow is his name? Tall fella, blond hair?"

"That's him."

"I remember him. Knew a couple of girls worked out of there. Said he was a good lad." Violet tipped her glass towards Della. "I guess there's hope for us yet?"

Della giggled and swallowed back the remainder of her drink. "I suppose so."

They chatted a bit more about Mr. Barrow and shared

another drink before Della noticed the small brass clock on the mantel, its glass face split by a crack.

"I should be goin'. Have to prepare for tomorrow night."

Violet rose from the bed as Della made her way to the door and put a hand on her friend's arm. "You be careful at that party. People like them can be dangerous. If someone here does something stupid out of desperation, they go in the jug for a bit, but when someone like a duke does something out of desperation..."

"I know, Vi, I know. I can take care of myself," Della said, patting her friend's hand. "I'll be careful."

Violet smiled and stepped back as Della opened the door. "You'd better. We have plans."

TWENTY-THREE

Cole's hand shook – just barely – as he poured himself a healthy measure of whisky and paused before raising the glass to his lips. She would be down shortly, and he would finally have to face her after her last words to him. *There is no future for us that I can see.*

But he did. He saw that future, as clear as day before him, and she was firmly in the middle of it. He frowned down at his glass, trying to see everything around her in that vision, and there was only one other thing there that seemed as clear as she – his life's work. There it was, side by side with Della, who had been brutally, pointedly accurate in her words. *I can't be Della Rose unless people know who you are.* And who had, rightfully, expressed the fear of a world who saw people like her as little more than refuse – not to be trusted, not to be welcomed.

His two greatest passions warred with one another, and he closed his eyes for a fleeting moment as though it would help him to clarify his vision, but one never materialized over the other. It was then that Cole knew, with heart-sinking certainty, that he would have to make a choice. And if he chose her over everything he had worked for, would she even want him in return?

He turned when the door to the parlor opened and she stepped inside, her expression unreadable, resplendent in pale pink satin and lace. Martha had swept her rich, dark tresses up into an elaborate chignon and her pale eyes gave her ordinarily sharp-featured face an ethereal air. She drew in a deep breath as the door closed behind her, then took a hesitant step forward.

"Good evening, Miss Rose," he said, keeping his tone formal. He gestured to the decanters behind him. "May I get you a drink?"

The relief in her expression was palpable. "Yes, please."

He turned to fill a glass for her and when he faced her once more, she had moved closer and now stood within arm's reach of him. Ever the professional, he did not react to this, but merely handed her the glass. She accepted it with a nod before raising it to her lips and taking a deep, appreciative sip. A hint of her perfume reached his nostrils – something light and exotic, almost peppery, and he resisted the urge to inhale it. He had scrupulously avoided her the past few days, knowing that to be with her would require turning his back on a lifetime's work, and that she would have to sacrifice more than he could possibly comprehend. Perhaps she was right to tell him they couldn't be more than this. Damned if that thought didn't break his heart.

She gave him a blank look over the rim of her glass as she drained the last of the whisky, then handed him the empty glass. He reached up to take it from her, his fingers closing over hers for a moment and holding her there as her gaze locked onto his. The air seemed to spark between them, the tension of words unspoken, of desire unfulfilled. He cleared his throat and took the glass from her finally to set it down on the table behind him.

"I had an interesting conversation with Mr. Barrow this afternoon," she began, her tone careful. He faced her with a raised eyebrow, gesturing for her to take a seat.

"Did you now?" he asked as she perched upon the corner of the green watered-silk settee. He settled down opposite her in a wingback chair as she placed her hands in her lap and nodded.

"Indeed. You did not tell me he grew up in Seven Dials as well."

"He did. I did not think it pertinent at the time."

She frowned at him, a little furrow marring her smooth brow. "It might have been nice... knowing I was not alone here."

Cole tilted his head to observe her and the sharp blue eyes that stared back at him, unflinching, and he wanted desperately to reach out and touch her. Instead, he leaned back in his seat.

"You're right, I should have told you. Mr. Barrow understands well the urgency of our work and he did not wish to distract you. I understand he accompanied you to Seven Dials earlier?"

Her fingers tightened in the folds of her skirts, and she straightened her shoulders, her expression defiant. "He did. I must make plans with Violet for our new home. After tomorrow... if we are successful..." She trailed off, her expression faltering for a moment as Cole's jaw tightened and the knowledge of her imminent departure made an unbearable pain slash through him. His voice when he spoke, however, was cool and collected.

"We will be successful. I have every faith in you, Miss Rose. That is why I wished for us to meet tonight, so we may discuss our strategy for tomorrow."

Her throat worked as she swallowed, dipping her head in agreement when a knock suddenly sounded upon the door.

"Come," Cole called out, never breaking eye contact with her.

The butler poked his head into the room. "Dinner is ready, my lord."

"Thank you, Harris."

He withdrew and Cole smiled at Della. "Shall we eat?"

Della halfheartedly returned his expression and took the hand he offered. When he led her, not to the dining room, but to the garden doors at the back of the manor, she turned to him with a questioning glance.

"It's a beautiful evening," he explained, "and I thought dinner in the garden might be nice."

Her whole countenance softened then, and a small smile turned up the corners of her lush pink lips. It took everything inside him not to draw her towards him then and kiss those lips and beg her not to leave, but he continued through the doors and out to the massive oak tree where they had picnicked on her first day with him. A checkered blanket had been laid down with a spread of baskets, fine china dishes, silverware, and cushions. Cole watched Della carefully as they came upon the picnic and she turned to him, her smile fading and her gaze full of sadness.

"I hope you're hungry," he said, trying to keep his tone light as he gestured for her to sit. She made no reply but dropped to the blanket in an elegant billow of pink satin with Cole following suit. She plucked up a bread roll and took a small bite as the breeze stirred the branches above them, sending the shadows upon the ground dancing.

"So," she said, holding out a glass for him to fill with wine. "What's the plan for tomorrow? Suppose I'll be the distraction."

Cole paused as she took a sip before he answered. "Only until you can get Salisbury alone – after all, he'll want to show you off, and you will let him."

Her lips twitched at this. "And when I get him alone?"

Cole shifted then to withdraw something from his pocket before reaching out and dropping a small vial into her outstretched hand. She turned it over and read the label before looking up at him with a frown.

"Laudanum?"

Cole's expression grew serious now and he leaned closer,

lowering his voice when he spoke. "Salisbury must be out of the way for this operation, not following you about like some lovesick puppy. I need you to get those documents out of the safe – the window in the library overlooks Lufton Castle's gardens. I shall have plenty of cover outside. You just get those documents to me, and I'll handle the rest. There are dozens of names in those documents and if Salisbury is able to decipher any of them, their lives are all in great danger, to say nothing of what those letters to the Russian government might contain. That is why we need what's in that safe – we have nothing against him otherwise. He is very careful."

Della looked thoughtful as she chewed on a bite of her roll. "I can distract him... you can be sure he won't be any trouble."

Something about the flat calm of her voice, the cold glint in her eyes, assured Cole of the certainty of her words. "I have no doubt." He paused then, and his smile faded. He would have reached out to touch her hand, but her expression was guarded, and he continued. "But I do ask... please be careful, Della. Salisbury is no fool, and he can be dangerous."

Her features hardened. "I've dealt with men far more dangerous than he. I told you... you just have to know what a man wants, and you will have him wrapped about your little finger."

Cole breathed deeply to slow the dull thud of his heart. "All the same," he said, reaching out to touch not her hand, but her arm, covered in a froth of cream lace. "Do be careful. I could not be there for my father, but I will do everything in my power to keep you safe. If anything happened to you..."

Her glance was wary for a moment before it softened, and she allowed a faint smile. "You know, I've never had anyone really worry about me before."

A breeze blew through the garden, ruffling the curls which had slipped loose of her chignon. She pushed them away with an absent gesture and he couldn't help it then – he reached up and caught her fingers, squeezing them with his. Her gaze never wavered.

"Della, I..." he began, then stopped, and for the first time in a long time, he didn't know what to say. He couldn't tell her he would take his leave of the Home Office, give up a lifetime's work... but nor could he tell her to go, and all he could do was stare at her with his mouth open, waiting for the words that never came. Her lips pressed together.

"Come with me," she said suddenly, pushing herself up off the ground. He frowned at her for a moment in confusion before he, too, rose from the blanket and followed her, wordless, back into the house. He knew he should say something, but her determined gaze kept him quiet as she led him up to her room. She paused at the door and turned to face him.

"There is somethin' I have to show you," she said as she pushed open the door. Her room was quiet and smelled of her perfume. He followed her at a distance, bemused, as she walked to the bed and knelt to pull out her old valise. Sitting on the floor, her skirts forming a pink cloud about her, she looked up at him, expectant. He crossed the room and sat beside her without a word while she dug about inside the bag and withdrew a small silver picture frame. She hugged it to her chest for a moment as though reluctant to share it before she let out a sigh and thrust it towards him.

Cole frowned and took it from her, turning it over to see the photo. A couple stared back at him and as he perused the image, he began to see the striking resemblance between the woman in the photo and Della. He glanced up at her and saw she watched him with fearful eyes and a taut jaw. "Your parents?"

Her head moved slowly in acknowledgement.

"I thought..."

"I never knew my father? I didn't. He died before I was born." Her voice grew quiet, and he leaned close to hear her, sensing that what she was about to say was very difficult for her.

There was no more affectation in her voice. It was all Della Rose, seeming ready to lay herself bare before him. He resisted reaching out to touch her once more. She licked her lips and looked down at her lap before speaking again.

"My parents were married – a quite respectable couple. My father owned a bookshop, and my mother was pretty enough to get out of the rookery and wed him – and he died, right before I was born. He left her nothin'. My mother had no choice. She had a daughter to care for, and so she returned to Seven Dials, and she started sellin' herself." Della's voice grew harsh now – not angry, but defiant. Cole said not a word, but watched her lovely face harden and her hands ball into fists. He looked down again at the photo of the young couple, just beginning their lives together, and sadness stirred within him.

"She did her best... she did her best for me. But there was an outbreak. Consumption. A neighbor brought me to the orphanage after she passed. Better than dyin' in the gutter, I suppose. That's all I have left of 'em," she said, nodding towards the photo in his hands. "And I promised myself every day I was in that place, that I would depend on no one but myself. She had depended on my father and look where it left her. But no man would ever hold sway over me. I'd rather steal. I very nearly didn't accept your offer."

She looked up at him now, her pale eyes blazing in defiance. He stared at her for a moment, taking in all of her, from the dark mass of curls atop her head, to her face, beautiful in its coldness, to the casual way she sat upon the plush pink carpet, her skirts pooled about her legs. After a moment, he allowed a brief smile. "I'm glad you did."

A muscle in her jaw worked and she looked down again. "I'm glad I did, too. You've been... most kind. Too kind."

Cole's throat started to burn as he held back the flood of words he wanted to say to her. "I'm happy to have been able to help you. You are a good person, Della, and life has been unfair to you. I hope... I hope you will find some happiness after all this."

He couldn't be sure, but he thought he saw a tear creep down her cheek and when she cleared her throat, there was a slight catch. He remained unmoving, however, as though to reach out would be to frighten her away.

"I don't think I'll ever be happy." She looked up at him now, her eyes welling with tears. "How can I be happy knowing someone like you loves me, and I can't love you back?"

Cole's jaw grew taut, and his chest burned, and it took every ounce of his well-practiced self-control not to grab her by the shoulders and pull her lips to his. "Why not?" came his reply, a forced whisper.

Her mouth compressed into a hard line, and she shook her head. "I promised myself... I told myself that I'd enjoy your company, I'd wear your clothes and eat your food and... and take my pleasure with you if I could, because it would be a pleasant distraction. And in the end, I will have earned that money and I will have done it because of my skills, because I am Rosie Diver, the quickest hands in St. Giles. But... but what 'appens if we're together? What am I then?" Her chin quivered. "Just another kept woman? At the mercy of a man, beholden to his whims?"

Cole drew in a breath and the silence filled the air between them, heavy with tension. "No, Della," he finally said, his voice a strained whisper, "I don't want you as a kept woman. You are not a woman to be kept. You are so much more than that."

Her whole façade crumpled then, grief pinching her features as she squeezed her eyes shut and slowly moved her head side to side. And he did reach out then, unable to bear the small distance between them, to take her hand where it lay clenched in the pink satin of her skirts. If she noticed, she did not react, and when she finally spoke, her voice caught on unshed tears. "But not enough to be Della Rose. I know it... I hear it in your voice. You're not ready for that."

Her words, though spoken in a quavering whisper, hit him with the force of a cannonball and his grip tightened instinctively on her hand. He could deny it; he could tell her that he would give up all he had worked for and shout from the rooftops who she really was and that he loved her with everything in his being, but the words wouldn't come. There was still so much left he wanted to do, to accomplish just a fraction of what his father had and show himself worthy of the title of Earl of Bradford. Instead, all he could say was, "I'm sorry, Della. I do love you, for what that's worth – I would give you the world if I could, but I am not yet ready to abandon this path."

She was quiet – unbearably quiet, but as the silence stretched on, she slowly eased herself into the circle of his arms. Her head turned, tilted up, and her breath was warm against his neck. His heart drummed as she sat with her back pressed up against his side, her hair tickling his cheek, and he moaned as she let out a long, slow breath and touched her lips to his jaw.

"I have no need of the world. Right now, I only want one thing..."

He glanced down at her and saw the primal hunger in her eyes, the parted lips and the flush which rose from her chest.

"I want you." Her voice moved over him like a wisp of silk, sparking along the ends of his nerves, and his cock stirred as she twisted in his embrace to face him.

"Della..." he tried to protest, but her scent filled his nostrils, and her body was warm against him, and suddenly her lips were upon his neck and his whole body shuddered in response. God help him, he could not resist her and a low, guttural growl echoed in his throat as her teeth nipped at his ear and her hand came to rest upon his thigh. The little ember burning inside him roared to life and he suddenly caught her arms in his hands and pulled her to his lips. He crushed his mouth to hers, thrilled by the little gasping moan that escaped from her throat. Her hands were at his shoulders, pushing off his tailcoat, then sliding up his neck and into his hair. She pulled him backwards and they fell to the floor in a tumble of satin and lace. Her breath was harsh in his ear as his kisses moved along the smooth line of her jaw and down into the hollow of her neck. Cole's heart slammed against his ribs when her fingers caught the waistband of his trousers, tugging at them to free his erection and she was gasping against his temple.

"Please... I need you now."

He grunted as he propped himself up on one elbow above her, reaching down with his free arm to tug up her heavy flounced skirts and petticoats until she wrapped those long, shapely legs about his waist. His hand was on her thigh, skimming up until he found the gap in her combinations, and she was as warm and wet as he remembered. Her broken cry rang out as he slipped a finger inside her and her inner muscles clenched around him as she gave her head a vehement shake.

He withdrew his finger from her to push her thighs aside, then angled his hips and thrust inside her. Della's long, low moan of pleasure was cut off as he edged deeper, her skirts rustling beneath them with each movement. Her slick, wet core enveloped him, drew him in, and he couldn't stop. Didn't want to stop. If she loved him back or not, he still wanted her desperately and the sensation of her fingers curling into the material of his shirt drove him mad with desire. Her nails dug into his back as her breathing grew harsh, her legs tensing about his waist, and he buried his face in her neck as her cry of release echoed in the warm, soft evening air.

Cole didn't stop, he never slowed as the pressure built and the sensation of her climax wrapped about him, and as he was about to pull away to spill his seed, her legs clamped about him, holding him to her.

He gave a ragged groan of protest, but she threaded her

fingers through his hair, pulled him down to her eager mouth and murmured against his cheek, "Don't stop."

And then Cole, who had always worked so hard to maintain complete command over himself, lost control to the woman who held onto him as though she would drown. The climax burst from him, filling her as she writhed in ecstasy beneath him.

When the last shudder had passed and he held himself above her, staring down into pale eyes glassy with satisfaction and cheeks flushed from exertion, he knew he could not let her go. A hazy smile flickered across her lips, and she moaned as he pulled away and rolled onto the floor beside her, panting. Rich, golden light filled the room as the sun dipped towards the horizon and they both lay beside one another, quiet, breathless, Cole knowing what he wanted to say to her, but unable to form the words.

TWENTY-FOUR

Della stared up at the ceiling as she tried to catch her breath, her whole body burning with desire, unsated, even after Cole had brought her to that shivering, pulsing climax. Her hips twisted beneath the bunched-up heap of her skirt and petticoats, wanting more, wanting him. But, as always, her fear held her back, and the words she longed to say stuck in her throat until she was sure she would choke on them. Instead, she rolled onto her side to find him also staring up at the coffered ceiling. She inched closer, burying her face into his neck, and inhaling the intoxicating, masculine scent of him. A shudder raced through her. His seed was still wet upon her thighs, but she needed more, she craved him, and knowing her courses were due in another day or so made her confident that she was safe in letting him inside her once more, marking her before she was gone from his life forever. And she had to leave – it was clear he was not going to give up the Home Office for her. And she was not going to let her dreams go for him. There was no middle ground for them, no crossing the barrier between his being an earl and her being a nobody pickpocket. She would leave with her ten thousand pounds and never look back, but she could still take her pleasure of him before then.

His breath hitched as she pressed her lips to his neck, ignoring the sudden tightening of her throat, then lower, pushing aside the collar of his shirt, loosening the tie he still wore to touch her mouth to his collarbone. Her fingers worked at the buttons of his shirt, almost frantically, as though to push away the dull ache that had most inconveniently started gnawing at her heart. She tossed his tie to the side; the shirt came next, and a longing sigh escaped her as she traced her fingers over the hard muscles of his chest, of his stomach, and they grew taut at her touch. Her tongue flicked over one of his nipples and he let out a hiss of pleasure before his hands were upon her back, tugging at the tiny buttons of her dress. His back arched as she moved lower, kissing the flat, hard plane of his stomach, tongue skimming along his sweat-dampened skin. He was kicking off his trousers as she did so, removing the impediment to her wandering mouth. He was hard again, his cock thrust up proudly as her lips reached his hipbone, moving ever lower until he groaned in frustration. And then, with a fiery shiver of satisfaction, she took him in her mouth. His hips jerked beneath her touch and a low growl sounded in his chest as she traced her lips up and down the length of him, tasting the mingled flavors of their bodies on his skin.

With the ache now conquered by her growing lust, she pulled away with a gasp and, never looking away from him, tugged away her loosened bodice. She then stood on trembling legs and in the dying light of the day, undid the ties of her skirt and petticoats, letting them fall into a puddle at her feet. He sat up, leaning back on one arm, and watched with an enigmatic expression as she stood before him, hair in disarray, wearing only her combinations and corset. She reached for the hooks of the corset, but he stood suddenly in a ripple of muscle and put his hand over hers.

"Stay with me, Della. I cannot bear for you to go." His whisper was strained, his gaze imploring. The ache returned and now she replaced it with anger.

"Are you going to tell everyone who I really am?"

His fingers tightened just a little on her hand. "You know I cannot. It would compromise everything I have built..."

"Then I have no reason to stay. I will not live a lie. Can't we just have this, just this moment?"

"Is it enough, Della? Just this moment?" His gaze held hers, beseeching her, and her anger flared again.

"It's not enough. Of course it's not enough. But you are the Earl of Bradford, and you have your secrets, and I am Della Rose of Seven Dials, and there is too large a void between us, Cole. It's a bloody ocean." Her voice cracked on the last words. He reached up then and the touch of his thumb upon her cheek made everything in her crumble and she had to close her eyes for a moment as his whisper reached her ears.

"It is vast, indeed, Della. You are right. And yet, I still love you."

Dammit. Damn him. If he didn't let her go, she would break apart before him and never be able to put herself back together, and she hated herself then for doing that which she had promised she would never do – she had gone and fallen in love with him, too. She pushed away his hands in a sudden fit of rage and fumbled for the hooks on her corset.

"Just shut up," was her sharp whisper, and she glared at him as the corset loosened about her. His jaw tensing was the only sign he gave of any emotion; otherwise, he stared at her as she pulled away the garment and flung it to the ground. Somehow, being angry at him seemed to keep at bay the rising ache of denying him something she deeply wanted as well, and so she fed the anger. Chin jutting out, she pushed off her underwear and kicked it away, never taking her glare off him, defying him to say something. She was panting now, letting the rage build in her chest and the lust swirl in her belly and she wanted him to do something that would make it easier to hate him. Grab her. Push her down on the bed. Anything. When all he did was stare back at her, his broad chest rising and falling, she clenched her jaw.

"Will you not oblige a lady?" Her voice came out as a low hiss, all traces of Rose Winthrop gone, and suddenly, that always impenetrable expression of his broke, and now he scowled back at her. A gasp, somewhere between outrage and desire, burst from her when he reached up, put his large hands on her shoulders, and turned her around to push her onto the bed. She fell face first onto the silken bedspread and moaned into the cool fabric as the mattress shifted and he was kneeling over her. His hands dropped to rest on either side of her head and as he leaned down to whisper in her ear, the heavy ridge of his cock brushed her buttocks and a shudder racked her.

"I shall always oblige you, Della. You need only say the word."

She squeezed her eyes shut and closed her fists around the material of the bedcover. "Then take me... this is all I can give you."

There was a pause; she waited with bated breath as desperate desire pooled low between her thighs. Finally, he let out a low grunt and grasped her by the hips to pull her up off the bed. Steadying herself on all fours, she gasped when he thrust into her from behind and held himself there, letting her feel the length of him inside her, and she moaned as she pushed against him, desperate for release, desperate for him to do anything that would make her hate him, just a little. Just enough to make leaving a little easier.

His fingers dug into her buttocks and, still in possession of that iron will, he didn't move, and she gritted her teeth and wanted to sob in frustration. Suddenly, his breath was warm against the shell of her ear and every nerve ending in her body sparked as his finger brushed aside the curl that had fallen across her neck, and he touched his lips there.

"This changes nothing." His whisper was soft, and she growled.

"Please... please just fuck me."

He kissed the back of her shoulder, and she was sure then her heart would burst from her chest. "As you wish, Della."

And there was a moment where she held her breath as his fingers skimmed down her back, positioned themselves on her hips, and he pulled her against him. The bedspread muffled her gasping cries as he thrust into her, never slowing, never pausing, until she choked on a shout of pleasure as the climax washed over her, a throbbing, raw pulse of release that made her sob into the still night air. And before the last shiver had raced through her, his hands strengthened their grip on her waist and he drove himself to his own climax, grunting as he emptied himself inside her while she buried her face in the mattress and shook with desire.

They fell on the bed together, still joined, gasping for air. Della knew she should pull away from the delicious heat of his skin against hers, but she could not find the will to do so. His body, lean with muscle, felt too good, too comforting as his arms came about her and he held her close. His warm breath fanned across her neck and there, in his embrace, she did something she did not expect. She slept, a deep, dreamless slumber that made all the anger dissipate and she did not wake until the sun rose once again to touch her room with its cheerful, golden light.

Lufton Castle was an impressive sight in the evening. Every window of the massive Elizabethan stronghold blazed with candlelight and the strains of an elegant waltz drifted through the open casements as Cole offered an arm to Della. She hesitated before stepping out of the glossy black barouche, trying to summon her courage even as her hands shook and her stomach grew queasy. Swallowing, she dipped her head in a sharp nod and placed her hand into Cole's. His smile was encouraging as she slipped her arm through his, mindful of the heady fragrance of his cologne and the intense perusal of his golden eyes. She swallowed hard as they made their way up the grand stairs to the front doors of the home, flanked by guards and footmen in scarlet livery.

"Are you ready?" came his whisper as he tipped his hat to another guest.

Della, not trusting her voice just yet, bobbed her head and smoothed her free hand down the elaborate bodice of her pale silver gown. Cole had been careful in selecting it for her, knowing the shimmering material would catch the light and, hopefully, the eye of the duke.

"You didn't have to stay with me last night," she finally said as they passed through the massive iron-clad doors and into the grand hall, glittering with gold and silver and candlelight. Cole glanced over at her, unperturbed.

"I wanted to." He paused as though he would say something else but smiled instead and guided her through the throngs to the great hall.

"Do you have the key?"

She patted her elaborately trimmed bodice, inside which the copied key to the safe was safely tucked away. "All is in place."

Cole slipped his watch out of his pocket to confirm the time. "We have one hour. We just need to find Salisbury."

Della paused beneath the soaring domed ceiling of the great hall and let the crowds swirl around them. She heard the whispers already, carefully concealed behind dainty fans, as the guests chattered about the young woman said to have caught the attention of their host. She was a mystery to them, and Della could practically hear the old gossipmongers speculating about her. Again, the urge to laugh bubbled up inside her. *If only they knew.* Cole gave her hand a reassuring pat as she squared her shoulders and tilted her chin upwards, daring any of them to question her presence here.

"Let's try the ballroom," she suggested as she moved with serene grace through the room and closer to the sound of the music drifting in the air. Once they reached the doors to the ballroom, she knew she had found their target. A crowd had gathered near one of the window embrasures and at its center, taller than those surrounding him, stood Charles Lumley, ninth Duke of Salisbury. Della's heart stopped for a moment before she pulled in a calming breath and looked up once more at Cole, who gave her an encouraging nod.

"You can do this, Della."

She did not reply, but instead plastered a dazzling smile on her face and became, once more, Miss Rose Winthrop. They crossed the room together, Della noticing with a wry smile the appreciative glances of the ladies in attendance as they watched Cole, impossibly handsome in his fine suit and crisp white shirt, those amber eyes missing nothing, those sensual lips promising much pleasure. And oh, how they did bring pleasure. A twinge of yearning pulled at Della's loins as she recalled how he had bent over her in the dying light of the day and taken her with all that pent-up desire, bringing her to heights of ecstasy she had never thought possible. And then he had gone and told her he loved her. And she believed it, with her whole, foolish heart, though knowing it was not enough for him to let her into his life – fully, as Della Rose – made that foolish heart break just a little. And because she couldn't bear that, she told herself he was not obligated to do so, nor was she to make any concessions for him. Their business was at an end.

She peeked up at him one last time as they drew closer to the duke and his crowd of hangers-on and he looked down at her, not with that magnetic smile that she had so come to love, but with a gaze full of longing. She forced her attention back to Salisbury as they drew closer and finally, he noticed her.

He gaped at her for a moment as she paused on the edge of the dance floor and she stared back at him, the corner of her mouth turned up in a knowing smile. He gave an imperious wave of his hand to the couples surrounding him and they dispersed as he sauntered towards her, his intense gaze never leaving her.

"Miss Winthrop," he said when he reached her and Cole. "What an honor to have you in my home again."

"The honor is all mine, Your Grace," Della replied in a rich, husky whisper. She withdrew her arm from Cole's and offered her hand to the duke, who took it with a wolfish grin. He lifted it to press his lips to her, nipping her skin through the glove she wore, but if she was shocked, she gave no outward appearance. She merely batted her lashes and inclined her head in cool recognition.

"Bradford," he finally said as he released Della's hand, acknowledging her chaperone with a quick nod. "Thank you for coming this evening. May I borrow your lovely cousin for a dance?"

Cole's smile was benign as he gestured to the dance floor. "Of course, Your Grace. I see some acquaintances I should catch up with in the meantime."

Della caught Cole's meaningful look and swallowed back the nervous tremor that wiggled up inside her breast. It was time. She turned back to the duke with a wide grin.

"Shall we?" she asked, and he responded by tightening his grip on her fingers and pulling her out onto the crowded dance floor. As they moved in a graceful sweep, Della could hear it, the rise and fall of murmured voices, all wondering – who is this girl dancing with one of the most powerful men in the land? How did *she* get him to dance with her? Who is she, and where did she come from? And suddenly, perversely, Della was excited at the prospect of being an enigma, of being the center of chatter, and she could use this to her advantage. She lifted her face to Salisbury. "I fear we are becoming the subject of some gossip."

His shrug was nonchalant. "Let them talk. You are, by far, the most beautiful woman here tonight, Miss Winthrop. I should say they are sick with envy of you. The first to dance with the Duke of Salisbury – it's a wonder the ladies haven't all fainted from spite."

It took everything in Della's power not to roll her eyes at his vanity. She fluttered her eyelashes, carefully darkened by her with a stick of charcoal, and shook her head. "You are too much, Your Grace. I do not deserve your attention."

He laughed, but there was no joy in the sound. "I don't dance with just anyone, Miss Winthrop. I have very specific tastes."

The air grew close around them and the sound of the orchestra seemed to fade into the background as Della smiled and he pulled her tight against his body, his fingers digging into her waist.

"Really?" she said in a low whisper. "How lucky for me."

"Very..." He paused as the music ended. "I have known a great many beautiful women in my time, Miss Winthrop. But none can hold a candle to your loveliness."

Della's cheeks grew warm, and her hands shook. His touch seemed to be everywhere, overwhelming her senses, and though the music had stopped, he still had a hand about her waist. She let out a delicate laugh and tapped him on the arm with her fan. "You know, Your Grace, flattery will get you everywhere."

She watched his eyes widen as she put careful emphasis on the last word, then disengaged herself from his cloying embrace with a teasing cluck of her tongue.

"Indeed?" He followed her as she trailed to the edge of the dance floor, needing a moment to collect herself. She fanned herself as heat rose from her chest and seemed to suffocate her, and the quick breeze helped her catch her breath. She turned as he approached her once more, his lips turned up in a sly grin. "And where is that?"

She tilted her head to observe him with as sultry a look as she could manage, then smiled as the band struck up a lively polka. She held out her hand to him and as he drew her out onto the dance floor, she leaned as close as she dared and whispered in a voice only he could hear, "Anywhere you want."

She wasn't sure if she heard the low growl he made, or if she imagined it, but she knew she had him then. She just had to get him away from the ballroom.

"Perhaps we might get some refreshments?" she suggested as the polka came to an end. Salisbury nodded and presented his arm with a flourish, and she took it amid a flurry of whispers concealed behind flapping fans as they left the dance floor.

"Do you see, Miss Winthrop? They are positively green." The duke was not wrong – she saw the envious stares and the glares of the matrons who saw this unknown, pretty young thing on the arm of the Duke of Salisbury, and now saw no hope for their own daughters. Della bit back another wild urge to laugh.

Leaving behind the sharp whispers and the murmurs of discontent, they moved into the grand hall and passed beneath the immense, glittering chandelier hanging at the peak of the domed ceiling. Della made a surreptitious survey of the room, trying to find Cole among the throngs, but she saw no sign of him and returned her attention to the duke.

"If you would care to, Miss Winthrop, I have some very rare volumes by Euripides in my library I thought you might appreciate."

"No!" she said quickly. "No... perhaps somewhere a little more private?" she suggested with as coy a smile as she could muster. Salisbury's smirk widened.

"I have some very fine Burgundy in my study – perhaps you should like a private tasting?"

Della had to hold back a sigh of relief. *Perfect.* "Are you trying to compromise my reputation, Your Grace? I can assure you I am not that type of woman."

"Of course not," he replied, his voice low as he drew her down a quiet corridor. "I would expect any woman I court to have a sterling reputation. This is but a friendly invitation."

"Are you set on courting me, then?" Della tried to keep her tone light, but they were alone now in this dimly lit hall, and she wanted to look back to see if anyone had noticed.

"Perhaps, Miss Winthrop. It would be a fine match, don't you think?"

Della could only nod as he stopped at a set of paneled oak doors and pushed them open. The room beyond was dark but for a smattering of candles burning atop the large mahogany desk in the center of the room. The smell of smoke and leather reached her nostrils as she took a hesitant step inside. He had already crossed to the cabinet on the far side of the room and opened the inlaid doors to withdraw a bottle of rich red wine and two crystal glasses. He set them down on the desk and pulled the cork from the bottle in a single, expert motion, filling the two glasses. She took a few, nervous steps forward, though her face showed nothing but an eager smile.

When he looked up, however, her smile vanished. His expression was no longer full of foolish arrogance, but of menace. Her expression faltered and she fought to set it right again. "Is something the matter?"

"You're not going to tell anyone we were in here tonight." It was a command, not a question.

"Of... of course not. This is but a friendly invitation," she replied with a shaky laugh, echoing his words. He pushed one of the glasses towards her as she brushed a hand down the front of her bodice as though nervous.

"Try some, from the Côte de Nuits. It's quite exceptional."

Della drew in a ragged breath and plucked up the glass to take a sip. She barely tasted the wine as it slid down her throat, for his gaze never left her, and his grey eyes were full of suspicion.

"It's... it's lovely," she stammered, setting the glass down beside his and seeing her opportunity. It was a small motion she made with her hand – he wouldn't have seen anything but her withdrawing her arm, but her practiced fingers had slipped the dose of laudanum into his wine and her legs quivered with relief as she pocketed the empty vial.

He said nothing for a moment, and the guttering light of the candles made the planes of his face seem harsh. Suddenly, Della saw in him the same bully she had seen in so many men before, men who wanted everything and were quite happy to take it, no matter the cost. Those narrowed eyes, that pursed mouth, the clenched fists. A dose of laudanum was the least he deserved, and she settled in to wait.

"Your guests will be wondering where you are." Her tone was carefully benign.

"As long as they have their music and their champagne they won't care where I am. You have flirted and smiled and insinuated enough – I will take what I want tonight."

A flash of fear skated up her spine, but she forced it down. *You are not afraid of him, Della. There's more danger down one back alley in the Dials than there is from him. He's just a toff like the rest of them. He'll be asleep before you know it.*

"I thought you required me to have a sterling reputation." Her voice grew defiant now. He smirked in reply.

"People need only think you are pure as the driven snow. I require a sampling before I can commit to a courtship."

He moved around the desk now, and she watched with the smallest sense of triumph as he drained the remainder of his wine in a single gulp. She stared him down, feeling the persona of Rose Winthrop slipping away as he stopped in front of her, his expression full of menace, his body crowding into her.

"I am not afraid of you," she said, her voice low and deadly as she fought to keep the rookery from her voice, her hands clenched at her sides. She knew a bully when she saw one and she was not about to let him cow her into giving him what he wanted. "I know what you are. I know what men like you do. You are a lie. Nothing about you is true, or good, or right."

"Oh?" Salisbury was casual now as he returned to the cabinet and plucked up a heavy crystal decanter to pour himself a measure of whisky, seeming to abandon his fine French wine. He twirled the amber liquid in his glass before looking up at her. "And I know what you are."

Della's heart plummeted and her breathing grew shallow as she stared back at him, struggling to keep up that carefully impassive mask. "And what is that?"

His low chuckle was not amused, or friendly. It threatened and he leaned a hip against the cabinet. He continued to swirl the whisky in the glass. "A thief."

TWENTY-FIVE

Della froze. Her stomach churned with sudden, terrifying dread, but somehow, some unseen power kept her expression calm and her hands still as she glanced at his empty wine glass. "Consider your next words very carefully, Your Grace. I do take exception to wild accusations."

"I am almost certain of it," he said as he pushed himself away from the cabinet and came towards her. Panic rose inside Della, and she fought the urge to step back. He stopped in front of her, towering over her, too close for comfort. "What are you doing here, Miss Winthrop? After my fortune? Hoping to land the great duke and bleed him dry, make a fool of him? What else would the daughter of some forgotten nobody from the north be doing here? You didn't seriously think I'd consider you for a bride?"

The panic subsided as she realized that he did not yet know the real reason for her being here. She let a slow smile cross her lips and was careful to keep her gaze on his as she took a step towards him – close enough that she knew he would be able to smell the expensive French perfume she wore.

"It seemed like a good idea at the time," she said in a low

purr, tilting her bare shoulder towards him. Drawing upon every seduction technique she had seen Violet use, she subtly pushed her arms into her sides, pressing the soft curves of her breasts upwards and biting her lip. She knew she had him when his head slanted to the side, and he angled his body towards her. He set down the glass and the corner of his mouth lifted as he regarded her, his eyelids now seeming to grow heavy; he blinked rapidly as though to rouse himself.

"How is Bradford involved?"

Della let out what she hoped was a snort of derision. "He is nothing – he thinks I am here to find a respectable gentleman to marry. I have set my sights much higher. And there is none higher than the Duke of Salisbury. My cousin does not like me wasting my time on you. He has heard rumors."

"Rumors?" He inched marginally closer, and it took every ounce of her willpower not to back away. He blinked again.

"Yes..." She racked her brain for something to redirect his attention. "Regarding the sort of women with which you spend your time."

"Really?" He raised his eyebrow at this, but the word came out slowly. "I don't suppose you'd like to share?" His tone was joking, but just barely, and she let out a soft chuckle and reached across him to pick up the glass he had set down. He watched with bleary eyes as she downed the contents, her gaze never leaving his the whole time.

"I hear you like the chase. That you would pursue a woman as you would a stag, like a hunter and his prey. So, Your Grace..." She paused to lick the last drop of whisky from her lips and pressed the glass into his chest. His expression was positively wolfish by now as she leaned into him and he swayed against her. "Have I led you on a merry enough chase by now?"

His voice, when he spoke, was harsh, almost granular, but the words began to slur together. "Quite merry. But my...

mother would never approve of marriage to you. She has also set her sights a good deal higher, and for this, I am truly sorry."

"Oh?" She arched a brow and started when his hand came to rest upon her waist. His closeness threatened to overwhelm her, and she bit the inside of her lip to keep from recoiling and slapping his smug face. He was so close now, swaying against her as he tried to lean in.

"But there are other ways, Miss Winthrop, if you are amenable. Surely we do not require a marriage contract to… enjoy one another?" His lips were dangerously close to hers and she summoned a smile from somewhere deep inside her.

"Well now, that is tempting," she whispered, shivering as his hand traveled up her ribcage, coming to rest close to her breast. Too close. She forced out a giggle and slipped out of his overbearing embrace, stepping away to trail her finger along the surface of his desk, looking back at him over her shoulder with a coy grin. She then looked away to hide the shaky breath that emerged from her and said, "I shall have to think on that."

Suddenly, he was behind her, his chest pressing into her back, his hands on her stomach, moving up until he cupped her breasts through the material of her bodice. A burning rage roared through her, and she bit down on her tongue until she tasted blood to stop it bursting out of her. The tips of his fingers slipped under the low neckline of her bodice, tracing along the edge, tugging it lower. His breath was hot against the back of her neck, his touch insistent and her fists clenched so hard at her sides that her nails dug into her palms. She couldn't do it anymore – she had no more false smiles, no flirtatious giggles, nothing left in her. That laudanum needed to take effect – and soon. She swallowed back the rising bile as his lips touched her bare shoulder.

"What is there to think on? I… I can make an affair very worth your while."

And that was it. She couldn't fake being Rose Winthrop any

longer. Della was inside her, screaming with rage and just as she started to turn around, her hand itching to slap his arrogant face, he grew quiet. He shook his head as she faced him, and she stilled, not daring to breathe a word as he passed a hand over his face.

"Your Grace?" she ventured in a quiet voice. He shook his head again, then blinked at her. "Do you need to sit down? You look a bit wan..." The suggestion, whispered in a silken voice, seemed to agree with him and he nodded slowly.

"Yes... yes, just for... just for a moment."

Della whispered a soft word of encouragement and gently took his hand to lead him to the small settee tucked between two massive parlor palms. She then gently deposited him upon the seat and stood there, stroking his hand until finally, mercifully, his eyes closed, and she carefully tucked a pillow behind his head. Della stood there for what felt like an age, her heart racing, until she was sure he was asleep before slowly lowering his hand to rest it upon his lap. She snatched up the empty wine glass he had drunk from and shoved it into the large pocket sewn to the inside of her gown – leave no evidence, Cole had instructed her – before backing away to the door.

She stood there for a moment, her ear pressed to the oak portal, listening for anyone who might be lingering in the hall outside, but heard nothing. After one final look to ensure the duke remained asleep, she dug into her pocket for the watch Cole had loaned her. She had to meet him in ten minutes precisely. Holding her breath, she eased the door to the study open and peered into the corridor. Empty. Sighing with relief, she slipped out and pulled the door shut behind her.

Della made her way back towards the main hall, pausing in the shadow of the massive staircase to ensure no one was looking in her direction, before slipping into the hall and casually joining the meandering crowd that had gathered in the great hall outside the ballroom. Voices rose and fell, but no one paid her any mind as she snatched up a glass of champagne from a passing footman and took a slow sip, looking for all the world as though she were making her way back to the ballroom from the retiring room. As she drew closer, she began to angle her way towards the corridor on the far side which led to the library. Another sip of champagne, and she returned the empty glass to another footman just as she reached the corridor. Once again, a casual glance about the room ensured no one was paying her any mind, especially now that the band had struck up an elegant waltz, and she slipped into the shadows, unseen. And there, ahead of her, were the library doors.

Della's heart had slowed its frantic pace by the time she reached the portal, the end of the operation finally within her sights. She laid her hand upon the latch and pushed down. Nothing. She pulled up and pushed. Nothing.

The door was locked.

Della's stomach dropped as she stared in horror at the latch, knowing Cole would be on the other side, waiting outside in the garden for her behind a locked window, in just a few minutes' time. For a moment, she couldn't think for the swirl of thoughts in her head. They had come all this way for the door to be locked? It hadn't been locked during the dinner party. Her heart began to race again, pounding against her chest as she tried wildly to think of what to do next. *The key. You must get the key.*

She whirled to face the empty corridor, thinking now of Mrs. Cooper with that massive keyring at her side, jangling with every step she took, and started back towards the great hall.

Della stayed towards the edge of the crowd in the ballroom, darting behind pillars as she made her way to the set of concealed doors at the far side of the room which she knew from the plans she and Cole had assiduously studied led to the kitchens. Della spared a silent thanks for Mrs. Cooper and her many hours of lessons, knowing that a housekeeper's place during any event would be the kitchens, overseeing the other staff as they worked frantically to feed the guests.

Della reached the doors without anyone spotting her, but her heart was now pounding so hard it hurt as she felt about in her pocket and withdrew the watch. One more minute. She was going to be late. *No time to think about that*, she told herself as she eased the door open a fraction. It was a hive of activity beyond; footmen passing from one doorway to another bearing trays of champagne, scullery maids hoisting massive pots into the kitchen which hummed with voices, and there, standing in a doorway farther down the hall, pointing at one of the kitchen maids, stood the housekeeper. And, at her side, her massive ring of keys. Della stood frozen for a moment, not knowing how to proceed. A guest – the cousin of an earl – had no business in the servants' halls and wouldn't be caught dead there without a very good reason. A bead of sweat trickled down her back as her fingers tightened their grip on the door, unsure.

That was when the housekeeper, a short, robust woman of middling age with a head of auburn hair pinned back under a mob cap, turned and met Della's gaze. Her eyes widened in shock and Della froze for a moment before pulling herself up straight and striding into the corridor with all the confidence she had seen Cole use as an earl, closing the door behind her.

"Excuse me, are you the housekeeper?" she called out, shocked at the cool authority in her voice. Her mind whirred as the woman nodded and came towards her, brushing her hands down the front of her apron.

"Yes, I am Mrs. Paxton, the housekeeper here. My apologies, miss, but this is not the place for guests..."

"I must speak with you privately," Della interrupted her, summoning the persona of Miss Rose Winthrop, who would certainly not be afraid to speak so boldly towards a mere servant. She stepped closer now and leaned in as though to impart a great secret. The housekeeper, eyes still wide with shock, nodded as she twisted her fingers together, no doubt very worried for her position should someone find one of the guests speaking to her in the kitchen corridor.

"It regards the Duke of Salisbury."

That got her attention. She drew back with a frown, looking concerned now. "Is something wrong with His Grace?"

Della reached out now, touching the woman's elbow, and leaned forward to speak in a low voice. "I must first ask for your discretion. This is a delicate matter."

The housekeeper nodded vigorously, and Della's fingers closed around the dangling keys.

"The duke and I were in his study as he had an important matter he wished to discuss with me." Della almost went on to make up some nonsense about their assignation but realized that Rose Winthrop would certainly not explain herself, and so continued, "I'm afraid he began to complain of a megrim and became rather disoriented... I left him in his study as I did not wish to cause a stir among the other guests, but I think it best that you see to him immediately. Certainly, it would be wise to have someone take him up to his chambers to recover before anyone finds him."

The housekeeper gasped at this and turned without another word to make her way back to the kitchen. As she withdrew, the keys came away from her belt and Della slipped the whole lot into her pocket along with the wine glass and watch, disappearing from the corridor before the housekeeper returned with a pair of burly footmen to rescue the duke.

It took everything inside Della not to run, knowing that for every minute that ticked by their appointed meeting time, Cole would be growing more and more frantic with worry, and the operation became more and more likely to fail. And so, she glided serenely through the ballroom, letting the other guests see her now – it wouldn't do for her and Cole to disappear for the whole of the evening – before mercifully making it out of the ballroom un-accosted. She kept to the edge of the room once more, using the massive flower arrangements, which had been set upon huge stone pillars throughout the space, to conceal herself before making it back to the library doors.

Della was frantic now as she pulled the keyring from her pocket and stared in dismay at the dozens of keys, before gritting her teeth, selecting the first one on the ring, and slipping it into the lock. It stayed stubbornly put when she tried to turn it and, biting back a curse, she tried the next. No luck. One key after the other, Della began to grow desperate, glancing down the hall periodically to make sure she wasn't disturbed until finally, thankfully, a large brass key slipped into the lock and turned with a satisfying *clunk*.

Without a moment to spare, Della slipped into the room, closed the door and locked it behind her, and flew to the window on the far side. The blood was rushing at her temples as she turned the latches on the windows and threw up the sash.

"Cole!" she hissed into the darkness beyond.

There was a rustle in the shrubs beyond the window, fragranced with jasmine, and he was there, his expression inscrutable in the darkness.

"You're late," came his whisper – she couldn't tell if he was mad or relieved or joking, but she apologized profusely, nonetheless.

"I'm so sorry, Cole. The bloody door was locked! Had to lift the keys off the housekeeper, didn't I?'

A moment of silence before his sharp whisper. "The safe, Della."

Della said not another word, but flew across the room to the panel she had discovered only days before, pressed the latch and pulled the copied key from her bodice. And there, inside the safe, were stacks of the seemingly harmless leather-bound ledgers and letters in faded envelopes, tied in bundles with twine and filling dozens of boxes. Many lives would be saved. Cole would be safe.

Within ten minutes, the documents were delivered through the window and hastened away into the night by Cole's men on the other side of the boxwood hedge which surrounded Lufton Castle. Not another word was spoken between her and Cole and he was gone from his hiding spot in the garden before she had even withdrawn from the window after depositing the last of the letters on the sill. She stood at the window for a moment, breathing in the scent of the garden beyond, both relieved and... sad.

She pulled the casement down, locked the window, the safe, pushed back the panel, and returned to the ballroom, looking for all the world as though she had merely been visiting the ladies' retiring room to refresh herself. She spotted Cole standing near a pillar and moved to stand by his side. The duke was nowhere to be seen, but none of his guests seemed to take notice. The energetic strains of a galop filled the space, at odds with the tension now between Cole and Della. She glanced sidelong at him after a moment.

"Since you have what you need, can we go? I can't stand to be in this place for another minute."

He shook his head. "Very soon. We must keep up appearances, after all. But we should be gone before Salisbury comes to his senses. He will suspect you."

Her mouth twitched. "A shame Miss Rose Winthrop returned north with the dawn after finding London Society so disagreeable."

Cole was quiet as dancing couples swept by them. The music seemed to fade into the background as she stared out over the dance floor. A bead of sweat trickled down the center of her back and her head buzzed as the swirling gowns of the ladies dancing melded into a kaleidoscope of pinks and creams and blues. "I want to go home."

Cole faced her again, his golden eyes revealing nothing of his thoughts. "We need just one more hour, Della. I shall personally return you to Seven Dials in the morning."

Della hesitated; the music was beginning to make her head ache. What she didn't say – what she ought to have said – was that, over the past couple of months, though she had denied it to herself, she had come to think of Bradford House as her home. And that home included him. Why, then, couldn't she say it to him?

She sighed and nodded. "Yes. One more hour."

She loved him. Damn him, and damn her. She had not wanted this, not at all, but she was weary of trying to convince herself otherwise. She loved that man, with every part of her, and some mad, impulsive urge made her want to say into the drawn-out silence, "I will stay, Cole, because I cannot bear to lose you. Please tell me I am not too late." But she said nothing, and she hated herself for her cowardice.

Cole stood outside her room, heart ready to burst from his chest, knowing he should turn and leave, but unable to force himself away. They hadn't talked about what would happen now that the letters were safely in the possession of Cole's agents, though he knew he must let her go, as she had told him. The ocean between them, as she had despaired, was too vast. But, if this was to be their last night together, then he wanted it to be with her, loving her, holding the woman he knew would haunt his dreams for the remainder of his years.

He lifted his fist to knock upon the portal when the door swung open and she stood there, bathed in the glow of candlelight, her slender form silhouetted beneath the lacy nightgown she wore – the only thing she wore. Every nerve ending in his body flashed to attention as she stared at him, those pale eyes luminous, her hair falling in silken waves about her shoulders.

They said nothing for a brief spell until she finally whispered, "I was coming to see you."

He paused for the briefest of moments before his raging desire could wait no more and he strode into the room, took her into his arms, and kicked the door shut behind him. There was no hesitation, no waiting – they were just kissing. Kissing and kissing, deeply, longingly, knowing they might never kiss each other again. They had been granted one more night together, and Cole clung to her as though he would never let her go. Her arms tightened about his neck as they fell upon the bed, and she gasped as he pulled away to tear off his shirt and push down his trousers before he was upon her again. She welcomed him with eager kisses and spread thighs and threw back her head with a long sigh as he took her waist in his hands and buried himself inside her.

They knew there would be time for slow, passionate lovemaking later. Right now, they couldn't wait to come together; he needed her in a way that he had never needed anything ever before. The operation had been a success, the documents from the safe securely bundled away by Mr. Barrow to an office outside London. With all those names now safe from the duke, they could finally set about the arduous task of building a case against Salisbury himself, exposing him as the traitor he was. In his elation of having completed the operation safely, he had almost – almost – forgotten that she would be gone the next day. Now that she was here, legs wrapped about his hips, welcoming his frantic thrusts with harsh gasps of pleasure, he wanted desperately to forget that heartbreaking information. He wanted only her, all of her, and his back arched as he plunged into her, fast, hard, until her cry rang out and he covered it with his mouth. Her climax pulsed around him, spurring him to his own release and, once more, she held him there so that he filled her with his seed, growling in her ear as his hips jerked.

They fell apart, gasping, and for a long time, neither of them said anything. Rain began to patter on the windowpane, and the small fire in the hearth hissed and spat, until finally Cole turned his head and observed her, her skin like satin in the flickering light, her satisfied smile, and the fan of her dark hair upon the bedspread. He reached over, touched her hand where it lay by her side, and simply said, "Thank you, Della."

She cast her glance over to him, her icy gaze drowsy, and nodded. "You're welcome."

And he lay there for a long time, listening to her breathing growing steadier and shallower until she was asleep, curled up beside him on the big bed. He sat up then and watched the steady rise and fall of her chest, her mouth parted just a little, before reaching over to gather up the quilt folded at the end of the bed to pull over her sleeping form.

"I love you, Della," he whispered into the quiet night and saw her expression soften in her sleep before he pulled up the blanket and lay down beside her.

Della stood at the door to Cora's once more, valise in hand, staring up at the broken façade of the brothel with a strange yearning in her heart. Over and over, memories of the night before played in her mind, tormenting her with their sweet clarity. Of hers and Cole's rough, hurried coupling before they slept, waking in the still of the night to reach out to one another, and pulling that hard, masculine body close to have him enter her once more. Then, making love, slowly, passionately, all through the night, sleeping for shorts bursts before they drew each other close once again. Her belly grew taut at the memory of his eager kisses, of the weight of him upon her, the slick length of him inside her, of his fingers tracing over every curve of her body until she had growled in frustration. Setting her lips in a resolute line, she pushed open the door and made her way through the dimly lit hall to the staircase at the back of the house.

Her old bedroom door was ajar, the light from within spilling out into the hall, and as she moved forward, she saw Violet inside, paintbrush in hand, mulling over her current project. A battered suitcase sat in the corner, filled to bursting with her possessions. Della leaned against the doorframe and smiled. "How would you feel about showin' that at the Royal Academy of Arts?"

Violet turned at the sound of her voice and raised a skeptical eyebrow. "What d'you mean?"

Della smiled as she stepped into the room. "I mentioned your paintings to Lord Bradford. He's an Associate Member there – he has quite an eye for art, it seems. He'd like to see your work. If he likes it, he said he'll be able to include it in their Fall Exhibition."

Violet gaped at her friend, brush poised in midair. "He never would?"

Della set her valise down upon the unmade bed and smiled. "I told you, he's not like them. He was quite excited to see your paintings. I told him they were rather provocative, and he seemed intrigued."

Violet's face broke out into a wide grin. "He did? Oh, Della, thank you!"

She threw herself at her friend and wrapped her in a hug. Della laughed and hugged her back before withdrawing. "He said you could call at Bradford House this week."

A gasp. "This week? I'll have to gather my best – which ones should I bring? You'll come with me, won't you?"

Della hesitated. She had her money – all ten thousand pounds, and that gorgeous book on Plato. Cole had also insisted she keep all the clothes he had bought her. *I'll have no use for them now*, he had explained, his gaze yearning as she had gathered up her valise with its meagre contents. Violet would be thrilled to try them on.

"I dunno. I've made as clean a break as I can. If I have to see him again..."

Her friend frowned and set down the brush she held. "What happened, Della?"

There was a moment of silence, filled only by the muffled shouts from the streets below and the rattle of cartwheels on cobblestones.

"I... I let him know me. The part of me that isn't Rosie Diver or an orphan; the part of me I want to be. And... he *wanted* to know that part of me." She gazed over at Violet, who tilted her head.

"Then why are you here?"

Della sighed, sadness welling up inside her until her throat burned with it. "There's too much between us, Vi... a vast ocean." She paused and looked down. "For starters, he's an earl and I'm just the daughter of a Seven Dials whore – I'd never be accepted by his people. And... there are some things he's just not willin' to give up for me, nor I for him. And I'm so scared of what would happen if... if he was gone from my life. No... it's better this way. I belong here."

Violet pursed her lips and shifted her weight to one hip, arms crossed in front of her chest. "No one belongs here. Folks are only here 'cause they don't have a way out. But you – you have a way out. So do I. And I'm takin' it." She smiled. "You'll love our new flat – overlooks the park, with lovely big windows. And bookshelves everywhere. I told them we'd be there first thing in the mornin'."

Della allowed a small grin. "I think I'll enjoy being a lady of leisure."

Violet laughed. "You'd be bored senseless after a week."

"You're right. I'm much better suited to the scholarly life.

Bedford College is allowin' women to earn degrees now... I think I'd like to do that."

Violet reached for the bottle of gin on the table beside her easel and filled two small glasses before handing one to her friend. "Won't your earl be impressed, then?"

Della shook her head. "He's not a part of my life any longer. I have fond memories... but it's best we don't see each other again."

Violet shrugged and swallowed a mouthful of gin. "If you say so. Dinner at the Fox and Friar one last time?"

"Oh, yes."

They made their way downstairs, but Della stopped outside Cora's room. "I forgot my cloak – just give me a moment," she said, turning back. Violet waved.

"I'll meet you there."

Della nodded and went back upstairs to collect her cloak when she heard a muffled knock on the front door. She frowned as she stepped out onto the landing. Violet had taken the day off; so had the other ladies. Cora was out of town. A new client, perhaps?

The knock sounded again, louder this time, and Della sighed as she turned the latch and pulled the door open, ready to tell whoever it was to go away.

She never got the words out. There stood the Duke of Salisbury, expression livid, a revolver in his hand. Pointed right at her.

TWENTY-SIX

He pushed her back into the hall before she could react, and Della gasped as his fingers closed about her wrist and the barrel of the gun jammed into her side.

"Where are the letters?" His voice was low, deadly, and she shook her head. How the hell did he find her? And did he think this would scare her – as though she had never been accosted with a weapon before?

"How did you—?" Her gaze moved past him to the street beyond, but it was getting dark now as the sun slipped behind the rooftops and there was no one in the street she could call to. Her chest grew tight with rage and the smallest wisp of fear as he kicked the door shut and propelled her down the hall, the gun still shoved into her back. His grey eyes blazed with cold fury as he pushed her up the stairs at the back of the house, causing her to stumble. She tripped and fell, gasping as her knee slammed into the rough edge of one of the steps. He hauled her up and pushed her again, and she limped up the rest of the way with gritted teeth. When they reached the second floor, he thrust her into the first room at the top of the stairs, Violet's old room, now empty but for a brass bedstand and straw mattress, broken chair, and empty hearth.

"Is he involved?"

His grip was so tight upon her wrist that she was losing the feeling in her hand, but she refused to cry out.

"Who?" Her voice lashed like a whip.

"Do you think me a fool? I know who you are – Della Rose," he said as he slammed the door behind them. Her stomach sank as he said her name. When he rounded upon her once more, his eyes flashed with rage. But Della saw deeper than that. She saw the dark, desperate fear. Those letters were out in the world now, he knew not where, and all evidence of his father's treachery lay within. Perhaps, as well, of his.

"How did he help you? Do you work for the Home Office?"

"I don't work for anyone. And as for Lord Bradford?" She forced herself to scoff. "He's nothin'. He was a foot in the door."

"Liar. How the hell would you know anything about those letters?"

She spat at him, and he raised his free hand and struck her across the cheek. Della fell back onto the bed with a gasp, pain exploding through her jaw. She managed a defiant laugh. "You can do whatever you want to me, it won't get those letters back. They're long gone, and soon everyone will know you're a fucking traitor." She made a guess at that one, and the widening of his eyes told her she had guessed correctly. Like father, like son. She sneered at him. "And if you think I needed any help from that fool Bradford, you're wrong – I had dirt on him and used it to get him to help me."

There didn't seem any point in pretending any longer, and Della slipped easily back into her Seven Dials accent, finding comfort in the familiar. She flinched when he raised his hand again, but he didn't strike her. Instead, a slow, cruel grin spread across his lips, and he reached out to touch her cheek, still smarting from where he had hit her. She fought the urge to recoil from him as he traced his finger down her jaw, her neck, until he reached the tiny buttons at the neckline of her bodice. Instinct kicked in and she lifted her arm to slap at his wandering hand, but he caught her wrist once more and wrenched her arm up against his chest. She couldn't stop the gasp of pain that burst from her.

"I don't care about him. You tell me where those papers are, or I promise you will not make it out of this house alive." His whisper was harsh, and she squeezed her eyes shut as her mind raced to come up with a plan to escape. She forced out an impudent laugh even though she could taste blood in her mouth.

"You're wrong – it's *you* who won't make it out of this house alive. You think no one noticed you come in 'ere? All dressed up, with your fine coat and gold cufflinks? Do you know what those are worth in this place? I'm surprised you made it *in* 'ere alive. Lots of folk been killed for much less in these streets."

Della's stomach twisted when, instead of looking fearful, Salisbury merely pushed her away to perch himself upon the small, broken chair in the corner of the room, brushing a fleck of dust from his immaculate sleeve. "You would do well to study your adversaries better, my dear," he said as he crossed one leg over the other and propped the gun upon his knee, pointing it squarely at her. With his free hand, he loosened the tie about his neck and observed her as a snake might a small rodent. "I have men throughout this festering pile of bricks in my employ... how do you think I found you, dear Miss Rose? Or is it Rosie Diver?" She glared at him from the bed, still touching her stinging cheek. "I hear you have the fastest hands in St. Giles."

She smirked. "Fast enough to steal away those precious letters without you knowin'."

His jaw tightened. "I will get them from you, one way or another, Miss Rose."

More laughter bubbled up from inside her, half nervous,

half insolent. "You can't kill me. I'm the only one who can help you now."

A slow, forbidding grin spread across his face and Della shivered, instinctively drawing her knees up to her chest. "I don't need to kill you. I don't *want* to kill you, Miss Rose. But I don't imagine you live here alone." He glanced towards the door and a cold dread settled in the pit of her stomach. "When will Violet be home?"

Della swallowed back the lump in her throat and lifted her chin in what she hoped was a gesture of defiance. She reached behind her and felt for the pillow in its threadbare linen casing. "Are you trying to threaten me? As though the life of some whore has any meanin' to me?"

Salisbury clucked his tongue in disapproval and offered her a smirk. "Now is that any way to speak of your best friend, Miss Rose? The girl you've known since you met in that depressing little hovel of an orphanage?"

Della tried her best to conceal her shock, but somehow, a small gasp escaped her, and the duke chuckled.

"Oh, yes, I came across some quite revealing information whilst reviewing the ledgers for your former home. I am always very selective when it comes to the charities I support. I have suspected you since the Colchesters' ball. Who was this incomparable woman Bradford brought with him? I did have my eye on you after that – true, I thought it might be worth proposing. You would assuredly come with a large dowry. And of course, Bradford's line is respectable, and you are a woman of exceptional beauty... but it is not in my nature to be trusting."

"Oh?" Della added no more than this, hoping he would keep talking about himself long enough to distract him. Salisbury rose from the chair suddenly and she pushed herself into the corner of the bed as he approached to take a seat beside her. She flinched as he reached out and trailed a finger down the length of her arm before he met her gaze.

"I had one of my men follow you. And where should you take yourself one night but here?" He made a vague gesture to the room. "This filthy slum. Why? I pondered. Why would this young woman of exceptional breeding take herself into one of the vilest rookeries in London in the middle of the night? I gave you the benefit of the doubt and assumed you did charitable work here but perhaps your cousin forbade you visiting whoever it was you supported. Or perhaps your taste in men ran to the low-born and you were merely slumming with some laborer..." He sneered. "I had my men ask after a Miss Rose Winthrop – nothing." He shrugged. "Until last night, when I fell ill in the middle of my own event. What was it you gave me? Laudanum?" She said nothing. "And then I discovered that my safe had been emptied. And you were the last person I was with last night."

At this point, he reached into his left inner coat pocket and withdrew a small brass key. The same key she had both stolen and returned to him. She lifted her gaze to his, refusing to look away.

"And so, I investigated your background. And you had none. And I realized – this young lady is no cousin of an earl. She is a criminal. My men came back to ask, not for a noble-woman, but for a thief. And they were told of a legend – a pickpocket who had never been caught, known as Rosie Diver, who had grown up in the very orphanage to which I had pledged a goodly amount of money." He leaned in close now and she fought the urge to back away from him. "The matron was very forthcoming in revealing the life story of one Della Rose. And her best friend, Miss Violet Latimer. A whore. Living right here."

A growl sounded in Della's throat as she reached under the pillow to retrieve what she had been praying Violet had left behind. Her hand closed around a small, sharp dagger and the growl finally burst from her in a roar of rage as she snatched her hand out from under the pillow and thrust the knife in a blind arc before pushing herself off the mattress. She didn't wait to see if she had done any damage, but she did hear his bellow of pain before the pistol went off and the sound of shattering plaster and wood filled the room.

Della snatched open the door and skidded onto the landing before throwing herself down the stairs. Her heavy breathing echoed in the hall as she reached the front door and flung it open. She barely made it onto the worn stoop before a heavy, meaty fist caught her in the stomach and she tumbled into the filth of the street, gasping.

Night fell over the city and Cole stood alone in Della's former bedroom, quietly taking in the lingering fragrance of her perfume, and fighting back the rising wave of despair inside him. He fancied he could still feel her skin beneath his fingers and hear the harsh rasp of her breath against his ear, and heat stirred in his loins at the memory. He shook his head and moved to the bed, now made up with impeccable precision, all evidence that two bodies had worn themselves to exhaustion there the night before erased. A curse burst from him, and he turned away, furious with himself for not having done more to get her to stay. He had never felt so helpless, so lost, and without her in the house, he felt uncomfortably incomplete. Where were the furtive smiles and the snapping glares and the tart retorts that had made him feel so alive, so challenged?

But he had let her go. She had asked, and he had obeyed, realizing that the part of his heart he had kept guarded – guarded from Lady Evangeline, from the family and friends who knew nothing of the work he did to keep them safe, to bring meaning to his life when it had always just seemed a shadow of his father's, was still closed to her. And as much as he wanted to, he couldn't find a way to open it. But good Lord, how he missed her.

A knock at the door made him turn and standing in the dimly lit corridor outside her room was Mr. Barrow. Upon seeing his expression, Cole's heart shot into his throat and his stomach clenched. "What's wrong?"

"There is someone here to see you, a Miss Violet Latimer. She says it's urgent—"

Cole didn't wait for him to finish but darted out of the room and raced down the stairs to find a young woman, slight and blonde, waiting by the fire in the parlor. She turned when he entered the room, his heart slamming against his ribs now. Her emerald eyes were wide as he strode forward.

"Where is she?" he asked, dispensing with any formalities as the urgency in her expression suggested there was no time for such frippery. The woman drew in a sharp breath as she came toward him with hands clasped before her.

"We were goin' out for dinner, but she never arrived. I went back to look for her and there was a man waitin' outside. She came flyin' out of that place and he dropped her right there... there was another man who brought her back inside. Fancy-looking gent. I thought he might be that duke she told me about. This was the only place I could think to come..."

Cole was already turning away as she spoke, a cold, fierce rage beginning to burn inside his chest. If that man had hurt her in any way – by God, he would wish he had never been born. He gave a sharp nod to Mr. Barrow, who stood in the doorway. "My coat and hat please, Mr. Barrow. I want you to come along. Find Agent Tyndall. We shall need something to distract his man—"

"I can help you with that, milord."

Cole turned at the sound of Violet's voice and saw the cold calculation in her eyes. "I cannot ask you to put yourself in harm's way, Miss Latimer..."

"You're not askin'. I'm tellin'. She's my only friend, and I'll help her in whatever way I can."

There was no arguing with that tone of voice. "Is there any other way inside?"

"There's a back door – well, not a door, as such. There's a storeroom behind the house. If you go into the back alley, you can reach it through a couple of broken slats in the wall. Cora never had it fixed; she was sure it would come in handy one day if there was ever an emergency. I suppose she was right." That hard-edged voice of hers cut through him and he gestured for her to go ahead. Mr. Barrow had returned with his coat and hat and handed them over as they made their way outside and into the night.

"Where is Cora now?"

"In the country, visitin' her sister. The others took the day off – there's no one else there."

"Good."

A hand came to rest upon his arm as he made to turn and he glanced back at Violet, who now eyed him suspiciously. "Agent Tyndall? Is that what this has all been about? You a copper?"

Cole faced the young woman now and shook his head. "I am not with the police, Miss Latimer. Miss Rose has been helping me to get close to a suspected traitor in return for that ten thousand pounds and the assurance that she will come out of this with a clean record. I am an operative for the British Home Office." He saw the fear behind the surprise in her eyes and touched her hand. "They will not get away with this. I will get her out of there." His voice came out in a deadly whisper and Violet inclined her head and said nothing as the valet pulled a revolver out from the folds of his cloak and handed it to Cole, who slipped it into his pocket. A sudden, clarifying calm took over him, even though his mind envisioned the very worst happening to Della. It was always thus when he had an operation to complete. Better to focus his energy on how the plan was to be executed rather than what the outcome might be. And still, for all his carefully honed calm, he raged at the very idea that Salisbury might harm Della, and at himself for not having done more to keep her safe.

But as Violet climbed into his carriage and took the seat beside him, her jaw set and her gaze steely, he realized that if anyone were going to come to harm tonight, it would be Salisbury. Della would certainly not go down without a fight, and his chest tightened as he thought, once more, how much he adored her. He banged on the roof of the cab with his fist, and it lurched forward.

"She can take care of 'erself."

Cole turned at Violet's sudden words and she was staring straight ahead, a determined look upon her face. He nodded slowly. "Yes, I know she can. She saved my life, you know."

A ghost of a smile lifted the young woman's lips, but she never looked at him. "Funny, that."

Cole arched a brow as the carriage rattled through the quiet streets, passing under pools of gaslight which highlighted the tense line of Violet's jaw. She was every bit as worried as he, and he cursed himself again. "What's funny? Her saving my life?"

The same hint of a smile. "I've never in my life known Della to have any interest in helpin' anyone but herself."

"Not even you?"

Violet sniffed. "She knows I can take care of myself. That's the world we grew up in. You look after yourself first because no one else will."

Cole was quiet for a moment. "I want to look after her."

Another half-smile curled Violet's lips and she finally turned to face him. "You love her."

Cole stared right back at her, unflinching. "I do."

The young woman let out a soft chuckle and smoothed down a fold on her plain grey skirt. "She loves you, too."

Cole frowned at her as the carriage dipped when it hit a bump in the road. "Miss Rose made it very clear she did not feel the same way. That there was no future for us. I am ashamed to say that I played a part in that."

Violet shrugged and glanced at him once more. "I don't know about any future, but she does love you. I do know that."

Cole was silent for a moment as he contemplated this. A small part of him was overjoyed to know that Della felt that way about him, however little she had shared it with him. The other part... it broke, knowing that they might have had more and he still couldn't bring himself to give up on his father's work – on his own lifelong dedication to the Home Office. Wasn't there still so much more he wanted to do?

"If I gave it up... if I was just the Earl of Bradford... how do I show her that she would be my whole world? That she will never have to worry about going back to Seven Dials?"

The carriage stopped suddenly, and Cole glanced out the window to see they had arrived on Charing Cross Road, just outside the twist of roads that made up Seven Dials. In the moment before the driver stepped down to open the door for them, Violet held his gaze and offered him a sympathetic smile. "She never wanted much in her life and we grew up expectin' nothin'. She just wants to read her books and quit divin'. I don't want to be sellin' myself anymore. I'm a painter. That's all we ever wanted. You've shown her a whole new world that she never thought she could be a part of. It's daunting. And most folks in your world won't accept her. Is she to be shunned and ignored for the rest of her life just 'cause her mum did what she had to to keep her alive? She's not going to give up everythin' she ever wanted for that. And she's scared. She's scared to end up like her mother."

The door swung open then and Violet stepped out without another word. Cole followed, setting aside this little bit of information for the time being. They had a task at hand, and it was time to focus.

Della's friend led him through the dark, forbidding streets, sidestepping the occasional pool of filth or huddled mass of a person. She stopped where Della had brought him when they first met, asking him to wait while she gathered her precious few belongings. Violet turned to him and jerked her head in the direction of that faded red door.

"Is that his man?" she whispered. Cole peered through the gloom past her to the figure waiting beneath the flickering light of a torch. A huge man in a derby hat and tweed coat. Cole knew him as one of the duke's thugs and pushed down the incoherent anger that would have burst from him, knowing this man dared lay his hands on Della before he nodded and noticed a bit of movement down the dimly lit street behind a stack of old crates. "Mr. Barrow is back with one of my other agents – you call out if you need any help, Miss Latimer."

She smirked and reached up to unclasp her cloak before thrusting it into his hands. She then reached under her bodice and lifted her small, pale breasts high beneath the bones of her corset. "I've been doin' this a long time, sir. Too long. I know what I'm doin'. Round the back you'll find a few old barrels. If you move 'em to the side, you'll find a loose slat on the wall. Push it aside and you can get into the storeroom. There are stairs at the back of the house." She glanced over at the man hovering near the front door to the brothel. "I'll keep him busy as long as I can."

Cole took her hand for a moment, and she met his gaze. "Thank you, Miss Latimer."

She gave him a sharp nod and pushed him back into the shadows without another word before squaring her shoulders and slipping out into the street. She walked towards the man, hips swaying beneath her bustled gown. "Hello, luv. What are you doing about at this hour?" She laughed as she drew closer to him, and he turned to face her. "Feelin' lonely tonight?"

He said nothing but tipped his hat back a fraction to get a better look at her as she sidled up to him and traced a finger down his massive chest. "You're a big fella – I bet you know how to please a lady."

Cole almost smiled as he drew in a sustaining breath and retreated into the dark to make his way around the block of tenements to the alley that ran along the back. It was quiet here but for the splash of night soil being tossed into the street followed by a distant shout. Cole found the stack of barrels and glanced up at the windows above him. All were dark but for one and he narrowed his eyes as he searched for any movement within the room. Blood pounded at his temples, but his breath came steadily, and he set aside the barrels to find the loose slat.

Once he had made his way into the storeroom and quietly pulled the slat back in place behind him, he slipped out of his overcoat and drew the revolver from the pocket. He pulled the hammer back to cock the weapon and the click echoed in the quiet, dark space. He waited for a moment, breath held, to ensure no one had heard the noise before closing his eyes to still his thoughts. Time to work. The door eased open, and Cole made his way down a hall lit only by a single flickering sconce. When he reached the bottom of the stairs, he paused and strained his ears to catch any sound from the floor above. Long, silent moments passed, an eternity before he heard a sharp whisper followed by a dull thud.

His grip on the revolver never wavered and his breath never caught as Cole took his first, silent step to saving the woman he loved.

TWENTY-SEVEN

There was no way out now. Fear, an emotion mostly unfamiliar to Della in the face of violence, crawled up inside her as Salisbury's thug picked her up off the street after leveling her with a punch in the gut. She gasped as he took her by the back of her gown and pushed her back up the steps into the house where the duke waited for her, his face dark with rage. She spat at him as he shoved her down the hall, the muzzle of the revolver digging into the small of her back. Once they were back in the bedroom, Salisbury turned to her with terrifying calmness after shutting the door behind them. She saw now that her wild attack had made contact and a thin line of blood marred his cheek and she smirked, even as her heart pounded.

"That's gonna leave a scar," she said, nodding towards the cut. His smile was chilling, but she refused to look away.

"Where are the letters, Miss Rose?"

She pressed her lips together and glared at him, daring him to strike her again.

"I promise you shan't come to harm if you tell me where they are. I am simply trying to protect my family's good name.

Surely you can understand that – what if everyone were to find out who you really are?'

Della let out a harsh laugh at this, throwing her head back as he scowled at her. "As though I care what *any* of you people think of me," she finally spat at him.

He stared at her for a moment before raising his brows. "And what of Lord Bradford? What will people think of him?"

A flicker of doubt crept up inside her, but she lifted her chin and scowled at him. "What of him? I got what I wanted... I don't care what happens to him now."

He narrowed his eyes, and her heart began to thunder under his scrutiny. He mustn't know; he mustn't suspect anything between her and Cole. Her mind raced as she tried desperately to think of another way to escape. Violet had already gone – had she come back looking for Della? Her only weapon was gone. She had no idea where Cole had sent all the documents, but she was fairly confident that Salisbury wasn't going to buy that excuse. She suspected his patience would only last so long, and her whole body grew cold at the thought. No. She was not going to die here tonight.

"I *will* get those letters back, Miss Rose, one way or another." He gestured to the bed with the revolver. "Sit."

She swallowed hard, backing towards the bed without taking her gaze from him before sitting on the edge. He resumed his seat in the chair, propping the gun up once more to point at her. There was only one way out of this she could think of, and she summoned a steadying breath before facing him with a raised brow. "Perhaps we could come to some sort of... compromise."

He never moved a muscle, though his eyes did narrow slightly as he observed her. "What sort of compromise?"

She managed a sly smile and lifted a hand to brush an invisible irritation from her neck. His gaze followed the movement.

"I only stole those documents to sell to the highest bidder. You're a man of great means... what's your best offer?"

The corner of his mouth twitched and in the flickering light of the lantern he had lit against the darkness, his eyes appeared black. "Are you suggesting I buy back something you stole from me?"

She smiled again. "I am. You must admit, it's a solution which benefits us both. I get the money I want, and you get to keep your dirty little secrets."

His lips compressed into a hard line, and he stared at her for what seemed an eternity. She became certain that he would tell her she was mad to suggest such a thing, but then his head tilted to the side as he seemed to contemplate her offer. "How much do you want?" he finally said.

Della drew in a deep breath and threw out the one number that had occupied her days and nights for the past few months. "Ten thousand pounds."

Salisbury scoffed. "Are you quite mad?" he said, echoing her thoughts.

Della shrugged and gave him a devious smile. "A life for a life. Mine would be set with that amount of money – and your life won't be ruined. Seems a fair exchange to me."

His face broke into a wolfish grin. "Or I could just kill you and assume you haven't any means to decipher or distribute the letters. Does that seem fair to you?"

Della pressed her lips together to stop them trembling as her stomach quaked, but she still refused to give him the satisfaction of showing her fear. "Perhaps... or perhaps I'm more than just a common thief. How'd you think I knew what to steal? I could have taken anythin' from you..." Her gaze flicked down to his waistcoat. "Your pocket watch, for example." She gave him a knowing smile, and his frown deepened as a muscle twitched in his jaw. His eyes flashed with some dangerous emotion, and though she knew it was not wise to provoke him, she could think of no other way to stall for time.

"Ahh," he eventually said as he leaned back in the chair. "So that was you. I might have guessed."

She held up her hands and wiggled her fingers with a smirk. "Quickest hands in St. Giles. The cufflink was also fine – got a few quid for it, too."

He sniffed and shook his head. "And you still want ten thousand pounds from me?"

"I do." She leaned back against the wall and crossed her arms over her chest. "A life for a life. It's a fair trade, I think." She grinned. "You should have burned the lot when you had a chance. But debt's a hell of a thing, I suppose." A pause, a shrug of the shoulders. "I wouldn't know."

He stared at her for a long time then, his eyes cold and calculating. She stared right back at him, wondering wildly what she would do if he actually agreed to the sum.

"The letters first. Every sheet of paper, in my possession, before I hand over a single farthing."

Her stomach dropped, but she was careful to keep her expression neutral. "No. I can't access them now. You bring me a note of credit – right here. I'll wait and you'll have everythin' back tomorrow evenin'. That's my final offer, or I will see to it that every nasty secret of yours is revealed to the whole country. You know I know what's in them."

His lips twitched and his eyes narrowed, and she watched with cold dread in the pit of her belly as his finger came to rest upon the trigger of the revolver still pointed at her. She pushed her fingers under her skirts to hide that they trembled fiercely, but her expression remained calm, impassive, and she kept her gaze steady upon his. Finally, just as she felt her heart would burst out of her chest from anticipation, Salisbury nodded slowly.

"Very well." He stood and moved towards her, and she

raised her chin as he came forward. "Just to be done with this whole bloody business."

She flinched as he reached out and traced the line of her jaw and if looks could kill, he would have dropped dead right there in front of her. A slow smile spread across his face as he took her chin into his grip and lifted her face to his. "My man will be outside... if you should try to leave again, be assured he will not be as gentle as before."

Della allowed the corners of her mouth to curve upwards, even as his fingers dug into her jaw. "I'm not goin' anywhere. I want my money, and to never set eyes upon you again."

"It's a shame, you know," Salisbury began, pushing her head away and stepping back, the revolver now held at his side. "I would rather have liked you to be my mistress."

Della smirked. "I'd rather just have the money, if I'm bein' honest."

He sniffed and his scowl darkened, but then he cleared his throat and tugged at the hem of his waistcoat. The look he gave her then made her shudder. "You'll get your money. But I warn you, Miss Rose... if you try to leave this house, there is no place you can go where I will not find you. If you do not return every last letter you stole from me, I will hurt you in ways you cannot imagine. If you breathe but a word of what you know..." He paused and let the threat hang in the air between them, and she nodded slowly.

"I understand."

"I knew you would." He moved as though to make his way out of the room, and then paused with his hand upon the latch. He turned back to face her, his expression dark. "On second thought..."

Della's breath caught in her throat and fear once more skittered up her back.

"Maybe you ought to come with me. You are hardly a trustworthy sort."

The corners of her mouth lifted in the very barest hint of a smile. "No, I'm not."

He scowled at her and gestured with the revolver. "Get up."

Her jaw was clenched so hard now it ached, but Della's venomous glare never left him as she pushed herself up off the bed. She started to move forward as he pulled the door open, and before the gasp even left her lips, there was a flurry of movement in the darkened hall beyond and a gun pointed squarely at Salisbury's head.

TWENTY-EIGHT

Cole had no time to process the muffled voices behind the closed door when it swung open suddenly and he instinctively raised the revolver. Salisbury stood in the doorway looking back at him with an expression of shock which quickly turned into a sneering glare before he snatched Della's wrist and pulled her in front of him. He jammed the revolver he held into her temple with a menacing scowl. "I knew you were involved in this, Bradford."

"Let her go, Salisbury. She won't be getting the letters back for you."

The duke now seethed with rage; a muscle in his jaw twitched and his dark eyes flashed. Della stared back at Cole, her eyes wide in astonishment as though her very life weren't being threatened.

"Bradford, you fool, you've no idea what you're getting involved in. I have men all over this city. I have secrets about everyone who matters. I could bury you. Is this little bitch worth losing everything—?"

"Let her go." Cole's voice was restrained but laced with

rage. Della flinched as the weapon pressed into the side of her head and Cole's muscles clenched, fear and anger making his head spin when he would ordinarily feel only a sharp-edged calm.

"Put your gun down or I will kill her." Salisbury's tone was level, but Cole could hear the quiver of worry behind it. Della's gaze met his and for the first time since she had dragged herself onto Dionysus' back, he saw fear in her eyes. He gave her the smallest of nods and looked at the duke.

"I'm putting it down." He held up his hands in a gesture of surrender, keeping his voice calm. "All I ask is that you let her go. She took nothing from you. I stole the documents."

Salisbury's expression faltered as Cole bent slowly to place his revolver on the floor. "You?"

Cole swallowed hard as he rose, hands still up. "Yes. They belonged to my father."

The duke's mouth turned up in a sneer and Della squeezed her eyes shut as the muzzle dug into her temple. Cole's eyes narrowed. "The Home Office has a lot of questions for you, Your Grace."

Salisbury's face contorted into an ugly snarl, and he shoved Della to the side as he turned his revolver to aim at Cole. A split second passed as Cole's body tensed and he began to move forward, but Della's enraged cry split the air as she took the duke's arm into her grasp and wrenched it towards her. The resulting shot went wide and blew a hole in the ceiling over Cole's head.

"Bitch!" Salisbury shouted and swung around to land a heavy fist against her jaw. Della staggered back with a gasp as Cole launched himself into the bedroom, fury tightening his throat and making his muscles quiver. He caught Salisbury around the waist and dropped him with a heavy thud onto the floor before rising and striking down with his fists.

"Cole!" Della shouted behind him, but he barely heard her

as a sudden, violent rage overtook him and blood rushed to his ears. How dare this man threaten her? How dare he, this traitor, this liar? He reached back to drive his fist down once more, but the duke's eye caught something under the bed and his arm snaked out to reach for it. Before Cole could react, Salisbury's hand emerged, his revolver held tight in his grasp. Cole snatched for the weapon, but the duke rolled away with a grunt and jabbed his elbow backwards, catching Cole in the gut. He turned at Della's shout of warning and saw her scrambling for the gun he had laid in the hallway but stopped when a loud click echoed in the room.

"Don't move, Miss Rose."

Della turned with a scowl to face Salisbury, who raised his weapon. She stood slowly without taking her thunderous glare off him. Her dark tresses had come loose from her neat chignon, and she looked every bit the vengeful fury, her pale eyes blazing as she stared him down. Time stood still as the duke chuckled, a harsh sound in the silence of the room. Cole pushed himself off the floor as Salisbury's hand twitched and the muzzle of the gun inched up a degree to point to the woman standing behind him. *Not today*.

"Della, get down!" he shouted as he shot up and grabbed her by the shoulders. There was a click and the revolver fired as Cole pulled her down. Not in time. He felt the sting as the bullet whistled past his ear and grazed his temple. Pain exploded through his head and Della screamed as blood sheeted down the side of his face before she scrambled up from the floor and threw herself at Salisbury, raising her clenched fists to slash down at him with an inarticulate cry of rage.

"You fucking bastard!" she shouted as the duke tried to aim at her once more, but it was like trying to beat back a tidal wave. She scratched, she clawed, she kicked and screamed like an avenging demon, and though hot shards of pain spiked through Cole's head and blood hindered his vision in one eye, he pushed himself up off the floor. He drew in a shaking breath to slow the spinning of his head, found Salisbury with his one good eye, and hurled himself at the duke, catching him around the legs and propelling him to the floor once more. He caught Della's skirts as he fell, dragging her to the ground with him, and she grunted as her knee slammed against the floor and the pistol skittered back under the bed.

"Della!" Cole managed to rasp, holding tight to Salisbury as he kicked and twisted. She reached under the bed and shouted in triumph once she snatched up the weapon before pushing herself up off the floor and turning it back on the duke. Her pale eyes blazed, and it was then, in that one, brief moment, that Cole knew he could not let her go, and that he loved her with every part of him. He allowed a small smile as he reached up and placed his hand over hers. She started, as if she had not been aware of his presence in her focused rage and glanced down as he released Salisbury and rose from the floor.

"Give me the gun, Della. My men are on their way. He can't hurt you now."

Della sniffed and handed him the weapon without ever taking her glare off Salisbury, who lay sprawled beneath them, his dark hair disheveled. "He should consider himself lucky I don't hurt *him*," she said, crossing her arms over her chest with a huff. Cole wanted to smile at her biting remark but turned to the duke instead.

"Who'd have ever imagined?"

Salisbury's lips curled in a sneer. "What are you on about, Bradford?"

"I did not think it would end this way. I have dedicated years to exposing you, looking for a chink in your armor, and here we are today... the mighty Duke of Salisbury, brought down by a common pickpocket." Cole swiped at the blood drying on his cheek as he turned his fond gaze to Della, who stood in the darkened doorway. She didn't smile at his acknowledgement but swallowed and looked away. The creak of the door opening downstairs interrupted them and Cole called out, "We're up here."

Footsteps clattered up the stairs and there, in the dim light of the hallway, stood Mr. Barrow and Violet. Della gasped as she threw her arms around her friend. "Violet! Are you alright?"

Cole kept Salisbury in the corner of his vision as Violet nodded and pushed Della back. "I'm sorry, I couldn't think of anyone else to go to who could help you."

Della's gaze shifted for a moment to Cole and her expression softened as she regarded him. "There is nothin' to be sorry for. Thanks, Vi."

Cole wanted so very badly then to take her in his arms and kiss her until they were breathless, but propriety made him turn to his valet, who waited at the top of the stairs.

"You alright, sir?" Mr. Barrow asked, handing a handkerchief to Cole.

"Fine, Mr. Barrow, just a graze. Is Agent Tyndall here?" he asked as he blotted at the fresh blood seeping down to his collar.

"Yes, sir."

"Good – have the carriage brought round for His Grace." He spoke the last words with scorn as he turned back to the man in the bedroom whose lips curled up in a sneer.

"You are a fool if you think I will spend a single minute in prison, Bradford. I will be tried by the House of Lords and no one there would dare charge me. All this will have been for naught."

Cole said nothing to the threat but jerked his head in the duke's direction. Mr. Barrow nodded in understanding and moved by him into the room, where he withdrew a pair of handcuffs from his pocket. Cole managed a grim smile as the valet led Salisbury past him into the hall. "Perhaps you are right, Your Grace," he commented as he tucked the stained handkerchief into his pocket. "I cannot guarantee you will spend the remainder of your life in a cell, but I assure you, this has been well worth the effort."

His meaningful gaze caught Della's then as Mr. Barrow led the duke downstairs. Her lovely brow creased as she looked back at him, unsmiling. Violet caught the look and cleared her throat. "Suppose I ought to go find out how that big fella's doing after knockin' him over the head with a pipe. Mr. Barrow will probably want to take him along for the ride as well." With that, she offered Cole a telling smile and scurried down the stairs.

Left there in the hazy light of the hall, with the stagnant air close about them, Cole finally turned to Della, whose face was inscrutable in the darkness.

"Della, I—"

"I want to go home."

Cole's heart sank as he observed her standing in the doorway, hair disheveled, the hem of her dress torn. Her expression was carefully blank, but her eyes were red, and he swallowed. "Please don't go, Della. I... I love you." It was all he could think to say, as her throat moved and she closed her eyes.

"Lovin' me changes nothin'. I am still who I am, and you are still who you are. Love does not mend this rift." She opened her eyes, those fierce, ice-blue eyes and met his gaze. "I saved your life, and now you've saved mine. We're square."

Cole watched, helpless, as she turned away and paused.

"Thank you," she said to him over her shoulder, the words filled with sorrow. "For all you have done for me."

"Della..." he called after her, but she had already made her way to the stairs and after a moment he heard the front door open and close and then he was alone in her little room. He stared at that empty doorway as despair filled him with its aching tightness. *Love does not mend this rift.* Her words echoed in his mind, and he shook his head. Love alone couldn't mend it, but he knew what might. Determined, he strode out into the night and hailed the first hansom cab he could find and asked the driver to take him to Mayfair. Jane would be very put out being called upon at such an hour, but he knew if anyone could mend this rift between he and Della, it would be her.

Jane Hardaway, Marchioness of Colchester, looked alarmed as she entered her parlor not half an hour later to find Cole waiting for her. She dismissed her butler before closing the doors behind her and turning to face him, pulling tight the belt on her floral silk wrapper. "Cole, what on earth are you doing here at this hour? What happened to your head?" She gasped as she touched Cole's temple where the blood had dried into a hard crust. He was certain he looked gruesome.

"I'm fine, Jane, just a graze. Head wounds always bleed like a stuck pig. No need for alarm."

Jane frowned and reluctantly withdrew. "Very well," she said and gestured to the tray that had been left while he waited for her. "Tea?"

He nodded and accepted the cup she poured for him. She then turned and took up one of the linen napkins on the tray and dipped it into the pitcher of water that had been left, wringing it out to hand to him. He accepted it with a nod and pressed it to his temple.

"I am sorry to disturb you at this hour, Jane, but I require your assistance."

She frowned at him over the rim of her cup. "I am no spy, Cole – what use could I possibly be to you?"

He allowed a small smile as he set down the napkin. "You'll be happy to know I do not require you to spy for me. As a matter of fact, our operation went rather well. We have our suspect in custody right now."

Her brow arched. "Oh? Care to reveal who that might be?"

He shook his head. "Now you know I can't share that information. I daresay it will be in all the papers within the next week, in any case. No, I require something a little more personal."

Jane took a moment to observe Cole before she gestured for him to sit. She followed suit and set her cup and saucer down before facing him. "Very well, then – what is the trouble?"

Cole's chest tightened as he thought of Della giving him one last look before disappearing into the night and he bit back a sigh. "It is about my cousin."

Jane's expression remained carefully impassive. "Oh?"

"That is... she is not my cousin."

"Well, thank God for that," Jane remarked, taking up her cup once more. Cole frowned at her.

"Whatever do you mean?"

Jane's smile was knowing. "I saw the way you looked at her. I am relieved she is not your cousin. Good heavens, you can certainly do better than a cousin."

Cole chuckled. "Damn, I thought I hid it better than that."

"Master spy you may be, but you are hopeless when it comes to women. Who is she?"

Cole drew in a deep breath. If he was going to do what he had come here to do, then this would determine if he had even the slightest chance of success.

"She's a pickpocket. I found her in Seven Dials. I hired her to pose as my cousin to help me get close to a suspect." Jane said nothing, nodding slowly as she stirred a spoonful of sugar into her tea. "Her name is Della Rose. Jane," he said, and she raised a brow as he grappled for the right words. "I am... hopelessly in love with her. She is the most beautiful woman I have ever... and clever, and fierce. Jane, I want to marry her."

The marchioness's eyes widened at this declaration.

"But therein lies the problem. If we are to be together, then she can no longer be known as Miss Rose Winthrop. But if we do that... then I am no longer a spy."

Jane nodded in understanding, and he sighed. The teacup he held was beginning to burn his hands, but he took no notice as he unburdened himself.

"I would give up all of this — years of dedication. It would be a messy business; the Earl of Bradford revealing himself to be an operative for the Home Office. Messier even for her. She knows what it would mean to marry me. *I* know what it would mean to marry me. But I love her. I want to give her everything. And... I think I am ready to be what she needs me to be."

Jane was quiet for a moment. "That would be a messy business. But I must ask... does she love *you*?"

And this was when Cole grew quiet, for he did not know the answer to that. Della had never declared as much, and it was so hard to know the mind of his mysterious pickpocket. He shook his head and stared down at the clear amber liquid in his cup.

"I... I don't know. We have... been together. But I cannot say if she feels the same."

Jane drew in a long breath as she returned her cup to the table before she met his gaze.

"Ought you not to find out how this woman feels for you first? If I am correct, you are here to ask me to ease her way into Society, no? I can get most of them on her side, especially if she has assisted you with some important operation—"

"She has. I have in custody a traitor to this country thanks to her," Cole said, quick to allay Jane's doubts. The older woman nodded.

"Leave it to me, then. But Cole... I cannot see the point of coming to me for help if you do not yet know how she feels. Will she speak with you?"

Cole raised the teacup to his lips and took a slow, thoughtful sip. "Perhaps." He set the cup down suddenly and rose from his seat. "I must go then. Thank you, Jane — and please do accept my apologies for calling at this hour. I knew I could count upon your help."

"I like her, Cole. Be assured she will be as welcome as any well-bred debutante. But you must convince her first of the merits of being the Countess of Bradford. And that you are well and truly ready to make some sacrifices for her – it sounds as though she will have to make many for you."

Cole gave her a smile as he reached the parlor door. "I will do my utmost. Good night, Jane."

<h1 style="text-align:center">TWENTY-NINE</h1>

Della had walked all the long distance from Seven Dials to the small flat Violet had rented for them in Marylebone, and by the time she let herself into the small parlor overlooking a little park, her feet ached, and her heart was heavy. Violet had no doubt returned to the brothel to collect her things, and so Della rummaged about in the tiny kitchen at the back of the flat and found a bottle of gin. She took the bottle and a glass back to the parlor and, not bothering to light a fire, sat in the moonlight streaming in through the casement and poured a glass. She sipped it as the clock on the mantel ticked away, hardly noticing the tears trickling down her cheeks. *He came for you*, she thought as she raised the glass to her lips. She had done everything in her power to push him away, and still he had come for her. Della had been certain she was alone in that little room, had not expected help and had been certain at one point that she would not be leaving. But he had come for her.

It changes nothing, she told herself once more, though the growing ache in her chest told her otherwise. She frowned at herself and downed the remainder of the gin. Della Rose did not cry. She did not pine. She did not love. Why, then, could she not stop the tears? Why did her whole being long for him as it had never longed for anything before?

A knock at the door started her from the grim thoughts chasing through her head and she sighed as she pushed herself out of the chair and made a half-hearted attempt to swipe at the tears staining her cheeks. Violet was home, and so she dragged herself to the door and pulled it open.

And there he was. Standing in her doorway, blood still crusted on the side of his face and staining his once-immaculate white shirt. They stared at each other in silence for a moment before Cole finally reached out and presented her with an envelope sealed with a glob of red wax.

"What are you doin' here?" she finally asked, hearing the strain in her voice. Her heart, mutinous betrayer, swelled at the sight of him.

"May I come in?" he asked in a low voice, still holding the envelope out to her.

She blinked to clear her thoughts and nodded before stepping back. "I suppose."

She moved ahead of him and lit a branch of candles in the parlor before turning to find him standing in the doorway. "What's that?" she asked, gesturing towards the envelope.

"A letter. Mr. Barrow will deliver it to the offices of *The Times* in the morning. If you want him to."

Della frowned as she stood staring at him from across the room. She dared not move any closer. She didn't want to see the rich amber color of his eyes, nor smell his wild, masculine fragrance. "I don't know what you mean."

He drew in a deep breath. "I love you, Della. I love you more than I ever thought I could love a person. To never see you again would be the greatest pain I could imagine." He paused and set the letter down on the table between them before lifting his golden gaze to her once more. Her breath caught in her throat and the longing became painful as she clenched her hands at her sides.

"I don't know how you feel about me. I don't know if what we shared meant anything to you." *It meant everything.* "I don't know if you want more now that our professional relationship is at end. But if you did" – he nodded towards the envelope on the table – "I want it to be on your terms." He drew in a shaking breath. "My letter of resignation. I will give all of this up, tell the world who you really are and that you are a hero, Della. That you helped bring a traitor to justice. And I want you to know that I will stand by you, whatever comes of it. And so will Jane."

Della frowned at him, and he elaborated.

"The Marchioness of Colchester. She is a dear friend, and she has influence. I have told her who you are, and she understands your fears of our world. She would help. Della," he said, his low voice strained, as he took a step towards her. She remained rooted to the spot, her heartbeat echoing in her ears. "You have helped me to keep a promise I made long ago. I never would have been able to bring in Salisbury without you. I thank you for that. And if we never see each other again after tonight, know I will be forever grateful."

Della's lips parted as though she would say something, but the words wouldn't come as Cole took another tentative step towards her.

"The letter tells all. Who you are. Who I am. If I have this delivered tonight, the whole of London will know by the morning. If I don't... I remain in the employ of the Home Office, and Miss Rose Winthrop returns to Northumberland. Della Rose goes on to become a scholar." The barest hint of a smile crossed his lips at this, and she glanced at the letter on the table. "You will never have to go back to Seven Dials... I will never let that happen to you, Della. Anything you want is yours if you will but let me love you. I only want to know if you feel the same."

Della stared at him for what seemed an eternity as the darkness closed around them with only the flicker of the candles she had lit to highlight his fierce amber gaze. "Damn you, Cole, I do love you," she whispered, shaking her head. It took a monumental effort to hold back the tears pricking at the corner of her eyes. "But I can't ask you to give up your life's work for me."

"I don't need it anymore, Della." He took a step towards her, a grateful smile beginning to play about his mouth. "I did what I set out to do. I have brought the Dukes of Salisbury to justice – with your help. I am ready to close this chapter of my life and begin a new one." He smiled. "With you. If you'll let me."

There was a long, tense moment of silence as Della closed her eyes and let his warm breath move over her cheek and his rich, woody scent fill her lungs. This felt right. So very right. And never in her life had Della Rose, the quickest hands in the Dials, ever felt right. She closed the distance between them to put her hands on his chest and raise her lips to his.

"You'd best find Mr. Barrow and tell him he's a letter to deliver, then," she murmured against his mouth as she raised her gaze to his. His eyes widened and that smile – that dazzling smile that made her melt – lit up his face.

"Truly?" She nodded eagerly and he lowered his head to press a fierce kiss to her lips, pulling her up against the length of his body as she gasped in delight. "Marry me, Della," he whispered against her cheek before kissing her again, his hands sliding up to cup the back of her head before he pulled away to look down at her. Della let out an uncharacteristic giggle and touched her mouth to his.

"I will, Cole – I will marry you." She smiled. "But you are going to have a lot of explainin' to do to your friends and family as to why you are engaged to a lowly pickpocket."

Cole shook his head with vehemence and clasped her shoulders to draw her gaze back to his. "No, not a lowly pickpocket.

The woman who helped bring down the Duke of Salisbury, a traitor to this country and its people. You will be a hero, Della. You are a hero, and I shall consider myself lucky every day that you grace me with your presence – the thief who stole my heart."

Della's own heart grew so full she was sure it filled her whole chest, that once cold, hard little thing that had refused to feel, and she smiled. "Quickest hands in the Dials."

The headlines ran the next morning with the shocking news that Charles Lumley, the Duke of Salisbury, had been arrested on suspicion of treason for selling information to the Russians to pay off his massive debts. The whole of London tittered with gossip, most of it related to the duke, and everyone's shock that such a well-respected peer had been a traitor to his own country and people. In the weeks that followed, as he and his father's correspondence with the enemy came to light, the gossip grew even more fervent.

Even more shocking to people, however, was the news of the couple who had exposed Salisbury as a turncoat. Everyone knew the Earl of Bradford's reputation as a steady and clever, if quiet, man, but shock rippled through the city upon discovering that Miss Rose Winthrop was not, in fact, his cousin, but his partner, a woman of some renown in the rookery, occasionally known as Rosie Diver, a Miss Della Rose.

Della had always feared that once the news broke that she, an ordinary criminal, had helped to expose a man as powerful as the Duke of Salisbury, she would be shunned by the very people she had worked so hard to become one of. But true to her word, the Marchioness of Colchester used her considerable influence to paint Della as a hero and make her a subject of much fascination among Society, and her skill as a pickpocket seemed to charm them. Della and Jane would grow to become close friends in the months that followed. It was no difficult feat, then, to announce her and Cole's engagement in the weeks following the duke's arrest.

But as much as Della had found new hope and new friends among Cole's circle, she still did not entirely feel as though she belonged. A year after they were wed in a quiet ceremony with Violet and Mr. Barrow standing as maid of honor and best man respectively, along with a few close friends, including Lord and Lady Colchester, Lord Perrin and his brother, and even Lady Evangeline, as well as Cole's family, they returned to Headingly Hall.

THREE YEARS LATER

A soft summer evening had come to Headingly Hall, filled with the sounds of crickets and sparrows and Della smiled as she entered the library, lit with the warm glow from a crackling fire. Cole sat in one of the wingback chairs near the hearth, newspaper in hand, and looked up when she came towards him.

"I think I'm ready," she announced. "I'm going to sign up to take the examinations at Oxford. I can't be formally admitted to the University, but I can gain honors. I want to do it before she comes," she added, patting her rounded belly as she moved across the room to one of the shelves. Cole's appreciative gaze followed her as she drew a finger across the varied spines of the books. Her free hand sat upon her ever-growing belly as the first tell-tale flutters of an infant's kick stirred within. She smiled at the sensation and glanced across the room to her husband, whose golden eyes tracked her movements, and never failed to take her breath away with their intensity.

"I'm so very proud of you, Della. I know you shall be top of your class. But are you so certain it's a she?"

Della laughed and stopped at a book with a red leather

cover. "Oh, yes. She knows what she wants... I hope she'll have your eyes."

"I hope she's just like you." Cole smiled that wide, warm smile of his that made her heart flutter, even after all these years.

"Mr. Avery said he'd arrive tomorrow morning for my lessons, so I had Martha prepare him the guest chamber. Oh, and I received word from Violet... she said we should go visit after the baby comes. She wants to show me all the sites. Her exhibition has been a great success, evidently. She even got to meet Monsieur Renoir."

"Really? I must admit I am envious of her keeping such company."

Della raised a brow as she glanced at him over her shoulder. "I think you keep rather fine company, if I may say so."

Cole chuckled as she turned her attention back to the book upon which her finger still rested. She slipped it out from between the other volumes and bit her lip when she read the title. *The Complete Works of Plato.*

Cole looked up then and the corner of his mouth turned up. "I have not seen that book in years."

Della shook her head as she brought it to the settee and settled herself down with her hand upon her belly.

"Nor have I." She flipped open the pages and skimmed one at random, smiling as she read the words. "'*Every heart sings a song, incomplete, until another heart whispers back. Those who wish to sing always find a song. At the touch of a lover, everyone becomes a poet.*' And to think – I once thought all of this sentimental nonsense."

Cole tilted his head as he contemplated her. "It is a beautiful song you sing. I hope you never stop."

Della smiled at him. "I never will, my love."

A LETTER FROM THE AUTHOR

This book started out as a single scene with a pickpocket and a gentleman catching her in the act – Della and Cole evolved from that and I would like to thank you, dear Reader, for taking the time to follow their journey – I hope you enjoyed reading *The Lady Thief of Belgravia* as much as I enjoyed writing it!

If you would like to join with other readers in hearing all about my new releases and bonus content, please do consider signing up for my newsletter:

www.stormpublishing.co/allison-grey

Additionally, reviews – even short ones – go a long way in helping other readers discover my books. If you have a few spare moments to leave your thoughts, that would be hugely appreciated!

I hope you'll stay in touch – I have many more stories to share!

Allison

ACKNOWLEDGEMENTS

I would like to begin by thanking Kathleen E. Woodiwiss, without whom I might never have written this book. I found a copy of Shanna belonging to my grandmother when I was an impressionable teenager and read that thing until it fell apart. I wanted to tell stories like that – about sweeping romances taking place in different eras, about people who would go to the ends of the earth for the one they loved, about places I had never seen but loved to study. It took a while to figure out how to do it well, but she gave me the inspiration I needed to put pen to paper myself.

A massive thank you, as well, to my editor Kate and the team at Storm Publishing, for taking a chance on a little story about a pickpocket and the earl who falls for her – I spent many years with these characters and knowing they are in good hands has made this publishing journey a lot less stressful. Kate's ideas and direction have made this book even better than I could have imagined.

I would also like to extend my gratitude to the many beta readers and critique partners who helped me over the years to polish my writing and improve my storytelling. Their advice and guidance have been invaluable.

And finally, thanks to my family and friends for supporting me and encouraging me to pursue writing and publishing. I couldn't have done it without you!